Morgana Wynd

By J. Herrera Kamin

Three Ravens Publishing
Chickamauga GA USA

Morgana Wynd By J. Herrera Kamin
Published by Three Ravens Publishing
threeravenspublishing@gmail.com
P O Box 851, Chickamauga, Ga 30707
https://www.threeravenspublishing.com
Copyright © 2025 by J. Herrera Kamin

Publishers Note: This is a work of fiction. Names, characters, places, and incidents are a product of the author's imagination. Locales and public names are sometimes used for atmospheric purposes. Any resemblance to actual people, living or dead, or to businesses, companies, events, institutions, or locales is completely coincidental.

Credits:

MORGANA WYND was written by J. Herrera Kamin
Cover art by: getcovers.com
Morgana Wynd By J. Herrera Kamin/Three Ravens Publishing – 1st edition, 2025

Ebook ISBN: 978-1-966507-37-6
Trade Paperback ISBN: 978-1-966507-38-3

Table of Contents

Acknowledgements

The author would like to thank the following people for supporting the creation of this book: Lisa Herrera, Dan Kamin, Craig Bowlsby, Magnus Hvidsten, Allie Lapin, Tara Rogic, Ryan Bevelander, Paul Dawson, Zain Shivji, Marina Bevelander, Mikalyn Trinca-Colonel, Jillian Herrera, Maria Herrera, Gavin Boyd, Rahim Moosa, Ben Avery, Mikaela Fuqua, and surely others whose names I have regretfully overlooked.

I would also like to thank the folks at Three Ravens Publishing for believing in this story, and helping me to bring it to the highest level of quality I possibly could.

Without all of this support, this novel would not exist.

Arc One: Gathering
Prologue

The storm came crawling out of the greyness left in the setting sun's wake and scuttled over the ocean toward the Morgana Peninsula. It caught the townsfolk off-guard: without warning the evening turned on them, ice and frigid rain blasting sideways over the clifftops and through the trees, lightning bleaching the sky, thunder rolling close behind it. And underneath it all a mad blustering wind shrieked and wailed.

As the townsfolk of the peninsula cowered in their thatched log houses, it sounded to them less and less like a storm, and more and more like peels of deranged laughter echoing through the electrified air.

By morning it was over. The townsfolk gathered on the beach to behold a tremendous sight: the lighthouse, which for years had stood on a rocky islet just offshore, had fallen. Toppled by the might of the storm, it lay crumpled like a sundered tree on the islet's rocks.

The surf swallowed the ruins over the next few days, dragged them bit by bit into the mouth of the sea until there was nothing left of the lighthouse.

The townsfolk grew restless. They wanted to build a new lighthouse. Without one, they knew, the peninsula would become a perilous destination for merchant vessels. Gradually the traders who had made Morgana Wynd prosperous would forget about it.

But the townsfolk couldn't do it. They couldn't rebuild the lighthouse.

It wasn't for lack of trying: at a town meeting, plans for a new lighthouse were presented, and a construction team rowed out to the islet the very next day to begin work. But in the evening they returned, eyes downcast, and explained in hushed tones that they simply couldn't build a new lighthouse. It couldn't be done.

"Why?" the mayor demanded.

The builders and architects couldn't explain it. All they could say was that the sound of the storm was stuck in their heads, even weeks after it had passed. They just couldn't shake it. That lingering echo, a cackling wind that was more than just wind.

And then, one day, the lighthouse grew back on its own.

Nobody saw it happen. One morning it was just there, silhouetted against the horizon again, as though it had been standing unchecked for a million years. Assembled once more on the beach, the townsfolk gaped in awe at what could only be described as a miracle.

It's back.

But something wasn't right. It wasn't anything the townsfolk wanted to put into words. The lighthouse was just... *wrong,* somehow. It leaned into the hollow of the wind, and anyone who glimpsed it out of the corner of their eye would say it looked slanted. Crooked.

Whenever people went down to that beach, and stared at the lighthouse for too long, they would always say the lighthouse was staring right back at them.

And even with a regrown lighthouse, it wasn't long before the merchant ships stopped coming. After a few years, the Morgana Peninsula had been entirely forgotten by the world. Years became decades, decades became centuries, and through it all the lighthouse stood sentinel on the rocky islet—or as the townsfolk took to calling it, *the Cursed Rock.*

They told stories about it, stories whispered by candlelight,as though the lighthouse could hear them in the walls of their homes:

"They say they saw her on the rocks."

"Who says that?"

"The crabfishers. They say they saw her, at dusk."

"What did they say they saw?"

"A woman, or a girl, or—*someone*. Standing at the foot of the lighthouse, in a white dress."

"A woman in a white dress?"

"That's what the crabfishers said."

Over the years, only a handful of people would dare to enter the lighthouse. Two of them came on a midsummer night, at twilight. They brought a lighted candle made from human tallow and hemp wick, and something heavy in a dark canvas sack. Dressed in dark clothes, hooded and wearing masks, they took the offerings in a little motorboat and cruised across the water to the Cursed Rock.

As they neared the little islet, one of them turned off the boat's engine. They coasted the rest of the way, and by the time the motorboat bumped up gently against the rocks, the engine had fallen completely silent.

After tying off the motorboat, the masked men climbed over the rocks to the foot of the lighthouse. One of them placed the foul-smelling candle at the base of the lighthouse door. The other dumped the contents of the canvas bag out next to the candle.

They both stepped back, and waited. Soon the lighthouse door cracked open, and *something* peered out at them.

When she spoke her words sounded as though they had been whispered long ago, in an echoing cavern, and the echoes had never stopped.

'What have you brought me?'

The masked men shared a glance. "A boy," one of them said, his nervousness muffled by the mask. "His name was Andy Keirian."

The lighthouse door swung open further. The two masked men did their best to watch as the folded-up corpse was pulled back into the darkness. The candle flame went out without a sound. Smoke coiled up into the thickening night.

"We wanted to ask you—"

'I know why you have come. I have watched you.' A rattling, desiccated sigh. *'You think I can help you.'*

The masked men shuffled their feet.

"…can you?"

For a moment there was just the hoarse chuckle of the cool ocean wind, the giggle of waves breaking on the rocks, and the heavy breathing of the men in masks. They peered into the darkness on the other side of the open doorway, but could no longer see anyone or anything left.

Then, at last…

'Bring me another one. Alive, this time. And young. A young mind is essential.'

The men nodded quickly in unison. And the lighthouse door swung shut with a CLANG.

The two masked men returned to the motorboat in uneasy silence. They untied it without saying a word, climbed in and revved the engine. Soon they had left the Cursed Rock behind.

It was full dark by the time they reached the shore.

Back in the place called Morgana Wynd, out of sight of the lighthouse, with their masks off, one of them finally broke the silence.

"I know who we should use."

The other smirked. "Yours, or mine?"

5 | P a g e

The other smirked. "Yours, or mine?"

Chapter One: Sleepyhead

"**M**eet me at the beach on the other side of the woods and I'll tell you a story you've never heard before," she said, and then she was gone.

Jack woke with a start. The coarse grass of a sloping lawn dug into his back. Blinking the sunlight out of his eyes, he pushed himself up on his elbows. There was a name on his tongue, but even as he tried to say it he found he couldn't remember what it was.

What?

Something about a name… *Forget it.* Jack looked at his watch. It was a quarter past three. But what *day* was it? He tried to fish the memories out of his mind, but in the place where he knew they should have been, all he could find now was a dull, smudged emptiness.

His skin crawled. His heart started beating faster. His throat was sore, his mouth dry. The grass of the lawn scratched his legs.

There was something written on his arm, two words scrawled in black marker:

WATCH HIM.

Frowning, Jack licked his fingers and rubbed at the words. But the ink only smeared, it wouldn't come off.

"Watch who?" Jack murmured. "Why?"

He got to his feet and looked around. There was only one car on the street, a black Jeep parked several houses down.

Morgana Wynd.

He turned to look at the house behind him. It was tall and old, all dark cherry wood and slanted shingle roofing.

A rusted brass 7 hung from the door. A set of wind chimes hanging beside the door clinked a subdued melody in the lazy summer breeze.

Jack sighed. "Home sweet home," he said, half-heartedly trying to coax the excitement into existence. But it wouldn't come. How long had it been now, four years? Five? Almost five years in the cold grey city, yearning for the Wynd—and now he was back, *finally* back, for real this time. But—

But this wasn't the grand return it was supposed to be, the one he had scripted in his head over and over.

No, this was all wrong. It didn't add up.

Jack crossed the lawn, knocked on the front door of number 7. Nobody answered.

He was breathing rapidly now, sharp, uneven, ragged-edged breaths. He moved onto the sidewalk, tipped his head back to gaze up at the house. *Five years.* He squinted as he scanned the curtained windows of 7—but he couldn't see any signs of life behind them.

Five years since he had spoken to any of them. Uncle Gabe. Dylan. Skye. Even his own father.

Jack screwed up his face, trying to cast his mind back, but it was no use. He couldn't even gauge the size of the hole in the filmstrip of his memory. How much time had been smudged out of his head? Was it a few hours missing—or was it days? Weeks?

He remembered his mother slipping out the door of their little apartment, her hasty promise echoing in the air behind her:

"I'll be back before you know it, sweetheart," she had said. "And then we're gonna get out of here."

He remembered sitting in the passenger seat of a truck careening down a highway. Someone next to him in the driver's seat. But not his mother—someone else.

Dad?

"Is this it?" Jack had asked.

And then... nothing. That was the last thing he could recall. After that it was just a dark vortex, a black hole that distorted the memories on either side of it.

It occurred to him that he might have hit his head somewhere. He ran his fingers through his tousled hair, along his scalp, down the back of his neck, searching for a telltale bump or bruise or... *something. Anything.* But he found no sign of a head injury—nor of anything that could explain why his mind seemed to be malfunctioning.

Fifteen years old, and I've already lost it.

All right. Trying to puzzle out the situation clearly wouldn't work right now—it was only making things worse.

Get moving, then. Do something.

He set off along the street. It was a beautiful day, clear skies overhead strewn with bunny-tail clouds and feathery sunlight. The street was curving around; behind him, 7 was already out of sight.

And there wasn't a soul to be seen.

He passed houses with random numbers on their doors. 18 next to 367 followed by 5 across from 92. Purposefully designed to confuse strangers. He passed a shabby convenience store with a flickering neon OPEN sign. A flower stand, closed for business. A pawn shop. A bakery. A café. A grocery store. A two-storey hotel: STURGESS SEAVIEW—*Rooms on the Wynd.* Jack remembered the hotel, but was certain it had been called something else the last time he had been here.

All the buildings in the right places, right where they were supposed to be. Still, something wasn't right. It was like he was looking at cardboard cut-outs of the homes and businesses of Morgana Wynd.

Wait—who was that up ahead? An old lady with a broom, delicately sweeping the sidewalk. Jack approached her. Her face looked like it had been patched together from newspaper clippings: he could read headlines on the folds of her skin, tales of ancient scandals and outdated miracles. The whole history of the Wynd displayed there for him to see, crowded around a pair of frosted eyes.

"Excuse me," said Jack.

The old lady turned her head slowly to look at him. She said nothing, and Jack realized he didn't have any questions ready. So he brushed past her and hurried on his way down the street.

Typical old person encounter, he thought to himself. *Was I supposed to recognize her?* You could never really tell with seniors, could you? Well, no matter; she was already passing out of sight, vanishing around a bend in the road.

Jack passed more houses, bungalows, overgrown gardens. His mother's voice echoed in his mind. *I'll be back before you know it, sweetheart.*

He wondered where she was now—and winced, a shard of guilt twisting in his gut.

He would apologize for everything, the next time he saw her. It was the very first thing he would do.

He thought of her gaunt face, dark circles rimming her bright grey eyes. Jack had inherited the dark circles from his mother, but not the colour of her eyes. Nobody had eyes like Mira Brecker. Twin lakes beneath stormy skies. Her hair tangled and unkempt, light brown streaked with seams of snow.

"I acted like a child," Jack began, muttering under his breath. "I was selfish and thoughtless, and I let you down. I'm sorry. I promise I'll…"

The rehearsed apology trailed off as the street came to an end. A forest reared up before him, towering trees rustling in the breeze. Evergreens. Pines, firs and camphor trees. Oak, beech, arbutus, cherry. The earthy scent filled his nostrils.

A narrow dirt trail cambered off into the woods where the street left off.

Someone was standing there, just behind the treeline. Jack squinted. Something red slipped through a patch of sunlight, the trees swayed and bent their knees, and whoever had been standing there wasn't there anymore.

"Are you lost?"

Jack jumped, and whirled around to face the person who had just spoken: a tall, burly kid wearing a striped tank top and swim trunks. He had a close-cropped buzzcut and was smoking a cigarette.

Jack wondered why he hadn't heard the kid approaching. "No," he said. "Just going for a walk."

"A walk." The other boy's eyes narrowed. "Are you from around here? I don't think I've ever seen you before."

"I used to—I mean, yeah, I'm from around here." Jack realized he was slouching, a bad habit of his, and he straightened up, inadvertently puffing out his chest. "I've been away for a while. My name's Jack."

"Simon." The boy stubbed his cigarette out on the bottom of his boot, and put the butt in a Ziploc bag which he folded and slid into his pocket. Then he strode toward Jack and extended a hand. "It's nice to meet you, Jack."

They shook hands. Simon's grip was sturdy, and he shook vigorously, a smug smile on his face.

"You must've moved here recently," said Jack.

"Four years ago," Simon replied. "Not exactly recent, no." He snorted. "Sorry about the smoking, by the way. I know it's off-putting. I'm trying to quit."

"I don't care," said Jack, though Simon was right, it *was* off-putting.

"Are you looking for somewhere to stay? There are rooms at my father's hotel. Sturgess Seaview, number 1024. They're not bad. You won't find any other rooms on the Wynd, since Barnacle Inn's shut down."

"Oh. Thanks, but—I've already got somewhere to stay."

"Really? Where?"

Jack's breath caught in his throat. Suddenly he was acutely aware of how much smaller and skinnier he was than Simon.

"If you don't mind my asking," Simon added coyly.

"With my cousins," said Jack.

"Your cousins?"

"Yeah." Jack shuffled his feet. "Maybe you know them. Dylan and Skye."

Simon's face darkened. He laughed a, humourless laugh. "Interesting," he murmured, smiling an icy smile. "Good to know. The thing is, Dylan and Skye are—where are you going?"

Without realizing it, Jack had started backing away from Simon. "Oh," he said, fumbling for the right words, "yeah, it was nice meeting you. But I've... gotta go."

He turned on his heel before Simon could respond, and hurried toward the treeline with his hands thrust stiffly into his pockets. Simon called after him a few times—"Where ya going, *Jack?*"—but to Jack's relief the other boy didn't follow him into the forest.

Once Simon was completely obscured by trees, Jack broke into a light jog along the dirt trail. But he was soon out of breath, doubled over, gasping for air. *Pathetic.* He remembered spending hours and hours at a time gallivanting through the woods and along clifftops all day, morning noon and night, sweat-soaked and breathing hard but not *winded.* Not like this.

He slowed to a walk. How had he gotten so out of shape? Had five years in the city really softened him this much?

Relax.

He looked down, and discovered that there was no trail under his feet. What? He was *sure* he had been following the dirt path. Pivoting on one foot, he turned slowly in a circle, three hundred and sixty degrees. But he couldn't spot anything that looked remotely like a trail.

Then something caught his eye. Jack approached the broad, towering oak, squinting at the jagged words scored into the trunk:

follow the Skein

"The Skein," Jack whispered.

Around him the forest murmured softly, the trees and plants stirring in the rich heat of early summer. The air was heavy here, beneath the sun-slammed canopy. It crawled up Jack's nostrils and into his brain, a smell like woodsmoke and saltwater mixed together.

He sighed. He picked a random direction and started walking.

As the forest drew him in he decided to try something, a trick his mother had shown him. "You are not the things in your head," she had explained to him once. "Remember this, Jack: whenever you feel like you've lost yourself, all you have to do is find two things. Your breath, and your heartbeat. *That's* what you are: the rhythm of your breath, and the beat of your heart. They'll guide you home."

So he forced a smile, breathed deeply, and tried to put the day's impossibilities out of his mind. Waking up in Morgana Wynd, the hole in his memory, the missing time. The writing on his arm. Nobody home at number seven. All of it, out—

And it worked, at first. He managed to melt into the rhythm of his steps, and for a few minutes it was just thick tree trunks and the leafy canopy overhead, and one step at a time, one foot in front of the other, crunching through moss and brambles. He emptied himself out into the woods: a hollow boy with nothing but leaves and branches in his head. Just a vague person-shaped wind-up toy marching steadily toward nothing, and away from nothing.

But as his feet pulled him deeper and deeper into the trees, something began to bubble up from the yawning darkness inside him.

No. Go away.

He focused on his footsteps, on the drumbeat they made with the steady kick of his heart. *Dum-dum. Dum-dum. Dum-dum.* Step after step after step. *Not now.*

But it rose up in him all the same, like acid flowing from a seam deep inside him, out into his veins and arteries. And when the acid found its way to his heart his fists clenched, his teeth ground against each other, his pace quickened to a frenzied stagger. Above him the canopy grew thicker, the patches of sunlight dimming between broad swathes of shadow.

Jack tried to focus on the knobbly tree trunks surrounding him, on the sun-dusted shimmer of leaves above him. But his inward gaze had turned to something else: a rusty steel door hidden at the bottom of his mind, beneath his fogbound subconscious. It was padlocked shut, this door, but someone or something was behind it, trying to force it open—something he knew he could not allow to see the light of day ever again, though he couldn't recall what it was, or even what it looked like.

It pounded on the other side of the door, a steady relentless knocking—a demented, off-kilter echo of his heartbeat. It was trying to throw his heart off track—and it was succeeding. His heartbeat thrashed in his ears now, off-rhythm, faltering, then speeding up too fast. Dum-DUM—dumdum-DUM—*dum-dum—DUM—DUM DUM DUMDUMDUMDUM—*

"Shut up!" Jack shouted.

He was immediately jerked back to the woods, to the eerie half-light beneath the ever-thickening canopy. He glanced around, worried for a moment that someone might have witnessed him shouting at thin air.

But he was still alone.

Where the hell am I?

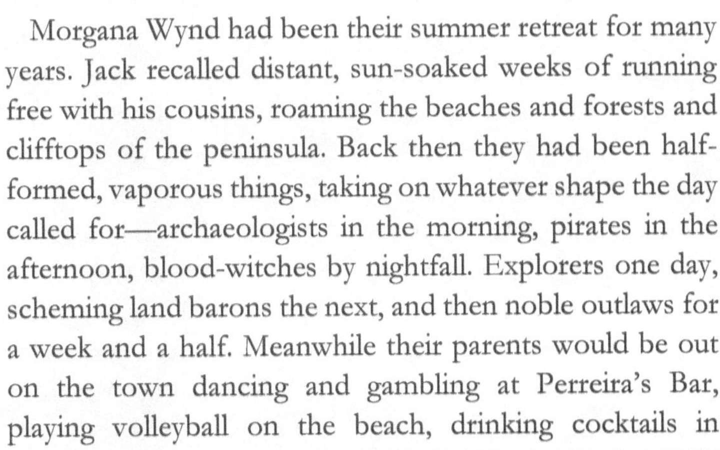

Morgana Wynd had been their summer retreat for many years. Jack recalled distant, sun-soaked weeks of running free with his cousins, roaming the beaches and forests and clifftops of the peninsula. Back then they had been half-formed, vaporous things, taking on whatever shape the day called for—archaeologists in the morning, pirates in the afternoon, blood-witches by nightfall. Explorers one day, scheming land barons the next, and then noble outlaws for a week and a half. Meanwhile their parents would be out on the town dancing and gambling at Perreira's Bar, playing volleyball on the beach, drinking cocktails in recliners on the front lawn of number seven, or—their favourite— cruising the blue crystal ocean in rental canoes, kayaks and jet skis.

Back then, Morgana Wynd had been a scintillating gem, a coveted secret amongst those who had known about it. A summer paradise tucked away on a half-forgotten arm of coastline.

Back then Mom and Dad had still been in love.

Right?

And Uncle Gabe had been there too. All three of them laughing and grinning together. A gang, a mischievous trio just like Jack and Dylan and Skye.

"Think they'll ever let us in on their cocaine orgies?" Skye whispered hoarsely, one time, a sick grin on her face as she shared her latest conspiracy.

"God damn it, Skye," Jack muttered, while Dylan groaned, "Why would you *say* that?"

Jack sighed. It seemed absurd, now, to think that such a time could ever have really existed.

He thought back to his very last memory of Morgana Wynd. A sluggish end-of-summer afternoon. They had been detectives that day, he and Skye and Dylan: hardboiled investigators hot on the trail of some beguiling mystery. It had seemed so important at the time. Something to do with one of the abandoned houses?

Yeah, that was it. Skye had seen a stranger sneaking into an abandoned house through a boarded-up window.

For a moment Jack was back in time: holed up in Dylan's bedroom, the *de facto* headquarters of the Rogue Detectives of the Wynd. He and Dylan and Skye were discussing ways of getting into the abandoned house unseen, when Jack's mother barged into the room, and informed Jack that they were leaving Morgana Wynd.

He didn't think he would ever forget that argument, a vicious debate which quickly devolved into a screaming match right in front of Skye and Dylan. His cousins stood to the side and watched, slack-jawed, shuffling awkwardly with second-hand embarrassment—but unable to look away, like morbid gawkers at a car crash.

"I don't *care* what it is! I said go *away!* Can't you see we're in the middle of something?"

Despair crept into his mother's eyes as he cursed her—but now that he had started, he wasn't able to stop himself.

"Jack—please just—"

"You said we're staying one more week. You *said!*"

"Jack, please just listen to—"

"Listen to you? You lied to me! You said a week! You *said!* So why should I listen to you ever again?"

"Because I am your mother—"

"If you want to leave so badly then just *go!* Just leave and never bother me again for all I care!"

"Jack. Jack! *Look* at me."

Tears in her eyes, Mira Brecker turned and swept out of the room.

Jack steadied himself, took a deep breath, and turned to face Dylan and Skye. But all the excitement for their investigation had evaporated.

"Jack," Dylan said gently. "You have to go with her."

It wasn't until they had left the Morgana Peninsula, and were cruising down the highway, that Jack noticed the welt on his mother's face, on her cheek underneath her left eye. A small area of concentrated red that soon took on the undeniable purple of a bruise.

Jack saw that bruise a lot, when he closed his eyes. Blood pooling dark under his mother's silver gaze. She never told him exactly what had happened that morning on Morgana

Wynd. All he knew was that, at the very moment when she had most needed a teammate, he had abandoned her.

She cried all the way back to the city, her knuckles white as they gripped the wheel.

That had been almost five years ago.

The ground beneath his feet was sloping downward. He was in some kind of hollow. The tree trunks were much thicker here.

He glanced at his watch. Quarter after three, it said. Only then did he notice that the hands weren't moving.

"Perfect," he sighed wearily.

Above, through the canopy, the sun was descending steadily from its zenith. Jack listened, but there was nothing except echoing calm around him, swallows chirping and seagulls screaming in the distance.

"So," a girl said. "Do you remember our deal?"

She was standing nearby, a bit deeper in the shade, and maybe it was because it was darker under the trees, but Jack couldn't tell what colour her hair was. It looked ginger, almost, but also brown and blonde, and it fell in curtains in front of her face. Her amber eyes shimmered like cat eyes in the shade.

She was wearing a jean jacket over a tattered shirt. Frayed shorts. An emerald headband. As Jack rose to his feet she smiled a sleepy smile. She looked familiar. He had seen her somewhere before, but for his life he couldn't remember where.

"I'm Neria," she said. "You forgot, didn't you?"

"Neria," he repeated.

Had he forgotten?

"Don't worry. I didn't expect you to remember. It's this *place*." She gestured to the trees around them. "It's like there's dust everywhere, or sand or something, and it gets in your ears and mouth and up your nose. And in your *head*. Like flies getting caught up in a spider-web, but they're clever flies the spiders can't catch, and they drive the spiders mad—" She broke off. "Never mind. Anyway, bit of advice: I wouldn't mention your affiliation with Skye and Dylan Brecker to anyone, if I were you."

"It's not an *affiliation*. They're my family."

"They're bad news." Neria chewed her lip. "Sorry. That's just what I've heard."

"It's fine. Maybe I'm bad news too." Jack paused. "If that's how it is." *Careful.* "My name's Jack, by the way," he added quickly.

"I know." Neria fixed him with a sly gaze, a simmering half-smile. "So. Our deal."

"Deal?"

"Yeah. You said you'd help me find the Angel's Trumpet."

The Angel's Trumpet? "I don't…" Jack sighed. "Look, to be honest with you, my memory hasn't been that good lately. I think—I think there might be something wrong with me."

Neria's smile flickered.

But then something occurred to Jack: *This is it.* This was exactly what he had been yearning for, what he had spent all these *years* pining for—he was back in Morgana Wynd at last, and a stranger was standing right in front of him, offering him a strange adventure.

A chance to forget the ugly things, to cast them aside and play a game with the Wynd again. While he still could.

"Okay. Wait. I—I think I do remember," Jack lied. "Yeah. The Angel's Trumpet, I mean." A cool breeze tugged at him, the tantalizing wind of adventure. It stoked the bead of fire lodged deep inside him, the Jack that had gone to sleep years ago when he and his mother had left Morgana Wynd. "But I don't know what it is. I don't know anything about it."

Neria blinked. Then—"Good," she said, looking almost relieved. She started walking, motioning for Jack to come with her.

"Thank you," she said, softly, as Jack fell into step beside her.

He couldn't help but stare at her as she led him through the woods. She appeared to know exactly where she was going, but as far as Jack could see they were deep inside dense, seldom-trodden, old-growth forest. There were no human-made pathways here.

But Neria's bright amber eyes were narrowed in concentration, and she reached up every once in a while to brush locks of hair out of her eyes as she scanned the woods… and Jack trusted her. He wasn't sure why. At that moment, he didn't want to think too deeply about it.

"The Angel's Trumpet is a flower," Neria said. The ground was getting steeper, the sound of rolling surf growing louder by the second. "It's exactly what it sounds like, it's white and it looks like a trumpet. Or there's Datura—which looks the same as the Angel's Trumpet, but it grows up from the ground, and it's got these little pod things on it, they're spiky and green. Got that?"

"And why are you looking for these flowers?"

"You mean, why are *we* looking for them?"

"…yes."

"If we find them, you'll find out."

"But why do you need my help to find them?"

Neria stopped walking. She turned to face Jack. Her eyes shimmered, a quiet, steady blaze. "*Because,*" she said, softer now, almost a whisper. "It's this place. Trust me, I don't really understand it either. But my map's all wrong. It's something in the air. Maybe it's 'cause we're near the sea. The sea does weird things to people."

Suddenly she looked embarrassed, like she had spoken too much. "Listen, I know you don't *really* remember, but last time we met you promised you'd help me, and that's the truth. I can't tell you why it's important, but it is."

Jack wavered. "Okay," he said.

He paused. Then:

"I believe you."

Neria's sleepy smile flickered like candlelight. "Good."

She turned and started walking again.

Up ahead Jack could see patches of glimmering blue water through the foliage. The trees were starting to dwindle, the ground leveling into a swathe of bright sand that curved out of sight.

Neria crouched behind a fallen tree and pointed. "There."

It was right on the edge of the treeline, almost on the beach itself: a thickset little cottage, with log walls and a wood-shingled roof. A cold, eager dread blossomed in Jack's chest.

"Think anyone's home?" said Neria.

Jack noticed a little chimneystack sticking out of the roof. "No smoke. Look."

"But it's summer. He wouldn't need a fire. Unless he's cooking something."

"Who's *he?*"

"What?"

"You said *he. He*'s cooking something."

"Barkface. That's what *they* call him, anyway. But they're too scared to investigate this place."

"Who's *they?*" said Jack. "The police?"

Neria frowned. "The locals," she said."They won't admit it, but it's true. They think he's gonna eat them. They call him the Child Eater. Which might be true, for all we know. I mean, nobody ever found that missing kid."

"The *Child* Eater? I thought we were looking for a flower?"

"We are."

Jack stayed put as Neria moved out from behind the fallen tree and approached the cottage slowly. She got a few paces before turning around.

"You coming or what?" she snapped.

"You're going in there?"

"*We*'re going in there. Together."

Jack blushed. He looked at his feet, then spotted a piece of driftwood shaped like a club.

"You asked me why you had to come," said Neria. "This is why."

"I—"

"You're not gonna let me go in there alone, are you?"

Jack sighed. "Fine," he said.

He knelt and picked up the driftwood club.

"What's that?"

"A weapon."

Neria grinned. "*That*'s the spirit."

They walked around to face the front of the cottage. Jack stared. The soot-blackened windows flanking the door were a pair of dark, blind eyes, the door itself a rectangular wooden mouth.

It's the cottage, he thought with dread, *not Barkface: the cottage is the Child Eater.* "This is a bad idea," he muttered. He blinked, and before his eyes the cottage blurred, became a massive sea-beast which had scuttled out of the depths of the ocean and settled on the beach.

"This is a *really* bad idea."

"Yes," said Neria. "Yes it is." She pointed to the door. "Go knock."

"What? No, I—"

"Dare you." Her amber gaze bored into him.

"Fine." Jack gritted his teeth, brandished the driftwood club and started up the porch steps. The wood sank and groaned beneath his feet.

And the door started to open.

For a hair-breadth second Jack was frozen—then his legs kicked into motion, he fell back, threw himself around the side of the cottage. He crouched down, one hand clamped over his mouth to muffle his breath, the other keeping a white-knuckle grip on the club.

He poked his head around the corner.

He could just see the porch. And the Child Eater. *Barkface.* An old, old man: stooped and scrawny and leather-skinned, with a gale of white hair swirling about his pitted face, and brownish eyes sunk so deep into his skull that Jack could barely see them. His skin was tanned, the roasted look of a lifetime spent in the sun and the weather.

Jack grimaced. It looked so agonizing, being that old.

Then he noticed that Barkface was carrying a bulging black garbage bag in one hand.

Where was Neria?

A melody floated over to Jack, like something the wind would hum. Barkface's lips were moving. Jack watched as the old man closed and locked the front door, then shambled with an angled gait down the porch steps. He strained to make out the words to Barkface's tune, but he was too far away to discern anything concrete.

To Jack's relief the old man turned and set off into the trees. The shadows swallowed him, and he was gone.

Neria was standing next to Jack again. "What d'you think was in the bag?" she said. Jack's heart lurched; she smelled like some kind of flower whose name he didn't know.

"Probably little kids' heads," she said. "Don't you think?"

"Well—"

"Or intestines." Neria moved around the corner to face the front door of the cottage. "Now's our chance."

"Our chance for what?"

"To get inside!"

"*What?* What if he comes back?"

Neria whispered something under her breath—it sounded suspiciously like "Pansy." She went up onto the porch, knelt before the door, and from the inner pocket of her jean jacket she pulled out a thin L-shaped tension wrench and a metal pick.

Jack watched as Neria slipped first the tension wrench into the lock, and then the metal pick. She jiggled the pick this way, that way.

Click.

"Aha!" Neria stood, turned the doorknob, pushed against the heavy wooden door, and it swung inward unhurriedly, with a long, drawn-out *creeeaaaaak*. Darkness gazed out from inside.

"How did you do that?" Jack demanded.

Neria grinned and held up the tension wrench and the accompanying pick. "Magic." She motioned inside. "Ladies first."

Jack closed his eyes, and on the undersides of his eyelids he saw grisly things. Corpses dangling from the ceiling, bones scattered about the floor, blood dripping down walls. *A fire burning in a garbage can.* Instinct made him glance at his watch, but the hands were still frozen. Quarter after three.

He wondered vaguely where his mother was, but...

No, it didn't matter.

Brandishing his driftwood club, he shot one final glance at the forest around them, at the beach and the glimmering sea.

Then he crossed the threshold, into the sea-beast's jaws.

The door swung to behind them but didn't close entirely, stayed open by a few precious inches. Warm musty air wafted over them, reeling them in like an invisible tongue.

"Shh," Neria whispered.

"I didn't *say* anyth—"

"I said hush, Jack!"

It was dark as tar inside. There was a moth-bitten sofa against the nearest wall; next to it, a bookshelf stuffed with clothbound books. Next to that an empty hearth. In the far wall a doorway led into a kitchen.

They went slowly. The floorboards protested, squealed and rasped beneath their feet. *Get out!* they moaned in crumbling voices. *Go! He'll eat you!*

"What are we looking for, again?" Jack hissed.

"Shh! Focus. The Angel's Trumpet. Or bodies, if we find any."

"*Dead* bodies?"

"Is there another kind?"

"Well," said Jack, "there's living bodies, and undead bodies, and I guess probably un-living bodies too." He paused beside the bookshelf, squinted through the gloom.

One of the titles gleamed in shiny silver lettering. "*The Sciomancer's Pharma—Pharmacopoeia?*" he read. "Wow, that's four vowels in a row." And the book next to it—"*The Loa of the Bokor.* By F.T. Errvall. What's that mean?"

Then a smaller, thinner paperback caught his eye. On the side, in letters that had almost completely faded: "*Cadaver Preservation.*" He looked up. "Cadaver preservation?"

Neria shrugged. Gingerly Jack weaseled the book out from between the clothbound ones. The pages were yellowed, the cover crumbling and loose. The picture on the cover was a skull, smiling cheerfully, with its glaring eyeballs still in place.

"It's just a book," said Neria. She went through the doorway into the next room. Jack set the book back on the shelf, and followed her into a dingy little kitchen. A sooty gas stove sat against one wall, next to a small wooden table with two chairs.

"This is probably where he eats them," she said. "Look."

There was a bowl of... *something* on the table. Jack approached it tentatively.

"Looks like oatmeal," he said.

"Human oatmeal?"

"Just regular oatmeal." He checked the cupboards: nothing there but a few chipped bowls, plates and utensils, and several jars full of dried herbs and powders, bearing labels like *Belladonna atropa* and *Brugmansia.* Two of the jars contained white powder which looked like fine flour. Their labels said *Scopolamine.*

Jack furrowed his brow. "There's no fridge."

"No bathroom, either. I guess he just goes in the woods."

Then Neria nudged him. Jack looked up. She was jerking her head at something: another door, slightly ajar.

Jack raised his club. They approached the door slowly, cautiously, keeping on their tiptoes to staunch the floorboards' complaints. Neria pushed the door; it swung slowly inward. *Crrrrrr…*

…eeeeeaaaak.

The room beyond the door was brighter than the rest of the cottage. The windows in the opposite wall were just as stained and sooty as the rest of them, but there was a skylight in the ceiling that let in a few extra rays of dusty sunlight.

The room was mostly bare. A mattress huddled in one corner, opposite a small table. There was a framed painting hanging from one of the walls, a portrait of a smiling red-haired woman. And…

"What is *that?*" said Jack.

It was sitting on the table: an hourglass, smooth and polished, with an ornate golden frame. It seemed to Jack that the object had a gleam to it, that it was brighter than it should have been—glowing with light that wasn't coming from the window or the skylight.

A pile of white sand sat motionless in the bottom bulb of the hourglass.

Neria gasped behind him, but the sound was muffled, it seemed to have come from far away. Jack turned. She was staring at the painting on the wall.

"I've seen her before," she breathed. "I *swear* I've seen her before…"

Jack looked closer at the painting. He saw now that it was old, the paint cracked and fading—but the image was still clear. The woman was young. Beautiful, he supposed, but with an aloof, spectral look to her.

Her name floated above her head in thin ghostly letters: *Anora.*

"She looks like you," said Jack.

"What makes you say that?"

But Jack turned away from Neria before he could even hear her question. There was a humming in his ears. A voice? No, not exactly a voice, but something that *wanted* to be a voice.

A melody drifting on the wind. *Look…*

He turned back to the hourglass. *But there's no wind in here.* The gold frame was impossibly shiny. The fine white sand sparkled like powdered crystals. It looked *valuable.* Jack reached for the hourglass, cupped his hands around it, and lifted it. It was heavy, much heavier than he had expected.

His fingers were greasy with sweat. He turned the hourglass over, and the sand began trickling slowly down into the lower bulb.

Something stirred deep inside him. No, not inside him—

"Jack!"

He looked up suddenly, startled by Neria's shout—and the hourglass slipped from his fingers. It fell, missed the table, smashed onto the floor—CRASH!—shattered into pieces, and was nothing but a pile of glass-shards and sand and bits of twisted gold.

Jack reeled. An invisible icicle pierced his chest, and he knew he had done something very, very wrong.

Neria put her hand over her mouth. "Oh my god," she exclaimed. "What did you *do?*"

"I didn't—" Jack spluttered. "I didn't think it—"

"You broke it!"

His heart was way up in his throat. "Let's get out of here," he grunted.

"We've only been in here for two freaking minutes and you've already broken the most expensive-looking thing in the whole—"

Thump.

The sound came from outside. Neria fell dead silent. The two trespassers froze.

Thump. Thump.

"He's on the porch!" Jack hissed.

"Hide!"

They darted out into the kitchen. Jack watched as Neria dropped to the floor and crawled under the table. He heard the squeal of the front door opening. Glancing over his shoulder, he glimpsed Barkface in the doorway, silhouetted by blades of sunlight.

Ducking down, Jack shoved himself under the kitchen table next to Neria, pressing in close to her. He knew he had been too late to avoid being seen. Her breathing was quick beside him.

"For the love of god, Jack," she muttered.

The old man's voice drifted over to them, like coarse sand stirred up by a rogue breeze. "Anora? Is that you?"

Then Barkface was standing in the kitchen doorway.

"I see you under there," he growled. "There's no point trying to hide from me. Come on out, or I'll have to drag you"

Chapter Two: The Angel's Trumpet

Neria hauls herself out from under the table, stands up straight and plants her feet wide. She brandishes her pocket knife and snarls, "Don't come any—"

She freezes, breaks off. The old man is staring at her, his mouth hanging open. She stares back, at the deep lines spider-webbing across his face. At the way his flesh sags as though the weight of his snowstorm beard is pulling him down.

"It's you." Barkface's voice is a frosty murmur. "You're home."

"What are you talking about?" Neria demands, sounding far less sure of herself than she would prefer.

Then one of the chairs shifts beside her, and Jack rises slowly from under the table, driftwood club in hand. He moves to stand beside Neria.

"D-don't kill us," he whimpers. "Please."

Perfect. Neria almost laughs, but she knows she has to stay focused. They have to get out—and fast.

"I'm not going to kill you," says Barkface. "However, there are some items of considerable value in here, so if you're looking for a place to play hide-and-seek, I request that you do it elsewhere." As he speaks, he turns and walks toward the bedroom door.

"Wait!" Jack shouts.

Uh oh.

Barkface pauses at the door.

"You shouldn't go in there!" Jack stammers.

Seriously? Neria jerks his hand, and the cry escapes her lips before she can stop it: "RUN!"

They sprint, crashing through the doorway into the living room. Gripping Jack's wrist, Neria drags him after her. They slam into the front door—Neria flings it open and they're out, naked summer air enveloping them.

They tumble away from the cottage, onto the glaring bright sand that pools between their toes. They squint against the sudden onslaught of sunlight, and Neria leads Jack down the seaweed and shell-laden shoreline. Once it's clear that Barkface isn't following them, they settle behind a sand dune to catch their breaths, and Neria begins to feel a bit silly about the whole thing.

He wouldn't really hurt us, would he?

The midday sun soaks them, warms them. In the distance seagulls scream and cackle.

To the north and west the water stretches out, a glittering cove opening into the sapphire-bright ocean. Several leagues out is a rocky islet on which a lighthouse stands tall, silhouetted against the glare of the sun reflecting off the ocean.

Suddenly Jack starts laughing. "Creepy old bastard," he says.

Neria frowns. "You blew it," she murmurs. "Why did you mention the bedroom? He didn't know you broke anything until you said that."

Jack stops laughing.

"Remember: silence is a beautiful thing. If you can't improve on it, then you should contribute to it." It's something Auntie August has told her many times, but she's not sure it sounds half as wise now coming out of her own mouth.

Jack chews his lip and looks abashedly at his feet. "Sorry." He sounds genuinely remorseful. "Well—you're the one who wanted my help in the first place. And we haven't found the Angel's Trumpet yet."

Something stirs in Neria's chest. Jack is wearing a funny expression, forlorn and hopeful. *He wants to redeem himself.*

He points to the trees. "When Barkface left the cottage," he says carefully, "he went into the woods. Right *there.*"

Neria beams.

A menacing quiet hangs like dripping moss from the boughs of the trees. Neria starts toward them, with Jack following close behind. Wind rustles the leaves.

Anora…

The foliage sucks them in, and they're walking along something that was once a path, long ago, but is now so overgrown and drenched in greenery that they would never have spotted it had they not known where to look.

It's a different path from the one that leads into the woods from the Wynd. This, Neria knows, is a much older, much more secret path.

The woods chant softly, the trees croon things in ancient whispers stitched together from leaves and strands of lichen. Most of their trunks have faces, lumps of drooping fungi for noses and owl-holes for eyes and mouths. The air grows heavy, and something that's almost a smell and perhaps even a sound begins to curl and twine and burrow its way into Neria's head.

Decay.

Evening sunlight sifts through the leaves, coils around tree trunks like golden serpents. *Map it out,* she thinks as they walk. *Know the path.* But her head grows heavier with each passing minute, and the thought of maps soon flees to the back of her mind. There are more important things… the shape of that stump, it looks so much like a giant frog… and what are those lights twinkling off in the shadows? Fireflies?

Slowly but surely, the forest becomes a bog. Their shoes sink into mud, cold mud soiling their socks. The sour scent of peat scrambles up their nostrils.

"Look." Neria points. It's a cluster of mushrooms, big, bulbous toadstools growing on the side of a fallen tree.

"Eat one," says Jack. "I dare you."

Eat one. Absently Neria grabs one, twists it off the trunk.

"Don't actually," Jack mutters.

Then something else catches Neria's eye: a walkway, just visible through the trees. Wooden slats covered in moss and vines, raised a foot above the ground. She drops the mushroom, crosses over to the walkway, climbs up on it. Jack follows. They spread their arms out for balance as they walk. The wood is wet and spongy beneath their feet.

"Neria," Jack hisses. "D'you know where we are?"

Something buzzes in her ears. She swats lazily at the air. Flies. Her eyelids are drooping. Each step she takes is slow, measured, and though she knows her feet should be sore and achy, she can barely feel them.

"Dunno," she says.

The bog ends, and so does the walkway. They descend from it to find the ground firm beneath their feet.

Over here. Neria can't tell if she said it out loud or not. Above them, the canopy has gotten thicker. It's still sunny, but neither of them can say exactly where the sun is in the sky—it's off somewhere else, minding its own business. Neria senses that the sunlight in this part of the forest has always been here: ancient and undying, trapped beneath the spread of leaves.

How long have we been here?

The trees part before them, revealing a yellow-grass clearing. A breeze scampers through the grass, pauses before Neria, then twists itself into a set of fingers, grabs her by the hand and pulls her forward. Jack follows her across the clearing, into the thick of the trees on the other side.

There, the breeze says. *Over there.*

Jack and Neria come to a halt.

There's someone standing there, between the trees. Perfectly still. "Hello?" Neria calls tentatively.

No answer. Her skin crawls. "Hello?" she calls again. "Barkface?"

But it isn't Barkface. She approaches it slowly... *slowly...*

"Neria!" Jack hisses.

The thing is leaning against a tree trunk. It's slumped and unmoving. Neria knows instantly that it isn't alive.

"I don't like this," Jack mutters. "I don't."

It's a woman. Or it used to be. It's dressed in a ragged cloak of moss. Its hair—but not its real hair, it *can't* be real hair—hangs down in front of its face.

They approach it from the side. It's tied to the tree, Neria realizes. Lengths of rope have been pulled tight around its midriff, fitted around its wrists and tied to the branches above, holding its arms up limply. It has a strange kind of smell about it, too. Not the stink of the bog, but a quieter, fouler stench, like an expired perfume. Its face is pallid, ashy. It looks like one of the dummies Neria has seen in wax museums, only...

Only this wax isn't smooth, it's cracking in spots, and poking out from beneath it is something coarse and grey. And its wax mouth is sewn shut. And its eyes are glass eyes. Amber eyes.

They look like your eyes, the breeze sighs in Neria's ear.

The thought makes the nape of her neck prickle. "No they don't," she grunts.

Jack frowns at her. "What?"

"Uh—nothing." Neria moves closer, reaches out tentatively and prods the waxwoman's chest. It shifts under her touch—Neria leaps back. "Agh!"

There are other things, too. Candlesticks jammed into the mossy ground. A ring of blood-red mushrooms circling the tree. Did they grow there on their own? And nailed to the trunk, above the waxwoman's head: a dead seal, desiccated and shrivelled.

Neria steps back. "I think," she says slowly, calculatingly, "this is Anora." She shivers as the name leaves her mouth. *Anora.* It *is* her. It has to be. The wax face is the same—well, *almost* the same—as the one in the painting.

Then Neria remembers something. The bookshelf in Barkface's cottage.

"Oh god," she says.

"What is it?"

"That book." She backs away from the thing tied to the tree. "The one Barkface had. *Cadaver Preservation.*"

"Doesn't that mean"—Jack's voice cracks—"oh, *god.*"

"I think we should get—"

But Neria freezes mid-sentence.

The waxwoman's head isn't hanging down anymore, it's looking up, nothing to support it, its amber glass eyes staring straight at Jack and Neria.

One by one, the seams holding its mouth shut begin to split. Its glass gaze pierces through Neria's eyes into her soul.

The waxwoman's mouth opens.

'Jaaack,' it groans.

One of its arms gives a sudden jerk. The rope holding it up snaps.

Jack and Neria are already running, even as the air fills with the sound of heavy footfalls. *Come on, Jack! Faster!* They trip and fall through swathes of dappled sunlight, streaks of shadowy green. Branches tear at their faces, crunch beneath their feet—trees scream at them as they fly by, faces ripping out of the bark, taunting them with moldering, cobweb-caked tongues.

"Lost their way!" the trees cackle. *"Lost their way!"*

Then Neria's feet vanish from under her—she's flying, falling—plunging into mud and lying still, her clothes and skin soiled with swamp.

She spits mud out of her mouth, hauls herself to her feet. She's standing in the shade of a weeping willow. The forest has gone into bog mode again. Jack is nowhere to be seen.

"Jack?" she calls.

She's alone.

"Hello?"

A snarl of fear. Something's wrong. When she and Jack first made their way to the cottage, they descended a hill— didn't they? But *where's the hill?* The ground is flat all around, in every direction as far as Neria can see.

She pulls her way through a patch of overhanging branches, and finds herself in another clearing. Yellow grass-stalks. But this isn't the same clearing as before. Is it?

No, it can't be—because *this* clearing is lined with white flowers. White petals opening to the sky. And more white flowers hanging pendulously from the thick-growing verdure lining the sides of the clearing.

The shape of the hanging ones is unmistakable. Trumpets.

"A*ha.*" Neria approaches the nearest white flower, which grows from the ground. Crouching beside it, she spots the spiky green pods lining the base of its stem.

She tears the white flower out of the ground, pods, roots, and all, and shoves it into the inner pocket of her jacket. Then she walks over to one of the hanging flowers, and plucks it from its stem, slipping it into her jacket pocket as well. She notices that the hanging trumpet-flowers have pods growing in their midst, smooth pods. Neria plucks a few of these, and places them in her jacket pocket with the rest.

Then she stands up, goes to the nearest tree, and clambers up into its branches. Balancing herself, shielding her eyes with one hand, she squints into the surrounding forest.

But suddenly a wave of dizziness overwhelms her, and all she can see are leaves everywhere, shimmering in the cold light. A sky of leaves, stitched together like a rippling tapestry. Neria reels, slips—hooks her arm around a knobby branch as her feet swing out beneath her. "Shit," she mumbles.

She has no choice: she lets go, tries to brace her body as she falls. She lands clumsily on the ground and staggers several yards before managing to right herself.

What's going on? She turns to look at the tree; it peers sternly down at her, like it's scolding her.

What's happening to me?

"Neria?"

She wheels around. "Jack!"

The front of his shirt and trousers are covered with mud, his arms tattooed with scrapes. "I was looking all over for you!" he exclaims. "For *hours.*"

"Hours?"

Jack falters. "Well, I dunno how—" He breaks off, glances at his watch. "Do you know what time it is?"

Neria shrugs.

"Well, where are we? Do you know the way?"

Neria looks around. Where's her map? She closes her eyes, but there's no map, not this time. Opening her eyes again, she turns in a circle, but she can't even tell which direction she came from. The woods look the same, *exactly* the same, on all sides.

Something tightens in her chest. "We're lost," she says. She isn't sure how she's supposed to feel about it. She can't even remember the last time she got lost.

"I don't understand," she adds sheepishly.

They sit down with their backs against the trunk of a tree. "That… *thing,*" says Jack slowly. "Is it following us?"

"It was tied to the tree."

"But the rope broke. And it said my name. Did you hear it?"

"I heard it."

"Why did it say my name?"

"I don't—"

"Why didn't it say *your* name?"

"I don't *know,* Jack!"

He goes quiet for a minute. "This is all real, isn't it?"

Neria doesn't respond. *Think.* The forest buzzes around them. *Use your head.* But no matter which way she looks, the trees are the same. Some of them have white trumpet flowers hanging upside-down from their branches. Jack plays with one of the upside-down trumpets, tracing the petals with his fingers.

"We found it," he says distantly. "Now what?"

Neria buries her face in her hands. "I dunno. I *dunno!* I thought it would prove my theory, but—"

"What theory?"

"That Barkface is the one behind it. You know, behind what happened at the Fifth Season and everything, but—it still doesn't make any sense!" She growls into the palms of her hands. "It doesn't make *sense.*"

"Well, we shouldn't stay here. That thing might get us." Jack says it absently, as though the prospect hardly bothers him anymore. "Which way should we go?" He's still stroking the trumpet-flower.

"I don't know!" Neria can no longer keep the panicked tremble out of her voice. Why is it so hard to remember anything? She thought she knew this place—thought she had it pinned down on the map she keeps between her ears. But these woods are *different.* They can't be trusted.

We've gone astray.

"Uh," she says. "That way?"

It's a guess, nothing more, but Jack doesn't seem to have any better ideas. They both scramble to their feet and head back under the tree cover, where the sunlight scours to a coppery green. Neria's breath is coming quicker now, and something inside her chest has tightened into a knot.

"Hurry," she whispers, quickening her pace. She can hear something behind them—footsteps. "Faster."

"What?"

"*Faster!*" She grabs his hand, squeezes it tight. "You lead the way. And don't let go of me, whatever you do."

"But I don't—"

"I said *lead!*" The footsteps behind them are quickening to match theirs. Can Jack even hear them? He takes the lead, pulling Neria along, and she closes her eyes as he guides her.

Where are we going?

Morgana Wynd.

How do you know Morgana Wynd is Morgana Wynd?

Then it comes to her. It's not a sound, really, or a smell, but a little bit of both. Like the scent of rain on dry earth if it were a sound, or the rustle of people snoring gently if it were a smell.

The forest loosens its grasp on the blackness behind Neria's eyes. Roots retreat, uncoiling from around her mind.

Her eyes snap open. "*This* way!" She points. "Quick!"

They're running again, whipping through the trees—and then without warning the ground drops away before them, and several yards below them is the dirt trail. The *real* trail.

There's no time to waste. They slip over the edge, and the slope scoops their feet out from under them: they plunge into the underbrush beside the path. Neria glances back up the incline, but the sunlight's in her eyes now, coming almost horizontally through the trees. She squints against the glare, but there's no incline above them.

To either side the ground is flat, mostly, but for a few bumps and dips.

The Skein changes.

Jack is lying sprawled a few yards away. He sits up, dusts himself off—and something fills Neria's chest, a surge so strong and achingly familiar that she can't bear to look at him anymore. The footsteps trailing them have faded now, but she can still hear them, somewhere not-so-far away.

I've dragged you too deep into this, haven't I?

As Jack climbs to his feet, Neria makes her decision.

Spare him.

Jack turns to look for Neria—but before he spots her she dodges behind a tree, catches her breath. *I'm just an afternoon daydream in the shape of a girl,* she thinks. *I dissipate with dusk.*

She half-hopes he'll try to follow her, but she knows he can't. He's not like her.

We're both safer this way.

So Neria slips away behind a curtain of syrupy evening sunlight, leaving Jack alone amid the trees, even as his bewildered voice begins to call out her name.

Chapter Three: The Changeling House

"Neria?" The impassive trees threw his voice right back at him. "Neria!"

No answer.

He scowled. Well, at least he had made it back to the trail. *She found it for you.* His watch still read quarter past three, but it was starting to get dark—it must have been around seven or eight o'clock. The bits of sky he could see through the canopy were still bright, but the trees and the foliage were starting to turn into silhouettes.

Jack heard footfalls on the path behind him. He turned to see someone running toward him, another boy who stopped suddenly several yards away with a startled "Whoa!"

Jack squinted. In the gloom he could make out curly hair, and a reedy, dark-skinned, bespectacled face.

"Look, I'd love to stay and chat, but I think it's caught my scent." The boy brushed past Jack and set off again at a remarkably fast clip.

'Jaaaack…'

The moan came drifting through the gathering dusk. Jack's heart skipped a beat. He scanned the darkening forest. At first he couldn't see anything…

But then he spotted it, a shadow lumbering through the trees, its movements jerky and stiff. He broke into a run. *Stay on the path!* He couldn't see the other boy anywhere, and a quick glance behind showed him that the waxwoman was on the trail now, shambling aberrantly toward him, an unnatural obscurity melting through the deeper darkness of the woods.

'Jaaaaack…'

The other boy's voice drifted down to him:

"Hey! You! Get in the trees! It can't climb!"

Jack stumbled to the nearest tree. He threw himself up the trunk—slid back down, his knees scraping on the bark. "Help!" he gasped.

"Come on!"

A hand reached down. Jack leapt again, grabbed a branch—the hand gripped his shirt, yanking him upward until he could grab onto another, thicker branch. Something brushed the bottom of his foot. He looked down, and even in the gloom could make out the waxwoman standing at the base of the tree, its head tilted back, staring at him.

'Jaaaack…'

He pulled himself higher into the branches. The other boy was perched several feet above him. "I don't get it," he muttered. "Why does it keep saying that?"

The cold, creeping dread returned. "It's me," Jack whispered.

"*You*'re Jack?" The other boy let out a loud, barking laugh. "Ha! Bad luck, man." He paused. "Have we met before? I'm Lucas."

Jack wavered. "No. But you might—" He broke off, remembered Neria's warning and the look that had crossed Simon's face.

"Might what?"

Jack decided to take the chance. "Might know my cousins. Dylan and Skye."

"Dylan and Skye? Yeah, I know them. They're certifiably insane, you know that?"

'Jaaaaack…'

"Jesus, that gives me the creeps," said Lucas. "What the hell is it? And why does it keep saying your name?"

"You're asking *me?*" Jack looked down through the branches. It was getting darker by the second. The waxwoman was still standing at the foot of the tree, but they could barely see her now. "I don't even—"

Suddenly Lucas pressed a finger to Jack's lips. "*Shh!*"

They could hear other voices. Deeper voices.

"Great," Lucas whispered.

Narrow beams of light cut through the trees. At least three people were coming down the path, all holding flashlights. Gradually their voices became discernible. "…swear to god," one of them was saying, "even the Cormora Creek cops are afraid of this place. You can tell they just want to get away as quickly as possible. I was talking to them this afternoon—trying to convince them, you know, that we *need* to crack down on all this lunacy— I *told* them I'm pretty sure someone put something in the water supply, but they weren't having any of it, you know—"

"So it's up to us, then."

For a moment one of the flashlight beams illuminated the waxwoman's cracked, clammy face. To Jack's relief it was finally moving away from the tree.

'Jaaaack…'

"Exac*t*ly," said one of the approaching men "Who are we supposed to be looking for, again?"

"I already told you," said another. "This little shit named Lucas Alvarez. He lives in ninety-four, but he hasn't been there all afternoon—I tried talking to his parents but they're—"

"He's the one who got into the Fifth Season?"

"According to Simon, yes. I've got him watching them. He says Lucas is in on all of this—he's friends with the Brecker kids, after all. He might even have…" The man trailed off.

Jaaack…'

"Did you hear that?"

"Hear what? Listen, though, I have a theory about—"

"Sol. Did you hear that?"

"Hear *what?*"

Jaaaaack…'

"That!"

"Jesus Christ! What the hell is that?"

"Go back. GO BACK!"

The forest exploded with sound: screams of terror, bodies trampling through underbrush, and those steady, stilted footfalls. *Jaaaack…'*

The noises began to fade. "Now's our chance!" hissed Lucas. "We've gotta get somewhere safe."

"Like where?"

"Your cousins' house. I think it's the only safe place left." And before Jack could object Lucas swung himself down from the tree and landed deftly on the forest floor. "Come on!"

Jack dropped from the tree, slid down the trunk—crashed to the ground.

"Stay close to me," Lucas hissed. "And whatever you do, do *not* leave the path. If we lose the path now we're as good as dead."

———— •·◆·· ————

It would go like this:

"Hide!" Lucas would whisper, and every time he did they scampered to the nearest tree. Jack needed a hand getting up every time, while Lucas scaled the trunks like it was the easiest thing in the world.

A few moments later the waxwoman would lumber past. Or the man called Sol or one of his friends would come sprinting by.

Or nothing would happen.

Then Jack and Lucas would climb back down and keep going.

Soon enough the trees were thinning. They were nearing the edge of the woods. The trail ahead was clear—

"THERE THEY ARE!" someone shouted—the man named Sol. "I SEE YOU!" Flashlight beams came chopping through the dark.

"Oh god!" Lucas wailed. He and Jack broke into a sprint… they were *so close* to the edge of the woods…

The waxwoman emerged from the trees onto the trail ahead, blocking their way. *Jaaack,'* it moaned.

"Just give it what it wants!" Lucas shrieked. "Take one for the team, Jack!" But then he tripped, sprawled on the path, and Jack stumbled over him—something went *crunch!* underneath his feet. He froze.

"My glasses!" Lucas was fumbling around on the ground, and in horror Jack knelt and picked up the crushed frame he had stepped on. One of the lenses had popped out—

"No time," he growled. He shoved the mangled glasses into his pocket. On one side the waxwoman was bearing down on them, Sol's frantic footsteps closing in on the other side.

Jack grabbed Lucas's hand tight and dragged him off the path. "My glasses!" Lucas cried, as the waxwoman veered from the path to follow them.

"I got 'em," Jack gasped.

"GET DOWN!" someone shouted.

A girl melted out of the shadows. She had black hair hanging low over her eyes, and her face was illuminated by a sparkling flame. The flame was attached to the end of a long cylinder, which she held in her hand.

As the waxwoman stomped toward them, the girl pointed the flaming cylinder at it.

"*Skye?*" Jack gasped.

"You have five seconds to pray," his little cousin hissed. "Motherf—"

She had mistimed it, though, because suddenly there was a flash, a squeal of heated air—BANG! A blast of iridescent sparks, blues and golds and reds splintering through the air—the sharp tang of gunpowder—and the waxwoman let out a horrific howl and stumbled back. Jack couldn't see, his vision branded with the purple afterimage of the firework. Acrid smoke enveloped him.

"Jack! Your cousins! Follow them, quick!"

It was Lucas who shouted it, who grabbed onto his forearm, and they were both sprinting through the smoke. The path was just ahead of them. They kept running and suddenly they were clear of the trees: before them was Morgana Wynd, the lights of the houses just coming on under a deepening twilight sky.

Behind them, shadows were emerging from the edge of the woods. "They're getting away!" someone shouted.

Jack and Lucas dashed for the Wynd, and glancing around Jack saw that two others had joined them: Skye was sprinting just ahead, and her tall, lanky, shaggy-haired brother was keeping up the rear. The four of them ran down the Wynd as it curved, more and more houses popping up on each side.

We're losing them.

Another curve in the street, and there were the storefronts, the café, Sturgess Seaview, The Fifth Season. They ran further, to where the street curved again, and there were more houses ahead of them.

Finally they arrived in front of the house with the brass 7 on its door. Skye got there first, unlocked the door, yanked it open, and gestured for Jack and Lucas to get inside.

They piled in. Dylan came in last. He closed the door and locked it behind them.

"Well!" he exclaimed. "Well, well, well."

Jack pulled the broken pair of glasses out of his pocket and handed them to Lucas. "Thanks," Lucas grunted. He looked up at Skye and Dylan, then pointed to Jack. "This kid saved my skin."

"*Did* he?" said Skye. She was a strange sight: fourteen years old, black-haired and slight, with dark rings around her eyes. She wore a leather trenchcoat that was far too big for her, so big it pooled in folds around her feet. Her brother Dylan, on the other hand, towered over all of them, sporting a mop of unkempt hair that kept falling in front of his face. Besides being the tallest of the four, he was also the oldest, at seventeen.

"We've been looking all over for you, Lucas," Dylan said. "Where have you been?"

"To the ends of the earth and back." Lucas was trying to cram the lens back into the warped frame of his glasses. Jack realized that he didn't recognize Lucas at all—maybe he had only recently moved to Morgana Wynd. He looked to be about the same age as Dylan.

As Jack watched, Lucas managed to click the lens into place. He put his glasses back on and stood up. "I hope it's okay if I stay here for the night," he grunted. "And before you say anything, the answer is yes, it is okay. D'you know why? Because Solomon Sturgess is after me because he knows I'm friends with both of you. Apparently he went looking for me at my parents' house."

"So you're in hiding," said Dylan. He shrugged. "That's fine. We're in hiding too." He turned to Jack. "And what about you?"

"What—what about me?"

Dylan smirked. Then he spread his arms and said, "Welcome to the Changeling House. The rules have changed a little since the last time you were here."

He started down the hall from the lobby, gesturing for them all to follow him.

Jack yawned. *What a day it's been.* Still, he couldn't deny the shiver of excited energy unfolding inside him.

Home sweet home.

As he followed his cousins into number 7, which smelled like ocean winds and was cluttered as though a tornado had blown through it, Jack saw why they had started calling it the Changeling House. 7 Morgana Wynd had been swapped for an impostor house, an inexplicable, otherworldly simulacrum. The lobby hadn't changed, but the first door on the right led into Dylan's old bedroom— peering in through the door, which sat invitingly ajar, Jack saw that the furniture had been removed, the room filled wall-to-wall with brown and black soil. The soil reached about knee-height around the edges of the walls, but bulged mountain-like in the middle of the room, a great hill of dirt whose crest nearly reached the ceiling.

A loamy, earthy scent filled Jack's nostrils. It was not unpleasant.

"It's a long-term project," Dylan said with a shrug. He, Skye and Lucas had started up the stairwell which lay just past Dylan's old room. But Jack crept further down the hall, to peer into Skye's former bedroom.

He was greeted by a jumbled storage room of half-abandoned hobbies. Amid the clutter he spotted a violin, an acoustic guitar, an electric keyboard, and a trombone. There was a medium-sized telescope. Several easels displaying sinister paintings. A bow and quiver with rubber-tipped arrows strewn about the floor. Two skateboards. A paddleboard. An empty aquarium containing the skeleton of a lizard. A tent set up in a far corner of the room; in another corner, a pile of modeling clay coiled into a half-formed castle, dried, dusty and forgotten.

Most of it had been scavenged from junkyards in Cormora Creek, or bought at generous prices from the pawn shop on the Wynd. It all belonged to Skye: hobbies she had taken up and promptly become disenchanted with. Jack remembered the summer when she had driven them all up the wall with the violin… until she had learned it would take *years* of practice to sound the way she really wanted to. He remembered how she had found that aquarium with the lizard skeleton inside it, abandoned by a dumpster in Cormora Creek. Skye had vowed to resurrect the lizard—hadn't a whole August been wasted on that futile endeavour?

Jack remembered the look on his cousin's face when she had discovered that she wasn't allowed to shoot at people with her bow and arrow set.

"Your expectations are too high," Dylan had explained to her. "Things take time, and practice."

Skye had answered that with a snort. "Life's short," was her reply. "And I'm busy."

"You're the least busy person I know!"

"Jack!" Skye called to him from the stairs. "What's the hold-up?"

Doubling back into the present, Jack left the junkyard bedroom and followed the other three up the stairs. Directly on the right, at the top of the stairs, was the room which had formerly been Uncle Gabe's bedroom-study. Dylan and Skye led Jack and Lucas into the room.

"Behold!" chirped Skye.

Jack's jaw dropped. Lucas made a sound that was half-groan, half-gasp.

"I call it the Stowaway Garden," Dylan said.

Dylan and Skye had dismantled the bed, carried the pieces out to the backyard one by one, and burned them on a bonfire. Then they had brought in buckets and buckets of soil, stones and clay gathered from the beach and the woods. Once the hardwood floor was completely buried under thick layers of earth, Dylan had planted dozens of seeds, which he had been collecting for years in a jam jar in his underwear drawer. He had arranged wooden lattices for the plants to grow along. The large bay windows, which looked out east over the forest cradling Morgana Wynd, had their curtains drawn wide, to let in as much sunlight as possible.

Things were already starting to emerge from the soil: plucky little sprouts that would soon carry tomatoes, blueberries, green beans, garlic, squash, carrots and cucumber. There were mushrooms and there was sage, thyme, mint, and lavender; there were future violets and delphiniums lining the walls "just for fun" and an embryonic sequoia sapling planted in the very middle of the room. Dylan had put hooks on the walls to hang watering cans. He had rigged the garden hose so that it crawled up the side of the house, emerging into the bedroom from a ventilation grille beneath the bay windows.

Finally Jack understood the purpose of the mountain of dirt in Dylan's old bedroom, which sat directly beneath the Stowaway Garden.

"If things go according to plan," Dylan declared, beaming with pride, "the sequoia will eventually grow so big it'll tear right through the roof of this house and soar into the heavens."

"What's Uncle Gabe gonna do when he comes back?" Jack asked.

"*If* he ever wakes up from his coma, and decides to come back… he'll be a little pissed off, I think," Dylan surmised.

"No shit."

"I don't care what he thinks, though. He's the old world. He's fading." Dylan smirked. "Trust me."

After standing back to give Jack and Lucas an appropriate amount of time to be awe-struck, Dylan and Skye pulled their guests out of the Stowaway Garden and led them out into the hall and up another flight of stairs, up to the attic: a small room at the top of the house, with a sloped ceiling striped with rafters.

"Skye," said Dylan, "make sure all the doors and windows are locked."

Skye nodded curtly, and disappeared back downstairs.

Jack surveyed the attic bedroom. He thought back to the days of the Rogue Detectives of the Wynd, when this had been the base of operations. *Our secret headquarters.* He saw now that to Dylan and Skye, those days had never ended.

Every surface in the attic, including the bed, was hidden under books, newspaper clippings, discarded clothes, empty coffee mugs.

There was a pistol sitting on the bedside table. "Is this real?" said Jack, picking it up gingerly. It was way too light to be real.

Skye appeared in the doorway. "That's a dangerous line of questioning," she said.

"'Course it's not real," said Dylan. "Who do you think we are?"

Skye cleared away a spot on the bed and sat down, then fished around in her pocket and pulled something out: a blue plastic pipe. She stuck the end of the pipe in her mouth and blew out a bubble, which hovered delicately in the air in front of her—then burst silently when a summer breeze gusted into the room.

The window was ajar. It offered a sweeping view: Morgana Wynd unfurling before them, aglow now as it coiled through the darkening forest, its lights coming on like a swarm of fireflies. A train of fallen stars, their brightness waging a desperate, never-ending war with the darkness of the woods that crowded around on all sides.

And beyond the peninsula: the cobalt ocean. The western horizon opened before them, fired up with the light of the sinking sun.

Jack shivered. *There.* He found the lighthouse he had seen from the beach, perched on its rocky islet just off the tip of the peninsula.

Suddenly he felt as though a pair of cold eyes had turned toward him. He shivered, and looking down he saw that the words WATCH HIM were still faintly visible on his arm.

"So where's Uncle Gabe?" he said.

Dylan and Skye shared a glance. "In the hospital," said Skye after a protracted moment. "In Cormora Creek. We're looking after the house till he gets better."

"Oh." Jack winced. "Sorry."

"Don't be sorry."

"Well, what does—is he sick?"

Dylan, Skye and Lucas shared a glance.

"Do you know what happened at the Fifth Season?" said Dylan.

"The restaurant?" said Jack. "No."

"Dad ate some bad food," said Skye. "Now he's in a coma."

"*What?*"

"Man," said Lucas, "there's food poisoning and then there's *food poisoning*. Eh? Right?"

"So," said Skye, ignoring Lucas's contribution, "what were you doing on our lawn, Jack? And why are we supposed to *watch you?*"

Jack glanced at the smudged ink on his arm. It was a good question.

"I think it's meant for Uncle Gabe," he said.

"Okay," said Dylan, after a moment's silence. "Let's get this cleared up. We don't hear from you or Aunt Mira for—what? Five years? Not since"—he broke off, hesitated—"since you left. And then you just show up in the middle of the weirdest week of our lives? I'm having a hard time believing that's a coincidence. So. What're you doing here?"

The others were staring at him, three pairs of eyes fixed on him.

So Jack made something up. "I just… Mom sent me here. For a vacation, I guess. I think she wanted a break from me for a little bit."

It was a total lie, of course. But he didn't want them to know that he couldn't remember, that his mind was riddled with holes like Swiss cheese. What would they think of him if he told them *that?*

Maybe they'd be afraid of him. Maybe they would think he was insane.

You **are** *insane.*

He saw it, for a moment, before his mind's eye. *An hourglass shattering on the floor of a cottage in the woods.* And there was something else: two pearl-white eyes opening. A pair of ancient, rotted lips pulling apart. A ragged throat drawing in a deep, rattling breath.

Something stirring in the darkness in the lighthouse just off shore.

A name on those primordial lips. The name that had distracted Jack enough to drop the hourglass: his own.

Jack,' said the thing in the lighthouse, and not so far away, something that had once been a woman named Anora echoed the name.

Jaaack…'

Jack shivered

"You all right?" said Dylan.

Jack nodded, and found it curious that even a motion as simple as a nod could be a lie.

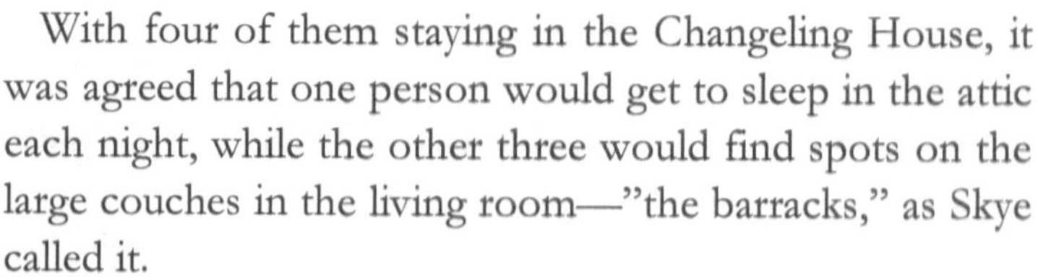

With four of them staying in the Changeling House, it was agreed that one person would get to sleep in the attic each night, while the other three would find spots on the large couches in the living room—"the barracks," as Skye called it.

Jack lay on the cluttered bed, staring at the rafters. The window was open. A cool morning breeze bustled in and out of the room.

He had dreamt that he was back in the city. Dreamt he was stuck in a dingy little apartment with flickering lights and relentless invasions of black mold, in a building that smelled like stale cigarettes. In his dream he had watched his mother as she sat at the kitchen table, staring out at the impassive brick wall across the alley.

"Mom," he had tried to say.

"It's behind us now, sweetheart," she replied, turning to look at Jack, and even in the depths of his dream the sight of her exhausted, sunken-eyed face had made him want to cry. "All behind us. We move forward. Only forward."

Only forward.

Jack turned onto his side, so that he could see out the attic window. He could just make out the dark green of the woods, and a few of the houses near the end of the Wynd. The sky was blue and empty.

Focus.

He tried to find a memory of his father, but the last time he could remember interacting with the man who had given him his name was five years ago.

He closed his eyes. "Where are you, Dad?" he whispered.

But all he could see was Heath Haltow, his mother's new boyfriend.

"Oh, come on," Jack groaned.

Heath Haltow was nice enough, okay? In fact, "fine" would be the perfect adjective to describe Heath. He was absolutely fine, but he and Jack had nothing in common, because Heath was a sickly middle-aged deportations officer whose skin was grey from lack of sun exposure— who needed a cane to get around, who fretted about everything—the weather, the traffic, his health, Jack's health, Jack's mother's health.

"Why are you even dating him?" Jack had raged to his mother's face, obnoxiously loud, fully aware that Heath was in the next room, within earshot. "What do you *see* in him? He's pathetic. Just looking at him makes me sad."

The Jackal's loose. He hated when the Jackal got loose, but he couldn't stop it when it happened.

"You always make *stupid* decisions, Mom. First my father. Now this prick… I dunno. I just think you can do way better."

Jack winced. *I'm such an idiot.*

His heart juddered off-rhythm for a moment, and the sound of someone pounding on a steel door echoed in his ears.

No. Not here.

"Jack!"

His eyes snapped open. He was looking at the window again, at the Wynd as it brightened with the day.

Not here.

Jack sighed. Then something caught his gaze, right next to the window. A map tacked to the wall.

He got out of bed and went to study the map. It was folded, torn, stained, but he recognized it all the same: a hand-drawn map of the Morgana Peninsula. He and Skye and Dylan had drawn it up one summer, years ago.

In dark ink the map depicted the peninsula, shaped like a jagged arrowhead; the winding street called Morgana Wynd, the numbered buildings, the docks, the woods, and the reservoir near the woods.

There was the islet with the lighthouse just off-shore, labeled THE CURSED ROCK.

In the patch of woods that sat indistinctly, unsure of its size, between the Wynd and the beach, was a phrase scrawled carefully in Dylan's unmistakable, spidery handwriting: *follow the Skein, if you dare.*

Jack frowned. That part must have been added recently. He didn't remember it from before.

"Jack!"

The call came from downstairs—Skye's raucous shout. Probably summoning him to breakfast.

Jack's stomach grumbled. What would they be starting their day with this time? Cold leftover pizza? Maybe even fresh hot pizza. Or perhaps someone had finally managed to convince Lucas to cook something proper.

Jack hurried down from the attic, leaving the window open behind him. He forced a smile, but then realized that he didn't need to force it: he was already beaming as he sauntered downstairs to join his cousins for a new day in the Changeling House.

Interlogue: Faces in the Shadows

A stretched late-afternoon shadow peers out from behind the dumpster bins, fixing a pair of pearly eyes on the restaurant doorway.

Someone left the door ajar.

This is too easy.

The shadow emerges into the evening sunlight, and as it does its face catches the light and blurs slightly… and then features sharpen: a plump round face, reddened nose, eyes like dark pebbles.

The man goes through the door, which says STAFF ONLY on it, and down a narrow stone hallway. Through the second door on the left is the kitchen, just as he's expecting. It's empty save for one cook, a chubby acne-scarred teenager hovering over an enormous steaming pot of gumbo.

"Oh," says the boy, feigning eagerness. "Evening, Sammy."

"Evening," Barkface murmurs. "Let me see that for a moment, will you?" Voices are far more difficult than faces, but his familiarity with the Nordine brothers has paid off: the boy nods eagerly and moves away from the gumbo. Barkface goes over to it and draws something from within the depths of his coat: a little brown paper bag which he empties into the pot.

"Just had these herbs shipped from Peru," he says. "Black mint and *chincho*. Just to add a little *exoticism*, you know? Chef's special."

The boy nods disinterestedly. Barkface stirs the brown powder into the gumbo, and out of the corner of his eye he watches the boy. *Good.* The lad can't tell the difference between Peruvian black mint and the ground-up seeds of the Angel's Trumpet.

"Take good care of this gumbo now, will you?" He steps back from the pot and gives the boy a clap on the back. "And save a big bowl of it for yourself too. On the house."

The boy's eyes light up. "Oh. Thanks!"

"Don't mention it."

With that Barkface sweeps out of the room, his face sliding only a little as he grins a garish grin.

Chapter Four: The Wynd

It's almost dawn when the brown car pulls into the driveway of number eighteen. "They're not in order," Neria whispers. Her breath fogs up the passenger-side window. "The houses. Did you notice? The numbers aren't in order."

Auntie August puts the car in park and heaves a deep, tired sigh. "I noticed." They've been driving all night, and all of the previous day. "Let's just get our things inside."

They don't have much in the way of things. Each of them has a duffle bag and a box of groceries, but aside from that there's nothing. They've learned to travel light. "Don't get too attached to *things*, Neria," Auntie August told her when she was little. "Things break. Things get lost. Things don't care about you, so you'd best not care about them."

As promised, the key is waiting for them under the flower pot on the porch. Neria opens the door and steps into 18 Morgana Wynd. It smells like sawdust inside the dark house.

"Now, how about some rest?" Auntie August's voice is slurred with fatigue, but even in the pre-dawn gloom Neria can hear the smile in her voice. "You've been up almost thirty hours."

But sleep is the last thing on Neria's mind. "No way. I'm gonna start my map. And I get the bigger bedroom this time, by the way—remember?"

Auntie August laughs. "At this point I'd settle for a nice bit of floor." She crosses the room and tumbles onto the sofa. "Goodnight, Neria."

"It's morning," says Neria, but Auntie August's eyes are already closed, and if she's still awake, she's doing a great job of hiding it.

————— •·◆·• —————

Every map begins at home. It takes Neria all of ten minutes to commit the new house's layout to memory. Two bedrooms on the second floor, a flight of stairs, a corridor branching off into a bathroom, a kitchen, a living room, and a patio with a north-east-facing view. *Not bad.* Better than the last few.

Now, the inventory. The sun's rising at this point, painting the wide-windowed rooms of eighteen in pinks and golds. Aside from several old pieces of furniture, a plump brown spider hanging in a web in a corner of the bathroom, and a few chipped dishes in the cupboards, there isn't anything noteworthy in the house.

But *outside*...

The air is ripe with thrush-song and the cries of seagulls, and there's something else, too. A smell? Or... a feeling disguised as a smell?

Have I been here before?

No, it's not that, exactly... but for the first time in her life, Neria feels as though she's *exactly* where she's supposed to be.

She sets off along the street, and every house she passes, every signpost, every curve in the road, gets fixed to the map, like flies sticking to flypaper.

She makes her way past the entrance of the Wynd, all the way to the highway, then backtracks. She goes slowly. Unhurried. *Take it all in.*

Gradually, piece by piece, the Morgana Peninsula takes shape.

The ragged coastline stretches on for miles and miles to the north and south: earth and ocean colliding in a dramatic tapestry of beaches and cliffs and forests. And there's the Morgana Peninsula, interrupting the coastline—jutting out into the ocean like an arrowhead stabbing into the flank of a blue giant.

The peninsula is covered in thick old-growth forest, cedars and sequoias and firs and other green things all vying for space, rocketing from the spongy lichen-carpeted ground to impressive altitudes. Some of them, the sequoias especially, reach so high they've got snow on their uppermost branches, even now in early summer.

Neria squints at the tops of the trees. She blinks. *No, that can't be.*

An optical illusion, then. Either way, they're tall as hell. She wonders if they're the tallest trees she has ever seen.

Focus.

She turns her attention back to her map. *Morgana Wynd.* Her new home—for now, at least.

How many people know about this place?

Neria passes the scratched, faded wooden signpost that says WELCOME TO MORGANA WYND. Soon the houses begin to pop up—spaced far apart at first, and staggered unevenly. But after the first sharp bend in the road the buildings start arranging themselves more regularly, a curving arc of painted colours against the backdrop of thick, snarling forest.

Morgana Wynd cuts and swerves through the woods like a river of concrete and wood and brick. It seems to Neria that these buildings couldn't have been built here, not with the forest pressing in so close and eager on all sides. No, she decides: Morgana Wynd is a vagabond street. It once belonged to a bigger town, a faraway city of some sort. But long ago it made its getaway, and hid itself cleverly in these woods, on this little-known peninsula, in this hard-to-find nook of coastline.

There are about a dozen businesses mixed in among the cottages and villas and bungalows of the Wynd. Neria takes stock. There's a large restaurant called The Fifth Season. A bakery called Maestro Pastries. A café with no name. A convenience store, a grocery store, a pawn shop, a hotel. A laundromat with an ice cream stand in front of it. An auto repair shop and a bike rental shop, both of which look like they're going out of business.

The street curves around once more, and the buildings become staggered and unevenly-spaced again. These ones, the houses at the furthest end of Morgana Wynd, look abandoned. Boards covering their windows and doorways. Caved-in roofs. Rotting fences.

The forest presses in on all sides, and the Wynd splits in two. Up ahead the street continues on until it becomes a narrow trail and gets eaten by the woods. The other path veers to the left and rolls downhill to the water.

Neria wanders down to the water, hoping to find a beach—but the shore here is ragged and rocky, and instead of a place for her to cool her toes in the ocean, the path ends at a large, garish wharf and several ancient-looking piers sticking out into the surf.

A boatshed sits at the end of the wharf. In front of it, a tall, burly, bald man in swim-trunks sits in a folding chair, and waxes a surfboard. Neria approaches him slowly. She can't help but stare at the tattoo on the man's muscular right arm—a shark and a squid in blue and black ink, locked in some kind of death-match. He's also got tattoos crawling over his bald scalp. He looks up at her, and Neria smiles her sunniest smile.

The man frowns back. "Who are you?" he demands.

Neria's smile doesn't falter. "Is there a beach here?" she asks innocently. "I'm looking for sand."

Above his untrusting eyes, the old man's forehead furrows. "You have to go through the woods first," he says. "Past where the trail ends." His frown deepens, and for some reason this makes Neria's smile widen.

"Who are you?" he repeats.

"You're dreaming, old man," she fires back, without planning it, without thinking—and before the man can respond she turns on her heel and speed-walks back up the path, back to the Wynd, giggling to herself the whole way.

———— •·◆·• ————

It's just past sundown. Neria's map is almost complete.

She crouches behind a blue-flowered hydrangea bush, gazing at the strange stone building before her. The ornate wood-carved sign above the entrance reads:

THE FIFTH SEASON
the finest dining on the Wynd

There are people dining on the patio beneath coloured ornamental lights strung on wires, and more people inside. Buzzing chatter fills the air, conversation and cutlery clinking against plates, laced with a jaunty melody spun on a violin.

This is where it begins.

The voices never lie. Neria creeps closer to the patio, bites her lip, and waits. *Where what begins?* she asks silently, though the voices never answer questions, at least not directly.

By the time she notices that something is happening, it's already in full swing.

Some of the diners have left their seats and are wandering around with strange expressions on their faces. "What are you *doing?*" somebody demands. A man with long black hair and haunted eyes starts walking in circles around his table, while the man he's dining with—a brawny man with a black beard—seems to be lost in conversation with the half-eaten wedge of steak speared on his fork.

Neria follows the black-haired man with her gaze as he wanders over to the wall. He starts talking to the wall. Neria tips her head to the side so she can hear better. She manages to pluck his voice out of the tapestry of sound: a low, throaty murmur. "Where are you I can't see you I can hear you what's going on I'm thirsty dear lord I'm so thirsty please get me some water where's the water whereisitIcan'tseeyoushowyourself..."

Neria walks to the oak tree right beside the patio. With a running jump she hauls herself up into its foliage. She finds a perch, a cradle of tangled branches: from here she can see clearly into the main room of the restaurant.

What the hell?

Some of the diners are lying on the floor—several of them are laughing hysterically, and one of them, a middle-aged woman, sobs uncontrollably, tearing at the floorboards. "I know you're under here!" she moans. "*Please* stop hiding *please* I miss you I *miss* you!"

Another diner is standing on top of his table—is he trying to dance or having a seizure?

Yet another vomits onto his server, who sports a look of sheer panic. And the clamour of confused voices rides above it all:

"…it's the end times it's judgment day I knew this day would come I knew it I knew it I *told* you…"

"Sammy? *Sammy!* The hell's going on?"

"I dunno, I dunno!"

"…he's coming he's coming I hear his footsteps quickly quickly eat your sins before he sees them…"

"Somebody call 9-1-1-1-1-1-1-1!"

"…I'm dizzy I'm so dizzy so so so dizzy…"

"Oh *shit,* this guy's not breathing—"

The man with long hair moves away from the wall and collapses onto the floor, he's foaming at the mouth and convulsing. His friend, the black-bearded one, turns and stares straight through the restaurant window, straight at the tree beside the patio, straight at Neria, and his eyes are wide and bloodshot, his pupils larger than any she has ever seen, his mouth a great big screaming O.

Neria half-leaps, half-falls from the tree, and starts running as soon as her feet hit the ground.

She runs all the way back to number eighteen.

Auntie August is sitting on the sofa, balancing a bowl of salad in one hand and a book in the other. She glances up as Neria slams the door shut and locks it behind her.

A wave of relief washes over Neria at the sight of her guardian. Auntie August is tall and broad-shouldered, with coffee-coloured skin and frizzy dark hair that descends to cover her ears. She has a special kind of look to her, the kind of look that makes you feel like she's going to make everything okay.

"Finish your map?" Auntie August asks.

"Yes. No. Sorta." Neria starts up the stairs to her bedroom—but then Auntie August sets her book down, and frowns at Neria.

"Yes, no, sorta," she echoes. "Well, it can't be all three of those at once, can it?"

"Apparently it can. G'night."

Neria races up to her room. She locks the bedroom door behind her.

This is where it begins.

For reasons she can't quite explain, she starts laughing.

———— •·◆·· ————

The next morning there's caution tape all over the Fifth Season's entrance, concerned-looking cops milling around in front of it. When Neria asks one of them for information he tells her brusquely to stay away. "This is a crime scene," he growls. "Keep your distance."

So Neria keeps her distance. She crosses to the other side of the street, where a tall boy is sitting on the curb and smoking a cigarette. He's got a funny look to him: his buzz cut is so thin he's basically bald, and his lower jaw sticks out, making it look like he's pouting.

Neria sits down next to him. "D'you know what happened?"

The boy looks at her strangely for a moment, like he's sizing her up. Then:

"Something bad."

"I figure."

The boy flicks ash off the tip of his cigarette and narrows his eyes. "They're saying it's murder," he says sinisterly.

"Murder?"

The boy nods impressively. "The Nordine brothers." He draws a finger across his throat.

"I dunno who the Nordine brothers are."

The boy gestures to the restaurant. "They own the Fifth Season—*owned.*" His frown deepens. "You're new here, then?"

"I moved here yesterday. My name's Neria."

"Ah." The boy proffers her the cigarette. Neria shakes her head. With a shrug he sticks it back in his mouth. "Simon," he drawls.

Then he leans in close to her—close enough that she gets a face full of tobacco-breath—and jerks his thumb over his shoulder.

"See that man there? The one talking to the police?"

Neria looks. The man in question is dressed all in black. Black coat, black trousers, black toque. Neria watches him converse with a pair of cops, who stand before him with their arms crossed, looking puzzled.

"What about him?"

Simon's eyes gleam dangerously. "I heard him say he was a friend of Sammy and Dacklyn. He was asking a lot of questions. Look."

The two cops are escorting the man away from the crime scene. As they push him past Neria and Simon, the two youths overhear what he's saying. "Like I said, whoever did this, they're gonna pay for it."

"Don't come back here again," one of the cops says bluntly.

Neria watches as they lead the black-clad man down the street to a beat-up Dodge. The man gets in and drives away. "What kind of questions?" she asks.

"What?" Simon grunts.

"That man. What kind of questions was he asking the cops?"

"Like, what kinda stuff they found in there, what's been impounded as evidence, whether or not there were any valuables."

The cops pass by Neria and Simon again as they make their way back to the perimeter of the crime scene. "You two have lingered far too long," one of them growls. "Get lost."

Simon stubs out his cigarette. "This is my home. My family's lived on Morgana Wynd for four years. I'll go where I please, thank you very much." He jabs a finger at the cop, who bristles and tenses. "*You,* on the other hand, are a stranger here, *officer.*"

With that, Simon turns on his heel and sets off down the Wynd before the cop can respond. Neria follows the boy eagerly.

"Hog," Simon scowls, once they're out of earshot.

Then he's smiling warmly at Neria. "Listen—it's Neria, right? I'm taking my dad's canoe out later with a friend, and there's a spot for you if you'd care to join."

But Neria isn't listening. She's just spotted something in the oak tree by the restaurant patio (the same tree she hid in the night before). She squints. *Who is that?* A dark mass clinging to the trunk behind curtains of leaves.

"It's a crocodile-hide canoe," Simon continues. "You should see it. It goes three times the speed of a regular canoe. And get this—it's made from the croc that killed my grandfather. Gramps took the monster out with him— stabbed it right through the roof of its mouth while it was chewing on his... Neria? Are you listening to me?"

Neria blinks, shakes her head. Turns back to Simon. "Er—what?"

Simon sighs. "We're taking a canoe out later, and seeing as you're new here, I thought maybe you'd like to join us. We'll show you round the peninsula."

"Oh. Right." Neria bites her lip. "Uh—sorry, I've gotta help Auntie with something." She's not sure why she says it. Maybe it's the way Simon's smiling at her…

"*Auntie?*" Simon half laughs, half jeers. "What does *Auntie* need help with?"

But Neria's already spinning on her heel and walking briskly away. *Why did I say that?*

"Hey, you're still welcome if *Auntie* lets you off early!" Simon shouts after her. "Think about it!"

But Neria doesn't look back. She closes her eyes, summons her map to the forefront of her mind, and lets it guide her feet along the curve of the Wynd as surely as if her eyes were open…

What use is a map if you don't know where you're trying to get to?

But Neria does know where she's trying to get to. She can already see where the map is guiding her. It's not just a map in space, of course, but a map in time as well—

And the time isn't quite right.

The path spools out before her, a vague, meandering trail, coiling through the sun-soaked hours of daylight, down to the end of Morgana Wynd, to the woods…

And eventually, hours and hours later, the path turns around, backtracks the way it came, and Neria retraces her steps all the way to the Fifth Season.

There's a cop standing sentinel at the front door, another in the back, and a third patrolling the perimeter. They're all muttering to each other through their walkie-talkies. Neria can't make out exactly what they're saying, but she can hear the unease rattling their voices.

She approaches the Fifth Season from the muddy alley that snakes behind it.

The officer stationed around the back sounds more on edge than the other two. It's not hard to tell why: there aren't any streetlamps behind the Fifth Season. Just a small circle of light from the lantern hanging above the restaurant's back door. In the gloom Neria can just make out several dumpster bins, an empty gravel lot, and the cop standing motionless in front of the door.

"Psst! Neria!"

Neria turns to see Simon crouched behind an old, rusted Volkswagen in the backlot of the café next to the Fifth Season. He motions for her to join him. Bent double, Neria slinks to the car and crouches beside Simon.

"How's your Auntie?" he whispers.

"She's fine," Neria whispers back.

"What are you doing here?"

"What are *you* doing here?"

"I don't trust these Cormora Creek cops. I'm keeping an eye on them. Consider me the neighbourhood watch."

Neria says nothing. Peering out from behind the old car, she watches the cop raise his walkie-talkie to his mouth again. This time she can actually hear what he says:

"When's next shift getting here? I don't wanna stay a minute longer than we have to. Over." A beat. "And actually, if you can tell them to kindly hurry their asses up, please. Over."

Then Neria spots something else: a man and a woman, dressed all in black, emerging from around the side of the Fifth Season—skirting the caution-taped perimeter and approaching the restaurant's back door.

"Simon—" Neria hisses.

"I see them."

Neria squints. *What's wrong with their faces?* It takes her a second to puzzle out what she's looking at. *Masks.* Pale masks with impassive slits for eyes.

"The hell?" Simon whispers.

Neria presses a finger to her lips. "Shh." The two masks are standing in front of the cop now.

"…crime scene," the officer's saying, a noticeable quaver in his voice. "I'll kindly ask you to leave." He raises his walkie-talkie to his mouth. "Harry, get over here now."

"No need for that," the masked woman says. She removes her mask—Neria squinches her eyes to try and make out a face, but all she can see is pale skin framed by long black hair.

The woman raises her hand to her mouth, palm up, and blows what looks like a cloud of white mist into the officer's face. The officer staggers back and falls against the door, spluttering in surprise. Then he looks up, and even from the next lot over Neria and Simon can make out the smile spreading across his face.

They hear him laugh, a giggle that starts low and ends high. He stumbles drunkenly toward the masked man, while the woman walks behind him and places her hands on his shoulders.

"Your friends have already gone home, officer," she says. "Go with them. Nothing's happening here."

The officer slips out of the woman's grip, then turns around to look at her. Neria almost laughs at the bewildered expression on his face. His jaw hangs slack, his shoulders slouched.

"On your way, officer," the woman says.

"Goodbye," the cop grunts. He pivots away from her and staggers off, vanishing around the side of the building.

The man offers a muffled chuckle from behind his mask. "That was easy."

"I *told* you it works best as powder," the woman responds as she puts her mask back on. They both approach the Fifth Season's back door.

"Let's do this quick, before it wears off and those cops come back."

"It won't wear off. This is one of Rika's batches. Those guys will never be right in the head again."

"Like Rika?"

"Like Rika."

Neria can't help it. "Let's get out of here," she whispers. She stands up—"Get *down!*" Simon hisses, grabbing her elbow and yanking her back to the ground next to him. "Did you *hear* what they just said? Lay low."

The masked man tries the back door—it's unlocked—and opens it, revealing the pitch-black innards of the Fifth Season.

And then a strident cry rings out like the chiming of a gong: "I SEE YOU!"

Neria's heart skips a beat. Auntie August emerges from the night, striding toward the two mask-wearers, her movements stiff with fury. She towers over the two of them, at least a foot taller than they are.

Fear blossoms in Neria's stomach like a spark igniting a gas cloud. *No—stay back—*

"The three cops you drugged are on their way to the hospital," Auntie August snarls, "and more are coming here. I suggest you leave before they get here. And never, *ever* come back. The Face of Pale is not welcome in Morgana Wynd."

The masks glow like twin orange moons in the warm lantern-light. Then the woman reaches up and pulls off her mask again, and leers at Auntie August. "We're not afraid of you," she growls.

"Where's the girl?" the other asks, glancing at the rusty car in the next lot.

"You'll never get your hands on her," Auntie August spits. "I *said*"—her voice swells with guttural rage—"LEAVE NOW, AND DON'T EVER RETURN."

The mask returns to cover the woman's face, and the two intruders hurry out of the circle of light. Neria loses sight of them in the darkness.

Silence falls. Then Auntie August turns to look at the rusty car in the café's backlot. "Neria," she calls, her voice returned to normal, "come out, please."

It doesn't even occur to Neria to disobey. She shares a petrified glance with Simon, then emerges from behind the car. Slowly she approaches the woman who has raised her and protected her all her life.

"You too, Simon," says Auntie August.

There's a scuffing of shoes on gravel, a terrified whisper: "Oh god, oh god, no freaking way, man," as Simon shoves himself out from behind the car and flees into the night.

Neria falls against Auntie August, and her guardian drapes an arm around her shoulders. "Let's go, Neri."

Neria grimaces and swallows.

"What… what just happened?"

But her guardian doesn't respond as she leads Neria back around the side of the Fifth Season, back to the Wynd. Neria only looks back once—and when she does she spots a sliver of shadow slipping through the open doorway, into the darkness of the Fifth Season.

Chapter Five: A Dead Man's Tale

It's only a bit bigger than a marble. It has a cobalt glow to it, like a pilfered piece of the moon, or a little stolen star. She finds it sitting on her pillow, and though the lights are out and the curtains are drawn, she can see her bedroom clearly, like it's the middle of the day.

But it's pitch dark outside.

She picks up the orb, holds it between her fingers. "Where did you come from?" she whispers.

———— •·◆·• ————

"Someone put something in the food," says Auntie August. "Listen to this: *Some of them were found talking to themselves, while others were vomiting, laughing or crying. Many reported seeing things that were not there, and complained of intense thirst and dizziness. Most appeared distressed, and several downright terrified.*"`

"Why, though?"

Auntie August shrugs, and returns to reading her newspaper. It's a local publication she picked up at the grocery store: *The Cormora Chronicle.*

Neria chews her lip for a moment. "Auntie?"

"Yes?"

"We've been here before, haven't we?"

At first Auntie August doesn't respond. Then: "I've said it a thousand times, Neri, and I'll say it again. There's only one rule. *Never return to a place you've been before.*"

It's the same answer every time, and every time it makes Neria angry. "Fine then," she growls, as she usually does. Most times Auntie August will follow up with something like "I know it isn't fair, kiddo, but that's just our lot in life," and her voice will be so tender and calming that Neria can't stay mad for long.

This time, though, Auntie August doesn't say a word.

———— •◆• ————

There's a library in Cormora Creek, which is a twenty-minute bike ride from Morgana Wynd. Neria borrows a bike from Simon.

It doesn't take her long to find the library. It's a modest pink stucco building that stinks of neglect. The librarian at the desk must be a hundred and fifty years old. "Can I help you?" he wheezes.

"I'm looking for information about drugs," says Neria. "Ones that cause hallucinations. And"—she consults the folded-up newspaper clipping she brought with her—"laughing, crying, vomiting, intense thirst, and dizziness."

The librarian glares at her. "I'm sorry," he croaks. "You'll have to look elsewhere."

Neria looks right into his sunken, beady eyes. "You *sure?*"

The librarian returns the stare. "Yes."

Neria shrugs. She wanders further into the library, down several rows of shelves. She tilts her head to the side and listens.

Libraries are good places for this sort of thing. People always leave things here—leftovers. Trails. Strung through the air like motes of dust. In an aisle between two shelves near the rear of the building, Neria finds something she recognizes: an ice-cold dread, the same she felt when she made eye contact with the black-bearded man at the Fifth Season.

The dread hangs there in the air, invisible and innocuous, and it makes Neria want to turn around and run.

But she can't run. Not yet.

She glances over her shoulder to make sure nobody's looking, then faces forward again. She stares down the aisle. The elderly librarian at the front desk crosses her mind. As far as she can tell, he's the only other person in the building.

He won't see.

She closes her eyes. She knows this game—the game of hidden gates. The game of secret ways.

"Come on," she whispers. "I need to know."

When she opens her eyes, a staircase rises from the middle of the aisle: twelve rotten-looking wooden steps leading up to a ledge, a narrow stone ledge that's not really there, that's just a trick of the light, hovering several meters above the library floor.

I'm a trick of the light, too.

Neria places her foot tentatively on the first step. The spongy wood sinks slightly under her weight, but when she puts her other foot down on the step it seems firm enough to hold her up. She walks up the staircase that shouldn't be there, up past the tops of the bookshelves, up to the ledge that nobody else can see.

Glancing back, she watches the steps melt away in her wake, dissipating into nothingness behind her. Then she reaches the top of the staircase, and climbs onto the ledge, wondering as she does so what she must look like from the librarian's vantage point. A girl floating to the ceiling and vanishing?

He'll probably just think he's going slightly mad. Most people do.

And Neria has more pressing things to worry about now. The hard stone beneath her feet is reassuring, but the ledge is much narrower than it looked from the library floor.

Pressing her back against the stone wall behind her, Neria shimmies along the ledge until she comes to a mouth in the wall: the entrance of a narrow dusty tunnel.

She starts down the tunnel, crouching under the low ceiling. The walls are tattooed with mildew and the floor is covered in thick black mud.

The dread nestled in her chest turns glacial.

The passage swerves this way, that way, and at the end of it a shadow is sitting with his back against a wall. He looks up at Neria. He's got no eyes, just charred pits where his eyes should be. His mouth is full of rotten teeth and his tongue lolls lazily out the side. He looks at her and tries to smile a ghastly smile.

"Nobody's come down this way in a while."

Neria approaches the shadow slowly. "I was in a library," she says, "and the librarian said they don't have what I'm looking for." She pauses. "What's your name?"

The shadow nods slowly, and with lightning-quick hands he grabs a cockroach from the floor and shoves it into his mouth, chews for a moment then swallows. "I am Cole Ferrox. I was a professor once. What are you looking for?"

Neria crouches beside Cole Ferrox and hands him the crumpled-up newspaper article. The professor unfolds it with blackened skeletal hands and scans it closely with the unseeing holes in his head.

"Ahh," he says after a moment. "I've seen this before. The breath of the nightshade." He looks up at Neria, and the rippling dread becomes so strong that she wants to cry. "What is your interest in this poison, child?"

"I just want to know what kind of thing would make people do that," says Neria. *Stay strong.* "What's nightshade?"

The shadow speaks slowly now, forming each word with careful deliberation. "A long time ago, when I was still a young professor, I fell afoul of a particularly… *strange* student. His name was Neil. He befriended me. He showed genuine interest in what I was teaching—I was a professor of pharmaceuticals—and he had an interest in the effects of plants that could, er, how to put it? *Alter* one's consciousness."

"*Alter?*"

"Alter, yes. His interest, specifically, was in the effects of the flowering plants of the nightshade family. He told me he was working on a project, but he wouldn't tell me what it was. But I was thirsty for knowledge, child. I was greedy. I pestered him and pestered him until eventually he caved." Here the professor's voice drops. "He was attempting to build a demon. And he needed something to help him. The flower he was looking for is called the Angel's Trumpet"— Professor Ferrox reaches forward, and in her mind's eye Neria sees it, a white flower exploding from a bank of green foliage—"or its sister, Datura. The seeds found in the pods which grow on these plants contain toxins which cause the effects that article describes. More or less. It is also lethal in high enough doses."

The professor smiles again, showing his blighted mouth in all its glory. "I did not realize until it was too late, but by revealing this to me, Neil had murdered me."

Neria shuffles her feet. The dread is screaming inside her, but her curiosity has been snagged. "Murdered?"

"He made me swear to keep it all a secret, of course. And then a week later he and some... friends of his, I guess you'd call them... well, they jumped me. Knocked me out. I think it was ether. When I woke up I was in a shed or a warehouse or *somewhere,* somewhere dark and wet, and they had tied me up." The professor is speaking faster now, his voice rising. "They did... *things.* They *cut* me and starved me, they wouldn't let me sleep, and—well, I shouldn't trouble you with the details. You have no idea how..." He trails off.

"That sounds so awful. I—"

"That wasn't even the worst of it. They weren't trying to extract information from me or anything like that. No, they were trying to convince me of something: that a creature called Pale was coming to take my soul. They called him their demon god. You must understand, child, that I would never have believed in such a thing ordinarily. I was a professor. I lived in books, in research and laboratories and proofs. In what could be observed and documented. But then, when I felt that I could take no more, that death must've been imminent"—he draws in a raspy, rattling breath—"Neil came to me and forced sixteen of the Trumpet's seeds down my throat. Then he stabbed my eyes out with a white-hot poker. As you can see."

Neria swallows loudly. "Right. Yes. And—and then what happened?"

Professor Ferrox smiles that awful, putrefying smile again. "The pain," he says, licking his lips as though reminiscing about a delicious meal he once had, "was unimaginable. Even now it's like remembering a horrible nightmare I had when I was young. But what was worse was the knowledge, the dead certainty, that I would never see anything again. It wasn't just darkness, child, like when the lights are all turned out. It was nothing. And nothing hurts like hell.

"I don't know how long I stayed like that for, but eventually I began to feel that I had been transported somewhere else. Somewhere far away. And then I saw him. *Pale*. He's real, my child. He came for my soul, just like they said he would. So now I'm here."

Neria's backing away now. "Well," she says. "That's really, really rough. I'll just—I should be going. Thank you, Professor."

"Not at all." He reaches out and grabs her arm with his blackened bony fingers. "Won't you stay a while, child? It gets lonely in here."

Neria tries to jump back, but the professor's grip is a steel vice. "Let go!" she shrieks.

The professor rises, a flowing mass of tattered robes, and his grip tightens around her forearm.

"Let! *Go!*"

"My flesh is dry and my bones are brittle. Perhaps I could use yours instead."

Neria remembers something Auntie August taught her. "You're *nothing,*" she spits. "You're a shadow of something that was once alive and real. But Professor Ferrox died a long time ago. You're not *real*. You're just somebody else's nightmare telling a dead man's tale. I don't believe in you!"

It's a lie, of course, a last-ditch bluff: Neria knows well enough that this piece of Cole Ferrox is as real as the real professor once was. But as Neria speaks the shadow shrinks from her, its grip loosens, enough for her to yank her arm away and scamper back up the tunnel—

But the tunnel's blocked off. The walls have folded in, sealed like the passage has been cauterized. She turns and Professor Ferrox is towering over her, he's swelled now to fill the entire tunnel, and he's got more arms than he should have, five, six, seven of them, and they're all reaching for Neria.

"Wait!" she shouts.

Three arms grab her, pin her against the wall.

"Wait! *Stop!* I can help you!" The professor's advancing on her, but she senses an opportunity. "I can get you out of here!"

One of the arms retracts, so that it's only two pinning her. "Can you?"

"Yes! I can! But only if you let *GO* of me!"

For a moment the professor doesn't move. Then his face twists into a vicious grin. "But I *like* it here," he rasps. Three more arms reach over, slam Neria back into the wall—and something falls out of her pocket, lands in the black mud of the tunnel floor. A tiny silver marble.

Where did you come from?

Neria squints and suddenly she can see more clearly—the professor is just a shroud, coils of darkness wound together in a writhing mass.

Maybe he **isn't** *real.* His grip has loosened, and Neria shakes herself free, drops down to her knees and scoops up the star marble. Rising, she turns, presses the marble against the cauterized wall before her, and the tunnel opens again with a hideous squelch. She staggers through, slipping in the black mud, up the sloping tunnel—and only once there's a considerable distance between herself and Professor Ferrox does she dare to look back.

He's still standing there, completely filling the tunnel, staring at her with his empty eye sockets. *"Your name,"* he says, but it's not just his voice, it's a dozen voices all tied up into one, *"is Neria Vale Faulken. Your father is Neil Faulken. He used to call you Neria Nightshade."*

Neria's knees buckle.

"The Face of Pale will find you," the many voices wheeze. *"Run now, little girl."* Crazed, maniacal cackling fills the tunnel, as though Neria is standing before a room filled with jeering spectators. *"You've been spotted. It won't be long. We will converge. We will finish what we started. Pale will be stronger than ever before."*

And then, beneath it all, another voice—Professor Ferrox. The *real* Professor Ferrox. "You said you could help! Please!"

Neria flips him the finger. "Go to hell!" she screams, and then she's running back up the tunnel as fast as her legs can carry her.

— • ◆ • —

She topples out onto the library floor, picks herself up, leans against a shelf and catches her breath. She's sweating, shaking, and her shoes and legs are caked in black mud. Her heart's going a million miles an hour.

"Excuse me."

She wheels around. The librarian stands before her, contempt etched into his potholed face. "You're tracking mud *every*where."

Neria doesn't trust herself to speak. She dashes out of the library into the late afternoon sunlight, hops on Simon's bike and starts pedaling frantically.

It knew my name.

The wind tears at her, her eyes stream, and the hot June sun slams the back of her neck.

It knew my goddamn name.

She pedals faster.

Arc Two: Splintering
Chapter Six: Wyvern

Waves lapped at the shore like sandpaper tongues, and under a sky dyed an unearthly red, Jack stood on the beach, dug his pale bare toes into the snow-white sand and stared across the water at the Cursed Rock, at the silhouetted lighthouse.

Someone was standing there, at the foot of the lighthouse.

Jack squinted. A woman?

He couldn't quite bring her into focus, but he was pretty sure it was a woman, wearing a white dress, and singing.

Singing?

He could hear the sound from over the waves, an ethereal voice moaning a solemn dirge. Or was it the wind?

Jack stepped forward, into the surf—waded through the quicksilver water toward the Cursed Rock—

And then he awoke.

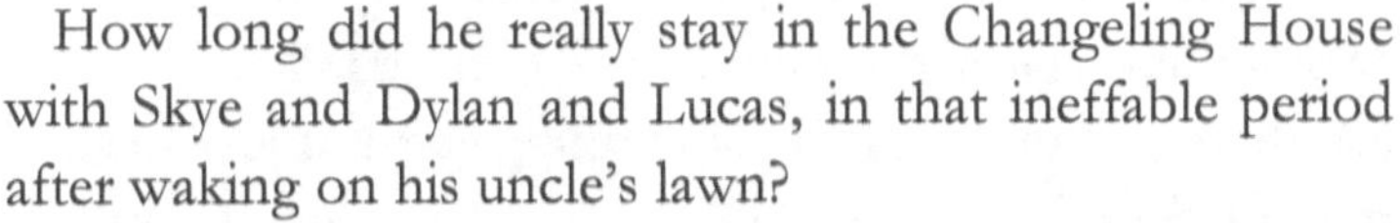

How long did he really stay in the Changeling House with Skye and Dylan and Lucas, in that ineffable period after waking on his uncle's lawn?

Later, when it was all through, Jack would look back on those days and remember them only as a blur, shadowy and moon-edged and hazy, like something glimpsed out of the corner of his eye. It was as though someone had strolled carelessly through his head and knocked his memories out of place, and when they had put them back together some of them had been missing, and others were twisted out of shape.

How long did he stay? Was it three days? Four?

A week? Two weeks?

Or was it just one night—one long, endless night during which the sun rose and set several times, off schedule, as it pleased?

You're losing your mind.

He watched Skye blow a trail of bubbles out of her plastic pipe. Watched the bubbles drift through the slants of rosy dusklight coming through the attic window.

"What's in the lighthouse?" he asked. The question was directed at nobody in particular.

Dylan looked up from the book he was reading, a thick tome about colonial history in the West Indies. "Nobody knows," he said. "Nobody's been inside. The door's sealed shut. We got there once, to the Cursed Rock—me and Skye, I mean—"

"And by that," Skye interjected, "he means Admiral Bloodskye and Dylan the Derelict made it to the Cursed Rock."

Jack forced a chuckle, but it was bitter, knotted up in envy and regret. *Another one I missed out on.*

"It's hard enough to get there as it is," Dylan continued. "Something about the tide, or the currents. But once we got there… I dunno, man, something about it just freaked me out. Something's not right about that place. I couldn't explain what it was—it was just a gut instinct. And they say you should always trust your gut in situations like that, 'cause it means your subconscious mind is picking up on something your conscious mind hasn't noticed."

Jack shivered.

"We didn't stay very long," Dylan added. "We didn't get in the lighthouse, and we didn't find anything else there. It was kind of a waste, to be honest." He glanced apprehensively out the window; Jack followed his cousin's gaze. He found the Cursed Rock easily on the shiny silver sheet of water, a distant black fist rising from the ocean, with the implacable lighthouse standing atop it.

"She'll grant you a wish," said Lucas from the corner of the room, where he had melted into a wicker rocking chair and momentarily phased out of existence.

"What?" Jack spoke absently, without looking away from the distant lighthouse.

"That's what some people say, anyway." The rocking chair creaked as Lucas sat up straight. "The woman who lives in the lighthouse—some people say they've seen her. They say she's beautiful. And she'll grant you a wish, but you have to bring her something. An offering."

"I heard she's a witch," said Skye. "I heard it's a sacrifice she demands. And then she'll give you whatever your heart desires."

"What kind of sacrifice?" said Jack.

Skye shrugged. Lucas opened his mouth like he was about to say something, but Dylan beat him to it. "Or maybe it's just an old lighthouse," he said.

Again Lucas opened his mouth to speak—but this time it was Skye who stole his moment. "Look at this, Jack," she said, setting her bubble pipe aside to grab something from the bedside table.

Finally Jack turned away from the window. He took the crumpled newspaper from his cousin and scanned the article on the front page. *"The End of the Fifth Season?"* He read slowly. "Warning: this story contains disturbing elements which might be inappropriate for some readers.

Discretion is advised?" He glanced at Skye, who made a *keep going* kind of face.

There was a picture of Sammy and Dacklyn Nordine printed above the article. Someone had crossed their eyes out with red Xs.

"Wait a sec," said Jack. "Murder-suicide? That means—"

Dylan reached over and flipped several pages ahead. He pointed to one of the paragraphs. "Read that."

"*Dacklyn Nordine, Samuel's brother, business partner and co-owner of the restaurant, was found dead in the bathroom on the second floor with a gunshot wound to the head that appeared to be self-inflicted, marking this case as a murder-suicide. It remains unclear whether there is any connection between this tragic event and the incident at the Fifth Season which occurred the night before.*" Jack looked up. "Dacklyn killed Sammy?" His voice was suddenly hoarse. *Dacklyn Nordine killed his own brother?*

He hadn't known the Nordine brothers *well*—but he had known them. Everybody in Morgana Wynd had known them.

"Except," Dylan said softly. "Except, except, except."

"Except *what?*" said Jack.

"Except Dacklyn didn't do it. Did he, Skye?"

Skye leapt in eagerly: "The morning it happened—okay, nobody found out it happened till later in the day. The police came at, like, eleven. So it must've happened early in the morning, right? And here's the thing. That morning I woke up way earlier than usual. Like, six in the morning. And I remember seeing someone out the window, going down the street. They looked like they were in a rush or something, and I thought—I thought they were dressed weirdly, like they were wearing a cloak or something, only it was shining like it was—I guess 'cause it was sunny or something. I thought at first it was covered in rubies. You know, embroidered. I didn't realize till that night. It wasn't rubies."

Skye fixed Jack with a lurid stare. "I might've been dreaming," she added, "but I don't think I was." She reached over and snatched the newspaper from him. "It's been a strange time for us too. And whatever it is that's happening, you're right in the middle of it. Whether you like it or not. So. You gonna tell us why you're really here?"

"I already *told* you!" Jack protested.

"Give it a rest, Skye," said Dylan.

"Give it a rest?" Skye leapt to her feet and flung the newspaper down onto the bed. "How am I supposed to give it a rest when the whole world's going completely sideways?"

"Skye—"

"First"—Skye pivoted on her heel to look each of them in the eye as she spoke—"a little boy and his dad go missing near Cormora Creek. Then people in masks start showing up all around the peninsula. *Then* Dad eats some 'bad food' in the Fifth Season and falls into a coma on the *same night* that Sammy and Dacklyn Nordine are murdered. And then *you* show up." Her gaze came to rest on Jack as though *he* were somehow responsible for all the events she had just listed. "And I'm supposed to give it a rest?"

Jack chewed his lip. "Who went missing?"

"What?"

"The boy and his dad, from Cormora Creek, who went missing. Who was it?" Jack braced himself for the answer. *Please don't say a name I recognize.*

"The kid was Andy Keirian," said Skye. "His dad was Adam. He ran a lumber shop in Cormora Creek."

Jack sighed in relief. He didn't know them.

"Andy's mother," said Dylan, "has offered ten thousand dollars to anyone who brings them home alive. *If they're still alive.*"

"Andy Keirian," said Lucas, dramatically slowly, "is in the lighthouse."

Skye, Dylan and Jack all turned to stare at him.

"Excuse me, good sir?" said Skye.

Lucas wavered, then adjusted his skewed glasses on the bridge of his nose. "It's a long story," he said, looking suddenly sheepish.

Skye rolled her eyes. "Oh, don't even bother then."

"Skye," Dylan warned. Then, to Lucas—"Go on, buddy."

"Okay, well, to start," Lucas began, "I got into the Fifth Season." His words hung impressively in the air, and for a moment the only sound in the attic was the wind knocking gently on the windowpane.

"For real?" Dylan murmured, right as Skye said, "And? Did you see the bodies?"

"Look, I'll tell you what happened," said Lucas. "But don't expect anything more from me, okay? I'm lying low after today." He sucked in a sharp, nervous breath. "They came back, all right? Those people in black, the ones who wear masks. They did something to the police—like, drugged them or something—and they were about to go in the restaurant, but someone chased them off. And then… well, there was no-one guarding the place, the cops weren't coming back, and the door was open, so… I went inside."

"You went inside," Dylan and Skye echoed in unison, their voices muted with awe.

"Yeah. I couldn't help it, it was like I *had* to see for myself. And I did. I saw all of it, man. The whole thing.

They left the crime scene cordoned off and, like, undisturbed."

"What was it like?" Skye pressed him with alarming eagerness.

"Dacklyn was in the bathroom upstairs. And Sammy was in the kitchen. Well, part of him was. The rest of him…" Lucas shuddered. "The rest of him was in the pantry."

"Metal," Skye whispered. "That's so metal."

She, Jack and Dylan were all leaning in toward Lucas now, wide-eyed, rapt with attention.

"They came back before I could get out. Not the cops— the men in masks. So I hid. I hid in a freaking broom cupboard, next to a wet greasy mop." Lucas chuckled dryly. "All I could do was sit there in the dark, try to breathe as quietly as I could, and listen."

"Did you hear much?" Skye butted in.

"I heard everything." An edge of smugness came into Lucas's voice now. "They were looking for something. At first I thought they were just robbing the place, but the more I listened… well, I'm pretty sure they were looking for something. Some kind of book, or a document, something like that. They found it eventually, whatever it was."

"What kind of document?" said Skye.

"I have no idea. But that's not even the craziest part." Lucas made a face that was half-grimace, half-smile. "They started talking about the kid who disappeared. Saying someone took him to the lighthouse on the Cursed Rock. And…" But then he trailed off, and fixed Skye and Dylan with a somber look.

"And what?" Skye pressed.

"And killed him?" Dylan ventured.

Lucas shook his head, and offered a forced chuckle. "They started talking about some weird shit, man. I don't even… they kept saying something about spilling the blood of a child from two worlds. And… putting a god inside a vessel."

Skye gave a low whistle.

"What else did they say?" Dylan asked.

Lucas was quiet for a moment. "Listen," he said, the fatigue now plain in his voice. "I would love to help you guys solve your mysteries, and—and stuff. But remember what I said.. I'm tuning out of this mindfuck." Another drama-infused pause. "Her name's Rusalka. The woman in the lighthouse. That's what the men in masks called her, anyway."

"*Rusalka.*" Jack, Skye and Dylan echoed the name at the same time.

"I tried to go there. To the lighthouse, I mean." Lucas readjusted his glasses. "But—"

"Why?" demanded Skye.

"Be*cause*. I wanted to see if it's true that Andy Keirian's in there. I thought maybe I could get my hands on that ten thousand dollar reward from his mother. So I could *finally*"—here a current of bitterness eroded Lucas's voice into a frustrated rasp—"get the fuck out of Morgana Wynd forever."

He massaged his temples with his fingers. "*Any*way," he resumed, "I decided today was the day I was gonna get to the lighthouse." He shook his head. "Bad idea. Really bad idea. It's far enough, even at low tide, and the water's *freezing*. I swam back to shore, and that's when that *thing* started following me. The woman made of wax. She was waiting for me on the sand. She chased me into the woods—and I couldn't find my way back. It's a good thing she can't climb trees, or she'd have gotten me for sure."

"What is she, though?" Dylan demanded.

"I dunno. Nothing good."

"D'you think she's Rusalka?" Skye ventured.

"No," said Jack. "Her name is Anora."

"What?"

"I think her name is Anora. The waxwoman."

"Why do you think *that?*" Skye muttered suspiciously.

"Whatever she is," said Lucas, "it's not *natural,* man. You can tell by the way she moves."

"Even if you had gotten to the Cursed Rock," said Dylan, "Rusalka wouldn't have let you inside. You said so yourself, didn't you? You need to bring her an offering."

"Or a sacrifice," Skye threw in.

Lucas buried his head in his hands, utterly defeated. "You're right," he whispered. Then his voice spiked in low fury. "And now Solomon Sturgess is out to get me too? Why? Because I'm friends with you lot? You realize you've both got a reputation here, don't you? Why d'you keep antagonizing him?"

"Because," said Dylan. "Solomon Sturgess is old, and delusional. He bought up a bunch of land here a few years ago—I guess he thought it was a good investment but it *wasn't.* I bet that's what drove him off the deep end. He thinks he's a gangster or something, now. Thinks he runs Morgana Wynd." He put a hand on Lucas's shoulder. "What I mean is, he's crazy. So don't worry about what he thinks, buddy. Just worry about staying the hell out of his way."

"Is that supposed to be reassuring?" said Lucas.

"Not really, no."

"Whatever. It doesn't matter." Lucas yawned. "I'm going to bed. Dibs on the big couch." And without waiting for any kind of response, he got up and left the room.

Silence fell.

"Weird guy," Skye offered.

Dylan turned to Jack, and when he next spoke it was with the subdued gentleness of someone wise beyond his years. "Jack. I'm sorry to bring this up, but we need to know. Have you seen your father at all in the last few years?"

Jack shook his head. "Mom got a restraining order. I haven't seen him since the last time I saw you guys. Why?"

"Because there's something wrong with our dad," said Skye. "Really, really wrong."

Jack glanced out the window again, furrowing his brow in concentration. For a moment he said nothing. He had been waiting for someone to ask him this for years. When finally he spoke it was careful and cautious and very very quiet:

"I think about that day all the time. My father, he—he hit Mom, hit her hard, in the face. But that's all I know. Mom never told me what actually went down between them. I dunno what you guys or Uncle Gabe know, but… but I've been thinking back, and thinking and thinking, and to be honest, I don't think I remember a time when there *wasn't* something just a little bit *off* about him."

Skye and Dylan shared a glance. "I told you," Skye hissed. "They're both up to no good. We have no idea where your dad is, Jack, but you better hope he doesn't find out you're here. If he finds out, he'll come for you."

Jack opened his mouth to speak—couldn't think of anything to say. For some reason the notion did not seem as absurd as it should have.

"They're up to something," said Skye. "Both of them. Dad and Uncle Jacob. Something's not *right!*" She blew hard into her bubble pipe, so hard that instead of bubbles gooey soap sprayed out.

"Something's not right," she muttered.

"What if they're also behind all that shit at the Fifth Season?" said Jack.

Dylan frowned. "No," he said. "No, I don't think they are. Why would Dad have gone to eat there that night if he knew someone was gonna spike the food? It just doesn't make sense. It's an impossibility."

"Yeah, well," said Skye. "Impossible things happen all the time." She paused. "For the Fifth Season, we've narrowed it down to two suspects so far. Barkface is one of them. You see him from time to time in the woods. Apparently he lives in some kind of cottage or something, but we've never found it."

Jack almost laughed. Something made him glance out the window again.

There she was, crouching on the sloping roof. It was her, unmistakably, on the other side of the glass—her ginger hair and her emerald headband, and her patchy jean jacket.

She winked at him and was gone.

"The other suspect," said Skye, "is Neria."

———— •·◆·• ————

Neria clings to the slanting shingles. *I'm nothing,* she thinks. *A shadow spotted in a reflection on a windowpane in the corner of someone's eye. Nothing more.*

She leans over as far as she dares and peers into the cluttered bedroom. Jack is sitting on the edge of the bed.

His mouth forms a silent word that she knows is her name. Then—

"Neria?" she hears him say innocently. "Who's that?"

What are you playing at? She presses closer to the window, holds her body so the fading dusklight hides her behind a shimmering veil.

"She's eerie, man," says Dylan. "The day she arrived on Morgana Wynd was the day it all started."

"It could be her mother, as well," says Skye. "The big woman, whoever she is. I only saw her once. She gave me the creeps."

Neria really wishes she could throw something through the window. *Are you gonna tell them anything, Jack?*

"So it's all right if I stay here for a few more days, then?" she hears him say.

Perfect.

Neria shimmies along the edge of the roof to another window—the bathroom window. She peers inside. The bathroom is empty. The window is unlocked.

Gingerly she pulls the window open. She pauses. Listens. *No-one's coming.*

Without making a sound, Neria slips into the Changeling House.

———— •·◆·• ————

Skye and Dylan had been using their father's credit card to order pizza from Cormora Creek. Besides that they had mainly been subsisting on cereal, bread, and ice cream. Occasionally Lucas would fix something up in the kitchen, lasagna or chili or piping hot soup. When Jack complimented him on his cooking, Lucas shrugged. "I learned it 'cause I was bored."

There was also a case of Deluxe Cormora Creek IPA in the fridge that they were all steadily polishing off. The warm drunkenness was new to all of them except Lucas, who had been secretly borrowing from his parents' liquor cabinet since his thirteenth birthday. To his knowledge, his parents still hadn't noticed.

"He won't remember he had this," Dylan assured Jack over breakfast one morning as he poured four glasses of frothy beer. "If he ever comes home at all."

Jack cleared a spot at the table in the kitchen and sat down. They were eating cold pizza left over from the night before. He grabbed a slice, dug in ravenously.

Skye had brought the map they had drawn of the peninsula down from the attic. She was drawing an arrow with a red marker, from the shore of the beach to the Cursed Rock.

"So," said Lucas. "I think Jack should do it."

"Do what?" Jack demanded through a mouthful of crust.

"Jack, the truth is, you're the only one of us who doesn't have a bad reputation around here. It's gotta be you."

"We're talking about breaking into the boatshed," Skye explained.

"*What?*"

"How else are we gonna get to the lighthouse?" said Skye.

"And *why* do we want to get to the lighthouse?" Jack demanded.

"To rescue Andy Keirian, obviously, and get filthy rich!"

"We need to bring Rusalka a gift if we want her to let us inside the lighthouse." Dylan gulped down his ale and burped loudly. "An offering. And besides that, we need a boat to get to the Cursed Rock. So how 'bout we kill two birds with one stone, and offer Rusalka the boat we bring?"

Jack snorted. "You think a *boat* would make a good offering?"

"Not just any boat," said Skye. "*Wyvern*. Solomon Sturgess's twenty-thousand dollar crocodile-hide canoe, made from the beast that ate his grandfather—killed by Solomon Sturgess himself, if you believe his story, right after his grandpa's shoe disappeared down the croc's throat." She paused. "They say his grandfather is as much a part of the canoe as the croc is. So I mean… that sounds like a good offering to me."

"And we won't let her keep the canoe, of course," Dylan added. "We'll just tell her she can have it so we can get inside the lighthouse, get little Andy, and get the hell back to shore. Then we return *Wyvern* to the boatshed with old Sol none the wiser."

"Sounds like a lot of trouble to me," said Jack. "Why? For a missing boy none of us knows?"

"Some hero you are," Skye snorted. "Besides, it's for ten thousand dollars, Jack." A mischievous glint came into her eye. "Think about it. That's twenty-five hundred to each of us. Technically that makes this a proper treasure hunt, doesn't it?"

"But—" Jack wasn't even sure why he was still protesting. Skye knew *exactly* what to say to persuade him. Treasure-hunting was the thing he had missed the most about Morgana Wynd. Wasn't it?

Wasn't it?

So what was wrong?

Maybe it was because every time he closed his eyes he saw the hourglass shattering on Barkface's cottage floor. Saw the waxwoman's head jerking up, her coarse straw-hair swinging over piercing glass eyes. Saw Barkface. Wrinkled sagging skin, sunken stare.

Saw a rusted steel door with a triple-deadbolt lock, shaking as something pounded on the other side of it.

Snap out of it. Jack shook his head, blinking rapidly.

"Come on," said Dylan. "Isn't Scurvy Jack still in there?"

"Who the hell is Scurvy Jack?" Lucas demanded.

"Scurvy Jack never once turned down a chance to go after some treasure," said Skye, smiling impishly. "Especially not when Admiral Bloodskye and Dylan the Derelict have a treasure map. I say it's time to commandeer Solomon's crocodile boat."

"You guys are insane," said Lucas.

Jack opened his mouth, then closed it. "And what about the freaking dead woman made of wax? Or Rusalka? What if she's dangerous?"

"She very well might be," said Lucas.

Skye turned to face Jack. So did Dylan and Lucas.

Three pairs of eyes gored him.

"So," said Skye. "You in?"

"But—wait—" Jack spluttered. "I'm so confused."

"If you're gonna stay here with us, Jack, then you're gonna have to help us out here and there." Dylan smiled, kindly but coldly. "So. Are you on board?"

Jack sighed. "*Fine,*" he growled. "But *how* am I supposed to get into the boatshed? And then after I get in, what? Do I carry this boat out by myself?"

"Getting *Wyvern* out is the easy part," said Skye. "The tricky part is getting inside without a key."

"Solomon Sturgess has a key," said Dylan.

Lucas snorted. "Good luck with *that.*"

"Maybe we can pick the lock," Skye offered.

"Neria can pick locks," said Jack. He said it automatically, without thinking, and instantly wished that he hadn't.

"Neria?" Skye spat the name venomously. "Why would she help us? And how do you know she can pick locks? I thought you said you didn't know her."

"I just—forget it," Jack mumbled. "Anyway—" But suddenly he broke off.

Neria?

He was sure he had just seen her, just across the room in the doorway leading to the stairs.

He glanced back at the others, but they didn't seem to have noticed.

She's in your head.

"So here's the plan," said Dylan, as Skye left her spot at the table and sauntered out of the kitchen. "Jack, you're gonna hang around outside the boatshed until someone unlocks it and goes inside. Don't make a big fuss of it, just slip inside after them. Casual. And, Jack. Don't. Be. Seen. By anyone. You're gonna have to hide out for a few hours—that'll be the roughest part, honestly. Bring a book. Then tonight Skye, Lucas and I will go down to meet you. You'll let us inside, and we'll all snag *Wyvern* together and take it down to the water. From there we get to the lighthouse. We find Andy Keirian, bring him home to Cormora Creek, and collect the reward money. Oh, and we have to make sure we bring the canoe back to the boatshed before the sun rises." He paused, frowned, and then nodded firmly. "Easy, right?"

"And if the waxwoman interferes?" said Lucas.

"We can climb a tree if we have to. And I doubt she can swim."

"We gotta wear these, too, when we're doing it," said Skye, bouncing back into the room. "In case we get spotted." She tossed four wooden animal masks down on the coffee table: a goat, a monkey, an elephant and an eagle, grotesquely distorted and misshapen, covered in fading paint.

"Dibs on the eagle," said Dylan.

Then Jack heard something from down the hall. A stray gust of wind, except it sounded an awful lot like his name.

"You guys hear that?" he said.

The others frowned at him. "Hear what?"

"Nuh—nothing. I'll, uh, I'll be right back."

He went down the hall, and paused by the stairwell. *Up there?* He climbed the stairs, and found himself in the bathroom. His stomach swooped. The mirror above the sink was fogged up, and there were words written on it:

I CAN HELP YOU

The bathroom window was ajar. Jack peered through, but all he could see outside was the neighbouring house.

He closed the window, locked it—glanced back at the mirror, but the words had already faded.

Did I imagine it?

He went back to join the others, grabbing the elephant mask from the coffee table. "Let's get this over with."

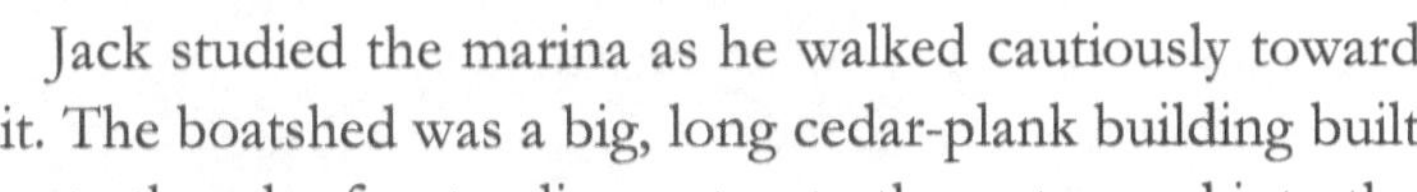

Jack studied the marina as he walked cautiously toward it. The boatshed was a big, long cedar-plank building built onto the wharf, extending out onto the water, and into the enclosed marina.

Waves rushed against sand. Sunstruck shells glittered in opalescent seams along the whiteshore. Seagulls and terns and kingfishers wheeled in the sky, crying and cawing. The air was thick with sea-stench, heady from the blaze of the midday sun.

Jack crossed the wharf to the boatshed entrance. The door was held shut by a large steel padlock. He tugged at the handle for good measure, but it didn't budge.

Jack stepped back from the door, and glanced around once more. There was nobody else to be seen. Not on the beach, nor on the wharf, nor on the breakwater enclosing the marina.

"Perfect," Jack grunted.

For a time he paced to and fro around the wharf. The elephant mask dug against his ribs under his jacket. Every time he heard something he jumped in alarm—a rustling from the nearby woods, a wave smashing against the stilted wharf supports, a distant wind that almost sounded like it was calling *Jaaaack…*'

Still nobody to be seen.

Some heist this is. Where was he even supposed to hide?

He sank down in a crouch against the wall of the boat shed. It hadn't been this hot yesterday – it took his breath away. Sweat glued his shirt to his skin.

Where are you, Neria?

He *had* seen her in the Changeling House, hadn't he? She *had* left a message on the mirror.

And then the afternoon sun threw someone's shadow over him. He squinted up at the silhouette.

"Can I help you, kid?"

Shit. Jack leapt to his feet. The man standing before him was bald, with a bristling black-and-grey beard. His scalp was riddled with tattoos. He was square-chested, broad-shouldered, and could easily have weighed two hundred and fifty pounds. He was wearing a tight black wetsuit and a suspicious glare. Jack swallowed loudly. *Shit!* He stepped back—bumped against the boat shed wall, and the elephant mask slipped out from under his shirt and landed on the wharf.

The tanned, tattooed man picked the mask up and scanned it. Jack reached for it, but the man held it away from his grasping fingers. "Who are you?" he demanded.

"I, uh—I'm new here—" Jack broke off. *Don't tell him your name!*

"I can see that. What are you doing?"

"I—I—I just wanted to see inside the boatshed—just to—um—see the boats." Jack squeezed his eyes shut. *Brutal.*

The tanned man dropped the mask onto the ground and brought his foot down on it, smashing it into little pieces. He leaned in close, smearing the stink of his fishy breath all over Jack's face. "*They* sent you, didn't they?" he sneered.

"Huh—who?"

"You know goddamn well who. I'm watching all of you." The tanned man stepped back. "I don't ever want to see you around here again, got that? And you can tell Dylan and Skye—I *know* that's who sent you down here—you can tell them Solomon Sturgess has a message for them. And that message"—his eyes narrowed to serpentine slits—"is this: *if I see any of you around here again, then you're gonna get hurt. Cease and desist.*" He smiled an equally serpentine smile. "Now *go.*"

Solomon Sturgess didn't have to say it twice: Jack was already sprinting for the Wynd. He didn't look back.

———— •·◆·• ————

"So basically it went about as badly as it could have."

Dylan sighed. "That bastard's gonna make this hard for us."

"Well," said Skye, "on the bright side…" But she trailed off. "*Is* there a bright side?"

"I, for one, am starting to think this might be a lost cause," said Lucas.

"It's not a lost cause. He broke my mask!" Skye cried exasperatedly. "This is war."

Suddenly there was a dull *thud* from upstairs. Four pairs of eyes shot to the ceiling.

"Is someone else *here?*" Skye whispered.

Dylan stood up. "Lucas, Skye—you two make sure all the doors and windows are locked. Jack, come with me."

Jack followed his cousin up the stairs. Together they combed the second floor: searched every room, under the beds, in the closets, behind the doors. They checked the closet in the Stowaway Garden, the bathroom, and the attic on the third floor. They didn't find anything out of place. Or anyone.

While Dylan was checking a closet, Jack breathed on the bathroom mirror to see if any words would appear, any secret codes or messages. But there was nothing.

Where are you?

Dylan appeared in the doorway. "What are you doing?"

Jack started guiltily. "Nothing."

Dylan sighed. "Look, I think we're all a little on edge. Let's order some pizza and figure out a plan. What d'you say?"

Jack nodded.

Then—"Dyl. Wait."

"Yeah?"

Jack swallowed loudly and stared up at his older cousin. Dylan's long, shaggy brown hair made him look wild, like someone who belonged in the woods. He already had smile-wrinkles around his lips, and twinkling turquoise eyes, and Jack figured that if he could trust anyone in Morgana Wynd, it was Dylan.

"Dyl, I'm—I think there's something wrong with me."

Dylan frowned in a grandfatherly way. "What are you talking about?"

"I think I might be losing my mind. I—I can't remember things. Like what I did last week. Or—or how I got here, or where my mom is, or—or—" Jack stumbled over his words. "I woke up on a freaking *lawn*. It's… it's like I was regularly knocked out for hours at a time, over the last few weeks."

Dylan pursed his lips, and furrowed his brow. "Do you remember anything," he said, slowly, carefully, "from while you were knocked out? Or asleep, or whatever it was? Do you remember anything at all? Or is it just blank?"

Jack scratched his head, and leaned against the sink. "You mean, like—dreams?"

Dylan nodded.

"Yeah. Yeah, there was one dream." Jack's frown deepened. "But I can't… I'm not sure what…"

"You don't remember."

"No."

"You have to *try* to remember what you dreamed, Jack. You *have* to. It's important. If you can find the dream, maybe you can follow it to… *the truth.*" Dylan put a hand on Jack's shoulder. "That's all I can tell you, I'm afraid."

"Oh. Well that's—thanks, Dyl."

"Don't mention it." Dylan motioned for Jack to follow him. "Come on. I *know* there's a way into that boatshed. Between the four of us we should be able to figure it out."

— • • ◆ • • —

But they didn't figure it out. The summer heat dripped from the walls and drowned them like insects in amber. Night fell, and the heat remained intolerable. They ordered pizzas from Cormora Creek, but no-one was really all that hungry.

Jack watched Skye as she attempted to play a simple melody on a silver flute she had taken from the schoolhouse in Cormora Creek, earlier in the year when school had been in session. She blew furiously into the flute's mouthpiece, her fingers grasping to cover the holes along the instrument's side. Jack, Dylan and Lucas all pretended to read as they surreptitiously watched her. Dylan and Lucas covered their mouths to suppress the inevitable guffawing.

To Skye's credit, she gave it several dozen attempts. By the end she was red in the face, and finally she gave a short shriek of rage and hurled the flute across the room, where it knocked a lamp from a shelf onto the floor with a *smash!*

Jack and Dylan both burst out laughing. Skye glared at them and stormed out of the room, snarling like a wolf. She stomped up to the attic, muttering mutinously under her breath the whole way.

One by one, the rest of the Changeling House's transient residents dozed off on the couches in the living room, bogged down by the weight of a wasted summer day. Only Lucas stayed awake, on one of the sofas, as Jack and Dylan's peaceful snoring filled the living room.

Lucas Alvarez tossed and turned, trying desperately to get comfortable. But it was no use, so he settled for staring at the ceiling.

The heat hadn't abated by morning. In fact it seemed to have gotten worse. Jack, Skye, Lucas and Dylan were all sweaty, and each of them had bags under their eyes as they gathered in the kitchen for another round of cold beer and colder pizza.

"Twelve steps past the dragon-shaped tree," Jack mumbled to himself—

"What did you just say?" Skye demanded.

Jack glanced up at her. "What? Oh, just—I had a weird dream last night."

"So did I…" Dylan said softly.

"What dream?" Skye's voice was rank with mistrust. "What happened in it?"

Jack frowned. "Well, we got into the boat shed. *I* did, at least. There were other people. It might've been you guys but I couldn't tell 'cause we were all wearing masks—*those* masks." He pointed to the coffee table where Skye had left the three remaining masks—

But the masks were gone.

"The hell?" Jack muttered.

The others stared at him bemusedly.

"What did you do with the masks, Skye?" said Dylan.

"Nothing!" Skye spoke in a hoarse whisper. "But you're not gonna believe this—I had a dream like that too. I was with these guys who had animal heads instead of people heads—there was a goat and a monkey, just like the masks, but there was also this cat—well it wasn't a *cat*, but it had a cat's face—and we got inside the boat shed."

"Okay, let's be real for a second," said Lucas. "Just because two of you had similar dreams doesn't automatically mean—"

"I wasn't *done,*" Skye continued. "We got into the boat shed, the door was unlocked and everything, and we got in, and we took one of them—"

"*Wyvern,*" Dylan hissed.

"What?"

"We took *Wyvern,* didn't we? Solomon Sturgess's crocodile canoe. We took *Wyvern,* and we hid it in the woods—"

"Twelve steps past the dragon-shaped tree"—Jack and Skye spoke in unison, and Dylan chimed in for the chorus—*"turn left and take three more steps and you'll see it."*

Silence fell. Jack, Dylan and Skye turned to Lucas, whose eyes were wide with bewilderment.

"Don't look at me!" Lucas exclaimed. "I couldn't sleep. It was too *hot.*"

"Neria." The name slipped out of Jack's mouth before he could stop it.

Skye wheeled on him. "What did you say?"

"I… I think Neria had something to do with this."

"With what?" said Lucas. "You guys just had really vivid dreams, that's all. We were planning on stealing a boat. You dreamt about stealing boats. It makes sense."

"But we were all there!" said Dylan. "The canoe. *Wyvern.* It's impossible, but—"

"Impossible things happen all the time," said Skye.

Dylan turned to Lucas. "You. You were awake the whole night."

Lucas shrugged. "Yeah, so?"

"So did you see anything *weird?* Like me or Jack sleepwalking, or—or any of us leaving the house? Or"—Dylan bit his lip—"Neria?"

"I didn't see or hear anything, man. And I was on that couch all night, like you said." Lucas jerked his thumb over his shoulder at the living room. "Dyl, you and Jack were both fast asleep. You both snore, by the way." He smirked. "Maybe the Breckers are losing it."

"I just—" Skye began—but she was cut off by a thunderous knock on the front door.

Chapter Seven: Spiders and Stars

The woman who calls herself Neria's aunt is reading a book on the patio, a battered copy of *The Odyssey* she found on the side of the road.

"Auntie," says Neria, "what's the Face of Pale?"

Auntie August looks up. She frowns. "Why do you ask, kiddo?"

"Just a dream I had."

Neria's guardian laughs. "I don't think you need to worry about dreams." She doesn't sound like she believes what she's saying. "Or about the Face of Pale."

She puts her book aside, stands up and walks back into the house. She puts on a jacket and heads to the front door.

"Where are you going?"

"For a walk. Stay out of trouble."

Auntie August vanishes out the door.

Neria goes to her room, lies on the bed and stares at the ceiling. Something appears before her, outlined on the off-white paint of the ceiling: a white flower.

For a moment the blank walls are covered in white flowers. White flowers rising, opening to the ceiling. *Datura*. White flowers hanging down, opening to the floor. *The Angel's Trumpet*.

If she can find the Angel's Trumpet, then maybe she can find the person who put its seeds in the food at the Fifth Season. Maybe then she'll find out what the Face of Pale is, and what it's got to do with her.

Pursuing this, Neria knows, is foolish. Ex*tremely* foolish.

Who knows what else she might encounter if she goes looking for the Angel's Trumpet?

Isn't one undead professor enough?

She fumbles in her pocket. The star marble. It's cool to the touch, but somehow its presence against her skin sends a pulsing, soothing warmth into her body from the tips of her fingers all the way up to her scalp, and down into her toes.

If I didn't have you, maybe I would be dead right now. Neria shivers. *I should just drop all of this.*

She closes her eyes and Professor Ferrox looms before her, with his sunken empty eye sockets and his rotten lolling tongue. She grinds her teeth.

Drop it.

But she isn't going to. It's too late for that. She's come this far already, and if she drops it now, she'll spend the rest of her life wondering.

Professor Ferrox, she knows, is only the beginning.

———— •◆• ————

The sky overhead is salted with stars, more than Neria has seen in a while. There aren't any big cities nearby, and Cormora Creek isn't much more than a village. Big enough to have its own police station and public library, and not much else.

If that's a village, then what's Morgana Wynd?

Neria arrives at the edge of the woods.

It's a street. Just a street that popped up in the middle of nowhere.

She holds up the star marble, and before her the darkness loosens its grip on the trees. It's not that she can see as though it's daytime—it's like she can see *through* the darkness.

She starts into the woods. The trees engulf her and immediately she gets a feeling, one of those primal, savage feelings, like she has crossed a threshold, and stepped out over an abyss. Something seizes her—a cold, rippling dread, like fingers thrust through her ribcage, pinching her heart. She grasps for her map of the Wynd but it's not there anymore.

Over the edge.

The viscous darkness stretches out around her on all sides. The voices swarm her like hornets. *You're alone*, they chatter cruelly. *Alone...*

She thinks of Auntie August. "I'm not alone." She says it out loud.

You are. The voices grow louder. *Auntie August wants to abandon you. You were forced upon her, and now she's tired of you. And she's closer to finally getting rid of you forever.*

You're alone, Neria.

She flails helplessly for a handhold or a foothold or *something*, but there's nothing. *You're alone and you don't stand a chance.*

———— • • ◆ • • ————

"Auntie," she says sheepishly. "I—I need help."

Auntie August stirs. Her voice is smudged with sleep. "What is it, kiddo?"

"I can't sleep. Can you make me a dream?" Neria shuffles her feet and hugs herself as she stands in the doorway of the smaller bedroom in number eighteen. "It's been almost three days."

Auntie August is silent for a moment. Then—"Mhmm," she mumbles, rising like a heavy vapour from the bed and drifting across the moonlight-striped room to her desk.

Neria moves to stand next to Auntie August. She watches her guardian grinding something with a mortar and pestle, down to an electric blue powder. "What kind of dream do you want, Neri?"

Tears creep into Neria's eyes. She turns her back on Auntie August, looking instead out the window at the inky night sky.

"Something bright and warm," she murmurs. "And—and happy, if you can."

Auntie August dumps the fine powder from the mortar into a small pewter teapot. She whispers something into the teapot's spout. After about a minute of whispering, she looks up at Neria's back. She opens her mouth. Closes it. Opens it again.

"Come on, kiddo."

Neria turns, wipes her eyes on her sleeve, and fixes her guardian with a tear-bright gaze. Her lip quivers. "Sorry," she whispers.

She accepts the teapot fromAuntie August, cupping it in both hands. Her guardian lifts the lid, and Neria holds the teapot up to her mouth, inhaling the blueish steam that rises from it into her mouth and nostrils.

"Thanks, Auntie," she says, once she has the dream inside her.

Auntie August gently ruffles Neria's tangled hair. "Someday I'll teach you how to make your own."

— • ◆ • • —

Neria was four years old when her mother died. She remembers so little of the woman who birthed her.

There's one night, though. A soft-sand beach under cloudless skies, the full moon blazing, turning the night sky a rich, endless indigo. Mom is sitting right beside little Neria, one arm around her, pulling her close and tight and warm.

Neria remembers it was a cold night, because of how warm her mother was.

She remembers the ocean waves rushing and crashing. And the ocean is so… *big,* and empty. Like a desert whose ground you can't walk on. And in the light of the full moon she can see the horizon, glimmering like dirty silver.

Overhead, the stars are bigger and brighter than she has ever seen before. It's like the whole sky is *lower* than it's supposed to be. Neria can see the Milky Way, the whole glittering arm arcing across the sky, bright and cold and distant.

Mom is singing a song to her. Neria leans her head on her mother's shoulder.

And then her mother reaches up into the sky, and plucks a star out of the dark. She gives it to Neria to keep. "Our little secret," she says.

Neria smiles, and snuggles in closer against the cold, cupping the star in her palms. It's no bigger than a marble, but it warms her like fire.

"You will never be cold, if you keep it with you," her mother says.

———— •·◆·• ————

The thing that was once called Neil Faulken watches the black-suited man pull up in a beat-up truck. Hanging innocuously from a streetlamp, he watches with eight marble-round black eyes as the man knocks loudly on the door of number seven. There's no answer.

Eight spindly legs dance excitedly along a silken strand.

Crouching low in the lobby of the house, the short girl with short black hair and the tall boy with long shaggy hair try to be as silent as possible. "It's Uncle Jacob," Dylan says, so quietly his sister's not even sure he said anything at all. "Don't answer him. Pretend we're ghosts."

The black-suited man retreats to the Jeep. He opens the back door of the truck and drags something out. No, not something, some*one*. A boy, by the looks of it.

The man sets the boy down on the lawn of number seven. Then, after glancing around slyly, he writes something in black marker on the boy's arm.

Then he gets back in the car and drives off.

For a moment the Wynd becomes as still as an oil painting.

Then the front door of number seven opens, and Dylan and Skye emerge. They approach the boy lying on the lawn. Skye prods his face, but he doesn't stir.

Bored of the sleeping boy, Dylan and Skye rush off down the street toward the woods.

Odd, thinks Barkface.

And now here comes Neria. She's striding carelessly down the street, and suddenly she stops. She's noticed the boy lying on the grass.

For a second a fleeting smile crosses Neria's face. She approaches the unconscious boy.

Good thinking, Neria Nightshade.

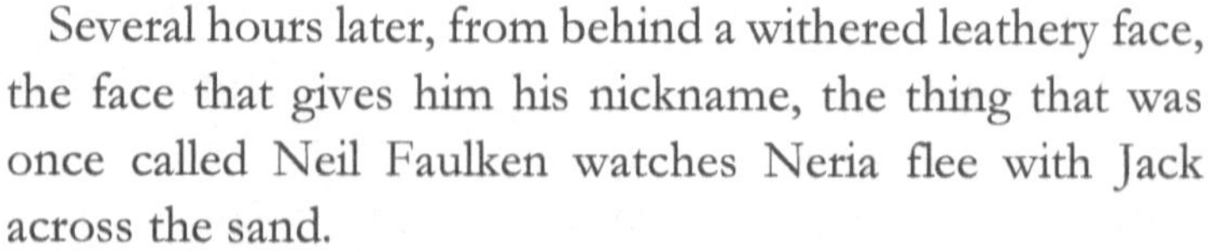

Several hours later, from behind a withered leathery face, the face that gives him his nickname, the thing that was once called Neil Faulken watches Neria flee with Jack across the sand.

They're afraid of me.

And with good reason. Barkface *could* easily catch up with them, if he wanted to.

Something spikes in him, then. A shard in his gut.

Come back.

He knows he must hold onto sensations such as these, lest he lose even more of himself than he already has.

Barkface watches until Jack and Neria vanish behind a sand dune. Then he closes the front door of his cottage, returns to his bedroom, sits on the edge of the bed with his hands folded in his lap, and gazes at the shattered heap of glass and sand and twisted metal on the floor.

He sighs. At the same time he soars above the peninsula in the body of a tatter-winged seagull, dips beneath the glassy waves in a seal's skin, and shivers as a summer breeze stirs the branches of a thousand-year-old sequoia.

Disengage from the Moment.

It's been years since he learned this trick. Now he watches everything from a distance. He knows, too, that he could not have learned this skill just anywhere; it's this *place*. These woods in particular. They're not fixed.

The Skein. He came up with the name himself.

He closes his eyes, glimpses the seasons cycling endlessly, a vast wheel turning, and he shrugs himself free of time like a snake shedding its skin. He can see something—it burns his eyes but he keeps looking. It looks almost like a spider, except it's made of pulsing, shimmering light, and it's sitting at the center of a vast rippling web. This is no ordinary web, though: this is *the* web. An infinity of strands branching off from the radiant core.

Barkface begins to suspect that what he's really seeing, when he beholds the web, is himself.

If Jack and Neria had been standing in the cottage right then, the man called Barkface would have looked less to them like a man, and more like a shadow reflected in a mirror. They would have known that he was there, but they wouldn't have been able to say where, exactly.

Through dozens upon dozens of eyes, Barkface watches the woods, the beach, the Wynd. He watches Neria and the boy called Jack, the boy she has chosen, as they clamber through the trees.

They're approaching Anora.

Let them. Barkface is prepared to intervene if necessary. But for now he's content to watch. An experiment.

He laughs. The world spins recklessly through cosmic corridors, the sun wheels through the sky, the season turns slowly, the days growing longer and hotter, and in the house with a brass 7 on its door, called the Changeling House by some, a motley crew takes up refuge, hiding from the swelter and the shadows outside.

Shadows… they swell, lengthen, shrivel and die, and an old man hobbles slowly through the trees of the Skein, humming a tune anyone would recognize. He's walking slowly, as though he doesn't know where he's going.

Has he ever known where he's been going?

Shadows… sometimes, if you catch them at the right moments, you can see them flutter and bend and flicker, like paper silhouettes blown about by a restless wind.

Nothing is set.

A twig crunches underfoot. A cold breeze gusts through the Skein. *Neil,* someone calls to him, a voice that comes bubbling out of the ground. A buried memory from the deep past.

"*Neil,*" the memory calls. "*You can't hide in there forever.*"

For a shiver of a moment he's thrown back: . a boy again, eleven years old. Short even for his age, and worryingly skinny, with a bird's nest of spiky jet-black hair and two plump purple bags under his eyes. It's hard to tell if the bags are bruises, iron deficiency or just a severe lack of sleep.

He's in the Old House again. The house where Pale first finds him.

Pulling his ratty shirt off, and staring into the cracked mirror, the boy named Neil winces at the sight of the welts and bruises forming an erratic constellation down the length of his arms. Not to mention the form of his ribs, like the blades of unsharpened knives pushing up through the dead -white skin of his chest.

He thinks of the man in the newspaper. Long unkempt black hair. A gaunt, wild-eyed pale face, with a look in his tar-black eyes like he knows the Devil's darkest secrets.

The man in the newspaper... Neil can't remember his name, but the article said the man laughed in court as they read the names of his victims. He laughed even harder when they projected the crime scene photos for the jury to see. He didn't even stop laughing when the father of one of the victims punched him full in the face while he was being escorted out of the courtroom—in fact, that was what made him laugh the hardest.

He even laughed on the electric chair, when they carried out his final sentence.

That face in the newspaper. *Pale,* Neil decides to call the face. The criminal to whom it once belonged is gone now, put to a well-deserved death. But that *face...*

Pale...

Neil sighs at his fragmented reflection in the mirror. A boy's reflection.

"Neil! Now!"

From the muffled sound of the drink-slurred voice, Neil can tell that his father is waiting for him at the bottom of the stairs. Which means that Neil still has a few precious moments left, before his day is ruined…

He steps backward, then forward, then backward again, and side to side, staring into the mirror the whole while. Depending on his distance and angle from it, he doesn't always look quite so boyish. Sometimes the cracked, chipped glass makes him look… older. More weathered, more… *dangerous*.

Like Pale.

Neil freezes, goes still as a lizard basking in the sun, as the face from the newspaper stares back at him, peering out from between the cracks of the semi-shattered mirror.

"Help me," Neil whispers. He can barely get the words out through the tremble in his voice.

"He's standing at the top of the stairs," Pale whispers from the other side of the mirror. "He's been drinking for hours. He's slow."

Now's your chance.

Eleven-year-old Neil closes his eyes, then turns away from the broken mirror and puts his shirt back on. Exiting the bathroom, he finds his father waiting for him at the top of the stairs. Belt in hand, face red from drinking, wearing nothing but his underwear. Matted grey hair tumbling in front of his face, hiding eyes that gleam with whiskey-spurred rage.

"Take off that shirt, boy," his father grunts. "Turn around. I'll give your arms a rest today. Show me your back."

Neil doesn't hesitate. "No," he grunts. *No more.*

Then he lunges, catching his father off-guard, jamming his elbow into his father's stomach so the man goes toppling backward down the stairs, down and down and down, landing in a twisted heap at the bottom.

The boy stands still at the top of the stairs, listening to the rain pressing its ghoulish fingers against the windows of his father's empty house. He watches until he's sure the twisted, grotesque mass at the bottom of the stairs isn't moving.

He's already rehearsing his explanation. "A man with a pale face," he whispers to himself. "He came in through the balcony window, and Dad tried to fight him off…" But the tears are coming, and the boy's shoulders begin shaking with sobs.

Pale wouldn't cry.

"Dad?" he murmurs, walking slowly down the great curving staircase that leads to the lobby. "Dad?" He's ashamed of the quaver in his voice, ashamed of the tears dampening his cheeks. "Dad, it's…" His voice peters out.

Dark blood crawls over the tiles at the base of the stairs.

Laugh at it.

The boy tries to turn his quiet sobs into laughter, tries to force a smile on his crumpling face. "Ha!" he barks. "Ha ha *ha!*" He begins to hiccup, then, which throws off the bizarre sound he's making—and the absurdity of it all trips a switch in his mind. He's laughing for real now, the sound echoing through his father's sprawling house as he stands alone at the base of the stairs with a corpse at his feet.

Be like Pale.

Neil Faulken gasps as he's jerked out of the past and dropped brusquely back into the Moment. It takes him a few seconds to orient himself in the old man's body again, with its sags and aches, and the inevitable sadness that comes with remembering what he truly is.

What? He blinks the woods into focus around him.

The Skein.

He understands why he's been pulled back: because someone is coming up on him. Rapid footsteps chomping through the undergrowth. Closing in—too close now even for Barkface to turn around and catch a glimpse of his assailant.

All he can do is brace himself, and prepare to leave the Moment once again. Something sharp plunges into the flesh of his upper back, right under his neck. Pain shoots through him, a blunt, burrowing pain. "Gah!" he cries, in spite of himself.

A voice in his ear: *'Jaaaaack…'* The forest spins around him. The ground rises to meet him.

Chapter Eight: The Skein

That morning, the residents of Morgana Wynd woke to find posters pinned up on every streetlamp and stuffed into every mailbox. They showed an image of *Wyvern* beneath a big bolded **STOLEN**, and offered a reward for its safe return to Solomon Sturgess of 1024. At the very bottom of the poster was a list of prime suspects: Skye Brecker, Dylan Brecker, Lucas Alvarez and Unknown Youth 1.

Some of the posters even covered up the MISSING bills for Andy and Adam Keirian, which had hung on the welcome billboard at the Wynd's entrance for months now.

As for Solomon Sturgess himself, everybody who saw him that morning would have said that he looked categorically murderous as he gusted down the Wynd like a monsoon and pounded on the door of number seven.

It was decided unanimously that Dylan, as the oldest and tallest Brecker, would answer the door.

Lucas hid in the attic, and Jack and Skye hung back to watch as Dylan opened the door to reveal Solomon Sturgess. The man was a formidable sight, it was impossible to deny: almost seven feet tall, wearing nothing but a tank top and swim-trunks, with his bald, tattooed scalp and his black beard. The tattoo along his right arm writhed, the battle between the squid and the shark intensifying, shifting with Solomon's bulging muscles.

He must have been at least forty years old.

"Oh!" Dylan's voice spiked to an abnormally high pitch. He cleared his throat, then brought it down to a simmer: "Good morning, sir."

"I'm gonna ask you this once, Brecker," Sturgess growled through his bristling black beard. "Where is *Wyvern?*"

"I dunno," said Dylan stiffly. "Why? Has something happened to it?"

"I'm not in the mood for this." Sturgess's gaze travelled past Dylan, and his eyes fell on Jack. "*You.* You have ten seconds to tell me the truth or I will *hurt* you."

Jack's heart notched up into his throat. "I have no idea what you're talking about," he squeaked. "That's the truth."

Sturgess turned back to Dylan as though Jack had suddenly blinked out of existence. "Is your father home?"

Dylan smirked and shook his head slyly. "He's still in the hospital."

"And you think that's funny, do you?"

"No, no. Not funny at all. I wish we could be of some help to you, sir. But we can't. So that's that."

For a moment Jack thought Solomon Sturgess was going to punch Dylan. But instead he took a step back. "The Cormora Creek police are coming," he said. "And I'm gonna be *watching* you. You and your sister and this whole thing you're doing—it's no good. You're both a couple of little pricks and you know it. Simon tells me everything.. You rub me the wrong way. And *you.*" Once again he looked Jack straight in the eyes. "Don't get mixed up in their shit. It's gonna end in tears. I promise you."

With that he stormed off.

Dylan shut the door and locked it.

"Well, that's not good," he said.

"You think?" said Skye.

"We really took it, man. We hid it in the woods." Dylan's voice was soft with awe, and so quiet that Jack and Skye couldn't tell whether he was talking to them or to himself. "I can't believe it. Twelve steps past the dragon-shaped tree... *Wyvern*."

"But how?" said Jack. "How could—I mean, Lucas said–"

"Jack," Skye admonished him sharply. "It's Morgana Wynd. Impossible things happen all the time."

"She's right," said Dylan. Then he frowned. "Hang on, I wanna check something." He went into the living room, crossed to the window and peered out through the blinds.

He groaned. "I don't freaking believe it."

"What's going on?"

"That cretin's watching the house."

"*What?*" Jack and Skye joined Dylan by the window. Sure enough, Solomon Sturgess was standing in the shade of the maple tree across the street, staring straight through the window, straight at the three of them.

"Shit! Get down!"

Jack and Skye dropped to the floor, while Dylan yanked the curtains shut. "That's really not good," he said. He leaned against the wall and sank into a crouch, his eyes wide with alarm."So we took *Wyvern*. It doesn't matter how—we just know it happened. And we know where we stowed it but we can't get to it. If we leave the house he'll see us and follow us.And if we stay here—the police are coming, and—"

"We can leave out the back door," suggested Jack.

"What about Lucas?"

"He's safe in the attic. Nobody knows he's here."

So Jack, Dylan and Skye went to the kitchen, and slipped out the back door. The three of them made it halfway across the backyard before noticing the tall, skeletal blonde woman standing right outside the back gate, arms folded sternly across her chest. She was wearing a faded brown leather jacket, and smoking a cigarette.

"Get back inside!" shouted Skye.

They sprinted back into the house. Dylan slammed the door shut, locked it. "Who the hell is that?"

"That's his *wife!*" Skye muttered. "That's Syrena Sturgess! We're trapped."

Something sank in the pit of Jack's stomach. "So… what do we do, then?"

"I dunno," said Dylan. "I really dunno. I guess we just have to wait."

———— •·◆·• ————

But *anything* would have been better than waiting. It was sweltering in number seven. Roaring sunlight blasted through the window, caked the walls, and the muggy air filled with the buzz of flies which Jack was only half-sure were really there. He, Dylan, Lucas and Skye played cards for a bit, but the games never ended properly, and the cards somehow ended up scattered everywhere.

They turned on the TV but it was only playing static.

They took their shirts off. It was too hot out for shirts.

Every once in a while, one of them would go to check the front window. And sure enough, Solomon Sturgess was there. Every. Single. Time. Sometimes he was sitting down, sometimes standing, sometimes leaning against the trunk of the maple tree. But he never took his eyes away from number seven.

Dylan went to the grocery store to get some drinks. When he came back he tossed Jack, Lucas and Skye each an energy drink, and said, conspiratorially, "He's got some of his friends watching too, man. They're doing *shifts*. One of them followed me to the store and back."

Jack said nothing. The drinks did some good to ward off the oppressive heat… for a few minutes. Then it swarmed back, angrier than ever.

There was a curt knock on the door.

"Don't answer it," said Skye, sneaking a surreptitious peek through the curtains of the living room window. "It's the police."

"*What?*" Dylan shoved her aside and looked out. It *was* the police—two uniformed cops standing on the porch. One of them knocked again.

"Don't even think about answering it!" Skye whispered. "I'm serious. If they find out what we're doing in here, everything's over."

"But they know we're in here!"

"They can't make us open the door. For all they know we could be asleep. Or we could've escaped by a secret underground passage. *God* I wish we had a secret underground passage."

"What if they bust the door down?"

"Everyone *shut up!*" It was the loudest whisper Jack had ever heard, and Dylan coupled it with a ferocious glare.

The doorbell jangled once, twice, three times. Then nothing. Jack crept over to the front door, crouched beside it, pressed an ear to the wood. He could hear Solomon Sturgess talking outside.

"…don't think you understand. It's a precious family heirloom."

"I'm sorry, I wish we could be of more help"—this was one of the police officers—"but there's really no evidence indicating that these… *children* are responsible, and we have no warrant to break down this door. Besides, Mr. Sturgess, you know we have more important things to deal with right now. I'm sorry, sir. We've filed the report. If anything turns up we will, uh, contact you right away."

Solomon again: "So what you're saying is, this matter is in my hands?"

"I would advise you to be patient, sir. Right now we don't have anything to go on. We've had a look at the boatshed. The best thing you can do is keep an eye on the other boats for now. Maybe the thief will return, if he was lucky the first time."

"Thieves," Sturgess spat.

They're not gonna help him.

Jack moved away from the door. "They're not gonna do anything," he whispered. "The police, I mean." He forced a weak smile. "So that's good, right?"

"It's either good," said Lucas, "or really, really, *really* bad."

After that they all dispersed throughout the Changeling House, each pulled in a daze into its depths, and Jack could have *sworn* that he heard Neria's voice calling him from the attic, but when he got there the attic was empty.

The window was open.

Suddenly the thought of Solomon Sturgess and his cronies seemed small and faraway. Jack turned off the lamp, swept a bunch of the clutter off the bed and lay down on the space he had cleared. Night fell, and the attic became a grey shadowscape, tinged by rays of moonlight trickling in through the window.

Jack's eyes fell half-closed, but for a while he couldn't get to sleep.

Somewhere between the folds of darkness and silver half-light, a glimmering amber stare fixed itself upon him.

Eventually sleep came for him. It was the same colour as the moonlight and it drifted in through the window, hooded and sewn from whispers and whistling softly—whistling a tune he had heard before. There were words to the tune, full lines… verses… but though Jack recognized how most of it sounded, he could not have said what any of it meant. And sleep pulled him down…

He was walking barefoot along a pale-sanded beach, looking for something. Or someone. *Who? Neria?* Above him the sky was blue and deathly still, and ahead the beach stretched on endlessly, extending into the hazy horizon.

Jack walked. He walked for ages, for eons, for glimpses of eternity. He walked for so long that the flesh sloughed off from his feet until only milk-white bones were left. Then it was twilight and he was climbing a narrow spiraling staircase up into the rose-fired sky. Up and up and up. *"Coming!"* he called desperately, but his voice dissolved like mist into the air. *I'm coming!*

And the staircase refused to end, it just kept going, the steps turning to glass beneath his feet. A glass staircase winding up and up and around and around, until only darkness surrounded him, a deep indigo darkness flecked with stars and a sliver moon…

Dylan, Skye and Lucas were fast asleep on the couches in the living room. It was cooler out, much cooler than it had been before. Jack went to the window and peered out.

Sturgess was still there, across the street, lying down under the maple tree, and...

Wait. Jack squinted. *No way.* Was Solomon Sturgess asleep? His eyes were closed, his hands clasped over his chest.

It never occurred to Jack to wake the others. The map of the peninsula was sitting on the coffee table; he grabbed it and left by the front door, pulling a gulp of cool breeze into his lungs as he emerged into the twilit air. What time was it? He looked at his watch but couldn't focus on the dial. The sky above him was a rich, steady blue, and to the east it was dark. The western sky, however, was lit up by a peculiar turquoise glow.

Dusk?

It didn't feel like dusk.

This way, Jack...

He made his way down the street to the woods, checking over his shoulder every few seconds to make sure nobody was following him. *You're in the clear.* It reassured him, for some reason, to have the map with him.

Follow the Skein if you dare.

He let the trees swallow him. Ignoring the path, he staggered in a daze along the curves and grooves of the forest floor.

"But what the hell is the Skein?" Jack murmured.

This *is the Skein.*

He started humming, a tune he had heard somewhere before. Up ahead, something danced through the dark canopy. Lights?

The ground sloped downward beneath his feet, the trees parted, and fine sand pooled between his toes.

He stopped.

Sapphire waves lapped calmly against the narrow shore. The western horizon opened up before him: the drowning sun striated it with gold and crimson and pink and green. And nearby was the towering lighthouse, dark like charcoal against the deepening sky.

Jack dug his feet further into the sand. *Do you leave footprints in your dreams?*

And then a bearberry bush beside him spoke: "I wasn't sure you were gonna come."

Jack jumped in surprise. *What?* He peered at the bush more closely. "Neria?"

With a noisy rustling she burst out of the shrub. She had a large kitchen knife in one hand. "It's a dangerous night," she giggled, plucking a strand of small red berries from her hair and brushing a fuzzy caterpillar from the sleeve of her jacket. "They used to call these kinds of nights *witching nights*. You can't be too careful."

"The hell is that for?" Jack demanded, eyeing the knife anxiously.

"I already told you. I helped you steal that canoe. You owe me."

"So it *was* you. *You* got us into the boatshed, but we never left number 7."

"Well, obviously that was me. What d'you think, that kind of stuff just happens?"

"So you really—you know, snuck into the Changeling House and—and everything?"

"You already know all that, Jack. Anyways…" She started walking, keeping to the sand of the beach but skirting the edge of the treeline. Jack hurried after her.

"Hey," he said. "Did you do that, back there?" He gestured vaguely toward where he thought the Wynd was (or where it would be later, anyway). "To Solomon Sturgess—did you put him to sleep?"

Neria laughed. "I didn't do anything." She was walking faster now, Jack hurrying awkwardly over the sand to keep up. "Ever heard of sleeping sickness?"

"*Sleeping* sickness?"

"You start to get tired—at first you think it's because you're stressed, or you've been working too much or something. And you sleep for longer and longer every day—the kind of sleep you just can't help. You can't fight it. No matter where you are, you just drop into this deep slumber. And it lasts for longer and longer every time. You start missing out on whole days, then weeks, and then one day you don't wake up at all."

"Oh." Jack chewed his lip. "And… are we awake right now?" He realized as the words left his mouth how stupid they sounded.

"I dunno about you, but I sure as hell am."

Jack smiled as a wave of giddiness swept through him. "I brought this, by the way." From his pocket he produced the map, the one which he, Dylan and Skye had made years ago. He handed it to Neria.

Neria tucked a strand of loose hair behind her ear and squinted at the map as she took it. "Follow the Skein if you dare," she read with a chuckle. "I like that."

"So you know what the Skein is, then?"

Neria stopped walking and squinted at the map in silence. "Well, not *really*," she said. "The Skein, it's… it's like a riddle. I'm still trying to work out the specifics, but… I mean, you must have noticed that this place is different every time. The path changes. It's not fixed. *Nothing*'s fixed here. Things move around, and even when I think I know which way I'm going I get lost… but somehow I keep finding my way back to the same places. Like this beach." She gestured to the sand. The water. The lighthouse. "And I keep running into *you.*"

It was the way she said it. *You.* Jack blushed. The giddiness came again, swooping from his scalp to his toes. *What the hell is wrong with me?*

"What about Rusalka, then?" he managed.

Neria shrugged. "Beats me. But, Jack—word of advice? Be careful. I dunno if you've noticed, but there's something *wrong* with the people here." She paused at the edge of the trees. "D'you hear that?"

Jack frowned. "No."

"*Listen.*"

He tilted his head to the side, like he had seen Neria do. And he did hear it, from a great distance away.

'*Jaaaack…*'

He shivered. "I can't stand that thing."

"That's what I brought these for." Neria brandished her knife and tossed one to Jack—except his wasn't a knife, it was a soup ladle. "The hunt is on."

"I'm supposed to fight it with *this?*"

"Auntie and I only have one knife between us." Neria shrugged. "Better than nothing, eh?"

Without another word she veered off the sand, slinking into the shade beneath the trees. Jack only hesitated for a split second. Then he scurried to catch up with her.

They walked in silence for a minute or two, side by side. Before long they had fallen into step.

"Neria," Jack began—

"Jack." The way she said his name made it sound incomplete. "What's that short for? Jacksmith? Jackery?"

"Um… it isn't short for anything. It's just short."

"Hmm." That ghostly, sleepy smile was playing on her lips again. "Jackdaw," she said. "Jackalope."

"What's a Jackalope?"

"You tell me. Your name's short for it."

"I don't think it is…"

"Do you like your name?"

"What?"

"Your name. *Jack.* Do you like it?"

Jack didn't know how to respond to that. No-one had ever asked him something like that before.

Then, before he could help it, he was talking. "It's—whatever. I don't really care one way or another." An edge of bitterness came into his voice. Truth be told, on some level he had always resented his parents for naming him Jack. It hardly qualified as a name—more like a placeholder. *Generic Boy 1.* Unlike his cousins. Dylan and Skye, now *there* were some interesting names. But Jack was just… Jack-of-all-trades, that's what it made him think of. *Master of none.*

Neria's bright amber eyes pierced him, prodded at the tangled knot in his chest. "So…" She bit her lip. "You don't care if I call you Jackdaw, then?"

"Jackdaw?"

Neria winked. "Or Jack the Ripper."

For a moment Jack thought about saying something snarky to rebuke her.

"Or Jumpin' Jack Flash."

"Jackdaw," Jack decided.

Then a scream tore the forest air apart. Except it wasn't just a scream, it was a *chorus* of screams coming from all around them—and most of them weren't human. There were seagulls shrieking, wolves howling, cats mewling, bears roaring.

Neria covered her mouth with her hand. "Oh my *god,*" she gasped.

Jack's heart jammed up into his throat. *Barkface?*

The old man was just up ahead, lying face-down on the ground. There was an axe stuck deep into the back of his neck, blood still spurting out, pooling under him, staining his white hair red, soaking his grey-brown cloak.

"Holy *shit.*" Neria crouched down beside the body. She grabbed the axe handle, tugged at it, and with a *pop* the handle came loose from the axe-head, which remained lodged in Barkface's neck.

Neria tossed the axe-handle aside. She crouched down, and with a grunt rolled Barkface onto his back. The old man was still alive—he was shaking and convulsing. Foam and blood bubbled from his mouth. His eyes were squeezed shut.

And then those eyes snapped open, sparkling green-brown eyes. "She's—lost," he gasped, blood spraying out from the corners of his mouth. "Get—back to—the Wynd. *Run!*"

Shakily, Neria stood. She backed away from Barkface. But she didn't run. She found Jack next to her again, and grabbed onto his wrist; and the two of them watched slack-jawed as Barkface's skin shifted, boiled, *melted.* For a split second his bones were showing through his flesh, his skull staring at them through tatters of dissolving tissue.

And then it was over, and they couldn't see him anywhere.

Where did he go? Jack spotted a shadow on the ground—no, that wasn't it. Barkface's dying corpse was nowhere to be seen.

Where did he go?

What just happened?

"GET OUT!" something screamed in their ears. Frigid wind blasted them. Jack spun on his heel, ripping free of Neria's grasp. He broke into a run, sprinting back the way the two of them had come.

"Jack!" Neria shouted after him. "Wait! Come back!"

But he didn't stop, and Neria was already out of sight.

Jack slowed. The trees swayed and rustled around him. They weren't the same trees as before. Or were they?

Why had he run away? That had been stupid. *Stupid!*

"Neria!" he shouted.

It's different every time—the path keeps changing, and things keep moving around, and even when I think I know which way I'm going I get lost…

"Neria?"

…but somehow I keep finding my way back to the same places.

There it was, just ahead, as though it had popped into existence the moment he had thought of it. Barkface's cottage.

———— •·◆·• ————

Neria can hear the waxwoman's lumbering footsteps up ahead. She picks up speed, gripping her knife, bent double, doing her best to make as little noise as possible. The forest floor is coarse on the soles of her bare feet.

The ground slopes in a familiar way.

There it is, up ahead. The cottage. Relief fills her. *If you wander for long enough you'll always find your way back.*

And there's the waxwoman. Standing completely still near the front door of the cottage, staring at Neria with those empty glass eyes.

Jaaaaaack…,' it calls.

Neria freezes. Her grip on the kitchen knife tightens to white-knuckled. "I'm not Jack," she tells the waxwoman.

Then the door of the cottage flies open like it's been rammed with a gale-force wind, and out storms a swirl of black robes. A hatchet gleams high in the air—then it's brought down *straight* into the middle of the waxwoman's forehead.

JaaaAAAAAIIIIIIIIIIIIII—'

The cry makes Neria's stomach churn. Still, she watches enraptured as the waxwoman stumbles backward, her arms flailing erratically.

The whirlwind of black robes has now resolved itself into a person. But he's too tall to be a real person. He's got pointed ears and a muscular, youthful face, and brownish-green eyes that glitter too brightly to be normal human eyes.

Not to mention the elk antlers protruding from his forehead.

In the man's other hand is a serrated knife, which slides horizontally through the waxwoman's throat. There's no blood—only dust comes pouring out as the saw crunches back and forth, back and forth until the waxwoman's head lolls sideways.

Then the head is yanked clean off, and the elk-antlered man turns to Neria, his eyes flash dangerously, and in a guttural tone that's unmistakably Barkface's voice, he growls: *"Go."*

He strides back into the cottage, dragging the waxwoman's body with one hand and carrying the severed head in the other. The door shuts behind him.

Neria rushes to the porch and pulls on the door-handle, but it's locked and doesn't budge.

So she descends from the porch. Circles the cottage. The grime-plastered windows have curtains drawn, and are too murky to see through, anyway.

Then Neria remembers standing in Barkface's bedroom. Sunlight dripping down from the ceiling.

The skylight!

There's a rusty metal eavestrough running down from the cottage's wood-shingled roof. Neria runs to the metal shaft, grabs onto it and hauls herself up onto the spongy shingles. She makes her way over to the skylight, crouches down beside it. The glass is smudged, but she can see through it, well enough into the bedroom below.

Nobody there. The room is empty.

A sound behind her makes her duck down in alarm against the shingles. Pressing herself flat against the roof, she cranes her neck to watch as Barkface emerges from the front door of the cottage again.

In one hand he grips the waxwoman's head by its disheveled wiry not-hair. In the other hand he's got a torch.

Neria bites her lip and watches as Barkface places the torch against the bottom of the waxwoman's head. She watches as the flames lick up around the head, as the wax starts to melt, the hair starts to shrivel and a hideous smell corrupts the forest air, along with a high-pitched whining noise that makes Neria wince.

She wants to cry. It's as though the noise is coming from under her own skin.

Then it's over. Barkface lets the smouldering remnants of the head fall to the ground, stamping what remains of it into the forest floor. Then he looks up. "Leave this place," he says.

Neria's heart lurches—but Barkface isn't looking at her. He's staring ahead into the trees. Someone coming through the trees toward him. *Jack?*

It is Jack, indeed. He's still carrying that stupid soup ladle, and he falters when he sees Barkface.

"Oh, shit," Neria hears him say.

Oh shit is right. Barkface is advancing on him. Neria throws herself towards the edge of the roof, swings herself over the side, slides down the eavestrough—lands heavily on the ground, bouncing to her feet, her eyes smarting from the shooting pain of the impact.

"Don't touch him!" she shrieks.

Barkface wheels around and spots her. His eyes widen. *His face slips.*

"Please!"

He's still much, much taller than he ought to be. In the half-light he looks far older than he did a moment ago. "Neria," he whispers.

Jack appears beside Neria again, and again she grabs him by the wrist, and slides her fingers down to interlace with his.

Barkface is walking slowly toward them. Tears spill from his eyes, carving pathways through his labyrinthine wrinkles and losing themselves in his snowy beard. He's an old man again. His elk antlers are gone. And he's staring at Neria now as though Jack doesn't exist.

"Neria," Barkface croaks. "I'm so, so *sorry*. You shouldn't have seen what you just saw. You deserve so much better." He pauses, then straightens up, draws a deep, rattling breath and wipes his eyes on the sleeve of his robe.

"Well," he says, forcing a hollow chuckle. His gaze flicks to Jack for a split second. "While you're both out here, why don't you come in for a cup of tea? You have a great many questions for me, no doubt."

He sweeps past both of them, up the steps and into the cottage. Neria hesitates for only a second before following him. She turns when she reaches the door, and gestures for Jack to join her.

"We have to stick together," she says. "Remember?"

It's not as gloomy in the cottage as it was the first time they were inside. There's a fire crackling in the hearth now, but Barkface leads them through to the hearth-less kitchen. He directs them to sit down at the table. "Don't worry," he says, finally addressing Jack to his face. "Old age trips me out, too." He winks. "Make yourself at home."

He takes a kettle down from its hook on the wall.

"What you saw today," he says, "was a failed experiment. That is all."

He starts filling the kettle with water from a jug.

"That's all?" Neria growls. "How about you tell me the truth?" She rises brusquely from her chair and crosses the kitchen to the bedroom door, which she kicks open. She points into the bedroom, to the painting on the wall.

"*There,*" she says. "That's Anora." She glares at Barkface. "The waxwoman—that was also Anora. And you're going to tell us that it was all a failed experiment? Tell the truth, *Barkface.*" She spits his name like it's a two-syllable poison. "Tell *me* the truth."

Barkface stares at her without saying anything. Then he takes the kettle into the next room, hangs it in the hearth above the fire.

He returns to the kitchen. "Sit down, Neria."

Neria stays right where she is, in the doorway to Barkface's bedroom.

"Why did it keep saying my name?" Jack demands.

Barkface turns to him in surprise, as though he already forgot Jack was there. "Because you broke the hourglass, kid." He can't help the cruel glimmer of a smile that crooks his mouth. "Rusalka saw you. I put her under an enchantment, but when you broke the hourglass the enchantment broke as well. She's free to play her games now."

"And—and who's Rusalka? The woman in the lighthouse?"

Barkface smirks. "More or less."

"So—so you're not mad? About the hourglass?"

Barkface and Neria both laugh at that, and Jack blushes, realizing how childish it must have sounded. Then both laughs are suddenly cut off, at exactly the same time, and the room goes dead silent again, except for the crackle of the fire and the rattle of the kettle heating in the next room.

They're both staring at each other. Neria and Barkface. Barkface is wearing an expression like he's being slowly gutted by an invisible knife.

"No," he says at last, turning to look at Jack again. "No, I'm not mad. But there will come a time when you'll have to face the consequences of your actions, Jack Brecker."

Jack opens his mouth to say something—but then it occurs to him that he never told Barkface his name. He lapses into stunned silence.

"What the hell's going on here?" Neria demands. "Who are you, really? Nothing's made any sense since I came to Morgana Wynd, and nobody's given me a straight answer yet. I want to understand."

Barkface runs his long, gnarled fingers through the whorls of his beard. "There's something I have to do tonight," he says, slowly. "Perhaps you should come with me when I do it. It may help you... understand."

"What do you mean?"

"We have to call the *Jericho Cascade*. Do you know what that means?"

"What?" Neria looks flustered. "No, I don't. But—but it's got something to do with me, doesn't it?"

Barkface's eyes flash like hazard lights on a car. "It's nothing you need to worry about, kid."

"I'm sixteen," says Neria. "I'm not a kid."

Barkface's mouth twitches into a smile, his curling white moustache twitching in tandem just above it. "Good. Good." A beat. "It is no simple feat to summon the *Jericho Cascade*. It will only come if it hears the summons, and the summons can only be carried out properly in another realm, very far from here. An impossibly distant point in time and space. Do you understand? It is a time that never was, a time that could never have been. We cannot go there ourselves. But we can take Morgana Wynd there. That is what we must do."

"Uh," Neria manages. "Okay. I don't really–"

"You will come with me," Barkface instructs, "and I will show you how we will do this." Then he turns to Jack. "You, Jack Brecker."

Jack quails before Barkface's gaze, sinking as far into his chair as possible.

Barkface chuckles, a hoarse, barky chuckle. "Don't worry, I mean you no harm. You believe me, don't you?" He glances sidelong at Neria for just a second. "But you have been harmed, Jack Brecker. You have holes in your memory. And worse than that: something buried. I have experience with certain substances of the *nightshade* family, and you appear to be a victim of scopolamine. If you want, I can make you an elixir to help you remember. It will bring back some of what you've lost, and heal some of the damage that's been done to your brain."

Looking back at Barkface, Jack nods jerkily, and says nothing.

"Good. You might as well get comfortable next to the fire. I'll whip up the elixir. You will stay here until I return with Neria—it's best to remain still while the elixir works its charms. Lying down on your back is ideal. And then, once we're all done here, I'll take you both home."

So Jack curls up in a corner of the moth-bitten sofa, and Neria sits next to him while Barkface bustles around the kitchen, brewing the elixir.

"I wish you were coming with me," Neria tells him.

Jack blinks. "Why?"

"'Cause I *trust* you." Neria flashes that candle-flicker smile of hers. She grabs his hand, squeezes it tight. Then Barkface enters the room with a steaming mug of thick, pungent tea. He proffers it to Jack, who takes it and breathes in the steam.

"Neria, come on."

Neria stares long and hard at Jack as he begins to sip the tea. Then she follows Barkface out of the cottage. Barkface closes the door behind him.

"This way."

She follows him away from the cottage, into the thick of the woods.

"You know," Barkface says, "we used to call you Neria Nightshade."

Jack was back in the city he hated so much. The city that made his eyelids heavy. Grey and cold and relentless, it sprawled inside him, clogging up his arteries and valves, filling up his lungs, choking him.

"Mom," he said. She was on her way out the door. "We need to talk."

A sharp intake of breath as his mother turned in the doorway to look at him. Her sterling silver gaze made him rethink what he was about to say.

"About?" she asked curtly.

"Morgana Wynd."

"Jack, I've *told* you—

"We have to go back. I think Skye and Dylan are in trouble."

"We're not discussing this."

"You can't"—Jack's voice started rising—"just shut me up like that. Skye and Dyl called me the other night. They said—"

"Your uncle will take care of them," his mother interjected. She wasn't looking at him anymore.

"Do you really think they're safe with Uncle Gabe?"

Mira Brecker sighed. "Jack, I—okay. Fine. If you call Heath and apologize to him for the other day, then I'll explain things when I get back. All right?"

Jack nodded. "All right," he echoed.

His mother forced a smile that Jack didn't believe. He knew it was meant to reassure him. "I'll be back before you know it, sweetheart," she said. "And then we're gonna get out of here."

She slipped out the door of their apartment and slammed it shut behind her.

Jack put off calling Heath. He set his cell phone on his bedside table, then lay in bed reading comics as rain pounded down outside.

An hour went by. Two hours. He read three comics cover-to-cover.

He glanced at the cell phone, and scowled. He didn't have anything nice to say to Heath. *What do you* **see** *in him? He's pathetic.* Jack had *wanted* Heath to hear those words, the ones he had said to his mother, knowing that Heath was listening in the next room. *Just looking at him makes me sad.*

He winced.

Just apologize. Get it over with.

He grabbed the cell phone, dialed the number. Then he squeezed his eyes shut and held the phone up to his ear.

The phone rang once. Twice. Three times.

Then a low, gravelly voice. "Who is this." It didn't sound like a question.

"Um… this is Jack. Is… is this Heath?"

A low-pitched chuckle. "Ah. You're calling for Heath Haltow. He's dead, I'm afraid. Freshly killed, in fact. If only you'd called, oh, an hour ago." Tinny laughter shook through the phone's speaker.

Jack hung up. He threw the phone onto his bed.

"A joke," he said out loud, to the empty apartment, to the black mold growing slowly across the ceiling, to the rattling radiator and the rain-hammered window.

A joke. A horrible joke. He realized he was shaking, so he laid back in bed and stared at the ceiling.

Whose voice had that been? Not his father's, he was almost certain of that.

"Serves me right," he grunted.

Then someone knocked on the apartment door.

Jack rose slowly from his bed, tip-toed out into the hall, over the cold floorboards to the lobby.

Whoever was standing outside knocked again.

Jack opened the door.

"Dad?" he breathed.

He hadn't seen his father in five years, not since that fateful day when he and his mother had left Morgana Wynd. Jacob Brecker was dressed in a shabby black suit over a black button-up shirt. He looked much slimmer than he had the last time Jack had seen him. Paler. His face was narrow and sallow, with dark circles under eyes that appeared to have lost all colour—the irises as black as the pupils. He had shaved his balding head, and his patchy grey beard.

"Good to see you, son."

Jacob Brecker raised a hand, palm up, to his lips, and blew a little whirl of white powder into Jack's face. A tangy chemical smell overwhelmed Jack. A wicked dizziness swarmed him. Without another word, his father grabbed his arm and dragged him out of the apartment, leaving the door open behind them.

———— ••◆•• ————

Jack had no idea how long he had been in the car for. His father put him in the passenger seat, and made sure Jack always had a drink to sip from. Sometimes he stopped the car to blow more white powder into Jack's face.

But now, finally, the Jeep was slowing down, swerving off the highway into a cozy little hamlet clinging to the side of a lake. A remote little borough, with its own watermill, several farmsteads and a tiny village square of shops and boutiques.

"Is this it?" Jack murmured hopefully, his voice slurred, the words heavy and unwieldy on his tongue.

His father parked the car outside a corner store. He went inside the store and emerged a few minutes later with an iced tea, which he handed to Jack. "Come on, boy."

Jack followed his father out of the Jeep, stumbling here and there, giggling to himself under his breath. Somewhere deep down inside of him, he knew that something was wrong. But all he felt like doing was laughing.

The sky overhead was blue, only a few clouds strewn about here and there, and the sun roared cheerfully.

Jack wished his father would blow more of that powder in his face. *Dad...* it *was* nice to see him after all these years, wasn't it?

His father grabbed his wrist. "Keep it together, son. Today's a big day for you."

He led Jack across the village square, down a narrow lane between two buildings and through to another, less inviting street, whose buildings all had boarded-up windows and holes in their roofs.

Down the street, to the front door of an old, dilapidated brick building.

Jacob Brecker kicked the door open and pushed Jack ahead of him, into a darkened brick hallway that smelled of mildew and asbestos.

"This way," he whispered to his son.

Jack could hear voices coming from down the hall. He felt *light.* Like a bird. *What's happening to me?* He started giggling—stopped himself when his father growled "Shh! Quiet!"

Jack glided after his father down the brick hall. The voices grew louder. Louder. They rounded a corner, and up ahead was a rusted steel door, hanging open. Ajar.

A gruff voice drifted out of the doorway, a man's voice. *"Do you hear him? His footsteps?"*

Somebody else was in there, too, but whoever it was wasn't saying anything, just making a strange, muffled, moaning sound.

"You do?" said the other voice. "You *do* hear him?"

"Come on, Jack." Jacob Brecker couldn't keep the excitement from his voice anymore. "Come look."

Jack joined his father in the doorway, and Jacob Brecker put an arm around his son's shoulders. The two of them stared through into the room beyond, a cement-walled room with a high ceiling and no windows, lit only by a fire crackling in the middle of the room, in a garbage can.

There was a circle of them, of men and women dressed in black. Black suits. Black hoods. Black veils. Black hats. Seven of them, and at the center of the circle was Jack's mother, sitting in a chair.

Her hands were tied with wire behind the back of the chair. More wire bound her bare ankles. Duct tape had been wrapped around her head in a thick band, covering her mouth completely.

Jack froze. His heart rammed up into his throat. *Mom?*

Tears streamed down her cheeks. She was breathing fast, *too* fast, hyperventilating through her nostrils, snot dripping from her nostrils. She sobbed wretchedly, brokenly into the duct tape.

One of the men in black, who sported a thick black beard, turned away from the circle and looked up at Jack and Jacob Brecker standing in the doorway. The bearded man grinned a crooked, maniac grin. "Aha," he barked. "Just in time."

Jack dropped his iced tea. The lid popped off the disposable cup and the iced tea spilled over his feet. Only then did he realize that his feet were bare. Somehow, though, he couldn't feel the wetness of the iced tea on his skin; he could only see it.

Where are my shoes?

The other black-clad men and women turned to look at the new arrivals.

"Dad…" Jack mumbled.

His father squeezed his shoulder. "Don't worry, Jack," Jacob Brecker said. "You'll be one of us soon."

But Jack had finally made eye contact with his mother, who had stopped crying now. Her storm-coloured eyes were peeled wide behind tangles of silver hair. She shrieked something into the duct tape, which strained her words into a muffled hiss.

Jacob Brecker brought his lips down to graze the crown of his son's head. "Don't look away, Jack," he whispered into Jack's hair.

Then he looked up at the others.

"Does she believe yet?" he asked.

"She believed in Pale a long time ago," the black-bearded man responded. "You did well, Jacob."

"Then it's time."

The black-bearded man crossed to the garbage can fire, and when he returned to stand in front of Jack's mother he was holding something: a butcher's knife whose blade was white-hot.

He shoved the blade into Mira Brecker's left eye.

Screams tore through the duct-tape. Mira's head jerked back, blood spurting from her mangled eye socket.

Jack felt the front of his shorts grow hot and wet. He felt stomach acid rising up in his throat. He stared as the black-bearded man jabbed the knife into his mother's other eye, then tore the duct tape off her mouth, stuck his face inches from her savaged face, and over the sound of her bloodcurdling wails he roared:

"HE'S COMING FOR YOUR SOUL! DO YOU UNDERSTAND?"

Blood pumped into the air from the twin gouges where her eyes had been, drenching Mira Brecker's face, spilling into her mouth. She gasped and choked and spluttered, rocking back and forth as she desperately tried to free her hands. "JACK!" she howled, a guttural, animal cry, a desperate final spasm of her soul. "RUN! *RUN! RUUUUUUN!*"

The knife had cooled to red-hot, and before she could say one more word the blade was on the flesh of her neck, burning her skin and then cutting through the muscle and sinew, all the way down to the bone. Her cries were drowned by gurgling blood, blood spraying onto the black-bearded man's black suit, blood coursing in rivulets across the cement floor, hot and steaming. The air filled with the stench of iron.

Jack threw his father's arm from around his shoulders and fell back through the doorway, back into the hall.

Everything was slowing down around him, the air turning to jelly.

Jacob Brecker's head swivelled on his neck. His eyes burned like coals cooked in the furnaces of Hell.

Jack ran. He was sprinting, gliding—*soaring* down the brick hallway, his heart slamming against the inside of his chest, off-rhythm, thrashing double-time. *They killed her.*

They fucking killed her.

Footsteps echoed behind him but he couldn't look back, didn't *dare* look back and risk seeing that maniacal look in his father's eyes again—

He burst from the darkness of the hallway into the afternoon sunshine, and suddenly a wave of aching tiredness slammed into him. He was laughing again, uncontrollably this time. Somewhere in the back of his mind he remembered that he had to hide, and *fast…*

But his legs were so heavy.

With each passing second they grew heavier.

He ran… walked… *dragged* himself toward a dumpster across the street from the dilapidated brick building. But he only made it halfway to the dumpster before his feet melted into the asphalt and he fell to his knees. *No!* He tried to stand up but the fatigue was pulling him down again, and his body was shaking with laughter, like he was possessed.

Help me, he tried to say. But he couldn't speak. His lips wouldn't form words. He collapsed onto his back and his head slammed into the asphalt. But the asphalt was soft, like a pillow.

Shadows towered over him. One of them leaned forward. "He pissed himself."

"Shut up, Axel." A pause. "I'm sorry, Jack. I thought you were ready."

They killed her.

And then, finally, a chemical tide pulled Jack into unconsciousness.

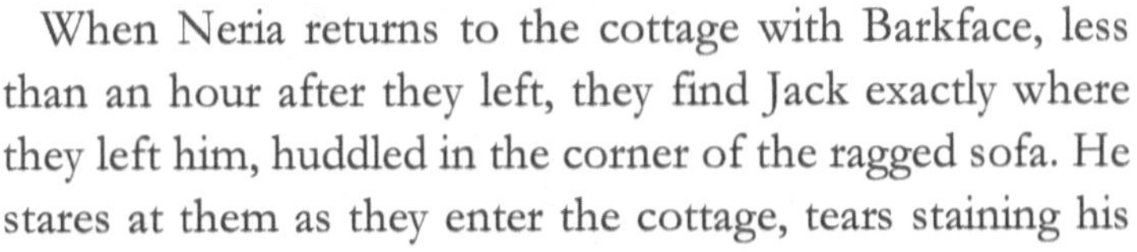

When Neria returns to the cottage with Barkface, less than an hour after they left, they find Jack exactly where they left him, huddled in the corner of the ragged sofa. He stares at them as they enter the cottage, tears staining his cheeks, sobs clogging his throat. At first Neria thinks he's choking.

"Jack," she begins, but then she breaks off. "Jackdaw." She crosses to the sofa, extends her arms. Jack flinches away from her, but he's got nowhere to go, he's just shrinking back into the ancient sofa.

"Come on." Neria puts an arm around his shoulder, and he falls into her, convulsing with sobs. "They're murderers," he rasps. His tears spill into her lap.

She pulls him in tight, wrapping both arms around him.

"I got you," she whispers.

Barkface towers over them. His face is contorted in anguish, his eyes burning like stolen stars. "Time to go home," he says.

Chapter Nine: Marauders and Marooners

After the cold, empty darkness came a foggy period in which Jack couldn't tell where he was. It took him ages to figure out what he was staring at. Rafters?

He was in the attic of the Changeling House.

Mom's dead.

He closed his eyes, and painted onto the undersides of his eyelids was his father's face, his clean-shaven head and empty black eyes, a violent heat suffusing his gaze as he smiled.

Jack opened his eyes. He stared at the attic ceiling. Stared at the window looking out over the Wynd as dawn blazed in the eastern sky.

But he didn't see the ceiling, or the window, or the sky. All he could see was a man in black with a black beard. A knife going through his mother's eyes. One eye after the other. One. Two. Gouged out. Blood spurting, spraying, spilling. The smell, so peculiar, like pennies.

He could see it so clearly—eyes closed or opened he could see it. His mother shrieking her final tortured words. *Run.* "RUN!"

"I'm sorry," he mumbled, his voice raspy and rusty, and he realized he was parched, his tongue dragging over dried lips. "I'm sorry, Mom. I'm sorry for what I said about Heath. I knew he could hear it. I wanted him to. I—I just—I dunno why I did it, but I'm sorry."

Somewhere far off there was a banging sound. Jack frowned, his eyes brimming with tears.

"And I'm sorry"—his voice started breaking, but he couldn't stop now—"for not standing by you like I should have, when you needed it most."

The banging came again, louder this time. Jack sat bolt upright in bed amidst a sea of clutter. A cold grey light filtered in through the windows.

"Mom," he gasped. "Tell me it's not true. *Please.*"

BANG! The sound came a third time, much louder and much closer, and he jolted. A sudden spasm of clammy terror. "Neria?" he said, for no particular reason.

He was alone in the attic.

Something outside the window drew his gaze. Someone running down the street. Lucas?

Jack rolled out of bed, crossed to the window. It *was* Lucas.

He was running away from the Changeling House.

From downstairs there came another sound—glass shattering. Someone screamed.

Jack crawled out of bed, and tottered unsteadily across the cluttered attic to the narrow ladder-stairs. He descended to the second floor.

As he emerged into the second-floor hallway, Skye came barrelling around the corner, a look of horror painted on her face.

"They're in the house!" she cried.

She shoved past Jack as two more people appeared at the top of the stairs. Jack froze. It was Simon and Solomon Sturgess.

"Get 'em," said Solomon.

Simon was holding a baseball bat. He snarled a war-mongering snarl.

Jack wheeled around just in time to see Skye vanish through an open doorway: the Stowaway Garden. "Come on!" she shouted.

He threw himself after her, lunging through the doorway. Skye slammed the door shut behind them, locked it, then trampled through the sprout-peppered soil to the window. She yanked the window open.

"Where's Dyl?" Jack demanded.

"No idea." Skye slipped out the window. Jack glanced back at the locked door. Then he followed Skye across the room and out the window, squinting as the glaring sunlight smashed into his face. The baking shingles burned the soles of his feet, but there was no turning back: behind them the bedroom door shook as the Sturgesses pounded on it.

Skye grabbed onto the nearest eavestrough and swung herself out over the edge of the roof. "We have to get to the lighthouse," she grunted.

"Skye," Jack said. "Mom's dead."

Skye turned and stared at him. Her jet-black hair swung in front of her gleaming green eyes.

"Aunt Mira?" she breathed.

Jack nodded.

Skye turned away from him without another word. She crept to the edge of the roof—swung out over the edge of the roof, grabbed onto the vertical shaft of the eavestrough and slid down into the garden below.

But even as Skye landed on the ground someone came rushing toward her from the street: Syrena Sturgess.

"Skye!" Jack shouted. His cousin glanced up at him, and so did Syrena—giving Skye the chance to dodge around Solomon's wife and run off down the street.

Syrena Sturgess pointed up at the roof and shouted something.

From inside the house there came a gigantic CRASH! Jack knew the door to the Stowaway Garden had just been kicked in. "Shit," he gasped. He shimmied along the sloping roof toward the bathroom window, which was ajar. *Thank god.* He waited until he caught a glimpse of Solomon Sturgess hauling himself through the window of the Stowaway Garden, out onto the roof.

Then, before Solomon could spot him, Jack slipped back into the house through the bathroom window.

He tip-toed to the bathroom door, poked his head out into the hallway.

The hallway was empty.

Jack rushed downstairs as fast as he dared, but slowly enough that he didn't make excessive noise. When he reached the living room he saw that the front window looking out onto the Wynd had been smashed, shattered glass lining the floor underneath the sill.

"Goodbye," Jack said. He couldn't have explained exactly why he said it.

Then out the front door and off down the Wynd. No looking back. No slowing down. Not anymore. He kept to the shaded part of the sidewalk. The asphalt chewed at his bare feet, but there was nothing for it. He couldn't go back for his shoes now.

He ran, as fast as the soles of his feet would let him.

Was that shouting behind him?

Whatever. It didn't matter. Soon Jack was in the woods, sprinting through rows of trees, dodging over tangles of roots and patches of brushwood. His feet thanked him for the relief from the searing slam of rock-hard pitch, the coolness of moss and soil underfoot.

He was panting, sweating, and there was a stitch in his side, but he didn't want to stop.

So far, running seemed to be the only thing that could displace the leaden anchor in his gut. If he stopped running, he knew it would all come flooding back.

I watched her die.

He ran faster, sprinting now, his aching soles hammering into the forest floor, his entire body stretched taught—

And then he couldn't run anymore.

He staggered to a halt and fell against the nearest tree, heaving and panting.

In the old days, he thought bitterly, *I could've run three times as far before having to stop.*

It took him a good moment to realize that the tree he was leaning against was the dragon-shaped tree.

Twelve steps past the dragon-shaped tree, turn left and take three more steps and you'll see it.

He stepped back. He had been drawn to it without even realizing it. The tree coiled above him, really two trees in one: a narrow trunk growing straight up, a leaning beech; and a coiling banyan spiraling around it, serpentine, a dragon strangling its prey.

It's different every time—the path keeps changing, and things keep moving around, and even when I think I know which way I'm going I get lost…

Jack squinted at the place where he knew the canoe was hidden. He could just make out a bit of *Wyvern*'s dark greyish-green hull showing through the tangle of branches. The unmistakable sheen of its scales.

Then—footsteps crunching through brambles nearby. Jack's heart rammed up into his throat.

"Jack."

He turned in the direction of her voice. "Skye?"

"That's Admiral Bloodskye to you." She approached him. "We've got work to do."

"No." Jack's lip trembled. "No." His throat tightened. "No, I can't—I can't just—they *killed* her, Skye. I saw it. I saw *them*. And Dad, he"—he gulped loudly—"he made me watch."

Jack could hardly believe he was saying the words out loud. As he spoke he locked gazes with Skye. He could see the storm raging behind her eyes.

Then his cousin closed the rest of the distance between them, and hugged Jack awkwardly, uncertainly. She pulled away quickly.

"We're gonna kill them," she said. "You're going to kill your father, and I'm going to kill mine. I want to choke that bastard to death with my own bare hands."

"Skye—"

"We'll make sure Aunt Mira's death is avenged. And Mum's death—'cause we know it wasn't a—a goddamn *car crash* that took her, was it?" She paused to catch her breath. "We'll make them pay for it. That's a promise, all right? Cousin to cousin."

"Skye—I don't want to—look." Jack breathed in as deeply as he could, closing his eyes and opening them again. "I don't ever want to see my father again. I just—I just want to forget everything. Do you understand?"

"But you can't—"

"Do you understand, Skye? I thought I wanted to know why there were holes in my memory, but it turns out things were so much better when I couldn't remember. If I can't forget it then I'm—I'm gonna see that knife going through her eyes and cutting her throat for the rest of my life. I want. To forget. *Everything.*" Stomach acid rising in his throat. His voice a growl. "Even Morgana Wynd, if I have to. Even *you*, if I have to."

He didn't know why he was saying it. It was spewing from his mouth like vomit. "I don't wanna play your little games anymore. I thought coming back here was going to make things better, but in actual fact it's ruined my life. Thanks a lot."

Part of him—the twisted, ravenous part of his soul shaped like a snarling dog—took vengeful pleasure in the way Skye's eyes widened, in the way her lower lip quivered. Then she turned away and rushed off into the trees, her stained trench coat trailing behind her.

Jack's heart was pounding, his blood hot in his temples.

Then he heard someone else approaching, through the foliage, somewhere nearby. He threw himself behind the dragon-tree… just in the nick of time, too, because moments later Solomon Sturgess entered the clearing with a portly man.

With a chill Jack realized that he knew the man's face: it was the black-bearded man from the cement-walled room. The man who had held the knife.

The man who had killed her.

That's my mother's murderer standing right there, in the flesh.

Jack ground his teeth, balled his hands into fists. Hot, furious tears sprang to his eyes. His knees buckled and he slumped down to a crouch behind the dragon-tree.

Meanwhile, Solomon Sturgess and Blackbeard were almost at the spot where the canoe was hidden. Had they seen it already? "God *damn* it," Jack hissed under his breath, peering out from around the trunk of the double-tree, watching as Solomon pulled a clump of branches aside. *Wyvern*'s scaly dark-green hull gleamed in the afternoon sunlight.

For a moment neither Solomon nor his black-bearded friend said anything. Then:

"YES!" Solomon cried.

The joy in his voice made Jack want to puke. He didn't linger a second longer. He jumped to his feet and ran.

———— •·◆·• ————

"Hey! Wait up!"

Only her voice could have stopped him. He ground to a halt, turned in a full circle. Neria came toward him through the trees, her hair glinting bright and orange in the morning light.

"They found it," Jack grunted. "They found *Wyvern*."

"Come with me." Neria took his hand and led him along a lane of trees and shrubs to a gigantic towering sequoia which grew treacherously tall, rising above the rest of the Skein's canopy.

"Up there," Neria said, pointing into the branches. "They won't find you. Trust me."

Then she was gone.

It took a few tries for Jack to get into the branches, but once he did he hauled himself up, up, further up, until the tree's branches thinned, so that they swayed and bent precariously under his weight. A hot breeze crawled over him.

"Jack?"

The shock almost made him let go. "Lucas?"

The older boy was perched further up in the tree. "How the hell did you find me?" he asked.

"Neria brought me here," Jack replied.

"Neria? Funny. She brought me here, too."

Jack scrambled up to Lucas's height and found a cluster of branches that he could rest comfortably on. They had a sprawling panoramic view of the forest; it stretched out around them, extending on all sides much further than it should have. A sea of rushing green. And far, far in the distance they could just make out the houses and buildings of Morgana Wynd, and the rest of the Morgana Peninsula. How had it all gotten so far away?

And there, below them, was the beach. Barkface's cottage. The lighthouse sitting just offshore.

The gaping, hungry ocean.

"What is she up to?" Jack wondered aloud.

"Hmm?"

"Neria. What's she up to?"

Lucas whistled, a low, ominous sound. "All I know is, I'd rather chill up here than get beaten to a pulp down there." He looked sideways at Jack. "You trust her, don't you?"

Jack nodded.

They both fell silent.

Then Jack burst into tears. Lucas stared at him, bewildered, and then he sighed and looked away over the vast forest toward the ocean.

Soon they heard more voices far below. More people climbing the tree.

Jack and Lucas waited. Sure enough Skye and Dylan clambered up to join them in the thick branches, followed closely by Neria.

Jack had stopped crying by this point, but his eyes were rimmed with red, and he had an expression on his face that said *Don't say a word to me.*

"What the hell?" Skye demanded. She glared at Jack. "What is this?"

"Good question." Dylan turned to Neria. "What's going on? What are you doing?"

Neria shrugged. "I figure you guys stand a better chance against the Sturgess clan if you're all together. Besides, I guarantee they won't find us up here."

"You're helping us?" said Dylan.

"Well, yeah," she said matter-of-factly.

"*Why?*"

For a moment Neria looked confused. "I just…" she began, but trailed off. "I dunno. I'm rooting for you guys. Besides, I got you all into this mess, didn't I?"

The sun was beginning its slow descent to the horizon.

"So how long are we gonna stay up here?" said Skye.

"Probably until they've searched the whole woods."

"How long will that take?"

"Dunno."

Silence.

Then—"Where are you going?" Jack demanded. Neria had started making her way back down the tree.

"To cause a bit of trouble." She didn't bother looking back up at him. "Don't worry about me."

As Neria descended through the sequoia's foliage, Jack glanced from Dylan to Lucas to Skye. Skye was still glaring furiously at him.

Jack started climbing down the tree after Neria.

"What are you doing?" Dylan demanded.

Jack ignored him. But Neria asked him the same question when he caught up with her, about midway to the ground.

"I'm coming with you."

"No you're not."

"But I wanna cause trouble too." He didn't know why he was saying it, but he continued hauling his way down through the branches after her. Neria sighed, grumbled something under her breath, then slowed her descent so that Jack could catch up.

When they were low enough, Neria dropped nimbly to the ground. It was about a seven-foot drop. She looked up at Jack. "Come on!" she whispered hoarsely.

Shit. Jack lowered himself onto a smaller branch beneath him—but it snapped beneath his feet—he lost his grip, couldn't recover it—

He fell. Landed on his side on the ground. "Gah!" he shrieked.

"Oh, you *idiot.*" Neria knelt down beside him. "What did I tell you, man?"

"Owww, god!"

Where was it coming from? His arm? No—his wrist, wedged firmly under his body.

He rolled to the side and sat up. Splinters of pain went up and down his forearm. *"Gah!"*

"Hide! Quick!" Neria pulled Jack to his feet by his collar—but Solomon Sturgess and several of his cronies were already coming toward them through the trees. Neria grabbed Jack's good wrist. "You'd better be up for this," she hissed. "Don't let go of my hand, no matter what happens. And don't say a word."

"I—but I—I think I'm hur—"

Then Neria dragged Jack forward into the shade of the trees, and they ran. Not in a straight line, but slanting through the trees at odd angles, *impossible* angles, weaving this way, that way, ducking behind curtains of slanting sunlight and leaping between patches of shadow like they were stepping stones. Neria had a vice-grip on his hand and didn't say a word. Jack's eyes were streaming, his vision blurry. His heart was on rapid-fire. His chest and lungs ached like they had been torn open. He had to pump his legs so hard that he forgot entirely about his wrist— nothing seemed to exist other than his bare feet and his searing legs and the root-tangled ground, and Neria's hand gripping his good wrist.

He could barely hear Sturgess and his cronies behind them. Without warning Neria jerked to a halt. Jack bowled into her—she staggered forward, but gracefully righted herself, turned, and pushed Jack into a blackthorn bush.

Jack's left wrist exploded in pain again as he crashed through the tangles of flowers and sloes and landed on the ground at the base of the blackthorn. His eyes smarted. Tears rolled down his cheeks. "Aoow! What the—"

"Shh! Sorry." As he came to a rest, crammed into the depths of the blackthorn bush, Neria knelt beside him and clamped a hand over his mouth. "Don't move! They won't see you here."

Jack squeezed his eyes shut in an attempt to suppress the pain.

"No-one's gonna find you here," Neria reassured him. "*Stay put.* I won't be long."

"But where are—"

"Shh! Don't worry about me."

"Are you coming back?"

But she was already gone.

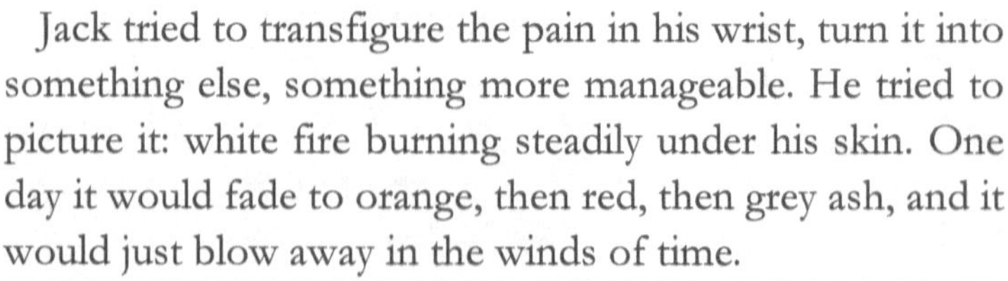

Jack tried to transfigure the pain in his wrist, turn it into something else, something more manageable. He tried to picture it: white fire burning steadily under his skin. One day it would fade to orange, then red, then grey ash, and it would just blow away in the winds of time.

A secret part of him was thankful for the sprain. The physical agony was a nice distraction from the soul-deep mutilation that his father had put him through. And huddled there in the tangles of the blackthorn bush, waiting for Neria's return, Jack knew he had to take what he could get.

He hoped Neria was right about nobody finding him here.

Still, as the light slowly leaked out of the forest, and the shade beneath the forest canopy faded to a deep bruised purple, his thoughts turned to the apartment he had shared with his mother, back in the city.

Back in time.

He and his mother, making dinner together. Jack chopping vegetables, his mother cooking the stew in a great big wok, while a tray of biscuits baked in the oven.

Then they were eating, ravenously, at their little two-person table at the biggest window in the apartment, which looked out over an alley.

It was their own private little alley, and they kept track of its denizens. Gave them names, backstories. The homeless man sitting at the end of the block was a former rock star. The dodgy kid who hung out at the corner of the alley was a baby-faced undercover cop. And the mangy brown dog that came trotting through every now and then was a weredog, cursed to live out its days in a canine body as punishment for some heinous crime.

Why is this all coming back to me now? Jack wondered. It was probably the elixir Barkface had given him, still working its way through the depths of his mind, dislodging other trapped memories and letting them drift to the surface.

———— •◆•• ————

"I swear those kids are messing around with witchcraft or something."

The ground's sloping. The beach is up ahead. Neria crouches behind a lattice of shadows and tangled foliage.

The clan is camped out on the sand. There's Simon and Syrena Sturgess, and two young women with short black hair, whom Neria suspects are twins, though from here it's hard to be certain.

There's an old, stocky man in a black hoodie. He's got long black hair and a white beard.

Over by the water's edge, Solomon and the man with the black beard have set *Wyvern* down on the sand. Now they lean against it, smoking.

"I knew she'd find her way back to me," Neria hears Solomon say, as he strokes *Wyvern's* side. "I knew it! She called out to me, and I answered."

Neria almost snorts. *The hell is wrong with this guy?*

"We going home now, Dad?" says Simon.

"No," Solomon growls.

"But you got *Wyvern* back!"

"Yes. And I'm very pleased to have her back. But let this be a lesson to you, Si: you never leave something unfinished."

"What... what do you mean?" Simon sounded exasperated. "Come on, I just wanna go home. We got what we came for. We—"

"We're gonna catch those kids," his father said, cutting him off. "And we're gonna *punish* them. For disrespecting us. For *hurting* my family, my magnificent wife and my beautiful son. And if what you saw last night is true—if that Neria kid really did put something in the reservoir, then, well—"

Neria grits her teeth. But Solomon is still going. "And you know what?" he continues. "I'm glad the police don't want anything to do with Morgana Wynd. Because that means we're the architects of our own justice."

You're the architect of your own bullshit, Solomon Sturgess.

"There are at least five of them. Two girls and three boys. That Neria girl is one of them. And you know the others, right Si?"

"Skye and Dylan Brecker," Simon mumbles. "And Lucas Alvarez. The new one is Jack."

"Well, I've got Dmitri watching ninety-four, Tom watching seven, and Maggie watching eighteen. They can't go home or we'll catch them. They've got nowhere to go. See how it works, Si? We're gonna get 'em. We're gonna get 'em good."

That's enough of that. Neria makes her way furtively along the treeline, away from the Sturgesses and their insanity, toward Barkface's cottage. Smoke pours out of the chimney, into the early evening air.

Neria steals onto the porch, approaches the cottage door.

She pauses just outside the door. Puts an ear to the wood. She can hear voices she recognizes coming from inside.

Wait a minute.

She twists the doorknob—pulls the door open quickly, so it doesn't make a sound, and slips inside like a vagrant breeze.

She freezes.

There's a fire in the hearth, and two people sitting on the old worn sofa, caught up in conversation. One of them is Barkface. The other is—

Auntie?

Auntie August has a look of concern on her face. She speaks in a strained, subdued voice.

"…when are you going to call it, then?" she says.

"I already have," says Barkface. "Last night. With Neria's help, I might add."

Neria's guardian furrows her brow. "I told you—"

"Hey, hey." Barkface raises his hands. "Neria found her way to me. All I did was try to give her some answers. Lord knows she was desperate for *something*. Don't worry. She doesn't know who I am. She doesn't even know my name."

Auntie August's voice is filed down to razor-sharp. "Just be careful."

Barkface smirks. "We have more pressing things to worry about. The Face of Pale is already converging. But we have to make sure enough of them are here when the *Cascade* arrives for it to be worth it. It's all a matter of timing."

"Just remember what the priority is, okay? Neria *has* to get on that ship. There won't be another chance."

"I know. I… I know."

Auntie August heaves a deep sigh. "I can't believe it, Neil. She's sixteen, you know."

"Of course I know." Barkface sighs, too, as though it's contagious. "Whenever I see her," he says softly, "whenever I look her in the *eyes*, I just want to tell her who she is—who I am. But…" He sighs. "I had a chance. I had a chance to fix things… I've had *so long* to make it right, and I just—I wasted it. I *wasted* it. So she can't know."

"The more she knows, the more her heart will break. But soon, if everything goes right—soon it'll be done. We won't have to worry about her anymore."

Something rises in Neria's throat, then. Something sharp. She wants to shout at them, but they've both spotted her now, and Auntie August is rising to her feet and saying something.

Neria doesn't hear. Her eyes sting with tears. She topples backward out of the cottage door.

———— ••◆•• ————

Simon's leaning against a tree trunk, frantically puffing away on a cigarette. He looks up, startled by the sound of Neria's quiet, steady sobs.

"Hey—" he says, through a fit of coughing as the smoke catches up to him.

"They're all fucked, aren't they?" Neria snarls, her amber eyes blazing. "I just wanna—" She breaks off, and growls in frustration. Then she and Simon's gazes meet, and neither of them can look away.

Neria's eyes are rimmed with red to match her red hair, and she looks more gaunt and haggard than Simon remembers. Simon, meanwhile, has an expression like two demons have possessed him and are wrestling for control of his face.

Without breaking eye contact, Neria steps forward, snatches the cigarette from Simon, and takes a long deep drag from it. Then she hands it back to him, and smiles humourlessly.

"Sorry," she sighs, slowly exhaling the smoke. She dries her eyes on the sleeve of her jean jacket. "I'm just—"

"My dad's insane," Simon mumbles, his gaze darting from Neria to the cigarette in his hand to the darkening canopy above them. "I mean, he's always been crazy. But he's gone over the edge now. Something's changed. And it's… it's all…" For a second anger contorts his face, and his free hand—the one not holding the cigarette—clenches into a fist. "It's your fault, isn't it? *You* pushed him over the edge."

Neria shakes her head, and instead of obeying her instincts and leaping backward out of Simon's reach, she steps forward and lays a hand gently on his fist. "Simon." She brings her voice down to a hoarse, smoky simmer. "Be cool."

The cigarette falls from Simon's hand and lands at his feet in a bed of moss.

"We all have to be cool," Neria says, removing her hand from Simon's and stepping back. "Because our parents—they're not going to be. They've shown us that. So now we need to be better than them."

She bends down, picks up the still-burning cigarette, and hands it back to Simon. He takes it without a word. Neria nods at him, and hopes he gets the message.

Then she rushes off into the woods to find Jack.

Jack's left wrist was swollen and puffy, but the pain was now just a vague dull throb.

A hand clamped over his mouth. A voice in his ear: "Don't scream!"

He reached up, pried the hand away. "Neria?" He could barely make her out in the gloom. "You came back?"

She made a sound halfway between a sigh and a giggle. "I can't just go leaving you stranded in the middle of woods, can I? We're in this together." She grasped him by the collar of his shirt and pulled him to his feet. "Let's find the others."

It was getting dark by the time they made it back to the sequoia. Skye, Dylan and Lucas were still hiding in the branches. Neria climbed up to fetch them, and guided them down to the sequoia's base. The five of them gathered in the impenetrable gloom of its shade.

Dylan started to collect stones and arrange them in a circle amid the sequoia's roots.

"What are you doing?" said Neria.

"Making a firepit."

"Don't." Neria spoke softly but firmly. "We don't need a fire. It would give us away for sure." She paused. "We can use this."

She reached into her jacket pocket and pulled something out, a polished orb with a silver gleam. And as she held it out before her for them all to see, something strange happened: the thickening darkness around them shrank back, and the five of them found themselves in a circle of what might have mistaken for daylight, if it were not surrounded by the darkness of encroaching night.

"What is that?" said Jack, his gaze fixed on the star marble.

"A star," said Neria nonchalantly. She leaned forward, and spoke in a conspiratorial whisper: "They're camping down by the water. They've got *Wyvern,* and they're planning to hunt us. No joke."

"So," said Lucas. "What the hell are we gonna do?"

"We can't go back to the Wynd. They've got people watching the houses."

"We can't get away from them," Lucas growled.

"No," said Neria. "But we can outsmart them. This is where it gets fun."

"This is *war*," said Skye eagerly.

"See?" Neria clapped Skye on the shoulder. "Someone has the right idea. It's just like Sturgess said—no laws out here. Just us and them. And I dunno about you guys, but I fancy our chances of taking them down."

"We could stay here forever if we wanted," said Lucas. "I don't wanna go back."

"Forever?" said Dylan.

"Yeah," said Lucas. "Honestly, I wouldn't mind if I never see my mum and dad again. I swear something's profoundly wrong with them. It's like they're sick or something. They watch TV all day. I don't think they even bother to eat. They just sit there on the couch and stare at the screen. One time I swear I caught them—there was nothing on TV, just static, just *fuzz*, and they were sitting there watching it. And then Dad turned to look at me, and his mouth was hanging open and he was drooling and there wasn't anything in his eyes. I don't know if he even recognized me."

"It's the same with us," said Skye somberly. "Our dad's not our dad. He's—I dunno. There were times I'd wake up in the middle of the night and my bedroom door was open and I'd see him standing there in the hallway—just a silhouette, but I *knew* he was watching me. He always said Mom's death was an accident, but I believe that less and less every day since the day she—" She broke off, unable to say it. "You know."

"It was so long ago," Dylan breathed. "I can hardly remember her face."

Dad.

"He killed her, didn't he?" said Skye.

Jack nodded in somber agreement. "Probably," he said.

Dad... what does that word feel like for other people?

"My father made me watch while my mother was killed," he continued. "A man with a black beard stabbed her eyes out, then cut her throat. She told me to run." There was no burn in his voice, no rage or grief. Just emptiness. *It's all one giant, wacked-out nightmare.* His eyelids were getting heavy. He leaned back against the trunk of the sequoia. "He's here tonight. In the Skein. The man with the black beard, I mean. He's one of the Sturgess clan. The muscle, I guess."

"Seems to me," said Skye, her voice simmering with rage, "that the older generation needs to go."

"Agreed," said Dylan.

Neria opened her mouth to speak—closed it without saying anything.

Jack sighed. "That's the problem, though, isn't it? They're not going anywhere, are they?"

In the circle of glow cast by the star marble, four pairs of eyes turned to look askance at him.

"It's all inside us," Jack continued. "They *made* us. That means we're made of the same stuff as our parents. What if—what if by the time I'm Dad'sage, I'm just like him?"

"You won't be." Skye and Neria said it at the same time. Dylan nodded in agreement.

"Yeah, you can say that," said Jack. "But watch it happen, anyway." The Jackal was poking its snout out from the sweltering room it rented in Jack's head; suddenly his voice was edged with guttural rage. "How many dribbling old men were once boys saying 'I'm never gonna be like *them*,' just like we're doing right now, and then they grow up and discover that's just what life does? How do we stop it?" His voice cracked, and dropped back down to a croak. "It's already inside me. The Face of Pale. I've already got it inside—"

He broke off.

"No you don't, Jackdaw." Neria leaned in to Jack so that their cheeks were grazing. "You're gonna make it through this," she whispered. "I'm going to make sure of it."

"I'm gonna…" Jack began, but then he faltered. He had been on the verge of saying something about what he wanted to do to his father—and to his uncle. *How he wanted to cut their throats the way his mother had died.* But the thought of the Brecker brothers seemed so faraway, so impossible… so he seized the chance to push the older generation out of his mind.

"Promise?" he said instead.

Neria nodded. "Promise."

What did Jack remember of that night?

He remembered Neria taking off her headband, using it along with a strip of fabric torn from her shirt, and a bundle of branches tied tightly together, to fashion a splint for his sprained wrist.

He remembered Lucas lighting a cigarette that wasn't "*just* a cigarette," and blowing smoke rings out of it, then passing it to Neria, who took a deep drag. He remembered the end of the cigarette glowing red, lighting her face for a split second. She winked at him, which made him feel juvenile and ignorant.

He remembered that she had offered the cigarette to him. He couldn't remember if he had taken it or not.

And then she was sitting next to him, resting her head on his shoulder.

"Why did you help me?" he asked. "With my wrist and everything?"

"Because I think we were supposed to meet," she said, "and even if we were never supposed to meet in a million years, I'm glad we did. Besides, I think you need my help… and I need yours."

He remembered their hands finding one another, fingers interlocking, as they watched Skye and Dylan sitting face-to-face, swept up in an impassioned whispered debate.

"You already have, what—six instruments back in the Changeling House?" Dylan was saying. "Why don't you stick to something for once?"

Skye bristled. "Don't you get it, Dyl? That's the whole *point*. I have to find the right thing. The right *cause*, you know? If I don't then it's all a waste. Isn't it?" Her voice hiked to a defiant growl. "Isn't it? I know I was put here on this planet for a reason. I've just gotta figure out what that reason is—"

"But what if you never find the *right thing?* You'll wind up old and grey with no talent at all, and a house filled with junk you don't know how to use."

Skye's voice spiked to a half-shout. "You don't get it—"

"Keep it down." Dylan put a hand on his sister's shoulder. "We're outlaws, don't forget. Maybe that's your reason."

And then Jack remembered waking up, wondering when he had fallen asleep. It was still dark. The cool pine-scented night air was filled with gentle snores. There were lights off in the woods, flickering lights. Growing lights. Coming toward them. And voices, too, getting louder and louder.

Someone was shaking him awake. "Wake up! Wake *up!*"

"THERE THEY ARE!"

Jack sat up. The five of them were all lying in a circle, surrounded by towering behemoths holding flaming torches.

Neria's voice rang out:

"Changelings!" she cried. "Scatter!"

The shadows whirled out of the trees and Jack was on his feet and running, sprinting again, pursued by distant voices and a muffled crackle of flames. The familiar burn in his muscles reassured him. *Fast as you can, Jackdaw.*

For a brief spell Lucas was running beside him—but then Lucas tripped and cried out and Jack left him sprawled on the ground behind him—

He was alone. The black woods towered impassively around him. He heard voices off in the distance, but they were far enough that he couldn't even tell from which direction they were coming.

His sprained wrist ached in its splint. Jack gritted his teeth. Someone was running toward him in the dark. Whoever it was halted several feet away.

"Jack?"

Jack's knees buckled with relief. "Skye! What happened?"

"They got Dyl. And Lucas."

"What about Neria?"

"What about her? I thought she was with you."

Jack groaned.

"Take one of these. Jackass." Skye thrust something long and cylindrical into Jack's good hand.

"Skye, I'm sorry for what I—"

"Just forget it. We all say shit."

Jack held up the narrow cylinder she had given him. "What is this? Is—?" Then it hit him. "Oh."

Skye held up another firework in one hand, and a lighter in the other. "It's war, remember? Come on."

They kept their ears peeled as they crept through the woods. Eventually they heard breaking waves, and saw the beach up ahead, distinguishable only by the faint glow of moonlight on the water.

They hid at the edge of the trees. "Holy," Skye muttered.

There was a roaring bonfire on the beach. Solomon Sturgess wasn't there, but Syrena Sturgess was, as well as a couple of their thugs. *Wyvern* lay overturned near the water's edge, near a pile of logs; Dylan and Lucas were sitting next to the boat, leaning up against the logs. They were tied to each other, back to back, their hands and feet bound with rope.

"So here's the plan." Skye stuck a firework into the ground and pointed it toward the Sturgess camp. She grabbed the firework Jack was holding and shoved it into the ground next to hers. "We're gonna set these off. Then you're going to count to ten, okay? And you're gonna run as fast as you can, you're gonna un-tie Dyl and Lucas, and the four of us are gonna commandeer *Wyvern*. Sound good?"

"What about Neria?"

"Screw Neria! She can take care of herself. I'd rather live as a marooner than die a marauder." Skye bit her lip. "You ready?"

Jack sighed. The sky was already beginning to bloom grey with the coming dawn. *I can't use my right arm.*

"Yeah," he said. "Ready."

Skye lit the fuses. "Ten seconds starting *now*." With a *hiss* the fireworks went wheeling off over the beach, bursting in midair. BANG! BANG!

Skye flew out from beneath the trees, running full-tilt towards Syrena Sturgess and screaming wordlessly at the top of her lungs.

Jack's heart slammed up into his throat. *Count!* He watched as Skye dodged to the side, narrowly avoiding Syrena's lunge; and as the other thugs began to chase after his cousin, Jack saw that there was nothing blocking his way to the canoe.

Was that ten seconds already? *It doesn't matter.* He sprang forward, dashing across the sand directly toward *Wyvern.* Why was it so hard to run on sand? He kept his eyes focused on the canoe, which sat several yards from the bonfire. He didn't let his gaze stray to Dylan and Lucas, who were still tied to each other, slumped against the pile of logs.

A voice behind him: "There's another one!"

"Shit!" Jack gasped. He reached *Wyvern,* grabbed an end of the canoe with his good hand, and threw his weight against it to heave it onto its side.

"Jack!" Dylan cried. "Oh my *god*—hurry!"

"WHERE DID SHE GO?" Syrena Sturgess screamed.

Jack summoned all of his strength, and with an almighty one-handed push managed to shove *Wyvern* across the sand into the surf. The water caught the boat's prow and began to pull it out onto the waves.

Jack looked around frantically—spotted Syrena Sturgess sprinting over the sand toward him.

"Quick!" Jack shouted at Dylan and Lucas. "Get in!"

"Untie us!"

"*Jackass!*" he heard Skye shout, though he couldn't be sure which direction the sound came from.

There was no time. It happened so quickly that Jack wasn't sure if he had made the decision himself. All he remembered was realizing that *Wyvern* was drifting further from the shore. He made a running dive for it—landed with a *splash!* in the surf. His knee caught on a rock; sharp, hot pain shot through him. His sprained wrist throbbed as it was jostled in its splint. Saltwater spilled into his mouth.

Spluttering, coughing, Jack clambered into the bucking canoe. He looked back at the shore. The tide was already pulling him out into the cove, and Syrena Sturgess and her cronies were standing by the bonfire, their vengeful screams filling the pre-dawn air. Dylan and Lucas were still bound and helpless against the logs.

Then Jack realized that he didn't have any oars. He leaned over the side of the boat, dipped his good hand in the water, and tried to paddle—but *Wyvern* was already picking up speed. There was already a gulf of dark chrome water separating Jack from the shore.

The bonfire was growing smaller and smaller.

There was nothing he could do.

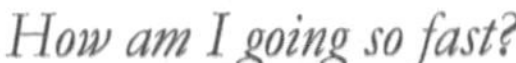

How am I going so fast?
The sky was silvering above him. The stars were fading. A chill wind picked up. The canoe bucked and swayed as it drifted further and further out into the cove. Something swooped in Jack's stomach. He had no way of steering, no way of controlling his speed. And beneath the rising wind he heard something. Something cold, distant, and cruel.

It's laughing at me. The lighthouse towered before him. Beside him. Behind him.

Still he was picking up speed, the wind getting louder and louder, colder and colder. The ocean was opening up ahead, vast and gaping and unending. Jack could feel the first sobs rising in his chest. He looked back, but the Morgana Peninsula was too far away now, just a black mass sitting uselessly on the water.

"HELP!" he screamed, but the banshee wind tore his cry away.

Jack,' something said.

The lighthouse vanished behind a wall of towering cliffs as *Wyvern* carried him further south. The waves were getting choppier now, the spray throwing itself into Jack's face, stinging his eyes, the wind so strong he could hardly breathe.

"SOMEONE HELP!" he howled, so loudly it tore his throat apart. He tasted something salty. Blood? Or seawater? "HELP ME!"

Then *Wyvern* bucked, tipped, and frigid water rushed in. Jack lost his balance, and the sea embraced him. It was bitterly cold. Colder than the water of the cove. He surfaced, flailing-frantically. Where was *Wyvern?* His hand struck something hard. There! There it was—

Dismay flooded him. The canoe had capsized. Jack grasped at it, tried to grab ahold, but the sides were too slippery. He caught the end, hooked his fingers under the rim of the canoe. "HELP!" he screamed. "HEAAAUUGGGLGGLGL—" Saltwater sluiced down his throat. His eyes smarted. Dizziness swarmed him—

Then a sound chopped through the air, a buzzing roar like a motorcycle.

For a moment water closed over Jack's head, and the roar was cut off… *Wyvern* was sinking…

He let go, pushed toward the surface…

Air!

A wave bowled into him, his head span, and something blurry and white and very, very loud filled his field of vision. Two hands grabbed hold of him, wrenched him out of the surf, and he was slammed down onto a solid floor. Solomon Sturgess's voice sounded in his ear. "This one's gonna cost you, kid."

— • ◆ • • —

Jack lay on the floor of the motorboat, curled up in the fetal position, shaking and shivering as they bounced over the waves back toward the beach. He hacked and spat up salt water—so salty it stung the inside of his mouth, stung his eyes so badly he could hardly see.

Solomon muttered savagely under his breath as he steered them around the Cursed Rock. "Entitled little *shits,* that's what you are. Think the world belongs to you, huh? Think it's all yours for the taking, eh? Is that it?"

You'll never understand. Jack wished he had the strength to say it out loud. He tried to push himself up on his elbows, but the motorboat's movement knocked him off-balance.

Before long they began to slow down, the buck and pitch of the waves becoming gentler, the roar of the motor softening to a low, steady purr.

There was a *splash* as Solomon dropped the anchor into the surf. "Come on," he grunted, grabbing Jack by the collar of his damp shirt. Jack spluttered in half-hearted protest as Solomon hauled him out of the motorboat. They crashed down into knee-deep water, and Solomon pushed Jack ahead of him toward the shore.

Jack struggled to gain some semblance of balance in the shallow water. Then—

"What the hell?" Sturgess grunted.

Jack squinted, peering through a nauseous haze at the scene that lay in wait for them on the beach. "What?" he gasped.

Skye, Lucas and Dylan were crouching together next to the still-roaring bonfire. The three of them had blankets draped around their shoulders. Three police officers were standing at the water's edge. One of them was holding Syrena Sturgess in handcuffs. The second was pointing a gun at Solomon. The third had a megaphone raised to his mouth.

Standing just behind the officers was Simon, his shoulders slouched, hands in his pockets.

Further back over the sand, near the trees, Jack could just make out more cops, detaining more people—the black-bearded man among them.

As Solomon Sturgess came to a bewildered halt at the water's edge, his gaze locked onto Simon's. His breathing quickened in Jack's ear, hoarse and ragged. Simon stared doggedly at his father, and Solomon stared back in silent fury.

"Let go of the kid, Sturgess," the third cop said through the megaphone.

Solomon's grip on the collar of Jack's shirt tightened. "Bastard," he snarled. Then he let go of the shirt and pushed Jack forward, so vigorously that Jack crashed in a heap in the inch-deep tide, , sending up a splash of water and wet sand. He gasped in shock, scrambling to get back up again—but one of the cops was already helping him to his feet, guiding him away from Solomon Sturgess, out of the water and onto dry sand.

"Got the last kid," the cop said into her radio. "Shaken up but alive. Minor injuries. Over."

Somewhere behind them, Jack heard a snap of handcuffs. Solomon's furious roars swelled to fill the fading night, like the cries of a wounded wolf. "YOU! YOU CALLED THEM! MY OWN SON, A FUCKING NARC! GOD *DAMN* IT!"

Jack shook his head to try to bring his vision back into focus, but the blurriness wouldn't loosen its grip anymore. The salt's doing, perhaps. He could make out the bonfire, and three shadows crouched around it, just up ahead.

"I saved his life," Solomon Sturgess spluttered. "I went out there and saved his life—let the record show *that,* officer."

You went out to save your boat, Jack thought. *You saved me by accident.*

"Steady," the cop murmured in his ear, her voice warm and motherly.

But Jack's legs had already given out, and he collapsed onto the sand at her feet.

Interlogue: Sleeping Beauty

How many times had they met beneath these trees, right where the Wynd ended and the woods began? How many times had his heart lurched as she emerged from the shadows, smiling that sleepy smile?

How many times had she assured him that everything was all right, that there was nothing to worry about?

"You don't have to trust me," she said. "But you should."

━━━━━━ •·◆·• ━━━━━━

In the semi-darkness Jack's breath rattled like a sputtering motor. He was cold—no, he was too hot, he was sweating but he was shivering too. Why was he *shivering?*

His teeth chattered feverishly. His head felt like it was about to split open. His sprained wrist still ached dully in its cast.

Water. Get water.

But he could barely move. An aching tiredness weighed him down, pinned him against the mattress. The ankle bracelet they had given him at the police station in Cormora Creek dug into his flesh. He had tried loosening it, but it seemed to tighten more with every attempt. His ankle burned from its sharp dig.

"Jack." Neria's voice drifted to his ears from the corner of the room. "Come in, Jack…"

"Neria?" Jack croaked, turning his head to see that the corner of the room was empty. "Oh, finally. God, you never pay attention, do you? I've been trying to reach you for ages. Are you coming or what?"

I'm definitely insane now. "I can't," Jack said to the corner of the room. "I'm… stuck."

"For godsakes, Jack, you have to try!" But he could hardly hear her voice anymore, anyway.Not with that goddamn whining noise in his ears.

He turned on his side to face the window, but looking through he couldn't even tell what time of day it was. The sky was dull grey.

The only *possible* silver lining was that being completely sedentary had allowed his wrist (still hanging in Neria's ragged splint) to set back into place. His whole arm still burned with a dull ache, but it wasn't nearly as intense anymore as it had been before.

When's Dad getting here?

Dread burrowed into Jack's chest. He still couldn't believe he had managed to forget what he had seen in that cozy lakeside town, behind that rusty steel door.

Going with his father into that abandoned building. Screams echoing down the hallway.

A circle of black suits.

Mom.

How much time had passed since Sturgess had saved him from drowning? Twelve hours? Two days? A week? It felt like eons since he had heard from anyone, from Neria or Skye or Dylan or Lucas. Where had they gone?

The only human contact Jack had had recently was with his uncle—and he wasn't even sure that could be qualified as *human* contact.

Gabriel Brecker had picked the worst time to wake up from his coma. Arriving at the door of number seven, he had found himself face-to-face with a police officer, who had calmly informed him that his children had gone conveniently missing. Besides that, his nephew was to be placed under strict house arrest, having incurred twenty thousand dollars' worth of debt by sinking Solomon Sturgess's precious *Wyvern*.

Besides that, the house was all out of order, and the master bedroom was now a garden.

And the front window was broken.

"The fuck happened here?" Uncle Gabe had stuck his rage-contorted face right in Jack's. "You should know by now that your father and I are not the kind of people you want to piss off."

And now Jack lay on the sweat-soaked mattress and he waited. That was it. Even if he had possessed the energy to haul himself out of bed, he couldn't leave number seven without his ankle bracelet alerting the police. He had no way of contacting Dylan or Skye, or Lucas. Or Neria.

He had no way of knowing when his father would be here to collect him, or what would happen when Jacob Brecker finally did arrive.

He lay on the bed in the attic of number seven and listened to his uncle shouting at someone over the phone two floors down. Or maybe he wasn't on the phone—Jack was never sure. Sometimes Gabriel Brecker just shouted.

Slipping his arm gingerly out of its splint, Jack wiggled his fingers, grinding his teeth against the dull, twitching pain that had settled in his wrist. He tried to imagine the tissue healing itself, the microscopic repairs slowly pulling the pieces of him back into place.

How much longer will it be?

Jack dragged his wrist back into the splint. He stared at the shadows playing on the wall, and bit his lip until it bled.

The blood surprised him. It was a bit pointless, really. He was already dead.

———— •·◆·• ————

"He won't move. I've tried everything."

"He's coming with us. I don't care what it takes. We can't leave him here!"

"Come on, Neria. Let it go. If we stay here much longer we're all dead."

Jack's eyelids flick up and down rapidly in the darkness. *Wake up!* Something important is happening, he *knows* he needs to be awake. But he can barely pull his eyelids up.

Her voice is in his ear, her breath pushing against his eardrums. *"Come on, Jackdaw."* He can feel her weight on him, her lips pressing to his, breathing something into him.

Smoke.

He chokes, splutters, pushes himself away from her but she locks her face against his and he has no choice but to swallow the smoke. It tastes cool. Fresh like pine. It's not smoke, it's *mist*. And then Jack remembers that while he can't walk, he can float.

"Wake *up!*"

A burst of energy courses through him. He jolts up in bed. "Neria?"

But the attic is empty. The door is wide open.

He's alone.

Jack leaps out of bed and rushes through the door… but there is no door, like there usually is, it's just a gaping archway. Stepping through it, he finds himself in a narrow stone passageway with a floor of black mud. There, up ahead—is that her?

"NERIA!"

"Come *on*, Jack!"

He follows the sound of her voice, scrambling down the passage as it winds steadily upward. Ahead, a distant light lends the tunnel a pallid glow.

The floor grows steeper. Jack can't see Neria anymore; her voice is distant now. *"Come on!"*

"Slow down!"

"Hurry!"

He's no longer following a tunnel: his feet are falling on steps. A spiraling staircase winding up, up, up.

"JACK!" Neria's voice is different now, shrill and petrified. "JACK! HELP! *PLEASE!*"

From way up above him, Neria screams a bloodcurdling scream. And then another. And another. Jack sprints up the steps four at a time, but the stairs keep going and going until he's too tired to climb, until his chest is heaving, his throat parched, and he collapses into a heap against the cold stone.

Chapter Ten: The Tale of an Eternal Summer Evening

"What do you mean, you spiked the reservoir?"

They're walking side by side through the woods. Neria speaks in a conspiratorial mumble: "When you stayed in the cottage," she says, "and drank the remembering elixir, Barkface took me to the reservoir. There's an opening, a tiny little crack. He wedged a funnel into it, and gave me a jug of this weird sludge, and told me to pour it into the funnel. I did what he said to do. And he told me…" She trails off. "Anyway. It's not important."

"It's not?" says Jack.

Neria smiles coyly. "No."

They wander. The hours slide slyly through their fingers like sand, but then they return,drifting back along the warm breeze, the way hours do on those endless summer evenings.

Music has been strung through the woods like party streamers, melodies coiling and twining through the air, harmonies finding each other, pulsing in radiant rhythm for a spell, and then breaking off, twisting away.

"What's going on?" Jack asks lazily. "How'd we even get here? I thought I was still under…" He trails off. Neria can tell he doesn't want to say it out loud.

You are, she nearly tells him. *You're still trapped in the Changeling House. But the rules are different now. For a little while at least.*

"Well," she whispers instead, "do you honestly think you've stayed inside your own body *every* single night of your life?"

Jack doesn't respond. Soon thewoods end, and they emerge onto the sand. "Whoa," Jack surmises.

On the twilit beach a festival has broken out against the blazing blood-gold light of the sunset. There are circus tents, aisles of booths and swarms of people: all sorts of people, dark people and light people, people who flicker like firelight and aren't there when you turn to look twice at them. People who don't look like people at all, because they have goat legs or elf ears or more eyes than they're supposed to have. "Tourists," Neria whispers.

Shadows brush past them as they emerge from the woods, misshapen things whispering to themselves. The sun hasn't even finished setting, it's taking its sweet time, but the stars have already come out, gleaming overhead far brighter than usual.

On the beach a banquet breaks out. People and banquet tables turn to charcoal silhouettes against the roaring light of the sunset.

"Something's calling them here," says Neria. "Something's—"

"You! Boy and girl. Come!" Someone beckons to them: a man who would be tall if he weren't so stooped. His skin is grey, he wears an orange turban, and his smile is wolfish and far too wide. He stands at the entrance to an orange tent.

Jack wavers, but Neria grabs his wrist and pulls him over. They follow the stooped man into the tent, and a powerful fragrance overwhelms them. Incense. Sandalwood. Their ears itch with the sound of distant singing, a dozen different songs, the voices intersecting, crisscrossing, harmonizing and diverging, too subdued for Jack to make out any words.

In the light of a dozen flickering candles he can make out shelves lined with…

"What *are* these?" Neria asks as she approaches the shelves.

"Spires," the stooped man says. "For sale."

They look like conch shells, only made of stone—smooth stone, swirled into spirals and points. Neria wonders if someone carved them this way, or if they formed on their own. *Maybe they carved themselves.*

Whatever they are, they're definitely the source of the faraway singing.

"What's a spire?" says Jack.

Neria bends over and picks one of the stone conches up. She holds the opening near Jack's ear so they can both hear it. The words which emerge from the conch are faraway, hollow, distant, as if they were spoken centuries earlier:

'I will see you again,' the spire says, *'at the place where myth and memory meet… I will see you again… at the place where myth and memory meet… I will see you again…'*

Jack moves away, grabs another spire. This one carries the sound of growling thunder, a deep, surging bass behind the captured voice: *'…the little ones were crying and I wanted to cry too, but I started laughing,'* the speaker recounts sadly, *'I can't explain it… I just wanted to laugh along with it, because I thought that maybe if I did it would leave us all alone…'*

Jack turns to the turbaned man. "I don't have any money," he says apologetically.

The turbaned man chuckles. "You need not pay with money."

"Well, we're not paying with anything *else,*" says Neria sternly. She reaches for Jack's hand again. *Careful.*

"That is your choice," the turbaned man responds indifferently. "But I ask one favour." He smiles sleekly, trundles to the other side of the tent, grabs a spire from a shelf and hands it to Neria. "It is empty." He makes a broad gesture. "Lend it your voice."

Neria nods, then hands the spire to Jack. "You do it."

Jack takes the stone conch from her, raises the opening to his mouth. He wavers. Glances at Neria. Then he reaches for her hand, grabs hold of it.

"I wish this moment could last till the end of time," he says.

Still clasping Jack's hand, Neria takes the spire from him and holds it up to her ear. Then she holds it up to his. '...*last till the end of time...,*' his voice echoes back.

Neria turns and gives the spire back to the turbaned man. She and Jack leave the tent. They wander through the throng of festival-goers, making their way slowly but surely toward the water's edge.

Neria points. "Jack, look! It's *him!*"

Jack looks where she's pointing. *Barkface.* It *is* him, definitely. He's young and tall and muscular, far younger than he has any right to look. He's got elk antlers protruding from his forehead, and he stands near the water where the sand is always wet, his arms raised to the sky.

And he *screams,* in a voice that's not one voice but a dozen, a hundred, a thousand different voices all tangled up into one.

"He's calling it," Neria whispers.

"Calling what?" But Jack doesn't need Neria to tell him. As he listens to Barkface's invocation he closes his eyes, and he can *see* it: seven masts stretching to the sky, sails shivering in the wind as it slices through the waves of a faraway ocean.

The Jericho Cascade.

What was it Barkface had said? *The summons can only be carried out properly in another realm, very far from here.* "We cannot go there ourselves," Jack whispers to himself. "But we can take Morgana Wynd there."

He opens his eyes, glances at Neria, and sees that her sleepy smile has vanished. She stares at Barkface with cold anger in her eyes.

"You all right?" Jack ventures.

Neria doesn't tear her eyes away from Barkface. "Let's go," she says.

They meander back to the Wynd. The sun is still working on its slow descent, burning the western sky golden pink. On the opposite side of the great dome of sky the moon wheels high in an indigo lagoon salt-flecked with stars.

The houses of Morgana Wynd loom darkly. For some reason they all look crooked.

Neria and Jack keep to the shadows. *What's happening?* The residents of the Wynd crowd the curving street: a throng of people singing at the tops of their lungs, drinking wine and rum straight out of bottles, juggling torches, dancing strange, woozy dances. Someone's playing a twisted tune on a fiddle, while nearby someone else plays a completely different tune on an oboe. The two melodies collide, twining round each other until the two sounds are inseparable but completely at odds. Someone else offers up a wordless howl in the background, an opera from another planet.

Others are skipping across rooftops, and others still are simply running, dodging through the crowd, giggling and cackling uproariously. Jack spots Dylan and Skye on a lawn across the street. He nudges Neria, points in their direction. "Let's go say hi," he says.

They approach the two siblings, Jack laughing and Neria frowning as Skye bends down to shove several firecrackers into the ground, while Dylan peers through a pair of binoculars at the crowd flooding the Wynd.

"Skye—" Jack begins, but Skye's already turning away from the fireworks, plugging her ears with her fingers. "For the love of the dread lords of mischief!" she cries, as the fireworks shoot off into the sky, exploding overhead in bursts of vivid blue and green. Around them passersby clap and whistle their appreciation, letting out a wave of "Oooh"s and "Ahh"s. Skye turns to face the onlookers, grins and does an exaggerated bow.

Dylan chuckles to himself as he stares through his binoculars. "That woman there," he says. "She was a bear when I looked at her a moment ago. Now she's a human again. But I bet if I keep looking she'll turn back into a bear." He purses his lips. "I wonder where she's from?"

Neria slips her hand into Jack's palm, interlaces her fingers with his. "Come on, Jackdaw," she murmurs. "Let's go."

But Skye is bounding toward them now, her black hair all frizzed up and wild, and she's grinning intoxicatedly. "What's going on, Skye?" says Jack, gesturing to the revelry filling the street around them.

"What's going on?" says Skye. "What's going on is, Morgana Wynd has gone *mad!* Isn't it wonderful?"

"Yes," says Jack. "Right. Wonderful."

Then Neria tugs him away from his cousins—"Please," she whispers—and they head back into the crowd, pushing through the multitude. The crowd pulls them along, an inescapable current of sticky, pungent-smelling bodies— and spits the two of them out in front of number 96, the tallest house on the Wynd. Four storeys tall with a flat roof.

Sweating from the end-of-day heat, Jack and Neria scale the fire escape and scramble from there onto the roof. They sit down on the sun-baked shingles. The roofs of all the other buildings seem to have crowds of revelers swarming on them. But Jack and Neria have this one all to themselves.

"It's the end of the world," Neria mumbles in Jack's ear. Her breath is hot on his cheek. The sun has just reached the horizon now, swollen to twice its normal size, crimson like blood. Below in the gathering shade the Wynd twists away from number 96 and loses itself in the deep, dark woods.

A deafening, aching silence pulls down on them.

"Jack," Neria whispers. "I'm sorry."

Jack seems to know instantly what she's talking about. "I love my mom," he says. "But she always seemed a little… broken. I know why now." He frowns. The notion of what happened, of what he saw, seems lifetimes away. *Eons* away. "She's dead."

"My father's name is Neil," says Neria. "But I think we should go on calling him Barkface."

Jack wavers.

"I dunno what to say, Jackdaw. It's horrible. It's all so horrible."

Jack nods. "It's like the world just gets uglier and uglier." He pauses, and when he next speaks there's a lump in his throat. It makes his voice crack. "My father's coming for me."

"I think you should—" Neria begins, but Jack cuts her off:

"Actually, can we talk about something else? Please?"

"Yeah, Jack. Of course."

"What's—" Jack breaks off, hesitates for just a moment. "What's your mom like?"

For a split second Neria freezes. Nobody has ever asked her that before.

Jack turns to look directly into Neria's face. Her eyes aren't amber anymore: the fading light has gotten trapped inside her, and now her eyes gleam with every colour of the sunset.

"My mother died a long time ago," she says. "When I was really little. I don't remember much of her. Except for one moment, I guess."

"One moment?"

Neria pauses. "We were sitting on a beach, at night, under the full moon, and the stars were all bigger than they were supposed to be. My mother was holding me, and then she reached up and plucked a star out of the sky. She gave it to me to keep."

Neria pulls the star marble out of her pocket. It glows in the palm of her hand, looking bizarrely faraway.

"Her name was Anora Vale," she says, her eyes scintillating with fragments of captured starlight.

"We should—" But Jack breaks off.

Are you going to say it?

"Don't you think it's funny," Neria whispers, "that you wanted to get to a place so badly, but you could never find it… and suddenly you woke up and you were just… *there?*"

———— •◆• ————

Jack was giddy. He couldn't think straight. "Well…"

"Jack, there's…" Neria trailed off. "Never mind."

He opened his mouth. Closed it. There were dozens of things he wanted to ask her, each question jostling for space halfway between his heart and his throat. *Where are you from? Why have you been helping me? How can Anora—how can the waxwoman be your mother?*

How could he be here, on this rooftop, now, with Neria, when he knew that he was really under house arrest, feverish and delirious, with a broken wrist, lying in bed in the attic of his murderous uncle's house?

(Or was it possible that Jack really *was* here, sitting on this rooftop with Neria? Clear-headed and giddy, with no broken bones at all?)

Instead of asking her any of those questions, he said, "Why is all of this happening?"

He expected her to laugh, but a look of grim doubt came over her face. "I wish I knew," she said. "Jackdaw, can I tell you something?"

"Er. Yeah, of course?" He didn't mean for it to be a question.

Neria looked down at her feet. "Sometimes I can see ahead. It's like I hear… voices, but they're not like people talking. They come from really deep underground and really high in the sky, from the trees and the wind and—and they tell me what's going to happen next. All my life I've heard them, and never once has any of them ever lied to me. Except here." She gestured to the Wynd stretching out below them. "And now I can't hear them at all. It's like they've stopped talking, like they all shut up because something horrible is about to happen, and they don't want me to know, and—" Her voice caught. She shook her head. "You've heard them. Haven't you?"

Jack opened his mouth, but then he froze. The urgency was so clear in Neria's voice, but he had no inkling of what she wanted him to say.

"It isn't only me," she said. She said it softly. Desperately. "Is it, Jack?"

Then, before he could answer, she pushed herself into him, met him in mid-air. "Come on," she whispered.

She clasped his hands and pulled—pulled him away from the rooftop in every direction at once, into the fleeing sunset and the oncoming night, up into the echoing emptiness above and down to the star-strewn depths of the ocean, and he was lying on the lumpy bed in the attic of number seven, sweaty, gripping the sheets tight. *What is* **wrong** *with me?*

He was dizzy. The room was spinning. *'You're dying,'* something said.

Jack sat bolt upright. Looked around. Nobody there. The room was dark.

When you die the things you love flash before your eyes.

Voices drifted up to him from the floor below. *Dad.* His father and Uncle Gabe. He could hear them talking. And there was a third voice, too. Who *was* that?

Then Jack saw her. She must have been a ghost, there was no *way* it was actually her. But her fingers went *tap-tap-tap* on the windowpane.

He clambered out of bed, lifted the window open. Neria crouched on the sloping roof. Jack didn't need to ask how she had gotten there.

She slipped into the room. "We're getting out of here," she whispered savagely.

"Wh—what?"

Neria frowned. "Are you crying?"

"What? No, I—"

"Jackdaw," she said, her expression softening. "Don't cry." She glanced at his right arm, still hanging in its splint. "How's your wrist?"

"It's—it's fine," Jack said hoarsely as he pulled the splint off and cast it aside. His wrist still sang with pain, but the adrenaline muted it to a dull discomfort. "Neria, what the hell is going on? You—you shouldn't be here. My uncle's gonna—and what about Dylan and Skye? And Lucas and—"

Neria's face darkened. "Jack. We can't stay here. We've got a chance to get away. But we have to go fast. And we can't be seen. By *any*one. So. You coming or what?"

"But… but I can't…" Jack fell back against the wall. "Just go without me. The police will know the instant I step outside of this house."

"Yeah, well," said Neria, slipping her hand into his, "fuck them. It's the end of the world, isn't it?" She pulled him to his feet. "We don't have much time."

Chapter Eleven: Outrun

Neria reaches into her pocket and pulls out the star marble. She's about to hand it to Jack—but suddenly there are voices in the hallway. Footsteps approaching the door.

There's no time to tell him.

"Alley," she hisses. She slips the star marble back into her pocket, then runs to the window and clambers out onto the sloping roof.

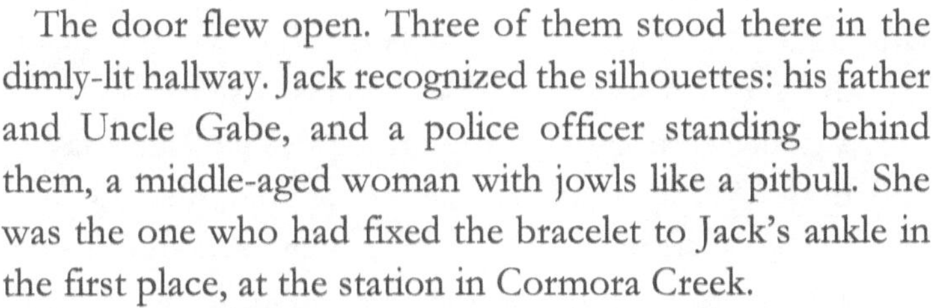

The door flew open. Three of them stood there in the dimly-lit hallway. Jack recognized the silhouettes: his father and Uncle Gabe, and a police officer standing behind them, a middle-aged woman with jowls like a pitbull. She was the one who had fixed the bracelet to Jack's ankle in the first place, at the station in Cormora Creek.

"Get that thing off him, will you?" Jacob Brecker growled.

The officer nudged her way past the two brothers, into the room, and approached Jack. She offered a weak smile, and Jack could see the beads of sweat on her brow, the quiver in her fingers as she pointed to his ankle bracelet. In her hand was the same small key which had locked it. Jack's heart leapt as he saw that little key. *Free at last. Well, almost—*

"I bet that thing itches like hell, eh?" the officer offered.

Jack stuck his ankle out over the edge of the bed, hiking up his pyjama leg so the officer could get at the tight metal-and-plastic anklet. Kneeling beside him, she quickly turned the key in the small lock on the mechanism. With a satisfying *click,* the tightness on Jack's ankle finally loosened.

"That's that," the officer said, rising to her feet with the bracelet in hand.

Jack stared past her at his father and uncle. They stood in the doorway, arms crossed, staring back at Jack, their gazes glacial and impassive. Uncle Gabe was taller than Jack's father, and skinnier. He had coarse, wiry, shoulder-length black hair, and part of his nose and lips were missing: they had been chewed off by a dog.

"Dad—" Jack began.

"Just keep your mouth shut. I think I've earned twenty thousand dollars' worth of silence from you." Jacob Brecker's voice barely rose above a growl. He jerked his thumb over his shoulder. "Take him downstairs, Gabe."

The police officer stood and turned to face Jack's father and uncle. "One moment," she said—but then Gabriel Brecker grabbed her by the back of her neck and pushed her face into a damp rag he was holding in his other hand. He held her head in the rag for what felt like an eternity, as the officer thrashed and kicked, until eventually her legs gave out. Uncle Gabe lowered her delicately to the floor, keeping the rag pressed over her mouth until she became completely still.

Jacob Brecker grabbed Jack by the collar of his shirt and dragged him off the bed, across the attic to the doorway. *"Move."*

"What—what the—what's going—" Jack spluttered as his father ushered him down the attic stairs to the second floor hallway, and down again to the living room on the first floor.

Jack's stomach lurched. The windows of the first floor had all been completely boarded up. The living room floor was covered with black garbage bags taped together to form a makeshift tarp.

There were three people leaning against the far wall—all tied up with duct tape, duct tape over their mouths. It didn't take long for Jack to recognize them: Solomon, Simon and Syrena Sturgess.

Solomon's eyes widened when he saw Jack. He made a muffled groan that must have been an attempt at a scream—

"Shut your mouth, Sol," said Uncle Gabe. "Or he'll take your soul first."

Jack felt vomit rising in his throat. *Not again. Please not again.* His father appeared beside him, pointed to the three captives. "I want you to watch this," he growled in Jack's ear. "This is your doing. I didn't want it to come to this, but I can't just dish out twenty thousand dollars because my shithead son happens to be a moron. Now, *watch.* Because once the Face of Pale has had its way with the Sturgesses, you're going to be the one cleaning it up."

Uncle Gabe had something in his hand: a long, serrated hunting knife. He approached Solomon Sturgess.

"NO! STOP IT!" Jack screamed. *"STOP!"*

Solomon writhed and kicked against his bonds. He was breathing manically through his nose, so manically he had a nosebleed, but he couldn't move.

Simon screamed into the duct tape.

Jack's knees buckled.

Uncle Gabe pressed the flat of his hunting knife against Solomon's face.

"I want you to listen carefully, Sol," he grunted, "or I'm going to draw blood. In fact"—he gestured to the others—

"I want all of you to listen. I need you to understand perfectly what I am about to say. If you don't, I'm going to let out a bit of blood and try again." He stepped back, and spoke in unison with Jack's father:

"The true face of Pale is the last thing you will see before you die."

All three Sturgesses were squirming frantically. Uncle Gabe leaned over and neatly pressed his blade into Solomon's right shoulder. Dark blood coloured Sol's sweat-soaked shirt.

"I don't think you understand. Pale is coming for your soul. He will not rest until he has claimed it."

Jack turned to run, but his father wrapped a single burly arm around him and held him in place. "Gabe!" Jacob shouted. "Tape!"

Uncle Gabe turned around, producing a roll of duct tape from the pocket of his stained brown coat. He tossed the roll to Jack's father, who caught it deftly.

"Dad!" Jack shrieked, as his father pinned his arms behind his back, and wrapped his wrists together so fast he had no time to wriggle free.

Thunk.

The noise came from upstairs. Jacob and Gabe Brecker both shared an alarmed glance.

"What was that?"

"You knocked the cop out, right?" said Jack's father.

"Yeah, she was—"

"Go check. *Now!*"

Uncle Gabe turned and rushed out of the room, leaving the basement door open. Then Jack's father kicked Jack in the backs of his knees. Jack collapsed to the floor. "HELP!" he screamed.

The duct tape came down once again, strapped over his mouth this time. He tried to shout for help, but the tape was too tight for him to even move his lips.

A burst of adrenaline pounded through him, and he jerked himself upright, dug his feet into the tiles and kicked himself across the floor, away from his father. Suddenly there was a crashing sound from the floor above. A cry from the top of the stairs:

"Jacob! Get up here *right now!* It's her! It's *HER!*"

Jack's father froze. He glared murderously at Jack, then turned and stomped out of the room, shutting the door behind him.

Jack pushed himself against the wall, shoved himself to his feet. His arms were cramping from being bound so tightly behind his back. He gritted his teeth and started walking toward the door.

A scream from upstairs.

"GOT HER!"

Jack's heart rocketed up into his throat. He froze. More screams—"Let *go* of me!"—and then footsteps coming back down the stairs. Jack didn't know what to do, so he didn't do anything—just stood there as the door burst open.

Both of them were carrying her, Uncle Gabe holding her in a headlock, Jack's father gripping her legs. She writhed and squirmed, but it was no use.

"Neria!" Jack wailed through the duct tape, but all that emerged was a stifled moan.

Neria bit into Uncle Gabe's forearm. "Bitch!" roared Uncle Gabe. But he held onto her. "Ether! Ether!" he howled.

Jack rushed toward them, but his hands were bound behind him: he could not defend himself when Uncle

Gabe turned and effortlessly swatted him in the chest. He collapsed into a crouch, gasping for air, and could only watch as his father pinned Neria against the wall and punched her square in the stomach. The blow sent her head and back crunching into the wall. She doubled over, then collapsed to her knees, wheezing for air, coughing, gasping.

Jack's father yanked Neria's hands behind her back; Uncle Gabe wrapped them in duct tape.

Neria's gaze drifted shakily around the room. Soon she found Jack. Her eyes simmered with defeated rage, like the dying embers of a stamped-out fire.

Uncle Gabe knelt down next to her. He spoke into her ear, so quietly that Jack could barely hear:

"Pale has waited so long for a soul of two worlds, Neria Nightshade. So long, in fact, that we're going to offer him three appetizers first. To whet his palate. Then we will give you to him."

Uncle Gabe looked up at Jack's father and gave a curt nod. Then he rose to his feet, and turned, and the two Brecker brothers approached the Sturgess family. Uncle Gabe held the serrated knife in his hand, at first. But then Jacob Brecker reached over and pried it from his grasp. "My turn," he said. "So, Sturgesses. Who first? Mommy? Daddy?"

The duct tape would have prevented any of them from responding, but Jacob Brecker didn't even give them a chance to try. He jammed the knife through the duct tape covering Simon Sturgess's mouth, through Simon's parted lips and down his throat.

Simon's head slumped forward as he gurgled his final attempts at breathing.

The metal stink of blood again. Thick, viscous iron, with that haunting underlying hint of meat. Jack retched into the duct tape. He was breathing violently through his nose, snot spurting out and spilling onto his lips.

Don't look. Don't watch.

From his place on the floor he rolled over to stare up at the living room ceiling.

Don't let them make you see it.

"Are you paying attention, Jack?" he could hear his father saying over Solomon and Syrena Sturgess's muffled shrieks. "*This* is what you do: feed them the brew of the Angel's Trumpet first—then take their eyes, so the hallucinations take over their minds. Make them *see* the demon god in the moment of their death." "

There it was: the unmistakable, unforgettable sound of metal sawing through flesh. Desperate, asphyxiating gasps. Solomon Sturgess's final words drowned, as he did, in his own blood.

"You see, Jack? We did this over and over again, and eventually the demon god became real. *Manifest.* Flesh and blood."

Jack squeezed his eyes shut, but he could still see the crimson blood sluicing over that tattoo on Solomon's arm, the squid entangled with the shark.

Once upon a time, he thought, *I had no idea what a throat being cut sounded like.*

"Don't look so grim, Neria Nightshade," Jacob Brecker said, his voice more soothing and fatherly than Jack had ever heard it.

Jack squeezed his eyes shut—and the Jackal took hold of him, rolled him up onto all fours, up onto his feet. He was seeing red, everything painted in shades of red, the same colour as the blood now spilling from the gouge in Solomon Sturgess's neck.

Syrena Sturgess was sobbing relentlessly, her anguish flattened by duct tape, tears spilling down her cheeks. She was staring at Jacob and Gabriel Brecker in disbelief. Jack knew what she was thinking. *This must be a dream.*

But it wasn't a dream. It wasn't even a nightmare.

"Stop what you're doing, Brecker."

The sound of Barkface's voice made Jack turn, but it was Jacob to whom Barkface was speaking.

Jack's jaw dropped. Barkface filled the doorway, more than seven feet tall, his face youthful, elk antlers protruding from his brown- and silver-streaked hair. He held a wooden staff in one hand.

Jacob and Gabriel Brecker both paused. Jacob stared straight past Jack, at a face he had once known, a face he had never expected to see again.

Uncle Gabe's eyes bulged. "Neil?"

"I'm going to kill you, Jacob," Barkface snarled. "You too, Gabriel. But if you let my daughter go first, I'll make it painless." He looked down at Neria where she lay on the floor, at the feet of the Brecker brothers. "Get up, Neria."

His words broke the Jackal's spell. Jack swayed on his feet. His vision blurred. Barkface strode toward him, grabbed him gruffly by the forearm and leaned in so that their faces were level. "Stick with Neria," he muttered. "*Please.* Take her to my cottage. Look after her. Make sure she doesn't do anything stupid. And for that matter, don't you go being an idiot yourself, either."

Jack's jaw dropped. His throat had sealed. He gave a jerky nod—for the moment it was all he could muster.

"Get outside," said Barkface. "Now."

Another nod. Jack stumbled to the door—then stopped, turned, to see Barkface crossing the room to Uncle Gabe, who was holding Neria on her feet, one great burly arm pinning her in place while the other held his serrated hunting knife to her throat. Jack's father, meanwhile, was holding his knife with the flat side of the blade pressed against Syrena's shoulder.

"Pale wants her soul, Neil," said Uncle Gabe. "You know that. Let's do it right now."

"You promised the demon god three appetizers, Gabriel. If you give him Neria after just two, he won't be sated, and you'll owe him your own blood."

Uncle Gabe wavered. Then he glanced over his shoulder at Syrena Sturgess, and nodded. Without hesitating, Jacob Brecker took the knife to her throat.

Jack stared at the knife blade Uncle Gabe was holding against Neria's neck. His gaze travelled up to her amber eyes.

She was staring straight at Jack.

Then Barkface jabbed the end of his staff into Jacob Brecker's crotch. Jack's father roared and collapsed against the wall, his knife falling to the floor even though the damage had already been done, and blood was already pouring from Syrena Sturgess's neck.

Swiveling on his heel, Barkface swung the staff with a *crack!* into Gabriel Brecker's elbow. Uncle Gabe screamed; the knife fell from his grip as his nerves shook to their roots.

Barkface stooped, grabbed the knife, then wrapped one arm around Neria in a bearlike grip, pulling her into the folds of his great black cloak. He hauled her across the room, to the door. To Jack. He tore the duct tape from her face, used Uncle Gabe's knife to sever the tape binding her hands behind her back.

"Go," he growled. "Hide."

Neria collapsed into Jack, shivering, every inch of her shaking. Jack took her arm and draped it over his shoulder. Then he helped her through the doorway into the lobby, to the front door, and out into the night.

The front door swung shut behind them.

⎯⎯⎯ •·◆·• ⎯⎯⎯

"Jack," Neria rasps. She coughs weakly.

They fall away from the Changeling House, stumble toward the alley behind it. Her breath is coming in rattling gasps, she's barely got her wind back, and she wonders if her internal organs are bleeding.

"Jack."

She drags her heel, forcing Jack to stop. Then she stands up, as straight as she's able, ignoring the pain in her stomach, the pain on her neck where the blade drew blood, the pain on her lips and cheeks and wrists where the duct tape tore away skin.

Jack's face is an orange mask in the light of the streetlamps.

Neria grabs his hand, jerks him toward her, and they both fall into one another, both of them sobbing uncontrollably, wrapping their arms around each other. Neria hides her face in Jack's shoulder.

Then she grimaces, wriggles loose, pushes him back.

"Breathe," she manages. "Breathe. It was just a bad dream. That's all."

She grabs his hand. Squeezes. Even in the dim orange light she can see the rage and confusion fighting for control of Jack's face. He knows she's lying, doesn't he? But sometimes it helps to pretend.

"We have to go," she says, her voice hardening.

"But—Barkface said—your—"

"*Jack,*" Neria snaps, her voice suddenly sharp and impatient. "We're leaving."

Her grip tightens on his hand, and she drags him around the side of the Changeling House, into the alley, where they're blasted by headlights. Jack recoils in panic, but Neria squeezes his hand again. "Friends," she whispers in his ear.

The *rrruuurrrmmm* of the engine grows as the Jeep pulls up alongside them. The back door opens. "Get in!" Skye cries.

Lucas sits in the driver's seat, Dylan in the passenger seat, and Skye in the back. But as Jack begins to climb into the back of the Jeep, Dylan opens his door and gets out. "You take my seat, Neria," he calls.

"*What?*" Skye snaps, as Neria circles the car to climb into the seat Dylan just vacated. Jack frowns. "Dyl, what are you—"

Dylan pokes his head in through the rear door. He smiles at Skye and Jack, and ruffles Skye's hair. "I'm staying," he says. "Someone's gotta continue the investigation."

"What?" Skye splutters. "Dyl–"

"Into Barkface," Dylan cuts her off, "and the Skein, and how it's all connected. I'm going into the woods, and I'm not coming out until I've got some answers. Hopefully it'll help. I have a feeling it will." He wavers. "You guys look out for each other, all right? Find somewhere nice to lie low for a while."

In that moment, he sounds so wise, so caring, so *grandfatherly* that Jack's heart punches up into his throat and he forgets how to speak. Tears spring into Skye's eyes as she stares at her older brother with a mixture of fury, affection and reverence on her face.

Neria shuts the passenger door.

"Go!" Dylan snaps. He steps back from the Jeep, and Lucas stomps on the gas. They lurch forward, and Jack quickly pulls his door shut.

Dylan stands in the shadows of the alley, watching them drive away, picking up speed. The Changeling House shrinks behind them, and then the car rounds a bend and the house vanishes altogether. The Jeep's hungry headlights swallow Morgana Wynd.

Then they're bouncing along the dirt road that cuts through the forest, and before long they're swinging out onto the highway. Lucas thrusts the car to ninety, a hundred, a hundred and twenty, and they roar off into the night. He rolls down the window, leans his head out into the wind. "*WOOOHOOOO!*"

"We made it," says Skye, turning to Jack. "We made it out alive."

"Alive." Jack repeats the word like it's the first time he has ever truly known its meaning. "Alive." His eyes are wild, possessed. "Where are we going?"

Neria turns and leans over the back of her seat to look him in the eyes. "Everywhere," she says.

She reaches for his hand, and they interlace their fingers. Jack grins a bewitched grin, the grin of a boy whose soul has been soaked in gasoline and set ablaze.

In the Changeling House, where it stank of blood, shit and urine—where three decomposing bodies still hadn't been moved from where they had bled out side by side—Jacob and Gabriel Brecker sat on sofas in the living room and sipped whiskey.

"Ridiculous." Jacob scowled, his eyes travelling around the room, from the broken front window to the clutter hiding the floor. "Sniveling little punks. What right do they—"

A timid knock on the front door cut him off.

"Door's broken down!" Gabriel called, in what could have been mistaken for cheer. "Just come in!"

Silence, for a moment. Then a scuffling of feet, and a wiry, stringy-haired woman emerged from the darkness of the lobby into the flickering candlelight. She was wearing what appeared to be a black bath towel with a neck hole cut into the middle, and tight leather pants which rose higher than her belly button.

"Evening, Rika," said Gabriel. "Welcome to my humble abode. Make yourself at home."

The elected High Chemist of the Face of Pale chuckled. "What in Pale's most unholy name happened here?" she said. "Friggin' lunatics. You guys take some dissociatives or something? Have a nice furniture fight?"

"You're the only person we know who takes dissociatives, Rika," said Jacob.

"Then what is it, coma-boy?" Rika turned her gaze on Gabriel. Her eyes were both different colours, one of them light blue, the other so dark you could hardly tell it was brown. "Get robbed?"

Gabriel's mouth creased into a smile which his eyes did not share. He shrugged. "Raising children, man. It's a journey of self-discovery. They teach you as much as you teach them."

Jacob snorted.

"Sit down," Gabriel said tersely, gesturing to the free space on the sofas. His hands shook slightly as he took another sip of whiskey. "We can use this place as headquarters from now on. It's my house, after all."

Rika wavered, but did not sit down. "I can't stay," she said. "I just wanted to tell you something. To make you feel a bit better about losing the girl *and* the vessel."

Gabriel straightened up from his slouch on the sofa, and Jacob turned to fix Rika with that trademark unblinking stare of his.

"I caught one of the kids." Rika spoke quickly now, sensing the spike in hostility. "Just for a moment, right before they all got away in that Jeep."

"Oh?" said Gabriel.

Rika nodded eagerly. "I did the usual intimidation spiel—you know. Planted an idea."

"An idea?" said Jacob.

"I said the Face of Pale promises not to hurt anyone who helps our cause, no matter what form that help takes. I said that's the only way for anyone to guarantee their own survival now—to *help* us. And I mentioned that… well, you'll see."

"Wait—what are you *talking* about, Rika?"

Rika's self-congratulatory grin widened. "Don't get too comfortable, boys. We've gotta go to the drop-off point. They'll be there to meet us."

"Which kid?" said Gabriel.

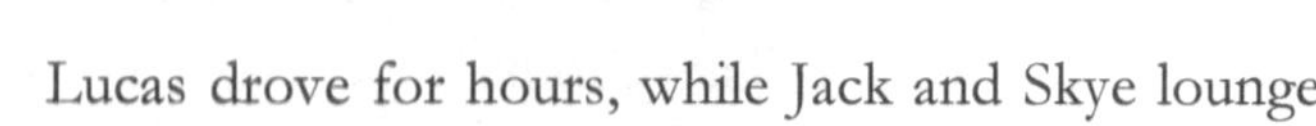

Lucas drove for hours, while Jack and Skye lounged in the back seats, first taking off their shoes, and then their socks as well. Lucas rolled all the windows down, let the cool night air blast through them and rinse them out.

Neria turned the radio on but Lucas shut it off after a moment. "Sorry. Reminds me too much of home."

A charcoal-and-navy patchwork of farmland streaked by on either side.

Eventually they pulled off the highway onto a straight gravel road cutting through an apple orchard. Lucas brought the car to a halt at the edge of a field. The clock on the dashboard read three-thirty. Lucas yanked the key out of the ignition, and they were plunged into darkness.

"We shouldn't sleep in here," he said. "Just in case, you know? Cars are easy to spot."

The four of them got out of the car and shut the doors. Lucas pointed a flashlight ahead of them and they wandered away from the car, through the rows of apple trees, through the warm aroma of cider, until they reached a low wooden fence marking the end of the property.

Over the fence, and down a slope of dry grass to a rickety wooden bridge crossing a dried-up riverbed. The four of them settled down in the riverbed, under the bridge. They curled up on the dry mud, and lay there in silence, each of them pretending to sleep, though not one of them would manage to drift off for some time.

———— •·◆·• ————

The sky was starting to brighten in the east, but the air was still crisp with the night's chill.

At first Skye wasn't sure who it was shaking her from her jittery half-sleep. Not until she felt his hand grab ahold of hers.

"Lucas?" she breathed.

"Shh! Come on."

Are we really doing this?

Lucas helped her to her feet, and they rose from the darkness under the little stone bridge. Quiet as ghosts, without so much as a glance back at the two other sleeping figures still lying there in the gloom, they scrambled out of the riverbed and hurried up the sloped embankment to the fence.

Over the fence. Through the apple orchard. All the way back to the edge of the field where they had left the Jeep.

Lucas unlocked the doors, and Skye lunged in a futile attempt to dodge past him into the driver's seat. But Lucas grabbed the collar of her shirt and yanked her back.

"No way," he said, still whispering even though Jack and Neria were well out of earshot, and most likely still asleep. "You don't know how!"

"How hard can it be?" Skye grumbled as she stomped around to the passenger-side door. "You press the gas and you go, and try not to hit things."

She clambered into the Jeep next to Lucas. For a moment they just sat there in silence in the semi-dark.

"You sure you don't wanna go back and get Jack?" Lucas whispered.

Skye wavered. She bit her lip, then winced the guilt away.

"No," she said. "He won't leave her."

Lucas sighed. Then he nodded, wordlessly, and slipped the key into the ignition. The engine woke with a rumble, and soon there was nothing left of them but tire treads in the dirt at the edge of the field, and the lingering aroma of exhaust.

Morning came sudden and painfully bright; Neria was shaking Jack awake and saying, "Jack! Jack! Get up!"

Jack stirred, pushed himself up on his elbows. His throat was sore and patchy. He couldn't open his eyes more than halfway.

"Jack! They're gone!"

"Wha—?"

He looked around in dismay. They were still under the bridge. The sky above was blue. The sun was hot and sharp. An acid sun.

Jack scrambled out from under the bridge and got to his feet. He and Neria climbed out of the old riverbed.

There was no sign of Skye or Lucas.

"Maybe they're waiting by the car," croaked Jack.

"The car's not there. I checked."

"What?"

Before Neria could stop Jack he set off at a run up the slope, hopped over the fence and started through the orchard toward where Lucas had parked. Neria ran after him, letting him lead the way.

They reached the edge of the field where the car had been. It was gone, like Neria had said. But the incriminating tire tracks furrowing the grass told them they were in the right place.

"It was right here," said Neria. "I remember it was parked *right here.*"

Jack's heart was in his throat. "D'you think—"

"Marooners," Neria spat. She scowled darkly.

"But *why?*"

She squeezed her eyes shut. "It's my fault."

"What?"

"I told them about—about the Face of Pale. About your father and their father, and—I told them I'm being hunted.

They didn't want to be involved, I guess." Neria sighed. "We don't need them anyway."

Jack drew in a deep shaky breath. "But what are we gonna *do?*"

Neria led him back to the riverbank. She sat down cross-legged in the dust and pulled him down next to her, so that she could lean in and kiss him on the lips.

Jack's lips were dry and cracked. He mumbled in surprise. Then he put his arms around her, and drew the kiss out, longer and deeper.

They settled down at the edge of the forgotten river. Neria opened a little backpack and pulled out some granola bars and a bag of beef jerky. "We can't eat too much," she said. "We have to save some till we can find more food."

They ate as little as they could. Then they started walking.

———— •◆• ————

The shoulder of the highway was lined with trees, so they walked in the shade, partially to escape the grinding sun overhead, and partially to stay out of sight of the highway. Every once in a while, to their left, a car would zip by. To their right, through the thin layer of trees, they could see farmland extending for miles and miles.

In the far distance purple-blue snow-capped mountains rose against the sky. The air dripped with plant fragrance. Honeysuckle and pine. Lavender. Summer berries. Poplar leaves.

Sometimes Jack and Neria held hands as they walked. Sometimes they stopped, to rest, and fold themselves up into each other.

But thirst clawed at Jack's throat. Around midday they came to a tiny creek trickling through the trees. The water tasted like soil, but it quenched their thirst.

"There must be a town nearby," said Neria.

Jack kicked at the ground listlessly. "Or more farms."

"A farm would be good. Farms usually have food, don't they?"

They kept walking. Ahead of them the highway shimmered as heat waves danced above its surface. Every few hours they stopped for a snack, but they knew they couldn't eat much. "We need to ration it, Jack."

A sign at the side of the highway read: *GREAVES—20 km.*

"How far is that?" Jack demanded. "How long will it take?"

"Dunno," said Neria. "It'll take as long as it takes."

"Think there's food there?"

"I don't know, Jack!"

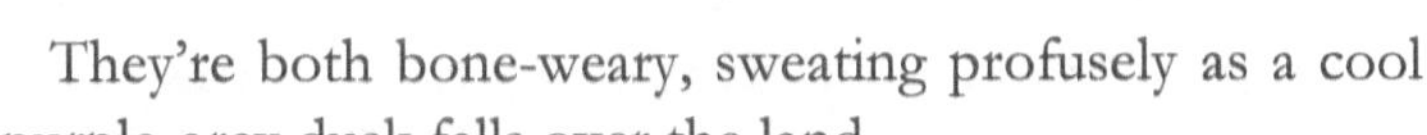

They're both bone-weary, sweating profusely as a cool purple-grey dusk falls over the land.

Neria leads Jack away from the highway. There's a field of whispering grass, and another brook nearby—or another part of the same brook.

They wash themselves in cold, fresh water. They drink deeply, plentifully.

Then Neria builds a fire. Jack watches as she gathers tresses of dry grass together, then twigs and sticks and clumps of brambles. She wakes the fire with her lighter, and they settle down beside it, side by side.

Jack's arm throbs with a dull ache. Neria tears a strip of fabric from his shirt to fashion a new splint for him.

The fire crackles contentedly. Around them, the field is a black abyss. Occasionally the headlights of a car barreling along the highway cast fleeting streaks of light through the grass stalks. Butapart from that it's just rushing darkness spiraling around them, the silver waxing moon and the reels of stars above, and the two of them huddled around their tiny fire.

Jack peers at Neria. She's got a face like she's trying to sort out the contents of her mind.

"D'you think—" she begins, then pauses, frowns. "Have you ever had that feeling, like… like you're a stranger here?"

Jack lies back and gazes up at the stars. "What are you talking about? We're in the middle of nowhere. Of course we're strangers here."

He can't see in the flickering amber light, but Neria's face is flushing red. "I mean, do you ever feel like humans are an alien species?"

"Uh… sure? I guess so, yeah, when you put it that way"

Something inside Neria hardens. *He's trying his best.* She's blinking rapidly. *The hell?* She angles her face away from Jack, hides it in shadow, so he can't see the tears. *Come on.*

"What are you doing?" Jack demands.

Neria wipes her eyes on her sleeve. "Goddamn smoke," she grunts.

She lies back in the itchy grass.

Jack falls down next to her. For a moment Neria can't think of anything to say. Then she points to the sky. "Race you to the stars," she says.

Soon the fire is just a puddle of red embers. They press together in the grass, warming their souls against one another.

But then Neria wriggles away from Jack, climbs to her feet and dusts her pants and jacket off. "I can't sleep," she mumbles.

Jack's on his feet beside her. "Me neither," he says, stifling a yawn.

Neria surveys the darkness around them. She finds Jack, in the darkness that has become almost total, and throws her arms around him.

"I wanna show you something, Jackdaw."

She takes his hand and leads him through the darkness, toward the dry grass. All that once remained of the fire is now gone; they're hovering in an abyss. Waist-height grass leaps up around them, scratching at them.

"You can only do it when the feeling's strong," Neria says.

"Do what?"

"Cross over," she whispers.

The darkness envelopes them both completely now, and still Neria pulls Jack further along. "Where did the grass go?" he says suddenly, his voice hoarse with bewilderment.

Neria giggles nervously, shakily. She stops walking. Keeps her grip firm on Jack's hand. Pulls him close. "I wanna know what's in your head, Jack," she says.

She kisses him, wrapping her other arm around him to keep him tight against her. She can taste the words caught in his throat, frantic half-assembled things he wants to blurt out, but she knows it would be a bad idea to let him.

He chokes the words back down and kisses her back, hungrily. His breath is hot, he tastes like blackberries, his lips are hot against hers; and around them the darkness recedes. She can feel Jack's heartrate crank up to double-time, triple-time—*daDUMdaDUMdaDUM*—thrashing in both of their ears like fists pounding on a steel door.

He tries to wrench himself away but Neria keeps a tight grip on him. "Jack," she gasps, but Jack's eyes are filling with tears. He's not looking at her anymore.

The hallway around them comes into focus. Dark. Abandoned. Reeking of asbestos and of mildew and of dust. And there's the end of the hallway, just up ahead. The rusty steel door, exactly where it should be. The lock with three deadbolts.

Jack stares at the steel door. It's ajar. Beckoning.

"No," he croaks. "No, no, *no.*"

Neria keeps her arms wrapped around him, keeps a tight hold on him even as he wriggles to free himself. "It's okay," she whispers, her lips right by his ear. "We're safe." It's not entirely true, but she *feels* safe here. "It's okay. I told you I wanted to see."

"No," he croaks. "It's *not* okay at all, it's—"

"Jack," she insists, grabbing him by his chin and jerking his head back to look at her. "Trust me."

"What?" Jack blinks away the tears. "What are you—?"

He breaks off. He can't help but turn back to look at the door. It could fly open at any second. Couldn't it?

At least nobody's banging on the other side. For now.

Neria lets go of Jack, and starts slowly down the hallway toward the door.

"Neria!"

But she doesn't stop. Jack moves to follow her, but his feet are stuck in place, and Neria is already almost at the end of the corridor.

"Neria, *stop!*"

Neria walks right up to the steel door. She runs her finger delicately over the triple deadbolt locks. Then she turns around and returns to Jack, and holds something up for him to see: three keys on a ring.

"Don't forget," she says. "You're the only one who has these."

Jack stares at the keys hanging from her fingers. "How did...?" The rest of the question gets stuck in his throat.

Later, when he tries to recall the details of that night, he finds he can't remember where Neria put the keys.

She grabs his hand again and tugs him backward—back out into warm darkness under a star-flecked sky. Tall dry grass whispering softly to itself. Scratching them through their sweat- and dust-stained clothes.

Jack realizes he's trembling, his teeth chattering despite the midsummer warmth.

"Jack, listen to me now," Neria says, and even she is taken aback at the seriousness in her own voice.

Jack stares agape at her—in her general direction, anyway, but it's too dark by now to make out anything against the gloom of the night except for patches of deeper darkness.

"That place," Neria presses on, "that door, wherever it is—*what*ever it is, it's..." She trails off, chews her lip, furrows her brow. "This is hard to explain, all right? But it's like... that place is a *part* of you. You have to accept that. Pretending it's not true isn't gonna get rid of it."

"How do you know?" Jack croaks.

"What?"

"How do you know it's a part of me?"

"Because the hidden gates were open, and I let you take me somewhere—and *that* was where you took me."

"But how—"

Neria knows the questions won't stop, so she throws herself into his arms again, pulling him into another kiss. It works to shut him up, while they both fall together endlessly, over and over and over into an oblivion of dry grass and sheets of darkness, hidden from all the world except the callous stars above.

Chapter Twelve: Delirium

Neria wakes to the sound of Jack's hacking cough. She sits up. The sky is veiled by a haze, and the day is already hot. It's humid, much more so than the day before.

Jack is doubled over in the grass nearby, coughing miserably. He jerks upright, startled, when he notices that Neria's awake.

He gets to his feet and tries to smile.

Neria's mouth is dry. Her throat's sore. Wordlessly she grabs her backpack, pulls out a bag of beef jerky and tosses it to Jack. She helps herself to the last granola bar, then zips the bag back up.

"That's it," she says. "We're out of food."

The sun's roaring at its apex when Jack sinks down to a crouch. "We gotta stop," he rasps. "Just for a minute."

Neria kneels beside him. "We can't," she hisses, failing to keep the impatience out of her voice. "I know you want to, but remember the sign? Greaves? Twenty kilometers? We can't be far now. We can get some food, maybe somewhere decent to sleep…"

"I can't, Neria."

The trees are thinning out here. They're standing in a copse of dead saplings, and ahead there's nothing but waving yellow grass. The stream is nearby, though; it's been keeping them company for a good two hours now.

It's something, at least.

"So *thirsty,*" Jack mumbles.

"Jackdaw," Neria whispers. "Okay." She squeezes her eyes shut, clenches her fists. "Okay. Listen. You stay here. Get some rest. Drink lots of water from the stream. I'll run ahead, and the first food I find I'll bring back. And then we're gonna keep going, okay?"

Jack looks at her. The expression on his face makes her feel sick. "Don't go," he croaks.

"Stay by the stream. I'll find you." She wavers. "Back in no time."

She sets off at a jog along the edge of the highway.

It takes her about an hour to reach Greaves. Whenever she hears a car coming she ducks down into the grass and waits until it passes. Several times she stops to find the stream and fill her stomach with water, both to quench her thirst and stave off the gnawing hunger.

When she finally reaches Greaves, she's certain that it's a mirage. It's like wandering into a postcard. The houses are all nice and tidy and gabled, the shops all have signs that say things like *The Olde Sarsaparilla Saloon* or *Vic's Vintage Sweets Emporium* or *Greaves Pies*. Most of the people she sees are old and stooped and slow—or young parents pushing strollers with screaming infants, while kids run ahead of them on the sidewalk with ice-cream cones in hand.

Neria doesn't like any of it. Not one bit.

She walks slowly, hands in pockets, head bowed. Occasionally her reflection glances back at her from a shop window she passes. Her hair is thick and matted, her skin and clothes coated in a layer of dust and grime.

It doesn't matter.

She scans the street, and something catches her eye: a Jeep parked down the block. A dusty black Jeep.

Unmistakable.

Neria picks up her pace, pushing through a gaggle of slow-moving parents and children. Approaching the Jeep, she peers in through its windows, hoping to spot a familiar face inside—but there's nobody inside.

She steps back, glances at the license plate. Yup, it's the right one. This is the same Jeep they escaped the Wynd in. Lucas's parents' Jeep.

Something makes Neria look up.

Directly across the street from the parked Jeep is a pub with a terrace out front, lined with umbrella-shaded tables.

At one of the tables sits a pair of dark-suited men. They're staring across the street—straight at Neria.

One of them mutters something. The other nods.

Neria spins on her heel and continues on her way down the street. *Don't look at them.* But she can't help glancing back.

They're watching her. *Definitely* watching her.

Don't look back. She's speed-walking now. There's a corner store across the street—she steps out in front of a car, which honks raucously as it jerks to a halt. Neria keeps her head bowed and rushes into the corner store.

A plump, middle-aged lady sitting behind the counter smiles widely at her. "Hello dear!"

"'Lo," Neria mumbles. She meanders to the back of the store. There's a door opening on a back room, which in turn leads out to the alley. *Perfect.*

She gathers a few bottles of Gatorade, protein bars, some bags of chips and a few candy bars which she slips into her pockets...

And then she hears it. The cashier's voice, hushed but frantic. "Hello? Hello? Yes, it's Zelda. From Zelda's Market—yes, yes, on High Street and Tenmor. Look, this is urgent—there's someone in the shop, a girl—I've never seen her in Greaves before but she's all dirty and she looks—I think it's one of the runaways on the news. The ones they're looking for in Cormora Creek. Yeah, one of the teenagers."

Panic claws at Neria's chest. *No!*

Then the lady says, "Okay, I understand." There's a *click* from the front of the shop.

She locked the door!

"Dear?" Zelda's voice drifts tremulously over to Neria. "Are you finding everything okay?"

Neria grabs a basket, throws all her food into it and sprints for the back of the shop. She goes through the doorway into the back room, and the alley door is only ten feet away, closer than that. *So close—*

But two men in black suits are already standing in the doorway.

"The Face is everywhere," one of them says.

Neria hucks the basket at them, Gatorade bottles and chips bags flying in their faces, and she turns and dashes back into the shop—only to find Zelda bearing down on her. The shopkeeper's expression is stern, but warm. "Sweetheart," she says, "I really think you—"

Neria ducks away from Zelda, rushes down one of the aisles. She throws herself toward the store's front counter—slams into the counter and looks around frantically. The front door key! *Where did Zelda put it?*

"Are you with the police?" she hears Zelda saying from the back of the shop.

"I am Detective Palmer," one of the black-suited men replies. "And that there is Detective Corder. We're here for the girl."

The girl. "But—"

Neria wheels around to see the supposed Detective Palmer sprinting down the aisle toward her. *Think!* She jumps up onto the counter, and crouching she lifts the cash register up, pulling its cord from the electrical socket on the wall.

She rises to her feet, and lobs the register at the black-suited man—it crashes into his head, and he tumbles backward into a sunglasses stand, which he drags down with him as he crumples to the ground. The cash register breaks open, loose keys, bills and change scattering on the floor around the unconscious man.

For a moment Neria just stands there on the counter, frozen, stunned. So stunned she doesn't see the other black-suited man walk up to the counter and grab her by the ankle.

"Detective my ass!"

There's a dull metallic THUD—and suddenly the black-suited man's grip on Neria's ankle is released; he stumbles forward and collapses. Zelda stands overtop of him with a grim expression on her face, and a steel baseball bat in hand. "What have you got yourself mixed up in, kid?" she mutters.

The shopkeeper's voice is fuzzy and distant. Neria shakily climbs down from the counter. She can see the cops gathering at the front door, three of them. At least *they* look like real police. One of them is holding a pair of handcuffs. The second has a gun in hand. The third is talking on a radio. The one with the handcuffs looks through the glass of the front door and gestures for Zelda to come unlock it.

Zelda starts in that direction, and Neria seizes her chance. *Go.* With all her might she forces herself to *sprint*—Zelda reaches the front door, she's too far to react in time now, and Neria dashes through the shop's aisles to the back —through the back room and out into the alley, where the sunlight strikes her like a hammer.

She sets off down the alley, and runs until she can't breathe. Until the pavement beneath her feet becomes parched yellow grass.

Is that shouting behind her? She glances back, but the world has gone blurry, she can't see anything except a blue strip of sky and a yellow band of grass beneath it.

Hide.

She gropes for something to grab onto—anything, a memory or a whisper or a string of emotion, but there's nothing, just dying grass.

Then she finds a ditch. She climbs down into the damp mud lining the bottom of the ditch, and makes herself as small as possible.

Stay awake.

She waits…

———— • • ◆ • • ————

…and when she wakes up it's almost dusk, and mosquitoes are eating her alive. It takes her a moment to remember where she is, why she's covered in mud—

Jack!

With a jolt she remembers that she was supposed to find food. She gets to her feet, climbs out of the ditch and tilts her head to the wind.

The grassy plain sprawls around her, an endless yellow ocean, broken only by the odd tree and the highway, and Greaves—a black mass crouching on the prairie.

Where did I leave you?

Behind a veiled distance she hears Jack's breathing. Right where she left him. He's about an hour away by foot. She knows she won't make it to him until after it gets dark.

And she has no food. Her stomach growls. No, wait—the candy bars she put in her pocket.

It'll have to do.

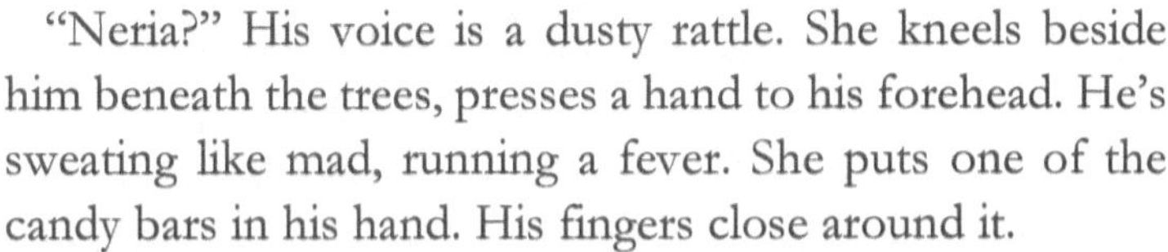

"Neria?" His voice is a dusty rattle. She kneels beside him beneath the trees, presses a hand to his forehead. He's sweating like mad, running a fever. She puts one of the candy bars in his hand. His fingers close around it.

"What's this?"

"I screwed up." That's all she can bring herself to say. "The Face of Pale was in Greaves, and we're all over the news—the runaway teenagers from Morgana Wynd. I—I'm sorry, Jack."

Jack laughs a scorched laugh and eagerly unwraps the candy bar. "There are some blackberry bushes just over there," he says, pointing off into the darkness. "They're not filling, but I think they're ripe."

Neria can't help it; she laughs too. "I'd say you did better than me, then." A pause. "How are you feeling?"

"Better. Better." He gets to his feet. "I thought you—I thought maybe you weren't coming back. I was thinking I'd wait it out then leave in the morning."

Neria swallows loudly. "Why would you think I—?"

"Maybe I'm dreaming right now."

"Jack. Come on."

"What?"

"There's—there's a farmhouse just a bit up the road. I think it's abandoned. We can sleep there tonight, if you're up for a bit of walking."

———— •·◆·• ————

The moon is waning, but it's still near-full, lighting the world with a sparkling silver glow. Neria and Jack teeter along the shoulder of the highway, then veer off down a dirt road, which soon leads them to a rundown barn.

"Shit," Neria grunts as she tries the door—padlocked shut. She steps back, scans the wall, and in the moonlight she spots a loose board.

Together she and Jack pull it aside, and squeeze one after the other into the barn.

It takes a while for their eyes to adjust to the darkness. The barn is mostly empty: there are some cardboard boxes stacked in the far corner, bales of hay lining the walls, but that's it.

Jack makes his way over to the boxes, pries one of them open. "Neria!"

"What?"

"Come look!"

Neria rushes over. Her heart leaps when she peers into the box: it's full of canned soup. Cream of mushroom, tomato, chicken noodle, Flemish stew.

"How do we open it without a can opener?" says Jack.

Neria skirts the perimeter of the barn. There's a rusty axe hanging from a bracket in the wall. "We can use this," she says. It's blunt, but after a few tries she manages to get a half-dozen cans open.

Then she makes a fire in the middle of the room, clumping hay together with shards of broken wood from the barn's disintegrating walls, and sparking it up with her lighter. She and Jack roast the soup cans until the labels have burnt away and the metal blackens.

They drink the hot soup. It's the most delicious thing Neria has ever tasted and bythe way Jack smacks his lips, she can tell he feels the same.

After filling up on soup, they extinguish the fire, find a bed of hay, and lie down together.

"What are we gonna do tomorrow?" Jack murmurs, pressing himself against Neria. She puts an arm around his shoulder, and lies on her back, staring at the ceiling.

"Keep going, I guess."

"But *where?* Where are we going?"

"I wish I could tell you that."

Jack lapses into silence. After a few minutes his head slumps down and he begins snoring gently in Neria's ear.

Gingerly Neria pushes him aside, just enough so that she can wriggle out of his slumbering grasp. She remains next to him on the bed of hay for a few minutes, her gaze roving slowly over the ceiling of the barn. Moonlight creeps through the cracks. Shafts of moonlight slanting through the air of the empty barn.

For a time Neria watches motes of dust drift through the striated moonbeams. Watches the motes light up with that blueish-silver glow.

Then she climbs to her feet, and steps back from Jack. She looks down at him in the gloom. He's still fast asleep, curled into a little ball in the hay. He must be so tired. Neria wonders briefly what it would take to wake him.

"Sorry, Jackdaw," she whispers. "We both know you're better off without me."

She half-expects him to stir, to sit up and ask her where she thinks she's going. But he remains completely, stubbornly still. Dead asleep.

At least he'll have a few hours to be oblivious, this way.

"I'm sorry. I... I'll always..."

Neria trails off. She sets her lighter down next to him, in the hay.

Then she leaves through the gap in the wall, and once she's outside and breathing in the silver moonlight she feels a little bit better, and a *lot* worse.

She starts walking.

———•·◆··——

Mountains loom in the far, far distance, tall, snow-capped monstrosities scraping the sky. How long will it take to reach them? A day? Six? Twelve?

It's midday now. She's got her jacket tied around her head like a headscarf, to keep the sun out of her eyes, and shield her face and neck from sunburn.

Greaves is far behind her; she hasn't passed any other towns since, and it's been several hours since she left the highway behind.

Neria spots another blackberry bush and rushes over to it, crams as many berries into her mouth as she can find. Most are tart and sour, but a precious few are juicy and sweet, and—

A sob rises in her throat. She pushes it down, smothers it.

Don't think about it. It's not like you had a choice.

No. She *knows* she didn't have a choice. Jack couldn't have continued on for much longer. And he's better off without her, anyway.

There's plenty of soup left in those boxes.

He'll be fine. As long as he can figure out how to build a proper campfire.

Another sob finds its way out of her mouth. It's been several hours since she passed the dead tree, with that *thing* hanging from its bone-grey, barkless branches.

Neria squeezes her eyes shut. It's too much—even now she finds herself hoping that her eyes lied to her.

She looks back the way she came, shields her gaze with her hand.

The highway's out of sight now. Thankfully.

Someone else will find the tree. They'll see it first through the heatwaves—just another dead tree along the side of the road, right?

But then, as they get closer, they'll spot the girl hanging from it, as dead as the tree itself. Her black hair falling in front of savaged eye sockets. Trails of blood-tears caked on her pale blue cheeks. Dark blood soaking into the tree's roots.

Someone will call the police. The police will take care of it. Within a day the highway will look normal again. As if nothing happened at all.

Back in Morgana Wynd, the news will spread slowly: Skye Brecker is dead. The Face of Pale got her.

Lucas Alvarez is nowhere to be found. He's probably dead, too.

Neria scowls savagely. It's all vanishing, like sand slipping between her fingers.

Stupid.

She realizes that her hands are clenched into fists. She wants to cry, but she can't anymore. She's run dry.

She turns her gaze to the mountains ahead.

There's no going back now.

Arc Three: Scattering
Chapter Thirteen: Rusalka

The sun woke him.

He lay on his side on his makeshift bed of coarse, moldy hay. Stared at the boxes of soup cans on the other side of the empty barn.

Sunlight stabbed through the cracks in the wall, drawing a mesh of crisscrossing light on the floor, throwing warmth on his face. Mosquitoes and horseflies buzzed through the air around him.

She'll be back.

He was certain of it. The ball of dread in his chest, that was… everything else. His father and uncle hunting them. The Face of Pale. His mother's death. *Murder.*

Neria had probably just gone to find a bathroom, or to get more food or scout ahead, or…

Any minute now.

He shifted in the hay. How long had it been since he had last had a proper shower? His skin was coated in a layer of grime. His hair was wiry and filthy..

He closed his eyes…

And heard something from far away, a voice he couldn't put a face to, but one he recognized.

'Jack,' it said.

He hoped Neria wouldn't take too long.

He helped himself to some cream of broccoli soup, heated on a shoddy little hayfire. Then he squeezed out through the gap in the wall and into the sweltering afternoon sun. It was much, much later in the day than he had anticipated.

He couldn't take it. "NERIA!" he shouted.

They got her.

"*NERIA!* WHERE ARE YOU?!"

The fields extending into the horizon on either side sucked up his cries, threw them scornfully back at him.

He sank down against the side of the barn. "Please," he croaked.

Then the puttering of an engine made him flinch, the crunch of tires on gravel. A maroon pickup truck pulling up to the barn. The driver's door opened and a plump red-faced man in overalls got out.

"Oh." The man's eyes widened. "What's your name, son?" He had a gentle voice, like old, rattling stones.

Jack thought about getting up and running. But he was so very tired, even though he had just awoken; it didn't seem worth the effort.

He leaned there against the wall of the barn. He didn't move.

The old man got back into the truck. Through the windshield Jack saw him talking on his cell phone.

The old man got out again and approached Jack. "You lost, son?"

Jack nodded.

"My name's Shelley Thompson. Funny name for an old man, eh?" Shelley Thompson proffered a gloved hand. Jack took it and let the old man haul him to his feet. He didn't trust himself to speak.

"Why don't you hop in"—Shelley Thompson opened the passenger door for Jack—"and I'll take you somewhere you can get some nice hot food and a bath. Then we'll get you home, eh? Looks like you've been on the road." His expression became stern. "Come on now, son."

Something throbbed in Jack's chest. *Son.* Shelley Thompson's smile was wide and warm. Jack nodded again, opened the passenger's side door and climbed in.

————— •·◆·• —————

They drove in silence. Shelley Thompson tried several times to strike up a conversation, but Jack answered exclusively in single syllables.

"What's your name?"

"Jack."

"What are you doing all the way out here, Jack?"

"Mmm."

"You must be starving."

"Yup."

Eventually Shelley gave up and put on the radio. Jack rolled down the window and leaned his head out. The wind threw his hair back. The highway roared by beneath them, and soon he could make out the ocean, the Morgana Peninsula jutting out into it, a dark mass against the ever-sinking sun. A sign at the side of the road said: *CORMORA CREEK—next exit.*

Suddenly something spattered across the windshield, streaks of red and brown. "Jesus Christ!" Shelley Thompson shrieked. He swerved wildly—for a moment Jack swore they were about to fly off the road into the trees—but then he recovered and brought the car to a stop on the shoulder of the highway.

"Um." Shelley Thompson turned in his seat to look wide-eyed at Jack. "Just a minute."

He got out of the car, leaving the door open, and walked around to the front. His face grew chalky and sickened. "Oh my *god.*"

Jack sat back in his seat.

'Jack,' someone said.

He started, glancing out the passenger window at the trees lining the shoulder of the highway.

A flash of red hair. A face in the dappled late afternoon shadows.

Neria?

A glance out the windshield: Shelley Thompson was talking on his phone again.

Jack opened the passenger side door slowly, quietly, and slipped out onto the highway. He glanced for a second at the thing on the hood of the car: a deer, mangled and twisted out of shape, its legs broken, its neck snapped. Its eyes black and lifeless.

Blood creeping down the hood of the truck and onto the asphalt.

Drip. Drip. Drip.

Jack took a deep breath, then ran for the trees until they enveloped him, and Shelley Thompson couldn't see him. Tall grass scratched at his legs. He ducked down into it, glanced back at the highway.

The old man was still on his phone.

"Neria?" Jack hissed.

She knocked against him, grabbed him, pulled him even further down into the tall grass. "Shh!"

She was there beside him, the sunlight all tangled up in her fox-coloured hair, the smell of her draped across him, that unearthly floral fragrance he couldn't identify.

"Neria?"

He scrambled to his feet. He was seeing things. There was nothing there, he was going crazy—

Except she was standing there before him, brushing the dirt off her jean jacket. The evening sunlight caught her amber eyes.

"So," she said. "Do you remember our deal?"

Jack couldn't breathe. His heart was on rapid-fire, slamming against the inside of his chest. "What—you—I thought—" he stammered. "What—"

She pressed a hand over his mouth and pulled him beneath the cover of the grass again. "It's something in the air," she whispered. "Maybe it's 'cause we're near the sea. The sea does weird things to people."

Something tugged at Jack's thoughts, in his peripheries. *Haven't I...?* But he brushed it aside. There were more pressing things to worry about.

"Neria," he said.

"Hey!" The cry came from the highway. They looked over: Shelley Thompson had finally noticed that Jack wasn't in the car anymore. He was scanning the trees—he was starting toward them—

"Scatter!" Neria took Jack's hand in hers; they bent double and ran. A chill wind whipped through the air around them, whipped *through* them, and Neria was running faster than a normal human being should have been able to. Jack kept a firm grip on her hand, and grinned to find he could keep up with her so easily.

He remembered this trick, from their time in the Skein.

They ran, and before long Shelley Thompson was far, far behind them. They ran through patches of trees, over brambles, through tall, scratchy grass. They soared through orchards, along creeks, over hills, until they were finally back on the Morgana Peninsula.

Somehow it was evening by the time they reached Morgana Wynd. The deep copper sun was already beginning to set. Jack and Neria stayed as far out of sight as possible, keeping to the alley that ran parallel to the main street, behind the houses. Jack stared at the Changeling House as they passed behind it. It towered against the evening sky, its windows dark.

What happened in there?

"Have you ever had that feeling, like… like you're a stranger here?" Neria turned to look at Jack. Her amber eyes shimmered with an eerie glow. "We can't stay here. We've got a chance to get away. But we have to go fast. And we can't be seen. By *any*one." She started down the street again. "So. You coming or what?"

"Where are we going?"

Neria smiled darkly. "You don't have to trust me," she said. "But you should."

Dusk was gathering in full, the houses of Morgana Wynd turning to purple-grey impressions behind them as they arrived at the woods. Neria was walking slightly ahead of Jack, and suddenly, inexplicably, he wanted nothing more than to turn back.

Part of him wondered where Shelley Thompson was now.

"Neria!" he called. "Wait!"

But Neria didn't even look back at him. She just plunged on ahead into the rapidly-darkening woods, leaving Jack with no choice but to follow.

He felt woozy. The ground was shifting under his feet like he was on a ship out at sea. He broke into a faltering speed-walk to catch up with Neria.

How did we get here so fast? he wondered vaguely.

"Are we going to find Dylan?" he asked.

"Come on, Jackdaw. Let's go."

They kept going, and they reached the beach much faster than Jack expected. It was deserted; the tide was out, way out, and over the water the lighthouse loomed before the setting sun.

"Neria! Will you at least tell me what's going on?"

How had she gotten so far ahead already? She had already crossed the expanse of dry sand and was splashing through the intertidal zone, as though she intended to swim to the lighthouse.

Jack decided that he wouldn't be all that shocked if she proposed swimming.

"You coming or what?" she called back to him.

He paused. Something was nagging at him, but… *what is it?* He couldn't put his finger on it.

"You coming or what?" Neria called again.

Jack's frown deepened. He shook his head, rubbed his eyes. *You're just tired, that's all.* He took off his shoes and socks and hurried over the sand, then splashed through a stretch of inch-deep water toward Neria. Seashells and barnacle-crusted rocks crunched under his feet, some of them breaking skin as he trod on them. "Ow," he groaned.

Neria was also barefoot, but she seemed to have no problem skipping ahead over the rocks. Finally Jack joined her at the water's edge, where waves broke ponderously against the shore.

"Where are we going?" he demanded, as he reached her side.

She pointed to the lighthouse. "Everywhere."

"Neria," Jack began.

"Jack." She turned her amber eyes on him. "Trust me," she said, and there was an edge of threat in her voice now.

Neria? Jack frowned – then nodded quickly. "Okay," he said.

Neria motioned for him to follow her, and led him along the water's edge, to where they found a raft waiting for them. It was a sparse thing, narrow tree trunks bound tightly together with greenish-brown rope.

How is there…?

But the question dissipated from Jack's mind before it even had a chance to form properly. He and Neria pushed the raft into the surf, climbed onto it, and sat back to back in the middle as it drifted out into the bay.

The raft drifted to the islet as easily as if someone were pulling it on a chain; neither Jack nor Neria did any rowing or sailing. When it bounced gently against the rocks of the islet they stepped carefully off the raft and climbed up the rocks to where it was dry.

They left the raft behind without a second thought. Left it bobbing listlessly up and down in the water.

Even when Jack turned, a moment later, to gaze over the water at the beach they had just come from, he didn't notice that the raft's bindings were coming undone, the ropes quietly loosening, the raft disintegrating.

He didn't see the logs drift apart in the waves.

All he saw was the beach on the Morgana Peninsula. The forest rising behind it, the rush of trees painted gold in the last light of the sinking sun.

He turned on his heel, tipped his head back to look up at the lighthouse. It was perched right on the edge of the rocks, its door facing toward the peninsula. It looked… crooked, somehow. Leaning over them. Peering down to scold them.

"So," Jack attempted. "Are we supposed to get inside, or something?"

Neria didn't answer. She climbed over the rocks toward the base of the lighthouse. Jack's gaze drifted from the distant beach to the rocks he was standing on. *The Cursed Rock*. He frowned. He couldn't see the raft anymore. Had it drifted away?

"Shit," he heard her say, as she rattled the door handle. Locked.

Jack's gaze swung back to the Morgana Peninsula, to the lights of Morgana Wynd twinkling through the trees. He pictured the Changeling House—eating cold pizza with Skye and Dylan and Lucas, in the attic, while the sunset blazed and the lights of the Wynd started to come on. And Neria sitting next to him, of course—

Neria.

He saw it out of the corner of his eye.

She was walking right along the water's edge, her arms stuck out for balance as she stepped over clusters of barnacles and starfish. A wave struck the rocks where she was walking.

She slipped. Fell. Her forehead went *crunch* against the rocks.

Jack's heart leapt into his throat. "Neria?" He started toward her. "Neria? You okay?"

She was lying still on the rocks, waves lapping indifferently at her feet. There was a dark spot on her jean jacket. Dark red.

"Neria! Look at me!" Jack fell to his knees beside her. Her head was split, blood pumping out of it, and her eyes were blank, frozen open in shock, her pupils shrouded with blood.

"NERIA!" He shook her but she wasn't answering, she was barely moving.

"No, no, no, no no no nononono—"

'Jack...'

Something made him turn, made him look up. There, in the lantern room at the top of the lighthouse: a pale glow.

CREEEEEAAAaaaaakkkk.

The lighthouse door swung open.

'Bring her.'

He knew what to do. Knew he didn't have a choice. "Come *on!*" He reached his arms under Neria's body, hoisted her into the air. She was unbearably light. *Don't think. Just go.* He staggered to the lighthouse door. "Don't worry," he sobbed. "It's gonna be alright, it's gonna be alright I *promise—*"

'NOW!'

Through the doorway: before him in the gloom a staircase spiraled up into darkness. Jack planted his foot on the first step and started to climb. The darkness reeled him upward, up and up and up, step after step, round and round and round. "I'm coming!" he cried. "I'm coming!" And that ancient voice was in his head. *Just up the steps, just a little bit further…'*

The world blurred around him. He was at the top of the stairs. Another door before him. No lock on this one; it swung open on its own.

Through the doorway, into the lantern room, and Neria's body was too light, far too light, it seeped through Jack's fingers like sand… it *was* sand, fine, pale sand, it wasn't Neria at all, just sand spilling into a pile at his feet.

The door slammed shut behind Jack with a metallic CLANG! A voice filled his head, coming from every direction at once:

'I've been waiting for you, Jack.'

She was standing there before him, next to the big shiny lantern in the center of the room. Except she wasn't standing, she was *hovering* several feet in the air. She was truly ancient, dressed in rags sewn from ship sails and fish scales and seaweed and shells. Her face was grey, creviced with wrinkles and folds, and her hair swung down in ghostly white curtains. Her pupil-less eyes gleamed like pearls. Her mouth was like a shark's mouth, hundred-toothed and frighteningly wide.

Rusalka.

In one hand she held an hourglass filled with sand.

'Jack,' she said sadly. Her voice was a thousand ancient winds gusting through forgotten sea-caves. *'It is truly wonderful to finally meet you.'*

Jack's knees buckled. He threw himself backward—his back slammed against the door and pain pulsed through him.

'I wouldn't bother, my love.'

She was coming toward him—she was surrounding him on all sides, to his left and right, in front of him and behind him. No matter which way he turned she was there, her empty white eyes boring into him. She was in the corners of his vision. He squeezed his eyes shut but she was still there, seared into the blackness behind his eyelids like a fiendish tattoo.

'I am Rusalka,' she said, *'and I found you before you found me, Jack Brecker.'*

He screamed, and it sounded to him as though the scream had come from miles away. Rusalka's hands were on his shoulders. She planted an arctic kiss on his cheek. His vision swirled, and he toppled to the floor, his head smashing against the floor, and the world strobed into darkness. The last thing he heard was *her*—was Rusalka cackling maniacally, a laugh that sounded like thrashing waves and forking lightning. And then one word, repeated over and over again, quietly, tenderly, as though she were savouring a morsel of some exotic delicacy:

Jack… Jack… Jack… Jack… Jack… Jack… Jack…'

Again and again she said that word. Over and over and over, for hours and hours, until he completely forgot what it meant.

Chapter Fourteen: Nightshade

Dylan hoisted his rucksack over his shoulder and gripped the map of Morgana Wynd tight as he strode toward the cottage on the beach.

Follow the Skein.

He tucked his shaggy hair behind his ears, ran his fingers through it to give some semblance of sophistication. Then he knocked on the cottage door.

A tall, broad-shouldered woman with dark skin and frizzy black hair opened it.

"Who are you?" she demanded, a low, impatient growl.

"Dylan Brecker." Dylan frowned. "You're not Barkface. *Are* you?"

"No. But I am busy." The tall woman started closing the door—but Dylan stepped forward and blocked the door with his foot.

"So am I," he snapped. "There are a couple things I need to know."

The woman furrowed her brow. "Like what?"

"Like what happened to the Sturgesses and a police officer from Cormora Creek, who all seem to have disappeared. Or why there are a bunch of people who dress in black and wear masks living in my house." Dylan's face darkened. "Barkface has answers. I know he does. So if you could tell me where I can find him, that would be great, because I'm figuring this mindfuck out today."

The woman peered contemptuously down at Dylan. Then suddenly her expression changed, her eyes flooding with warmth. She sighed. "Why don't you come in?" she said, much softer than before. "The man you call Barkface should be back soon."

She beckoned. Dylan hesitated for only a moment before following her inside. There was a fire crackling in the hearth, and the room smelled of sandalwood.

Dylan swallowed loudly. "So you're Neria's…" He trailed off.

"Guardian." The woman pulled a chair across the floor, and set it in front of Dylan. "I am called Ara Augustine. Would you like some tea, Dylan Brecker?"

"Oh," said Dylan. "Sure." He sank down hesitantly into the chair. Ara vanished into the kitchen, returning a moment later with a steaming mug. "This is ginger root, peppermint and hibiscus," she said. "Freshly picked."

"Thank you." Dylan took the tea and sipped. It was the perfect temperature—piping hot without burning his mouth. He settled back into the chair. "So when's Barkface getting back?"

"Any minute now." Ara Augustine sat down on the sofa next to the hearth. The fire illuminated the troubled lines on her face, and made her eyes dance like golden beads. For a moment she stared in silence at the boy sitting across from her. Dylan stared back.

"You know Neria, don't you?" Ara said at last.

"Kind of," said Dylan.

"Do you know where she might have gone? Any idea?"

"Well…" Dylan sighed. "She went with Lucas, and Jack, and Skye, my sister. They all just wanted to get as far away from here as possible. Lucas did anyway. I didn't want Skye to go, but I couldn't stop her. And Neria—I'm not sure why she went with them. But they'll be back. I'm sure of it. They're gonna realize there's nowhere to go, really."

Ara rested an elbow on her knee and her chin in her palm. "Neria's in serious danger," she said. "Whoever she's with is in danger too."

"Why? Does it have anything to do with"—Dylan wavered—"with my dad, and my uncle, and—?"

"It has everything to do with them."

Hot tea clogged Dylan's throat. He coughed. "Then for the love of god," he gasped, "can you please start explaining?"

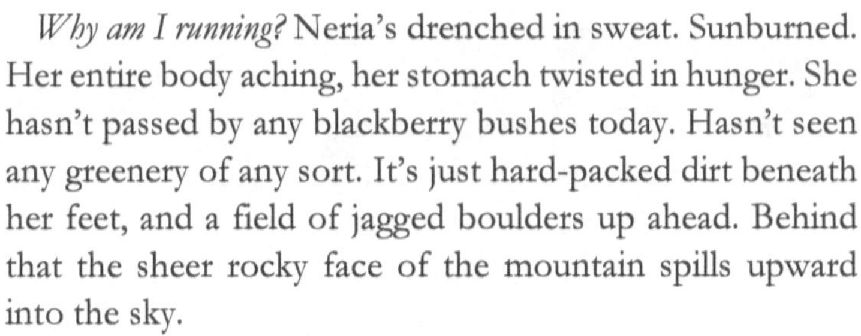

You're wandering, Neria Nightshade. Aren't you?

Barkface sits in a grassy clearing lined with Angel's Trumpets. He shrugs off the Moment—flings himself high above the infinite shining web, and watches the threads all twisting through one another with reckless abandon.

Wandering the wilder paths.

He combs the Skein. Morgana Wynd. The rest of the peninsula. But Neria is nowhere to be found.

In the body of an iridescent jackdaw, Barkface soars above the highway, riding tracts of cooked air.

I know you're around here somewhere. You can't have gone far.

The highway loses itself in the muggy horizon.

Why am I running? Neria's drenched in sweat. Sunburned. Her entire body aching, her stomach twisted in hunger. She hasn't passed by any blackberry bushes today. Hasn't seen any greenery of any sort. It's just hard-packed dirt beneath her feet, and a field of jagged boulders up ahead. Behind that the sheer rocky face of the mountain spills upward into the sky.

"I need water," she says to herself—*tries* to say, but her mouth's so dry she can hardly form the words. *And food.*

"Good thing there's nobody around to hear how crazy you've gone."

Heat waves obscure her vision, and for a moment she sees Jack coming toward her across the cracking slabs of hardened mud. She slows. "Jack!"

No, he's already gone. She's alone.

She blinks sweat out of her eyes.

I'm unraveling.

A hot, raggedy breeze licks at her. She sways, almost loses her balance. *Disintegrating.* "I need to eat." Without even thinking about it she's running again, her feet slamming into the packed dirt without making a sound. It's easier, somehow, than walking.

Soon there will be nothing left of you but a shadow, a swirl of dust, a parched whisper clinging to the wind.

The ground is sloping upward. The shadow of the mountain draws her in.

You're wasting away. Losing more of yourself with every step you take.

She grits her teeth, puts on an extra burst of speed, and soon she reaches the edge of the boulder field.

Reality is splitting apart, and your soul is slipping through the cracks.

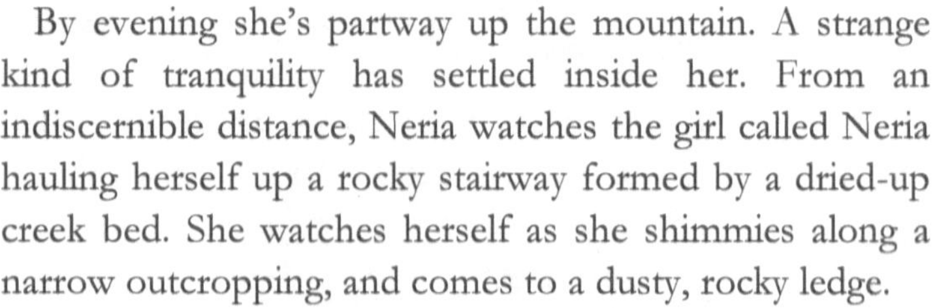

By evening she's partway up the mountain. A strange kind of tranquility has settled inside her. From an indiscernible distance, Neria watches the girl called Neria hauling herself up a rocky stairway formed by a dried-up creek bed. She watches herself as she shimmies along a narrow outcropping, and comes to a dusty, rocky ledge.

She pauses. Her wandering fingers find something in her jacket pocket. A flower—no, two flowers, dried and shriveled, along with several spiky pods.

There's no escape.

"Turn around," she hears herself say. "Look."

She turns, and for the first time since leaving the highway, she truly looks back. Before her the ground drops away, leveling out far below as the mountain slope becomes the boulder field, which in turn becomes the desert-like stretch of dry mud. Beyond that, the prairie of shimmering yellow grass, split by the highway. And to the west: the vast, dark, glittering ocean.

There's Greaves.

There's the barn where she abandoned Jack, just a tiny prick of darkness against the yellow plain. How long has it been since she last stood there and looked down at him? Lying curled up in the gloom of the barn, tucked into the little bed of hay they had shared.

Jackdaw.

And there, finally: the Morgana Peninsula. A wedge of darkness jutting out into the ocean. The lights of the Wynd are starting to come on, a winding train of golden specks shining defiantly out of the wedge.

There, just offshore: the impassive lighthouse, sitting on the Cursed Rock. Funny that she can still see it so clearly, even from this far away.

"You can't escape it. No matter how far you run, it'll just keep following you."

Neria totters on her feet, leaning into the hot summer breeze. She turns around, and Lucas is standing there before her. But it can't *really* be him, can it?

She tries to say his name, but her mouth is too dry. *Is this real?*

"Funny that you found this place too." Lucas sighs a raggedy sigh. He's skinnier than Neria remembers. And taller. Shirtless. His eyes are wild, sunken and bloodshot.

"Funny," Neria echoes.

Lucas sighs again. Then he reaches into the pocket of his shredded trousers and pulls something out. A little blue bubble pipe stained with blood. He holds it out in his upturned palm, and after a drawn-out moment of hesitation Neria takes it and slips it into the pocket of her jean jacket.

"Tell me what happened," she says.

Lucas squints at Neria, and she realizes that he doesn't have his glasses. *What can you see right now?* In all likelihood he can't see her as anything more than a blur.

"Tell me," she says again, when at first he doesn't respond…

⸻ •◆•• ⸻

The black Jeep pulls into Greaves shortly after sunrise, and two disheveled, wide-eyed teenagers emerge onto the pristine postcard street. There's the taller one, the boy with curly hair, whose scuffed-up glasses sit askew on the tip of his nose. And the small black-haired girl—hard to guess her age because she looks so bedraggled, wrapped in a dirt-stained trenchcoat that doesn't fit her.

The girl points across the street to a convenience store. Zelda's Market. But the storefront is dark, a CLOSED sign hanging from the shop window.

It's too early in the morning. None of the shops are open. Darkened windows and display cases leer at Skye and Lucas as they creep along the deserted street.

Too early in the morning. They're the only ones out on High Street. Condensation glistens on windows and awnings.

"Let's get back to the car," Skye mumbles. "We should keep moving." Her stomach punctuates this with a wretched grumble.

"But we need to eat," Lucas scowls as they pass by the gloomy doorway of a pie shop. "And we don't know how far the next town is. It might be a day's drive, or more."

Skye makes a small, hopeless sound, half-growl and half-sigh. "Lucas," she breathes. "Let's go. *Please.*" She comes to a halt. "I'm not joking."

Lucas grits his teeth. "Fine," he says.

They both turn and start walking back to the Jeep. The saffron sun starts to peek over the low buildings of Greaves. A golden-pink shaft of light crawls slowly along the street toward them. Skye and Lucas keep to the shadows under storefront awnings as much as possible, eyes peeled for any sign of movement. But it's as though Greaves has stopped, the whole town frozen still, locked in place. Holding its breath.

The creeping ray of dawnlight reaches the Jeep. The Jeep gleams in the morning light.

Someone's standing beside it, leaning against the hood. A tall man in a dark suit, his face hidden behind a chalk-white mask.

The mask is big enough to hide his entire face, but not his black, greasy, shoulder-length hair.

Skye freezes in her tracks and shudders, quails, her knees buckling, her face crumpling in terror. *Dad.* "Lucas—"

Lucas makes a muffled gurgling noise, and Skye spins around to see a ropy woman in a white mask pinning him in a chokehold with one arm, while her other hand holds a hunting knife to Lucas's throat.

"Skye," Lucas gasps.

"Don't worry, kid," Rika, the High Chemist of the Face of Pale, purrs in Lucas's ear. "Our deal still stands."

Skye shrieks as she's swept off her feet—shrieks as loud as she can, until her head smashes into the concrete of the sidewalk, and the damp pungent rag descends to muffle her mouth and her nose. Her assailant, the third masked man, pins her against the ground as she writhes and thrashes.

Rika holds Lucas hostage, and Lucas doesn't put up the slightest resistance. "I don't wanna see," he whimpers, squeezing his eyes shut.

Rika leans in to whisper in his ear:

"Thank you for bringing her." Her mask-muffled voice is soothing. "I know it can't have been easy for you. I know she's your friend. But it's not up to you. It's not even up to us. It's up to Pale."

The first masked man, the one with long greasy hair, walks slowly toward them. By the time he reaches them, Skye's resistance has broken, but she's still struggling sluggishly as the ether soaks into her brain.

"What are you gonna do with her, Gabe?"

Gabriel Breckerpulls off his mask, and his sunken eyes burn crimson in the morning light. He turns to stare at Lucas, smiling wide from ear to ear.

"If the only way she'll serve Pale is with blood," he says, "then blood it shall be. But you"—he jabs a skinny, jaundiced finger at Lucas—"you will watch, and learn, and I'm sure you will come to see that the best way to serve Pale is with your mind. Don't you agree?"

Lucas nods frantically, tears spilling down his cheeks, sobbing so hard he can't choke real words out. He squeezes his eyes shut as Skye Brecker stops moving.

"Does she believe in him, son?" says Gabriel Brecker, stepping over his daughter's unconscious body as he approaches Lucas and Rika. "Does she believe in the demon god?"

Through spluttering, quivering, hiccupping sobs, Lucas manages the only thing he's got enough energy for: "YES!" he screams. "YES! YES! SHE BELIEVES!" Then his voice crumbles to a defeated croak. "We *all* do."

"Good," says Gabriel. "As Pale wills it, this is good."

He crouches next to his daughter's limp body and tenderly eases her out of the crumpled, stained leather trenchcoat she's wearing. He puts it on—it fits him perfectly, the coattails coming down to his ankles, the sleeves precisely matching his arm length.

"Finally," he sighs. "I missed this coat."

———— •·◆·• ————

"...but that's what he said," Lucas concludes. "*I missed this coat.* He–"

Neria winds up and swings her fist into Lucas's mouth, clean into his gritted teeth. The blow sends pain ricocheting through her arm, and Lucas's teeth slice her knuckles, drawing blood.

He's on his hands and knees in the dust now, spitting out blood and bloody teeth. Neria turns to walk away. "Goodbye, Alvarez," she hisses.

She leaves him lying there in the dust. Clambers further up the mountain's jagged, rocky slope until she comes to another ledge, higher and narrower and all her own.

She collapses onto her knees, her kneecaps slamming into the rock, and falls onto her side in the dust.

Ferocious winds scavenge along the rock face above her. Eagles and ravens swing through the heated air, while on the ground chipmunks forage alongside hopping sparrows. Somewhere lower on the mountain slope, a lynx shrieks. Coyotes howl in the distance. The sun plunges toward the horizon, spinning its twilight colours through the sky, lighting strands of cloud like neon gossamer in its wake, before finally ducking behind the curve of the Earth.

The velvet sky overhead fills with stars, more of them than Neria has ever seen before. She finds herself staring out once again over the curving moonlit coastline.

Focus.

She reaches into her jacket's inner pocket, and pulls out the dried flowers. *Datura stramonium,* and *Brugmansia,* the Angel's Trumpet.

Holding on to a pair of spiky seed pods, Neria casts the rest of the decaying flowers aside. With the last of her strength, she spends a minute or so prying open the pods, extracting the hard black seeds.

Once she's got about a dozen little seeds, she cups her hands around them, and puts them in her mouth. She can't chew. Swallowing them whole is an enormous task, but she gets them down.

Take my hand and slip through the cracks with me.

She opens her mouth, breathes the wind and the moonlight into her lungs. The mountain air lacquers her insides. She closes her eyes, but finds she can see through her eyelids to the stars overhead, shining even brighter than before, if that were even possible. And beneath those stars: vast sweeping plains, the highway, the peninsula.

And to the west of it all, the ocean: a yawning portal to another realm, thrashing vengefully in the night.

Neria realizes that it's not her that's disintegrating. It's the rest of the world.

Slip through the cracks.

The sun is rising in the east, and ahead of her she can just make out two figures: a pot-bellied middle-aged man and his tall, lanky son. They're wheeling their bikes along the side of the highway.

Neria doesn't bother hiding. She knows they can't see her. She's standing in the middle of the road, and somehow she knows that no cars are going to hit her.

She watches.

Their names are Andy and Adam. A boy and a man.

A beat-up old van trundles past Neria, and slows down beside the father and son. The passenger-side window rolls down and a man with long greasy black hair and a narrow, sallow face leans out. "Hey!" he calls. "Flat tire?"

"You bet it is!" Adam calls back cheerfully.

"Where you headed? Cormora Creek?"

Adam hesitates, and shares a quick glance with his son. He decides to ignore the sudden flinching in his gut. "Yeah," he says.

"We'll take you there," says the long-haired man. "It's on our way. The bikes will fit."

"Oh! Fantastic!" says Adam. "See, Andy? There are decent folk out here in the big bad world."

Andy smiles up at his father.

The driver puts the van in park, climbs out and walks around to Andy and Adam. The long-haired passenger gets out, too, and pulls something out of his pocket: a vial of white powder. He pours a small pile of the powder out onto his upturned palm.

"Andy," Adam begins, but it's too late: Gabriel Brecker steps up to him and blows the powder into the man's face. Adam falls backward, coughing.

Gabriel turns, pours some more powder onto his palm and deftly blows a second cloud into the boy's face.

After a minute or two the coughing subsides, and Andy and his father fall still. They stare at Jacob and Gabriel with unnaturally dilated pupils.

"Are you prepared to do anything we say?" says Jacob.

Andy and Adam both nod.

"Leave the bikes. Get in the van."

Gabriel opens the back door of the van, and Andy and Adam climb in without a moment's hesitation. Gabriel slams the door shut, then gets back in the passenger seat. Jacob gets in the driver's seat.

The van pulls off down the highway, leaving the two bicycles lying on the side of the road.

———— •·◆·• ————

Neria waits till Jacob and Gabriel leave, then steals into the abandoned shed in Cormora Creek.

She finds the boy and his father slumped against the wall, unconscious. Their wrists and ankles are bound with rope. Crouching next to them, she tries to undo their restraints, but it doesn't work: her fingers pass right through the coils of rope.

I'm not really here, am I?

So she settles down next to young Andy Keirian, and whispers into his ear. *"I know you're scared,"* Neria says, *"but it's all gonna be okay in the end."*

Neither Andy nor his father show any sign of being able to hear her. Not a twitch nor a glance. Their eyes closed, their chests rising and falling gently.

They could only hear me if they were looking for me.

But she continues all the same: *"I know none of this is fair, but I also know you're gonna fight back. And that's all that matters anymore."*

She keeps talking to Andy and Adam—doesn't stop even when they begin to stir, to wake, to come to their senses and realize that they're in a cold dark place, cut off from daylight.

"I dunno where the hell they're gonna take you. The only thing that's important is that you keep fighting them. Don't give in. That's the only way we can ever hope to stop—"

"HELP!" The boy wails.

Neria lays a hand on his shoulder, and she knows he can't feel it. She barely manages to keep her voice in check:

"Good luck, Andy Keirian."

"HELP!" the boy screams. The father is trying to stay calm, for his son's sake. Neria sees on Adam's face that he simply won't allow himself to break. Not in front of Andy.

"Andy," he says quietly. "We're gonna be all right."

CRREEeeeeeaaaaAAAKKKK. The shed door swings open, framing Gabriel Brecker's long-haired silhouette.

Neria flings herself away from the Keirians. She's on her feet, rushing toward Gabriel Brecker—"The hell?" she hears him gasp, but she breezes right past him, through the door of the shed, and she's gone.

Later that evening, after Andy and Adam are dead, their bodies being prepared as offerings for the woman in the lighthouse, Gabriel explains what he saw to his brother. "It was the girl," he says. "Neil's daughter. I know it was. She'd be a teenager now, right? I'm telling you, she's around here somewhere."

A mangy black rat crouches in a corner of the shed and eavesdrops on the two brothers.

"But you said she wasn't there, when you went outside to look," says Jacob. "You said there were no footprints."

"I know, I know. I know what I saw. But—you know what, maybe you're right. Maybe it's nothing."

"Maybe it's the drugs," says Jacob. They both laugh at that.

The black rat scurries into the shadows, through a gap that opens in the rotting wood at the base of the shed wall, and out into the night. Making hardly a squeak, the little rodent begins to uncoil in the moonlight, ballooning suddenly to many times its former size, its fur retracting into withered old flesh.

Before long it looks like a loping dog; by then it's already out of sight of the shed. It continues to grow, bounding on two legs now, jerking up to its full height, a massive beard spilling from its face, elk antlers sprouting from its forehead.

"Maybe it's the drugs," Barkface mutters, laughing to himself as he sweeps along the highway on his way back to Morgana Wynd.

———— •·◆·• ————

In the creeping dawnlight beneath the forest canopy, Barkface meets himself. An old man with stormy white hair and an ancient face, sour and pitted, lined with shame and regret, stares down an imposing seven-foot-tall young man with elk antlers and a flowing brown mane of a beard.

"What are you doing here, Neil?" the tall one with elk antlers demands. He's clutching a bunch of Angel's Trumpets in his hand. "I'm in the middle of something."

"I know you are." The ancient one can hardly keep the disgust out of his voice. He hates being called Neil, and hates it most of all when it's coming from himself. "I'm looking for my daughter."

"Ara Augustine has her. They're far from here. They're in no danger."

The ancient one shakes his head. "Neria ran away," he says. "She left the Moment. She's sixteen years old, and she's hiding. Trespassing in a time she doesn't belong in. If I don't find her soon, nobody will." He points to the cottage. "She was in there."

The tall one looks confused. It's not an expression he's used to wearing; it doesn't fit his youthful face. "No she wasn't."

It's a lie, though: he *knows* he just saw her, not an hour ago. She ran past him, through a clearing in the woods, and when he ran after her he found that she wasn't really there.

"She doesn't want to be found," says the ancient one, his back straightening… and then his feet leave the ground and he rises further, until his face is level with the tall one's face.

He snarls. *"You."* He jabs a gnarled, accusing finger at the face of his former self as he bobs up and down in the air, like a buoy bobbing on the ocean surface. "You're a monster."

The tall one shrugs. "*We*'re a monster."

"So you haven't seen her?"

"I see her all the time. Whenever I close my eyes. *You* know that. You can remember everything I can. But"—for the first time the tall one's voice wavers—"you are wiser,

I hope, than I am." He sighs, then leans in close to the ancient one. "She went further back. To the Eye of the Storm. You'll have to hurry."

"Thank you." The ancient one drifts gently to the ground again, and the tall one puts a clawed hand on his future self's frail shoulder.

"Bring her home," says the tall one. "Make this right."

Without another word the ancient one turns and stalks off into the trees. The tall one stands there, fixed to the spot, staring at the mossy ground in silent contemplation.

━━━━━━ •◆• ━━━━━━

Neria left footprints. They're hard to spot, but Barkface knows what to look for. They aren't like regular footprints—these ones hover in the air, invisible to the eye but not to the mind. Little nodes of sadness, of confusion, and… a tiny pinch of hope?

He follows her trail. It cuts through a gloomy wasteland of distorted shadows, splinters of light and shade, and between the fragmented nightmares and forgotten memories, Barkface can make out moments he recognizes.

A young girl and an old man flit through the woods toward the reservoir, a vast concrete tank sticking out of the ground with several pipes branching off from either end. The two of them crouch down on top of the reservoir, at one end where one of the pipes sticks out. Soon they find it: the innocuous little crack in the pipeinto which Barkface sticks the funnel.

The girl empties the bottle of brown sludge into the funnel. Simon Sturgess hides in the shadows, one hand covering his mouth to silence his breath.

Barkface continues past that night, continues along Neria's trail.

He remembers...

He remembers how he came to know the forest intimately, its secret nooks and crannies, its hollows and heights. He remembers how he came to realize that the forest lived inside him, as he lived inside it. He acquainted himself with its wonders. Damiana, wormwood, mugwort. Mushrooms containing psilocybin, the fungus called ergot, the wondrous Diviner's Sage—useless to the uneducated masses who wouldn't recognize one plant from another, but for those who *know*...

Then there are the nightshades. *Datura stramonium. Belladonna atropa. Brugmansia,* the Angel's Trumpet. Plants that induce visions and fever dreams and a delicious delirium, and from which one might, if so inclined, and properly equipped, extract pure scopolamine, which some call the Devil's Breath.

"Scopolamine," he hears himself explaining to the hapless Professor Cole Ferrox, who would soon become a slave to the Face of Pale, a mutilated sentinel trapped forever in the dark. "It has the remarkable property of eviscerating a person's free will, so that he or she will do practically anything that is suggested. A rather ghastly thing. Of course, it is also highly toxic. If you were to swallow an entire vial of it, you would fall asleep and never wake up. Which is why it must only be used by those who know what they're doing. Like me."

I **am** *a monster.*

He sees himself pounding on the lighthouse door with his staff, stepping back as the door opens, and climbing the spiraling steps to the lantern room. "I'll do anything you ask of me," he tells Rusalka, "if you do something for me first."

'You come here just to offer your services to me, child?' Rusalka muses. 'Why?'

Barkface snorts. *Child.* It's been a long time since anyone called him that. "Why?" he replies, selecting each word with careful precision. "Because only you can accomplish this particular feat."

Rusalka fixes him with her lurid, milk-white gaze. '*Only I.*"

Barkface nods. He walks slowly toward her, his boots falling heavy on the stone floor of the lantern room. "I need you to help me retrieve a soul that has passed beyond this realm."

Rusalka chuckles mirthlessly. '*And what makes you think I can do this? It cannot be done.*'

"There's something you can do, surely."

'*There is nothing.*' Her face twists in sympathy, and she reaches toward him—and Barkface seizes his chance. His hand flies to his waist, to the sharpened dagger resting there in a leather sheath. He pulls the dagger out and swings it in one sweeping arc, cleanly severing Rusalka's outstretched arm at the elbow.

As she thrashes and wails he picks her severed arm off the cold stone floor, then turns and sweeps out of the lantern room, back down the spiral stairs.

Back in his cottage on the beach, he transfigures Rusalka's arm into glass, which he grinds down into fine white sand and delicately pours into an hourglass.

"There is something you can do for me after all, Rusalka," he says.

Several weeks later, the hourglass falls from a fifteen-year-old boy's hands and shatters on the cottage floor.

———— • • ◆ • • ————

Occasionally the past comes loose, stirred up by trespassers and tourists like settled silt billowing up to the surface of a river. Drawn out of forgotten time, lost memories can reach across centuries, grasping for that which is called the Moment, even as that very Moment flees at the speed of light into the future.

It is on a muggy June evening, long faded from memory, that the *Jericho Cascade* lands on the Morgana Peninsula for the first time.

The Morgana Peninsula is hidden from the rest of the world, almost impossible to find unless you already know it's there. The inhabitants of its small village live peacefully, without any desire for riches beyond what the peninsula provides. And the peninsula *does* provide: land to farm, abundant marine life to hunt, freely-growing spices and fruit to harvest. Wild dagga and sweet tobacco to smoke. Blackberry wine to drink in the evenings, as the villagers gather on clifftop meadows overlooking the ocean.

On the day of the *Jericho Cascade*'s arrival the horizon opens, a resplendent patchwork of exotic colours. The villagers gather on the beach, and the captain and crew of the *Cascade* appear before them, silhouetted against the irradiant sky.

They put on shows for the villagers. They play songs on odd, spindly instruments, and they teach the villagers to dance and sing along. They bring out food unlike any food the villagers have tasted before: hot and nectarous, laced with spices they can't even name.

They trade bizarre, otherworldly items for everyday artifacts: the villagers' paintings, instruments, and cooking utensils exchanged for colour-changing robes, books that talk, instruments that play themselves.

The visitors stay up long into the night, and in the tiny hours of morning they wake roaring bonfires, and sit around them and tell stories—unbelievable, absurd, lunatic stories. But as the visitors tell them, the villagers can sense the trueness of these stories. Stories about islands perched at the ends of the earth, dragons lurking in the waters off faraway coasts. Explorers who got lost and never really returned, though parts of them did, over the course of centuries…

The visitors are called oneironauts. Dream-sailors. They're known by many names throughout the cosmos. The photon farmers of the mirror plains call them angels, while the hidden folk of the floating forests of Aazdalan know them as *orda'al,* a word which can roughly be translated as "kind-hearted giants from the sky." In the scattered settlements of the Sandoval Starfields, they call themselves the Merchants of the Night, and in the Snow Jungle of Uncorona they're "the sunlight people," or "the good strangers," or simply "visitors."

The villagers wonder, of course, why the oneironauts of the *Cascade* have chosen this obscure, isolated little peninsula as a suitable place to visit. When they finally broach the topic, the oneironauts explain that they are refugees from a lost world, a beautiful realm that used to lie on the other side of the sunset, to which they cannot return. They explain that the Morgana Peninsula is one of the few safe places left on Earth. It is a place of beauty uncorrupted by industry, by avarice, by the cosmic imbalance which has become so rampant in the human world.

"If you keep it this way," the visitors say, "we will return."

The villagers wake up on the beach in the morning, and the *Jericho Cascade* and its crew are nowhere to be seen.

So the villagers build a lighthouse, the first one ever to stand guard on the rocky islet near the peninsula. By night the lighthouse's rays pierce the rushing darkness of the ocean; by day it's a silent sentinel holding up the sky, tall and proud and still. A monument to the oneironauts. A cry out for their return.

Don't abandon us.

And the *Jericho Cascade* does return. At first it visits the Morgana Peninsula once or twice a year. Every time, the villagers rejoice, and celebrate, and are merry. But as time goes on the gaps between visits increase. Sometimes years go by between appearances of the *Jericho Cascade*. Then decades.

Eventually, a visit from the oneironauts becomes a once-in-a-lifetime occurrence.

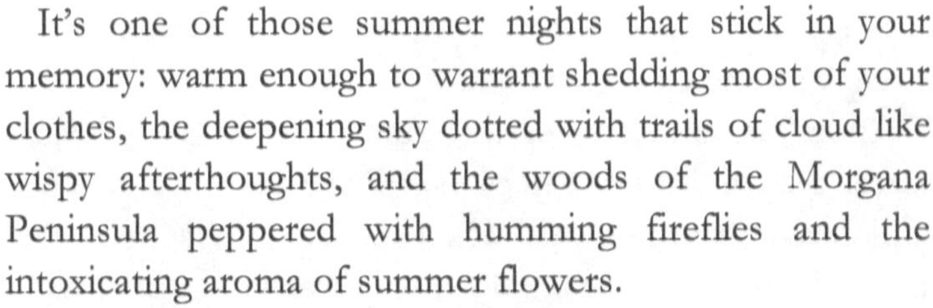

It's one of those summer nights that stick in your memory: warm enough to warrant shedding most of your clothes, the deepening sky dotted with trails of cloud like wispy afterthoughts, and the woods of the Morgana Peninsula peppered with humming fireflies and the intoxicating aroma of summer flowers.

The villagers know that the *Jericho Cascade* will soon be returning to the Peninsula. They have dreamt it, as their elders did when they were young. Some have seen it in waking visions. They gather on the beach in preparation, and sure enough the seven-masted galleon with a city on its deck appears on the widening horizon.

This is the first time in almost a hundred years that the *Cascade* has visited the Morgana Peninsula. The young, and middle-aged, who are seeing the *Cascade* for the first time, are awestruck. The elderly, who saw the dream-ship long, long ago, when they were small children, smile and weep and embrace their loved ones.

Until now, many of the older villagers feared that the oneironauts' absence hassomething to do with the regrown lighthouse, and whatever has taken up residence inside it. But now it seems that the dream-sailors of the *Jericho Cascade* are unbothered by the crooked lighthouse and the Cursed Rock.

The oneironauts arrive on the white-sanded shore, and the festivities begin.

That night, a young man named Neil, who lives on Morgana Wynd, meets an oneironaut named Anora Vale. Anora is spirited, wise beyond her years, with a glow in her amber eyes unlike any eyes Neil has ever gazed into before.

There's something about Neil that Anora can't turn away from; he's youthful and sharp-edged and he reeks of mystery and secrets, of a vast hidden darkness and a naivety strong enough to face it.

Anora has a laugh like a summer breeze, a smile that never truly fades from her lips. Her hair is thick and red, and descends to her waist when she lets it loose. Her skin is a shade or two darker than Neil's... but there's something else to it, isn't there? As though her skin has been tanned by the light of an alien sun.

Neil Faulken, a man of so many dark impulsions, manages to lose himself in someone else, for the first time in his life. Anora Vale sees the flickers of darkness at the edges of his eyes. She sees his dreams swirling about him in a nightmarish aura—as though he's trapped in a bank of roiling, lightning-cursed stormclouds, and he can't even see it.

The two of them get to talking. Before long it's more than talking. Much, much more.

———— •◆• ————

Barkface sighs. He understands, now, why Neria has come down this way. She's trying to make sense of it all.

You don't deserve this, Neria Nightshade.

When will she realize that none of it makes any sense, that it's all a mistake, just a colossal, agonizing mistake? She's trying to puzzle out an impossibility. An aberration. A contradiction.

Maybe she already knows that.

He finds her footprints in the snow in the depths of winter, and trails them to the sprawling estate that will one day be called the Fifth Season. Inside, he finds Anora Vale walking slowly (*gliding* would be a better word for it) down a hallway toward a set of double doors.

Barkface is overcome by that unearthly radiance he fell in love with so long ago.

He follows her through the doors, into a magnificent dining room.

In a far corner of the room, Neil Faulken stands with a glass of red wine and stares out the window at the snowflakes whirling outside. He's still young, slender and handsome, if a bit skinnier than he was on the day he met Anora. He's not clean-shaven anymore, his face marred with untamed stubble.

Anora pulls up a chair and sits down next to him. She leans her head against his side, and looks up at him with shimmering amber eyes.

She's got one hand on her belly, which has been swelling steadily for the past few months.

"Neil," she says, "I don't like this."

Neil nods slowly. "Me neither." He smiles. "But I won't be gone long. It's the last job. Two, three days at most. And then it's done. I promised, didn't I?"

"It's not that. Well, it's not *just* that. I'm worried about Neria."

"Neria?"

Anora strokes her pregnant belly.

"Right," says Neil. "*Neria.* Very beautiful name. A girl?"

"A girl. I've seen it."

Neil nods. "Neria."

"She won't be normal. Half of her will be like me, and half of her…" Anora looks out the window into the stormy night. "Don't be gone too long. Remember what's important."

"I'm doing it now, so that when the baby—when *Neria* is born I won't have to go anywhere."

Anora fixes him with that vivid, unignorable gaze of hers. "Promise me again," she commands.

So Neil does. He kisses her on the cheek. "I will finish this. And I will come back to you. I promise. On my life, Anora, I *promise.*"

Barkface can't help it. He stays in the shadows of the past, and for a time he forgets about finding Neria. He watches the woman he used to love. The woman he still loves, even though she only exists here, in this lost place.

And he watches the man he used to be.

I had a chance that nobody else on Earth has ever had, or will ever have again. They impressed this upon Neil when he and Anora went to Alaya—Anora's sister and captain of the *Jericho Cascade*—to tell her that when the *Cascade* next set sail, Anora would be staying on the Morgana Peninsula with Neil.

"Understand, Neil Faulken," Alaya cautioned him, "that you tread on sacred territory here. Never before has an Earthling held such sway over one of us."

I had a chance nobody else on Earth will ever have, and I wasted it. I wasted it like I wasted everything.

It's true. He knows it's true.

They host communal dinners sometimes, this young, striking, extraordinary couple who have taken up residence in the Big House. The dinners are Anora's idea. Invite the other residents of the Wynd over, cook them delicious food, befriend them. They can all feast in the huge dining hall, and Neil can charm the guests with his animated stories, tales from his university days, his favourite professors... shenanigans he and his friends got up to, that he wouldn't even *dream* of trying to pull off today...

And the whole while Anora sits back, half in the shadows, and she watches. She watches her husband and his friends all laughing together, getting drunker and drunker together, swapping tales that escalate in absurdity as the night wears on.

Why is it that they all gravitate to him, and so few of them seem to be able to say more than a few words to her at a time?

"It's because you scare them," Neil explains, one night, in bed.

"I *scare* them? How? I don't want to scare them."

"Because they're not—they're not used to seeing people like you."

"People like me."

"You know, people from other realms of existence. You're an *alien*, Anora."

This world was never for you, was it?

The illness begins almost imperceptibly: the colour starts to leave her skin. She talks slower. Then the coughing. She doesn't want to eat. She walks slow, not the graceful gliding from before, but sluggish, belaboured plodding.

Her red hair starts turning grey. "Don't go," she croaks. "Please."

Neil's been slipping away again. He'll be gone for several consecutive nights at a time now. He's always apologetic when he leaves, even more so when he returns. But Anora knows that he hates seeing her like this. He thinks the sickness is his fault, doesn't he?

"I'm not good enough for you," he whispers. "Really, Anora."

Anora draws away from him with a resigned sigh. "Just come back. And *stay*. That would be enough."

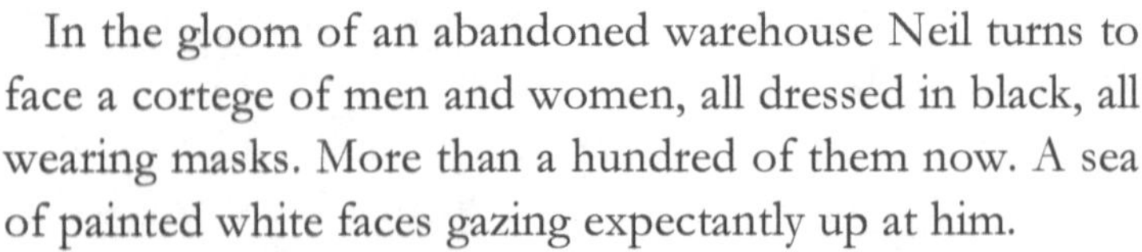

In the gloom of an abandoned warehouse Neil turns to face a cortege of men and women, all dressed in black, all wearing masks. More than a hundred of them now. A sea of painted white faces gazing expectantly up at him.

He wipes his bloody hands off on a towel. Clears his throat. Behind him a bonfire blazes on the cement floor, and dark billowing smoke spills into the air, bearing the smell of barbecuing meat. Neil stands silhouetted in front of the blaze, the heat scorching his back. Sweat trails slowly from his forehead down his chalky face.

For a moment he loses his words. His eyes rove over the faces of his disciples, taking in their rapt stares.

There's Jacob and Gabriel Brecker, the two no-nonsense brothers, Jacob with his tightly-shaved head, Gabriel with his long mane of black hair—both of them sporting wide, empty smiles.

There's Rika, the High Chemist, lean and skittish, a nail-biting psychonaut who ventured down a wrong, wrong path long ago. And Axel, the muscle, scowling over his bushy black beard—the scariest of them all. And of course the other set of brothers: Sammy and Dacklyn. Tall, handsome, solidly-built young men. Sammy has short cropped hair, while Dacklyn grows his out, tying it up in a neat ponytail.

Neil sighs.

"My friends," he says. "My comrades. We have perfected our craft, haven't we? Honed it to the point of beauty. I'm so"—he pauses briefly, almost imperceptibly—"very proud of you all."

The gathered cultists murmur their appreciation. Neil tenses his body in an effort to keep the tremor out of his voice. *Rip off the band-aid.*

"I'm sorry to say," he continues, "that this is goodbye. What you all saw today was my final offering to Pale."

Sammy Nordine turns to look askance at him. "What do you mean?"

"It means, Sammy, that you are now in command of the Face of Pale. I trust you to carry on my legacy. In witness of our faithful legion!" Neil turns to face the crowd again.

"The Face of Pale has vast potential, my friends. We built a god. We built a god from nothing but nightmares and rumours and *tiny* bit of blood. If we can build a god, what does that make us?"

The men and women gathered before him mumble and whisper amongst themselves.

"Why the hell are you leaving, then?" Rika demands.

"Because," says Neil, "Pale commanded me to rest. So I shall take rest now, and let others ascend to the glory which I have held as High Priest of the Face of Pale."

But Sammy Nordine isn't convinced. "Or maybe you're lying," he accuses Neil. "Maybe you're afraid to keep going. You're afraid of what this can become. But *I'm* not." He turns to face the other disciples gathered there in the stark orange glow of the bonfire, and the sweet smell of cooking meat. "*We're* not afraid of Pale, are we? We love Pale."

The others are starting to move slowly toward Neil.

"Maybe," Rika murmurs, "you're leaving because you're afraid of *us.*"

Neil laughs it off, but it's a hollow laugh. "Don't be silly," he says – a fumbled attempt at a scoff – but he fears it's all the proof Rika and the others need.

"If you leave, Neil," Dacklyn says, "you know what will happen. If you're not with the Face of Pale, how can we possibly be sure that you haven't turned against us?"

"Anyone who isn't with us," Jacob Brecker says, "is on our list. That's how we've always worked, right?"

For a split second Neil freezes up. Tongue-locked. Behind the sea of black suits and pale masks, in the smoke-hazed gloom of the warehouse… is that *him?* Cloaked in smoke and darkness, towering above the legion of faces…

A man-made god, in the flesh.

"You think we don't know what you've been hiding?" Sammy growls. "A wife and *child*, Neil?"

"And not just any child," Dacklyn adds, "but a child of two worlds."

"In other words," Gabriel Brecker growls, "the exact kind of sacrifice needed to give Pale dominion over the cosmos."

"*Anyone who isn't with us is on our list*," Jacob Brecker proclaims. "You don't seem to be with us anymore, Neil."

"Our god grows thirsty again," Rika cackles. "A demon god must drink!"

It will never stop. You can't finish it. You can't get away. "Rest assured," Neil says, wincing as the quiver finally finds its way into his voice, "that this is Pale's will, not mine."

It's over. They've already called his bluff.

"Get him!" Sammy Nordine shouts.

For the first time in many, many years, Neil gives in to the fear. He turns on his heel, bounds toward the warehouse door and kicks it open. Before the others even get outside into the parking lot, Neil's already climbing into his car, gunning the ignition and driving away.

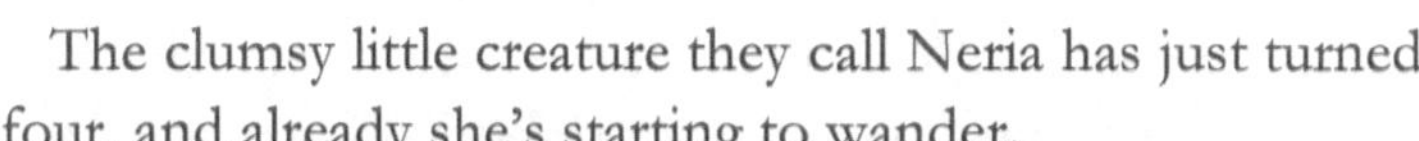

The clumsy little creature they call Neria has just turned four, and already she's starting to wander.

Barkface makes himself small, the eight-legged form he has come to love. He spins a silken web, its strands reaching all over Morgana Wynd, and he crawls along it freely, absorbing tremors which tell him all manner of secrets. And with eight beady black eyes, he watches Neria.

Sometimes, when nobody else is looking, he returns to near-human form and sneaks up on his daughter, and whispers things in her ear. Things like, *"Everything's going to be all right in the end."*

One day little Neria wanders away from the building that will soon be called the Fifth Season. Barkface stays behind. He watches the man he used to be trace a finger along the lines creasing Anora's brow.

"You miss it." Neil speaks softly. "Don't you?"

Anora nods. "I can't lie. I do miss it. But I love it here. And Neria does, too." A pause. "But this world turns, Neil. It *spins*. It makes me lose my balance."

"When the *Jericho Cascade* comes back, you have to get on board."

"Not without Neria. Not without you."

"I never said it would have to be without us." Neil draws in a deep, rattling breath, and then speaks the words he's been dreading: "We could come with you, couldn't we?" He glances through the window at the windswept darkness beyond.

Anora's face crumples, the tears coming thick and fast. "I don't know," she sobs. "They would let Neria come, but… I don't know about you, Neil. And even if they did let you come…" She draws a deep, rattling breath. "Well, you wouldn't really want that, would you? I know you're saying all that for me, and it's nice, but after a while…" She straightens up, suddenly, a look of alarm on her face. "She's gone too far. Someone's got her."

"*What?*"

"Neria!"

The two of them leap to their feet. "You search the house," Neil says. "I'll look—"

But Anora points out the door. "Out there."

They run together down the Wynd to the copse of trees at the end. Barkface tails them from afar, disguised as an ownerless noontime shadow. He watches with amusement as Neil and Anora comb the trees, calling out for their daughter. But the girl's nowhere to be seen.

"NERIA! Sweetheart!" Anora slows, and points to a large oak tree. "There, look!" She starts running toward it. "NERIA!"

But Neil doesn't see anything. "What?" He follows Anora, catches up in time to see his wife's red hair vanish into the roots. "Anora!" Neil peers at the tree's roots. They grow thick, and cover a wide radius of ground around the tree. Still, there aren't any gaps in the roots big enough for him to squeeze through—or for a full-grown woman to vanish into.

But Anora's already back, unfolding herself from a too-narrow gap between two coils of root, cradling little squirming Neria in one arm.

"Wretched imps," Anora growls as she clambers to her feet. "Go teach them a lesson, Neil, will you?"

She brushes past her husband without another word, making her way back toward the Wynd.

Neil turns to stare at the roots at the base of the oak tree. *How in the hell did she—?*

Barkface almost laughs as he approaches Neil from behind. He remembers how stumped he felt, in this moment, staring at that impassive tangle of roots.

So he grabs Neil Faulken's wrist.

"This way."

When Neil Faulken sees the face of the man grabbing his wrist, he blanches, begins to splutter. "What the—what in—what's—"

Barkface pulls his past self down into the conspiracy of roots, into the tunnel hidden beneath the oak. Suddenly the two of them are stumbling in mud, scrambling for balance. The tunnel stretches on ahead of them, and there's light at the end.

They make their way toward the light, and emerge onto a series of cliffs overlooking a blustery ocean. It's midday—how can it be midday?

Screaming winds claw at Barkface and Neil, and they spot a group of children. They look like they're around six or seven years old, and Neil can't spot any other adults around.

But something's wrong.

One of the kids has silver skin and pointed elfin ears. Another is riddled with scales, and her eyes are round fish eyes that protrude from her face. Another has hooves instead of feet, and horns growing out of the top of his head.

The fourth is covered in scabs, and his skin peels away in patches, exposing the muscle and bones underneath. He's smoking a cigar.

Neil falters, glances around frantically but finds himself alone on the clifftop with the four imps, who have now all turned to look at him.

"Who are you?" the one with silver skin demands.

"Not someone you wanna piss off." Neil clears his throat, draws in a deep breath, and starts toward them. "You think it's funny, luring little girls into danger? 'Cause that's serious business, and it has consequences."

"Luring?" one of the imps croaks, the one with scales and fish eyes. "She found *us*. We were just going to see the Singing Spires, and we took a wrong turn and ran into her, and we *asked politely* if she wanted to come and she said *yes*."

(Barkface crouches several yards away from Neil, in the body of a seagull, and squawks to himself.)

"So that makes it all right, then?" Neil grunts. It's suddenly painfully clear to him how small the imps are. He winds up to kick the nearest one—

But at that moment a strident voice cuts through the air: "Hello there!"

Neil wheels around, and sees someone striding along the edge of the cliff toward him. She's tall, extremely tall, and broad-shouldered, with dark skin and frizzy black hair. She's wearing a black cloak, and smiles an eerie smile at Neil. "Are my imps bothering you, stranger?" she asks coyly.

"Yeah," says Neil. "They are, as a matter of fact. They tried to kidnap my daughter."

The tall woman nods slowly. *"Did* they?" She looks down imperiously at the four imps, which have all gathered about her feet. The fish-eyed one and the hooved, horned one are hugging her legs. "And where is your daughter now?"

"Safe," says Neil. "With her mother. I just came here to teach these imps a lesson."

"A lesson, eh?" The tall woman nods again. Then she snaps her fingers four times. The imps turn and, without a word of protest, leap in unison off the edge of the cliff.

"I made them today," the tall woman says with a shrug. "I was bored." She extends a hand. "Ara Augustine."

"Neil." They shake hands. "Nice to meet you, Ara. Could I offer you some tea?"

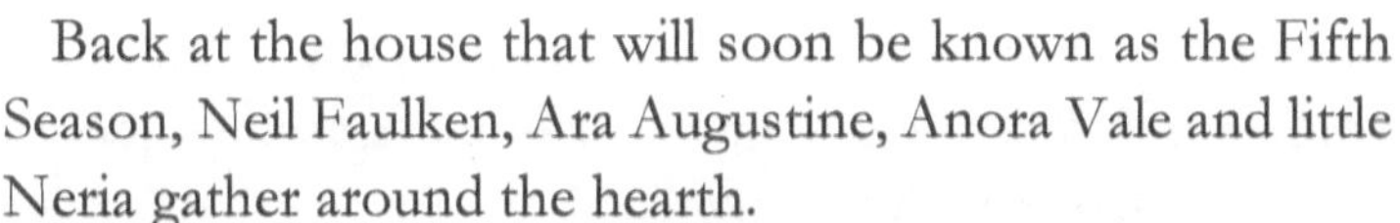

Back at the house that will soon be known as the Fifth Season, Neil Faulken, Ara Augustine, Anora Vale and little Neria gather around the hearth.

To Neil's surprise, Anora recognizes the newcomer: "We've met before!" she exclaims. "At the Sleepwalkers' Souk, on the island at the edge of the world. You were selling stolen nightmares."

Ara Augustine laughs a husky laugh. "Yes," she agrees. "I remember you. You came to the Souk with your whole crew, dozens of you. I almost convinced you to buy one of my nightmares, didn't I? You almost did, if memory serves."

Anora chuckles. "Well, are you still selling?"

She, Ara and Neil all burst out laughing at this, which makes little Neria laugh too, an excited high-pitched squeak.

Ara draws a feather from mid-air, and leans down to the child, teasing her with the feather before making it disappear, much to Neria's bewilderment. Ara snaps her fingers, making the feather reappear in Neria's hair, and waits for the little girl to notice.

"I'm glad to say that my nightmare-peddling days are over. It's nasty stuff." Ara shudders. "So what are you doing here, Anora Vale of the *Jericho Cascade*? This is"—she makes a gesture that somehow manages to encompass not just the room, but the entire Morgana Peninsula, perhaps even the entire world—"a rather boring place. And you'll pardon me if I say that you seem all the worse for wear lingering here."

Anora smiles gently. "This one right here." She ruffles Neil's hair, and Neil's pale face flushes red. "This is why I've stayed."

Neria erupts into giggles as she finds the feather sticking out of her hair, right above her left ear. She pulls the feather out and holds it up to examine closely—only to watch it evaporate in her hands.

Her jaw drops and she falls to her knees in stunned, bewildered silence.

"I believe you," says Ara Augustine. "And I believe I owe you something, Anora. I endangered your child. I created those imps purely for my own entertainment—it was irresponsible. Perhaps there's something I can do to make up for it."

Silence falls, save for the crackling of the hearth. Little Neria, having forgotten the Trial of the Vanishing Feather, curls up like a cat between her mother and Ara Augustine. She giggles again, sleepily.

"You don't need to make up for it." Anora sounds tired. "Neria's not like most children—most children cannot walk through the hidden gates. But maybe... maybe, if you can spare a couple of days, you can stay with us, and... help us keep watch. I would feel much safer with you around. You're... like me, aren't you? You're a kind of oneironaut, too."

A kindred soul.

Barkface watches from behind a coat rack. He bows his head. He can't stand listening to Anora's voice anymore. She sounds too resigned. Drained.

Besides, he knows that this is the night it happens. The night the Face of Pale catches up. He can feel it in the air, a kind of silent, crackling energy.

A witching night.

"Maybe you can help us watch over her for a little while, is what I mean," Anora says to Ara Augustine. "She is a child of the *Jericho Cascade*. Exploring is in her blood. It's bound to lead her into trouble. And there are troublesome forces about, these days. I fear they have caught her scent."

Ara nods. "I could stay for a few days," she says, as she strokes little Neria's blood-red hair.

———— • • ◆ • • ————

Less than an hour later, the Face of Pale descends on Morgana Wynd.

Barkface forces himself to stay and watch as they gather in front of the house. Shadows with white masks.

He watches, his entire being hardened against the harrowing sight, as they slip into the building and emerge, moments later, one of them carrying little Neria, and a pair of them dragging Anora's limp body behind them.

They take their captives to the trees at the water's edge.

A few minutes later, Neil and Ara come bursting out the front door, and without hesitating for even a second they both go sprinting as fast as they can down the Wynd. Barkface stays close behind them.

Ara is noticeably faster than Neil. Before long she's far ahead. She reaches the woods first, vanishes into the trees.

Voices drift to Barkface from within the trees. He stays by Neil's side—the two of them creep stealthily forward, and before long they can hear little Neria's hysterical, hiccupping sobs.

Sammy Nordine is talking to her. "Listen to me," he says, his voice calm and dementedly soothing. "His name is Pale, and he's gonna come for you. He's gonna take you to a dark place, and he's gonna keep you there forever. Do you understand?"

"STOP! STOP!" Neria wails. "*STOP!*"

"It's got to be you, my dear. You're perfect for him. A child of two worlds. With your soul, he will be immeasurably powerful. Don't you want to be a part of that?"

"HELP!"

"You don't understand. You can't. I know that's not fair. But your services to Pale will never be forgotten, little one."

Neil can see Sammy up ahead, kneeling in front of Neria, pinning her against a tree. The child wriggles and squirms but it's no use, she can't possibly free herself. And Anora's tied to the trunk of another tree—she slumps forward, her hair hanging down in front of her face, and she's not making a sound, not moving—not *breathing*—

It's too late. There are two bloody holes where her eyes used to be, blood spilling all down her front, onto the ground at her feet.

"He's on his way right now," Sammy hisses in Neria's ear. "Can you hear him?"

The other faces of Pale gather in a semi-circle to watch.

Then—

"Neil?" one of the cultists says.

With one hand Sammy keeps Neria pinned against the tree. With the other he draws something from his belt: a long, serrated hunting knife.

"NORDINE!" Neil shouts.

"Daddy!" Neria cries.

"Neil!" Barkface screams.

And then Neil's barreling forward as fast as he can—just as the ropes binding Neria loosen. Ara Augustine appears beside her for a split second, for just long enough to pull the child away into the darkness.

Sammy Nordine tilts his head back and screams a guttural battle-cry. Neil pauses several yards away from the man he himself chose to replace him as leader of the Face of Pale.

For a moment neither man moves.

Then Sammy lunges. He slides his knife smoothly between Neil's ribs, once, twice, three times, four times. Blood sprays into the thick forest air and Neil collapses to his knees, Sammy falling with him, straddling Neil's body now—and the knife comes down again, again, *again!* Sammy screams wordlessly at the top of his lungs, and Neil can only stare up at the man who used to be his friend, whose face is now twisted in psychotic rage.

He tries to laugh, but realizes he can't even breathe through the blood flooding into his lungs. He lifts his head to catch a glimpse of his own chest, and frowns as he tries to count the gouges. *Six… seven… eight… does that one count as two?*

"Look at me."

Neil lowers his head again, so that Sammy Nordine's face fills his field of vision.

"The Face of Pale," Sammy gasps, "is unstoppable." But then his expression becomes anguished. "Neil," he moans, grabbing Neil's shoulders and shaking them. "Oh *god*, Neil! Neil, buddy, it's—oh, god no, I'm sorry—"

Then he turns, sees that Neria's gone. Panic seizes him as he glances around frantically.

"THE GIRL!" he shrieks.

Commotion breaks out beneath the trees as the faces of Pale begin combing the darkness.

"Ara…" Neil tries to say, causing blood to spurt out of his mouth and nostrils.

"The girl's not here!" shrieks the portly black-bearded man named Axel. "We lost her!"

"FIND HER!" Sammy Nordine roars.

Like a murder of crows all taking flight at once, the black-clad men and women sweep out of the copse of trees, into the night.

She's not here.

Neil lies alone beneath the trees. Silence falls, save for the rustling of the foliage, the whimpering wind. He knows Anora's body is nearby, still tied to that tree. But he can't reach her. Can't move.

Ara Augustine crouches beside him in the dark.

"Neria…" Neil gurgles. His vision's becoming blurry. He can hardly see Ara at all. But he can feel her warmth beside him.

"I'm—dying," he manages, blood spurting out of his mouth with each syllable.

Ara shakes her head. "No, Neil Faulken. You're not going to die. Not exactly."

"Yes I—"

"Neria's safe. But Anora—well—" Ara's voice catches. "We weren't fast enough."

Neil can't form words anymore. Ara presses something into the palm of his hand, something the size of a marble. It glows like a stolen star, burns cool against his skin.

"Sleep," she whispers. "I'll keep the child safe. She cannot stay here. Don't worry. I'll look after her. I won't abandon her. You have my word." She rises. "Sleep well. When you wake up, you will have a lot of work to do." Her voice becomes razor-sharp. "When the time comes, we're going to make them pay."

Ara walks over to Anora's body, still tied to the trunk of a tree. She loosens the ropes, and vanishes into the trees before Anora even hits the ground.

It's only then that Barkface hears it: quiet, muffled sobs. Stepping over his nearly-murdered past self, he approaches Anora's body. "Neria?" he whispers.

The sobbing is coming from above him.

Barkface's guts twist into knots, tightening and tightening until he's short of breath.

He looks up. There she is, in the branches of the tree to which the cult tied her mother. She clings to the trunk. Just a snarl of shadow. Red-rimmed eyes. A chalky face streaked with tears.

"I'm sorry, Neria," Barkface croaks. "You deserve so much better than this."

She's glaring down at him, balling her hands vengefully into fists. "Your words mean nothing," she spits. "Why didn't you save them?"

Barkface shakes his head miserably. "I'm sorry." He reaches for her. "Come down. Come with me. We're going home."

But Neria recoils further into the branches. "I'm not here," she hisses.

"Neria, *please.*"

At first she's silent. Then: "I mean it, *Barkface.*" She wipes the tears from her eyes, but soon more spill down her cheeks anyway. "I'm on the slopes of Mount Carthage. I've poisoned myself with deadly nightshade. It's too late for me."

— • •◆• • —

Neil Faulken wanders.

He's forgotten how long he's been walking for. He lets his feet do the thinking. His sore, aching, bleeding feet. His head feels as though it's about to split, and he knows he should have bled out by now... but somehow he hasn't.

His stomach's still hanging open, his entrails spilling out, dragging between his legs along the forest floor. His face is all hacked up too.

Still he walks.

It's the thing Ara Augustine gave him. A marble glowing with the light of a tiny star. He holds it out in front of him; it lights the way.

He knows he should have reached the other side of the trees by now, but… *That's not how it works here, is it?* No, it isn't. If he were to keep wandering, he's certain that the forest would never end, that the trees would draw him in deeper and deeper and deeper and…

He keeps walking.

He walks for days. For weeks. For *years*. He walks until he's stooped and limping, until the trees surrounding him reach taller than any trees he has ever seen before.

He walks until his skin peels away like old wallpaper.

He walks until he's so weary that he can't take it anymore, and he falls to the ground and his body just *breaks*, clean and simple.

He lies on a bed of cool moss and watches stars spiral overhead through gaps in the canopy. He stares into the sun, and eventually he rouses some energy, and pushes himself up on his elbows.

Someone's sitting on a tree stump nearby, staring at him.

The man is tall, even when sitting down. He's got a luscious mane of brown hair and piercing earth-coloured eyes, and elk antlers protruding from his forehead.

"Who are you?" Neil demands.

The man licks his lips. *'I,'* he says unhurriedly, *'am the Heart of the Skein.'*

"The *what?*"

'The Heart of the Skein.' The man stands slowly, towers magisterially above Neil now, so tall he blots out the sun.

"What's the—what's the Skein?"

'Whatever it is that you are following.'

Neil tries to stand, but his legs won't let him. He looks down, sees that they're frayed like old rope, sinew and bleach-white bone sticking out.

"Oh god," he mutters.

'I must congratulate you, Neil Faulken.' The Heart of the Skein extends a hand. *'You have journeyed further than anyone else.'*

"Is it over yet?"

The Heart of the Skein laughs. *'Of course not. You have not gone as far as you might, and once you have gone that far, you must travel all the way back.'*

Dismay tightens around Neil's lungs, but he accepts the hand, allowing the Heart of the Skein to haul him to his feet. He staggers to a tree, leans against it. The Heart of the Skein watches him curiously, his head tilted quizzically to the side.

"I don't think I can go much further," Neil gasps.

'No,' the Heart of the Skein admits. *'Your body has been direly abused. Which is why, tonight, you and I will roast it over a bonfire beneath the falling stars, and feast on it until there is nothing left.'*

"But—" Snarls of fear lick at the base of Neil's brain, like tongues of flame. "But—but we can't—"

'You need not worry, my friend. You will borrow another body. A wolf, perhaps. Or a bear. A deer. It does not matter much to me, but perhaps you will have a preference.' The Heart of the Skein smiles widely, and runs a long-fingered, mahogany hand over his antlers. *'We will dine. And I promise you, Neil Faulken, that it will be the most delicious thing you will ever taste.'*

———— •·◆·• ————

And it *is* delicious.

Neil chews the meat ravenously from his hiding place inside a mangy silver fox. He's not the only one eating. The smell of roasting human flesh fills the woods, and on the edges of the golden circle of light cast by the bonfire, pairs of glowing eyes begin to appear. Slowly they stray into the circle: hunters. Lynxes, foxes, wolves. A black bear with a convoy of cubs. And then *others*. Shadows with shambling walks, misshapen things whispering to themselves.

Beneath stars gleaming far brighter than usual, a banquet breaks out: a gathering of souls from all throughout the cosmos. They tear into the roasted carcass that was once Neil Faulken: hot sizzling blood and juices and gleaming bits of meat, sucked clean and chewed up and totally consumed.

After the feast is over Neil lies on his side, his tiny fox belly so full he fears it might burst. *Where do I go now?* he tries to ask, but he can't speak. Thankfully, though, the Heart of the Skein hears him.

'You will know which way to travel, my friend. I cannot guide you any further.'

You're not coming with me?

'I am sure that you would make a fine travelling companion. But I have other work to see to.' The Heart of the Skein smiles fondly at Neil. *'Remember that you may turn back at any moment. But you have already come further than any other before you. You will follow the Skein to the ends of the earth, where we will meet again, and though I will be prepared, then, to teach you what it is you wish to learn, I suspect that by that point you will already know it.'*

With hesitation bordering on bashfulness, the Heart of the Skein reaches out and scratches Neil between his fox ears. *'Godspeed, my friend,'* he says. *'Though this is farewell, I promise that in time I will see you again.'*

Then he rises, and strides off into the trees, leaving no sign of the man that was once called Neil Faulken, save for some scraps of clean-scraped bone.

The old silver fox lopes quietly into the darkness.

A succession of eternities speeds by. Time and tide sweep the Skein, and then one day the trees curtsy and salute as the creature that was once Neil Faulken comes striding purposefully back to Morgana Wynd.

He stands tall, unnaturally tall. He's got elk antlers protruding from his forehead, a mane of curly brown hair, a long, flowing beard.

He's got glimmering eyes the colour of moss and of earth. His skin is weathered like tree bark.

He hardly identifies with the name they used to call him. He strides purposefully, the stride of a man who has travelled leagues and leagues, to whom walking is now as effortless as breathing. Eventually he catches a familiar smell in the air: saltwater and woodsmoke. He slides through a patch of shadow beneath a towering sequoia, and when he emerges he's just an old man: stooped, hunched, with a white beard and flowing white hair.

He catches sight of someone up ahead—a child, lanky and shaggy-haired, who immediately turns on his heel and sprints away. "Skye!" The child's voice echoes through the clean forest air. "Skye! Help! HELP!"

From that day onward the children of Morgana Wynd call the man who was once Neil Faulken by a new name: Barkface.

Barkface doesn't mind.

He waits for dusk, then summons a contingent of fireflies to light his way. He combs the woods until he finds what he's looking for: the place where the bog starts, where the stench of peat clogs his nose.

Eventually he finds it. A stone with an *X* scored into it, marking the spot.

Barkface digs with his bony hands, digs down into the peat. He digs all through the night, without resting, until eventually he finds a face in the dirt, a face he knew long, long ago. Her eyes are closed peacefully. She looks like she could be sleeping. The knot in his stomach tightens.

"Anora," he whispers. "Come on, love."

He can't be sure how long it's been. Weeks? Months? Years? *Decades?*

So far, though, the peat has done a good job of preserving her.

Barkface grimaces. *To work, then.*

———— ••◆•• ————

The next morning, the sun rises over a Morgana Peninsula that's been irrevocably transformed.

It takes the locals a while to figure out what's happened. They know something's wrong, but they can't quite put it into words.

After several days, a businessman staying on the Wynd decides on a whim to say something:

"Were these woods always here?"

The businessman's brother responds with, "What are you talking about? Of course they were!" But he's not as certain of it as he sounds. "Wasn't this just a little grove before? A dozen or so trees, no more? Where we were supposed to... never mind."

The residents of number 1—"the Big House," as it's often called—are missing. It's not a murder case, because there aren't any bodies. There's nothing to indicate where they might have gone. Except...

Except for something a little boy named Lucas claims to have seen at the edge of the woods, one cold, grey dawn:

"He looked sick and I thought he was hurt, and he was carrying something, I dunno what it was but it was *bloody*. I *swear* I'm not lying!"

"And where did you see him go, Lucas?" the boy's father demands testily.

"He was in the woods."

The woods?

Those woods aren't supposed to be there, are they?

Months trail by. Autumn rolls into winter, and by the time spring swings around most of the locals have grown accustomed to that strange feeling they get every time they pass by the forest.

It's always been like this, hasn't it?

Nobody brings it up in conversation anymore. It's too difficult to discuss.

Gradually, people move on.

Sammy and Dacklyn return in the spring and decide after some deliberation to purchase the Big House. "It's the perfect location for a cozy seaside restaurant," Dacklyn says. "A quaint little community nestled in the woods, right by the ocean."

They call their restaurant the Fifth Season.

Chapter Fifteen: Doldrums

In the body of a raggedy jackdaw, Barkface soars over the slopes of the mountain called Carthage. He finds the boy first, a teenager of around seventeen: his face caked with dried blood, dying of dehydration in the dirt. Struggling to drink from a murky pond with his dislodged jaw. The boy moans as Barkface swoops past him. At first the jackdaw appears to ignore him—but then the bird circles back. It alights next to the broken boy for just a moment, just long enough to whisper something into the boy's ear.

"You played your part. Now taste of oblivion."

A flapping of wings, feathers stirring the air, and the boy is alone on the mountain slope again, half-conscious—his mind suddenly crystal clear, emptied of shrapnel and sharp edges. Later, perhaps, he would rouse as from a strange nightmare, beset by clinging memories of a place he had once dreamed, and people who were there… people upon whose company he had grown drunk… but their voices and faces already dimming, turning to shadows against the fading purple-and-green afterimage of a moment in time he no longer recalled.

Later, beneath the stars, he would begin walking. A simple journey for him. He would reach civilization eventually; but by the time he did, he would have entirely forgotten that he once bore the name Lucas Alvarez.

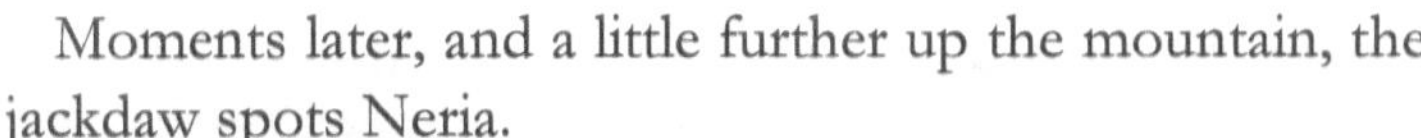

Moments later, and a little further up the mountain, the jackdaw spots Neria.

She's in much worse state than the boy. Foaming at the mouth. Convulsing. Thrashing. Barkface pries his daughter's jaws open, empties a canteen of saltwater down her throat.

Oh, Neria.

She starts heaving. Then she vomits. He turns her onto her side so that the puke spills onto the ground beside her. At first it's only saltwater that emerges. But after three or four heaves the seeds start to come up. Four, five, *six* little brown seeds.

Neria Nightshade.

"Everything's gonna be all right," Barkface tells her, rocking her frail body gently to and fro. "Everything's gonna make sense soon."

Her lips twitch in response. Her eyelids flutter.

Everything's gonna be all right.

———— •·◆·• ————

Neria looks up and finds herself in a strange moonlit dusk, an indigo sky overhead dotted with stars far too big to be real. Before her there's a pathway made of leaves, strung together like a patchwork quilt. The pathway leads between gentle rolling hills dotted with quaint, rustic houses.

She smiles sadly. She would recognize Auntie August's artwork anywhere.

"This way, love."

She follows the path as it winds, twists and dips through the peculiar twilight. Blissful warmth pools inside her. "Auntie?" she says…

A chilly breeze gusts over her. She sits up.

She's lying on the sofa in her father's cottage, and she appears to be alone. A fire mutters to itself in the hearth. The front door hangs open.

Neria sits up slowly. Her head hurts. She blinks several times in succession, but her vision refuses to focus.

"Auntie? Barkf—" She catches herself. "Dad?"

She hauls herself off the sofa. Stumbles to the front door, peers out.

Dylan Brecker's there, sitting on the front steps. He turns to look at Neria. "Hey," he says carefully. He's filthy, covered in mud and dust, his tangled, disarrayed hair falling in front of his eyes.

"Hey," Neria echoes. She slips a hand into her jacket pocket, and her heart notches up into her throat as her fingertips find…

Please no.

"Your, uh… Ara says you need to stay put," Dylan says. "Go lie down, Neria. You need to rest."

"Auntie August? Where is she?" Neria demands. "I don't need rest."

"Yes you do. You've been through a lot."

"Where is she, Dylan?" Neria's voice catches and quivers. "Please just tell me."

Dylan frowns, and bites his lip. Then he sighs. "She and—she and Barkface went to the Wynd. They'll be back."

Then he rises to his feet. He moves toward Neria—for the first time she truly appreciates how *tall* he is. He towers over her, the sunlight catching his turquoise eyes and turning them gold.

"Skye and Jack," he growls. "And Lucas. Where are they?"

It's like a blizzard blows through her and freezes her heart over inside her chest. She exhales through her teeth and *swears* she can see her breath billowing before her in the sweltering midsummer air.

"Dylan," Neria whispers.

Then she pulls it out of her pocket: Skye's bloodstained bubble pipe. She can't meet Dylan's gaze. She holds the pipe out in her upturned palm, and as soon as Dylan takes it from her, she brushes past him—hurries through the cottage door, down the wooden steps of the porch.

"What the hell?" Dylan croaks. "Neria—?"

Her face crumples. The shadows of the woods rear up invitingly, ready to swallow her. *I can't do this anymore.* Her shoulders start to shake.

"TURN AROUND AND LOOK ME IN THE EYES, NERIA!" Dylan roars from the porch.

That stops her. Like a red-hot poker stabbed through her ribcage, shattering her frozen-over heart. She looks over her shoulder at Dylan. He stands there on the steps of the porch, his gaze flicking from the bubble pipe in his hand to Neria. Back to the bubble pipe. Back to Neria.

She bites her lip. Dylan's trying to keep his voice level now, his expression impassive. "Please." He speaks with clipped desperation. "Just tell me."

Tears course down Neria's cheeks. *I can't do it.* She shakes her head, turns, and breaks into a run, sprinting into the trees. "Please," she finds herself saying as her feet pump into the ground, and she realizes she's speaking directly to the Skein. "Please take me somewhere nice this time. *Please.*"

The forest takes control—no need to think—*just run.* Her feet following a predetermined trail. Wading through greenery, trudging through brambles and over thick-creeping underbrush. Her nostrils pulsing with pine-smell.

Predestined.

She runs and runs until the woods run out, and the Skein spits her out onto the Wynd.

Panting heavily, she stops dead in her tracks, right where the woods begin.

They're coming down the middle of the street, a whole swarm of them, all dressed in black. So many of them—hundreds. All wearing expressionless white masks. Neria can't move. Her legs simply won't work. She can't tear her eyes away.

The cultists have already spotted her… some are starting to run toward her…

And there's Auntie August, darting out of the shadows to stand in the road between Neria and the Face of Pale.

"No!" Neria shouts.

Ara Augustine brandishes a long wooden staff in one hand. As Neria watches, her guardian swings the staff through the air, and the air around the staff distorts, shimmers, twists out of shape. There's a noise like a chord played on a detuned electric guitar, and the faces of Pale stagger and sway, losing their balance as their formation breaks.

Auntie August swings her staff at the cultist nearest to her—but even as she catches her target and knocks him down, another face is already coming up right behind her, raising a pistol to the back of her head, squeezing the trigger—

"NO!"

Neria doesn't even hear her own scream. It's like the sound came from far away. Her legs kick into motion, she barrels forward, but it's already over: Auntie August's staff clatters to the asphalt, and Neria's guardian collapses, her life spilling in torrents from the back of her head as the cult members close in around her.

Soon Neria can't even see her guardian's body, it's blocked by the thickening flood of cultists.

"Neria!"

Suddenly Barkface is standing between her and the advancing throng. "Run to the beach," he commands. With a snap of his fingers Neria's legs spur into motion. She turns, and her feet carry her back into the woods, with Barkface following right behind her, and the full might of the Face of Pale in pursuit.

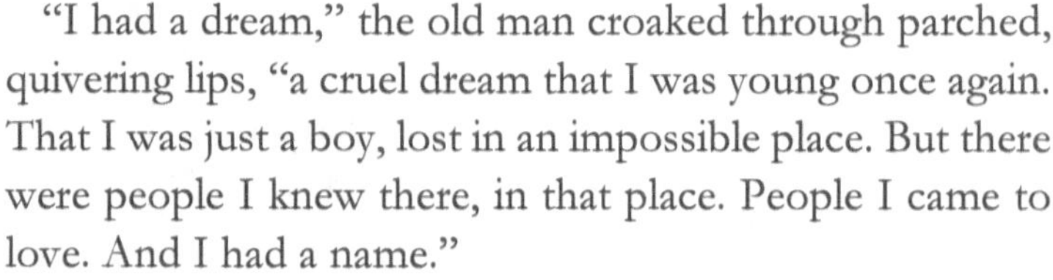

"I had a dream," the old man croaked through parched, quivering lips, "a cruel dream that I was young once again. That I was just a boy, lost in an impossible place. But there were people I knew there, in that place. People I came to love. And I had a name."

'You do have a name. Your name is Jack.'

He couldn't tell if she was lying or not. She lied a lot. But not always. She called it "playing games." And slowly, over the course of eons, the old man had learned that Rusalka, whatever she was, was keeping him as a pet.

He couldn't see her but she was always there, floating above him or hiding in the corners of his vision… or lurking somewhere inside him, gliding through his iced-over veins or slipping through the darkened, moldy corridors inside his head.

She laughed frostily. It was the same thing she told him, over and over again. She had been telling it to him for years now, decades. And once, long ago, he had believed her:

'Your name is Jack. You are a child.'

"LET ME GO!" he screamed. The cavernous abyss pitched his echo back at him. He tasted blood in his throat. He clambered laboriously to his feet; his legs were frail and trembling, but they held him up. He hobbled frantically away from Rusalka, into the darkness extending on all sides. He remembered dimly that there was nowhere to go. But he kept going all the same.

I'm gonna make it this time.

Her voice grew fainter and fainter behind him. The old man smiled grimly. He wasn't in the lantern room anymore—*couldn't* have been in the lantern room, because the lantern room was a tiny circular chamber at the top of a lighthouse, and he had been running for several minutes now. Running directly forward, into the darkness which unspooled endlessly.

By all logic and reason, he had gotten out. Somehow. He was free.

How long had it been? Hours? Days?

Seconds?

All of a sudden his legs gave out and he collapsed onto the cold stone floor. The sound his body made as it hit the floor was like stone striking stone.

He lifted his head... and there it was ahead of him, as it always was, as it always would be: the lighthouse lantern, shimmering with a cold, ghostly light.

Rusalka was there beside the lantern, her ancient face beaming ghoulishly. Her shark's mouth opened wide.

'Before long, my love, you will look just like me,' she said. *'And we will be wed at the ends of this world, under the divine light of a galaxy-rise.'*

She towered over him. The smell of her made him gag. Like rotting fish and creeping algae and putrefied seaweed.

'Consider yourself blessed. Not many of your kind get to live as long as you will. Few of your kind live beyond a century. But your eyes, my love, will see millennia.'

She held something up in front of his face. A shard of glass? No, a mirror.

He took the mirror, peered into it. His reflection stared back at him. It was pale and emaciated, tufts of thin white hair clinging in a desperate horseshoe to his craggy scalp. His skin hung off his face in folds, and his eyes were rimmed with red circles, and sunken so far back in his skull that he could barely see them.

Rusalka tossed the mirror shard away, stooped and kissed Jack. He drew back but there was no space behind him, he was pressed right up against a wall: the lantern room had shrunk back to its normal size again.

Rusalka puckered her shark's mouth and drew a second long, glacial kiss from his lips. A frigid wind swept through him, and he felt his skin tighten over his bones, felt it crack and split and flake away.

Blood in his throat again. Blood trickling out of the corner of his mouth. He touched a finger to his lips and it came away glistening and black like wet tar.

He could see his veins through the skin of his arm. Black veins.

He ran a finger over his scalp. The scant tufts of hair he had left came loose and fluttered to the floor like snowflakes.

'You're mine,' Rusalka hissed, and she stole away into the shadows.

She had built toys for him to play with. A plush doll as big as he was, with hair that changed colour, from red to brown to black to grey. It had two glittering opals for eyes and seashells for teeth, it wore a tattered jean jacket, and it ran from him whenever he got close to it.

He chased the doll away into the hungry darkness, and found himself surrounded by floating mirrors, hovering on all sides. Broken mirrors with jagged edges, reflecting his fragmented face back at him. They said things to him, the faces in the mirrors. *"This is the sleep you never wake up from,"* they said. *"This is the final sleep."*

"I don't *believe* you!"

He ran from them, the mirrors, but they were still there, dancing in the corners of his eyes. "Help!" he shrieked. "Someone! *Please!*"

And for a moment, just a moment, he would think of Neria, or of Dylan or Skye or Lucas, or sometimes of all four of them coming to his rescue…

But instead it was Rusalka. Only Rusalka. Always Rusalka.

'Don't be afraid, Jack. Fear paralyzes you.'

He knew her approach by the stench of rotting fish, and the feeling of ocean spray on his skin. And though he hated to admit it, in that moment it was reassuring to see her.

'You are a curious thing, my love.' She stroked his scalp, scratched his wrinkled, sagging skin with blackened nails. *'Curious, curious, curious.'*

The old man was ashamed to find that he was crying. "The mirrors," he choked. "The mirrors."

'Do the mirrors frighten you?'

He nodded miserably.

'Well, you will not have to worry about them anymore, my love.'

She was good on her word: the mirrors never troubled him again.

Rusalka left the old man alone in the dark after that, for a good long while. So he found a place on the floor at the base of the lantern, and lay there in the fetal position, listening to distant winds thrashing and colliding.

"Jack?"

The old man lifted his head an inch. A chill unlike anything he had ever felt before swept through him. Like a node of absolute coldness—zero degrees Kelvin—had been planted right in the center of his heart. He gasped, and saw his breath steaming before him in the pale glow of the lighthouse lantern.

She came limping toward him out of the dark. He recognized her face, vaguely, from an eroded memory of a dream he kept tucked away on a dusty shelf in the back of his mind.

"Jack," the girl croaked, and as the old man pushed himself up on his elbows he saw that she wasn't right. She had black hair, bangs low over her bright green eyes. She smiled a crooked, lopsided smile, and a trickle of blood emerged from the corner of her mouth, rolled down to her chin.

The name came to his grey lips. "Skye?"

She was wrapped up in her father's black trenchcoat, the one that was too big for her. The fabric was soaked with blood, and blood pooled out from under the folds of her coat, gathering thick and dark on the floor.

"You look awful," she said. And in the depths of the old man's mind something flared. *Her name is Skye. And I'm Jack.*

We're both Breckers.

"Don't be alarmed if I fall apart," said Skye. "It might happen. It's hard to hold myself together in this place."

"Skye," Jack murmured.

"Jack," said Skye.

"Jack…" the old man echoed, like it was a word he had never encountered in his life. Bracing himself on the lantern, he pulled himself to his feet. "Jack."

"Good god," said Skye. "What did she *do* to you?"

The old man furrowed his channeled, wrinkled brow. He glanced quickly from side to side, but he couldn't see Rusalka anywhere. *Is this another game?* he wondered.

Everything was a game to Rusalka.

"I… I don't know," he wheezed, squeezing the words out of a tightening throat. He scratched one of the bald patches on his scalp. "How did you get here? Why aren't you"—he gestured to himself—"like me?"

"Because I'm not getting any older than this," said the thing that was once Skye. She sighed. "They got me, Jack. In Greaves. Dad was there. They gave me to Pale." She paused. "For a while there, I swear I *was* Pale—or *part* of Pale, anyway. It's a horrible feeling, but—but it's also a *rush,* all of it. The screaming surrounding you on all sides. The pain while you're pinned in place—you can't move, you're paralyzed and god-awfully angry, so all you can do is scream along with the others."

"The others," the old man repeated. It was all he could muster.

"Yeah, well," Skye sighed. "My father killed a lot of people. So did yours. Like brother, like brother, huh?"

Jack said nothing.

"And Neria's father, he's the worst of them all. He *started* the whole thing. But anyway, it doesn't matter anymore. Not to me, anyway. 'Cause Rusalka came and got me. She found me and pulled me from the guts of the demon god, and trapped me here, before my soul could get to the After. She put me back together. She gave me new eyes."

The old man licked his parched lips. "Why is she doing this?"

Again Skye thought in silence for a moment before answering. "I don't think she means us harm," she said eventually. "But she... she doesn't understand. We're like pets to her." She wavered. "We have to get out of here, Jack. You know we do. She's not our friend."

The old man screwed up his time-ravaged face trying to puzzle it out. And then his eyes widened. "You left us," he gasped. "You and Lucas, you—you left us under the bridge."

A tear trickled from one of Skye's new eyes down her bone-pale cheek. "I'm so sorry, Jack. I dunno what to say, except..." She trailed off.

Jack's time-worn face shifted in the gloom of Rusalka's lair, and for a moment his wrinkles appeared to ebb, to fade. When he spoke his voice smouldered with the heat of youth. "Just tell me what happened," he said.

So Skye told him. She told him about how Lucas had shaken her awake... how she had gone with him, and...

As she told the story of what her father had done to her, the lines and the sag returned to Jack's face, until he was a slouched old man again, barely recognizable.

"We have to get back to Morgana Wynd," he whispered.

Skye chuckled, a dry, tragic sound. "Morgana Wynd is one place," she said. "There are other places out there. Better places. But—*listen* to me now. I want to make sure you remember who you are. You're Jack Brecker. Scurvy Jack. You have to remember that, no matter what else Rusalka does to you. Promise me you'll remember that."

"I—"

"Promise you'll remember. Don't let it slip away."

Jack approached Skye, raising his arms to embrace her. But Skye held her hand up. "No," she said.

"Why?" He couldn't help the question.

"Because I'll fall apart," she said. Her eyes were distant, unpolished gemstones. She reached for him. "Just—careful. Take my hand, but be very, *very* gentle."

Jack gingerly laced his fingers through his cousin's. Her skin felt strange, neither warm nor cold, and it didn't seem to have any texture. He could hardly feel her fingers against his.

"Skye."

"Yeah?"

"You can't be dead. You can't be. It's one of Rusalka's games, that's all. You—you *can't* be dead."

"I… I think I am, though." Skye swallowed loudly. "Having your eyes stabbed out *sucks*, by the way. Especially if it's your own father doing the stabbing. I don't recommend it. It's like—you know your body's permanently fucked up, all in an instant, you know what I mean? You know it's something you'll never get better from."

"Goddamn it, Skye—"

"Forget it." She gave a bitter, frustrated growl. "Just forget all of it." Scowling, she crossed her arms and pouted. "As if *that's* possible."

"Come on—"

"Whatever. Just—whatever, all right? Let's get out of here. I'm sick of this place."

"There's no way out."

"Of course there is. Close your eyes." Skye said it with such sudden tenderness that Jack couldn't have disobeyed. He closed his eyes.

"Remember that this is all just a big trick," Skye whispered, gesturing to the glowing lantern in front of them, the sprawling darkness surrounding them. "Nothing more. I know that seems impossible. But—"

'It is not a trick.'

Rusalka came drifting in from above like a feather, weaving unhurriedly back and forth through the air, her sail-sewn robes billowing as she lowered herself to the floor between Jack and Skye.

'Look at all I give you both,' she sighed. *'Such ungrateful* **wretches.***'* She landed on the floor before them. *'Go, then. You know the way out.'*

And in that moment they were standing in the lantern room of a lighthouse again, a room no bigger than the living room of the Changeling House. White-painted walls lit bright by the radiant lantern.

There came a squealing of rusty hinges: the old iron door swung open.

Jack stared agape at Rusalka. "This is definitely a trick," he mumbled.

"Shut up and hurry up," said Skye. "Don't look at her. Just—come on."

She tugged him gently over to the door, over the threshold to the landing. Jack couldn't help but glance back at Rusalka—twice.

Then they were descending the spiral staircase: slowly they went, cautiously, so that Skye wouldn't fall apart.

At the bottom of the stairs they found the door open, and emerged onto the barnacle-carpeted rocks of the islet. The air around them was heavy with the smell of the ocean, that acrid, salt-laced stench of algae and sea foam. A fat, swollen sun hovered just above the yellow-and-pink horizon.

Above, the sky was cornflower blue. Cloudless.

Behind them, the lighthouse door slammed shut with a groan and a CLANG!

This is too easy.

Jack inhaled the cool salty sea breeze. Colour began to return to his face, and his back straightened. "Skye," he said, and this time when he said her name it was with the voice of a fifteen year old boy.

Skye was standing over by the edge of the water, hugging herself. She didn't turn to look at Jack as he came to stand beside her.

"It's gone," she said. "It's all gone."

Jack squinted. She was right: there was no sign of the Morgana Peninsula. The rocky islet was surrounded by sprawling, empty ocean, beneath a sprawling, empty sky.

"I knew there was a catch," he muttered.

Standing at the edge of the rocks, staring through the water's glassy surface, down into the green depths, Jack and Skye lost themselves for a time.

"Where are we?" Jack ventured after a while.

"Outside of time and space as we know it," said Skye. "Somewhere *else.*"

Then she turned to him. "I have some time, before the cosmic winds carry me on to the next place." There were tears glimmering in her unpolished eyes again, blood dripping from her nostrils. "It's calling me, Jack. I wanna go back with you, to Morgana Wynd. But Morgana Wynd's in the real world. And I don't have a body there anymore." She sighed, wiping the blood from her face. "I'll stay here as long as I can, but… I dunno how much longer I can hang on for."

"What do you mean?"

"The After's calling. It's tugging at my soul. Like a magnet. You can't imagine what it's like. To feel it pulling at you, at every fiber of your being. I want to go…"

"No." Jack reached for her, but she flinched away. "Skye—you have to hang in there."

"It's like there's a part of me that knows what Skye Brecker would've said when she was alive. She would've said, 'I'll hang on with everything I've got, for as long as I can.' But that was when I had hot blood in my veins, and electricity running through my brain."

She was starting to flicker, like cold fire. Like static on an old TV. Jack turned to look at the lighthouse. He swallowed loudly.

"Come on, Skye. We can go back inside. Rusalka can— she can help—"

The words caught in his throat. His eyes stung.

Skye grimaced. "I'm not going back."

The sun was starting to slink below the horizon. Jack looked back at Skye, and the two of them lowered themselves down to sit on the rocks. They stared out over the water at the alien sunset, both trying to get ahold of their voices.

"I wish I'd spent five years hanging out with you and Dyl," Jack managed at last, trying to keep the quiver in his voice to a minimum. "Instead of wasting it, hiding from a lunatic in a place I hated."

"Forget about all that," said Skye.

Jack wavered. He chewed his lip. "Tell me what it's like, then. I know I won't understand, but—tell me."

"To be dead, you mean?" Skye offered a mirthless smile. "Well, it's cold. Everything's really cold. Besides that it's kinda the same as being alive, except… except you can hear this… *sound*. It's like distant singing, it's warm and welcoming, filled with light and—and love. I know it sounds corny, I don't think there's a way I could describe it that wouldn't sound corny, but… but I want to be there so badly, Jack. It's like it's the only thing I've ever wanted. And all I have to do, to be there, is *let go.*"

"Skye—god damn it, *no!*" Jack's voice spiked to a helpless shriek, and he turned to look his undead cousin right in the eyes, understanding even as the words left his mouth how unfair they were. "There's so much more we're supposed to do. Back in Morgana Wynd—we need Admiral Bloodskye and Professor Skye High and—you have to come back—you can't—"

"Stop. *Stop* it. None of this was ever a game, Jack. It's real life."

"For Dylan, then. For your *brother.* You *have* to."

She shook her head sullenly. "It's done. It's non-negotiable now."

Jack drew in a deep breath.

"Then I'll come with you," he declared somberly.

"Don't you *dare.*" Skye rose shakily to her feet, then carefully leaned over to stick her face in Jack's, so that he couldn't look away from her poison-green stare. "Don't you dare follow me, Jack Brecker. You have to go back to Morgana Wynd. Tell Dyl what happened. Tell him—tell him I'll miss him, wherever I'm going. And just—remember me, will you? Tell people about what happened. Tell 'em about what I did, when it all went to shit. Actually, you know what?" She smiled, and it was a real smile this time, full and ripe and glad. "Make something up. Tell a good story."

Jack tried to say something, tried to say anything at all. But he couldn't.

"Goodbye, Scurvy Jack," said Skye.

She turned away from her cousin and walked toward the edge of the rocks. The lighthouse door went *creeeeaaaAAAKkkk* behind them as the breeze toyed with it. Jack shot a fleeting glance back at it. He watched the door swinging side to side on its hinges. Beckoning him.

When he turned back to look at Skye, she was already gone. There was nothing left of Jack's cousin except the black leather trenchcoat floating on the waves.

The sun was gone. The sky was a crisp moonless black, speckled with plump stars. Before Jack the ocean became a vast mirror and reflected the night sky. He went to stand at the edge of the rocks. He let his gaze wander.

The stars. They wheeled and danced through the sky above him, and below him in the crystalline water's depths. There were constellations he had never seen or heard of before arcing across twin night skies, one high above, the other far beneath the waves.

It seemed to Jack that if he simply dove into the waves, and swam down far enough, he would be able to reach those stars.

His breath came sharply in the obscurity, jagged like the blade of a knife. He turned to look at the lighthouse, saw that the door was wide open. Rusalka was there in the doorway, her lurid gaze fixed on him.

A tattered old witch, advancing now toward him over the rocks.

I **knew** *it was a game.*

Jack turned away from Rusalka, and saw that in the place where Skye's trenchcoat had been a moment before, floating on the waves, there was now a familiar-looking raft. Tree trunks bound together with rope.

He walked right up to the edge of the rocks and squinted at the raft. It looked solid enough.

'Jack,' she said, behind him.

He stepped onto the raft. It bucked and listed under his feet—he dropped to his knees to regain some balance, gripping the bound tree trunks with both hands. Already the tide was pulling him out, away from the rocky islet. Away from Rusalka.

He stared at her as she stood there on the rocks, watching as the raft carried him further and further. He couldn't help but smile as Rusalka shrank and shrank, and before long she was gone, and he was alone on a vast, quiet, faraway sea.

The ocean breathed. Slow muscular waves rising and falling like the chest of a sleeping giant, buoying the raft, rocking it gently back and forth. Back and forth.

The stars howled silently in the moonless sky above. Jack lay on his back and stared up at them. He tried to pick out constellations he recognized, but found none.

Where am I?

He remembered what Skye had said. *Somewhere* **else**.

He woke to find that he had run aground: the raft had washed up on a sandbank, a little bar of pale beige sand crouching on the water, surrounded by endless blue prairies of ocean. The sun was rising like a sweet, rotting grapefruit, bathing him in pleasant amber light.

What?

Jack rolled off the raft, into warm, ankle-deep water, and clambered unsteadily onto the sandbank. Overhead the sky was clear. Everything was deathly quiet. There was no wind. The surface of the ocean was completely still.

Doldrums.

Jack licked his lips. *I need water.*

The sun heaved itself higher and higher, its light becoming harsher, less welcoming. He could hear his heart beating, skidding and thudding in his ears. *Thump-thump. Thump-thump. Thump-thump.*

It was getting louder. *Thump thump.* Heavier. *Thump.* Slower. *Thump. Thump. Thump… thump….* It wasn't a heartbeat anymore, it was horse's hooves. *Clop. Clop. Clop. Clop.* The sun deepened to a baleful orange as a smoky haze crossed in front of it.

Jack squinted out over the water. *There.* Coming toward him. A white horse.

It trotted silently on the surf. Its hooves didn't sink beneath the waves—they landed on the water as though it were transparent stone.

Someone was sitting on the horse's back. A man, it looked like. A bald man. He was wearing a grey cloak.

Jack's stomach plunged into his guts.

As the horse and rider drew nearer to the sandbank, he saw that the horse's hide was made of white scales. Its hooves squelched in the wet sand.

They stopped several yards away from Jack. Now that the rider was up close, Jack could see that he had no face. Just a featureless mask of smooth, bare white flesh, and two gaping black holes where his eyes should have been.

"Am I dead?" Jack asked. His voice was like sandpaper against rust.

The faceless horseman cocked his head to the side. Then he slid off the back of the horse, and landed gracefully on the sand. He approached Jack, pulling a flask from within the folds of his grey cloak. He uncorked the flask and handed it to Jack, who raised it to his lips and tipped it back.

Fresh cold water spilled into his mouth, slicked down his throat, coated the inside of his stomach.

"Thank you," Jack gasped.

Then he drank again. He drank and drank, and only once the flask was empty did he hand it back to the faceless rider.

The rider capped the flask and slid it back into his cloak.

"Who are you?" Jack asked, though he suspected he already knew the answer.

The horseman reached again into his cloak, and drew out something else. Jack's heart skidded. It was a knife. A long, shiny, silver blade.

The faceless rider handed the knife hilt-first to Jack, and then gestured to his own featureless head. He drew a line with a long, bony finger across his face, a few inches beneath his eye-holes.

Jack understood what he was supposed to do. Before he could stop to think too much about it, he brought the knife forward—dug it into the flesh of the horseman's featureless face, about two-thirds of the way down, and pulled it slowly through the flesh. Thick, red blood oozed out.

Jack carved a straight gouge from left to right across the rider's face. Blood spattered onto the sand at their feet.

The horseman took the knife back from Jack and placed it once again in the folds of his cloak. Then his face split at the gash Jack had carved, split wide into a ghoulish smile. A tongue emerged from inside the gash, long and snake-like, and it licked the blood from around the newly-carved mouth.

'I am Pale,' the horseman said. His voice was coarse and gravelly yet gentle, and Jack knew he had heard it somewhere before, a long time ago. Pale's snake-tongue darted out again, licked away another trickle of blood. *'Your father serves me well, Jack Brecker. Blood, body, mind, and soul. I could not have asked for more from a servant.'*

"Is he dead?" said Jack.

Pale gave a deep chuckle. *'No. My followers are not rewarded for their loyalty with death. While I live, they live.'* Pale tapped his naked breast with an ashy, nailless finger. *'Inside me. Part of me—I am them, and nothing more.'* As he spoke his face shifted, melted—blurred and filled with colour, and suddenly it was Jacob Brecker's face staring at Jack from atop the horseman's shoulders. *'And I am everywhere.'*

Jack's hands clenched into fists, and his field of vision was painted in shades of red. *Don't do it.* But he couldn't help himself—he was already striding across the sand, winding up, launching his fist into the side of his father's face. His knuckles connected with what felt like cold marble, and he screamed as the bones of his hand crunched out of place.

"I'm gonna *kill* you!"

His scream dwindled to a moan. He fell to his knees in the soft sand in front of the thing called Pale.

'You waste your strength. You cannot destroy me.' Pale was speaking with more voices than one now, several voices tied up thick and tight, like a dreadlock. He walked back to his scaled horse, swung himself effortlessly up onto it, and stared at Jack.

His mouth had vanished. Only his blank holes-for-eyes remained.

The scaled horse turned and trotted off over the surface of the waves. Soon both horse and rider sank beneath the waves, and were gone.

————— ••◆•• —————

Jack paced the sandbank from end to end, keeping to the water's edge, his feet submerged up to his ankles the whole way. The water was pleasantly warm.

The sky overhead was the steady blue of daytime, uninterrupted by clouds. Pure blue. But there was no sign of the sun—the sun had gone away some time ago. It had merely been a tourist sun, a visiting star strolling merrily through on its way to better places.

Still, it had left behind a pleasant warmth in the air. Jack looked down, frowned and blinked. Was his mind playing tricks, or was the sand at his feet *moving?* Currents of it coiling this way, that way around the sandbank?

Then, right in front of him, the sand began to shift. It bubbled, rising in small, formless waves, as though giant invisible hands were playing with it, shaping and molding it.

Soon the sand took on recognizable forms: sand-hands grasping for the sky. Sand-faces pushing up out of wet sand, screaming silently before dissipating.

Then she rose to her feet.

She was small, human-shaped, featureless like a mannequin. A girl made of sand. She drew herself gingerly to her feet. At first Jack thought she was going to collapse. She didn't look strong enough to support herself.

But she *was* strong enough. She limped toward him, and as she approached him her features began to solidify. A nose. Ears. A mouth opening in a bewildered O.

"Skye?" Jack breathed.

The sand-girl slowed. She sank to her knees, buried her head in her hands.

"Neria?"

She was beginning to crumble, pieces of her breaking away, the sand falling back into place on the beach.

Jack sat down cross-legged next to her. He put a hand around her sand-shoulders, and she rested her head against his leg. "I think I'm lost," he told her.

He wanted nothing more, in that moment, than to be back in Morgana Wynd, in the Changeling House.

The Changeling House, where Simon ,Solomon and Syrena Sturgess died. Where Jack had watched his uncle punch a sixteen-year-old girl in the gut. Where his father had wrapped him up in duct tape.

The Changeling House is over.

The sand-girl was almost gone now. There was barely anything left of her but a few mounds of sand that almost looked like a person. Jack craned his head back, and stared up into the interminable blue of the sunless sky.

Where am I?

The sand was cushiony beneath him. He curled up, pulling his knees to his chest, and let the gentle rustling of nearby waves lull him to sleep...

———— •·◆·• ————

He awoke in Rusalka's arms.

Her fingers gripped him tight, digging cold and vice-like into his flesh. She smiled down at him, sadistic joy creasing her sagging, papery skin.

'I've got you, my love,' she murmured. *'You've had ample time to play. It's time you came home.'*

Chapter Sixteen: The Jericho Cascade

Neria can't see straight. Her chest heaves with sobs. Her vision is all blurry.

"We have to go back!" she shrieks. "*Please!*"

But she can't move her arms. Her bewitched legs carry her forward, only forward. Barkface walks behind her, wearing a hardened expression. He's not a stooped old man anymore: he's tall and barrel-chested, with thick brown hair and a long brown beard. Someone who didn't know him might have guessed that he was in his thirties.

"I said *stop!* Let me GO!" Neria writhes against her invisible bonds, but it's no use. "SOMEBODY HELP!"

Barkface shakes his head sadly. The beach appears up ahead through the trees.

"We have to go back, we can't just *leave* her there! Barkface, *listen* to me! *Please!*" Neria's voice breaks, and Barkface's guts twist into bitter knots. "We can't just leave her there!"

"She's gone, Neria."

"I don't care, we can't *leave* her back there!"

"Ara Augustine," Barkface mutters bitterly, "died in service of a mission, all right? All we can do now is finish what we've started. I know it's awful, but it's what she wanted."

"Bull*shit!* What she *wanted?* She wanted to live! She wanted to get rid of me, and she wanted to live!"

They emerge onto the sand. Neria's breath catches in her throat as feeling returns to her legs and arms. *Run! Go!*

But she's rooted to the spot. She can only stare.

Out over the water, the sky has opened up. Never in her life has she seen anything like it. The horizon blazes with every colour imaginable, apocalyptic streaks of reds and golds, greens and pinks, purples, silvers, and shimmering blues.

"There," Barkface whispers, and even he can't keep the awe out of his voice. He points to the ship crawling over the waves toward the peninsula: a colossal galleon with seven masts, towering against the shrieking sky. The ship is large enough to carry an entire city on its deck, crouching beneath its seven spectral masts: an eclectic cluster of towers and mansions, shacks and huts, villas and temples.

For a moment Neria manages to forget that Auntie August is gone. Barkface guides her across the sand; they come to a halt near the water's edge. Neria stares, agape. Is it just her, or is the ship made of glass? Look, now, how the light of the impossible sky comes sieving through the sails, the masts, the hull, as though this impossibly massive galleon is only half-there.

On the ship's side, in great gleaming letters:

THE JERICHO CASCADE

The sun sails high above them on a sea of shadowy clouds, and a bridge of shimmering sunlight extends from the galleon to the shore.

And… is that a *person?* Neria squints. Yes, she's seeing clearly: a silhouette crossing the sunlight bridge, walking nimbly on the tops of the waves as though the bridge is actually solid.

"How?" Neria gasps.

"They're oneironauts," says Barkface. "They're from a different realm altogether, a wilder realm than this one. The rules of our world don't always apply to them."

"O-neiro-nauts," Neria echoes numbly.

Barkface smiles sadly. "It's time to go home," he says.

Neria's gaze flicks to the lighthouse sitting innocuously out on the water.

"No." She turns back to her father. "No way."

"I believe you will want to, Neria," an ethereal voice says.

Neria and Barkface turn in unison to see the newcomer step off the sunlight bridge onto the sand of the beach. The leader of the oneironauts strides purposefully toward them. She's tall. *Too* tall. She's got piercing amber eyes. She's bald, and beneath plated pale gold armour she wears sky-blue robes with golden-red trim, which ripple like enchanted water in the wind.

She proffers a hand. "My name," she says, "will be of no use to us right now. For all intents and purposes you may call me Alaya Vale." She speaks with some sort of accent—but it's not an accent, exactly, is it? No, it's a certain *curve* to her words, a bend, like she's straining to form them. Like she isn't accustomed to speaking with her mouth.

"I am the captain of the *Jericho Cascade*," Alaya Vale says. "Your mother, Anora Vale, was my sister. You are my niece. I have waited a long, long time to meet you."

Neria doesn't shake Alaya's hand. "My mother's dead," she snarls. "And so is Auntie August."

Alaya nods slowly. "By that you mean Ara Augustine. I am aware of her passing. Know that she did not die needlessly. Her sacrifice will serve a greater purpose." Alaya leans in closer to Neria, and lowers her voice in a way that Neria figures she's supposed to find reassuring. "Neria, please allow me to escort you to the *Cascade*. The rest of us have been eagerly awaiting your return. We have prepared a banquet in your honour."

A banquet?

Alaya turns to Barkface. "There is a place for you onboard, too, should you be inclined to accept it."

Barkface blinks. "Me?" he says.

"NO!" Neria's almost shouting now. "We *can't* leave! Not yet!"

Alaya turns back to Neria, stares imperiously down at her. "You're going home, young one. This world is not for you, just as it was not for your mother. You are one of us. You will sail with us, over the edge of the world, across the Circling River and into the Unspeakable Beyond." Alaya Vale smiles a kind, stern smile. *This is not negotiable.* "You belong with us."

Neria looks to Barkface for help. "But I still have to—"

"Quiet, Neria." Barkface speaks softly but firmly. Then he turns back to the oneironaut. "The Face of Pale is here," he says. "We have a chance to destroy them." He swallows loudly. "Will you help us?"

For a moment Alaya says nothing, just stares at Barkface with an expression of aloof bemusement.

"There are enough of you to make a difference," Barkface continues, gesturing to the massive ship out on the water. "That's why I called you here. To help us end this madness once and for all."

Alaya shakes her head sadly. "No."

"But…" Barkface falters, and in the unearthly light Neria can see the lines on his face deepening, his hair thinning as his eyeballs strain out of his head.

He's losing.

Neria turns to look past Alaya and Barkface, at the sunlight bridge stretching from the edge of the sand to the

Cascade. There are more people crossing the bridge. Neria squints. Six of them, she counts.

"Please." Barkface drops his voice to a whisper. "Help me."

"My people are not yours to order into battle," Alaya intones somberly. "You must remember that we are not peddlers of vengeance, nor agents of justice. We have tasted war before—many times, over many of what you would call lifespans. But we have since renounced all warfare. We are peacekeepers. It is what the Universal Continuum always intended for us to be. We are refugees from a peaceful world, long gone now. *Peacekeepers.* Not soldiers. We will do our duty as *peacekeepers.* And then we will be done with this world forever. It is a primitive, violent place."

Barkface wavers on his feet.

"They're here," says Neria.

Barkface and Alaya both look over their shoulders to see the Face of Pale emerging from the woods, a swarm of black clothes and white masks melting out of the trees and onto the sand. They walk unhurriedly. Calmly. Confidently.

They think they've won already.

Six oneironauts step off the sunlight bridge onto the beach, and gather purposefully behind Alaya.

"We will attempt to negotiate with the Face of Pale," Alaya growls, turning back to Barkface. "Keep the girl safe until we're through with this."

Neria winces. *The girl.*

"You can't negotiate with them," says Barkface.

"We are quite persuasive," Alaya Vale retorts. "We have had practice." She turns to the six oneironauts gathered behind her. "Go on," she commands. "I will follow."

The shortest of the oneironauts stands seven feet tall, the tallest pushing nine feet. They all sport colourful ankle-length robes, sky-blue with golden-red trim, over which they wear that polished unscratched armour of pale gold: breastplates, helmets, gauntlets, greaves and boots inlaid with glittering gemstones. Not one of them carries a visible weapon.

In unison the oneironauts turn and begin marching across the white sand, toward the cult waiting patiently down the beach, a dark, seething mass, like a stormcloud pulled down to Earth.

Tramp-tramp-tramp go the oneironauts' gold boots in the sand.

"We fought in the Battle on the Great Rings of Rah," Alaya continues. "We led a raid on the Snow Jungle of Uncorona to unseat a royal usurper. We took up arms against the Wicked King of Winter in the War of a Thousand Suns. We know war, Neil Faulken, so do not accuse us of shirking our duties or of cowardice. This is not war. This is a mistake. We will do what we can to help—but this is *your* mess to clean up. Do not forget that."

With that, Alaya turns and sweeps away, breaking into a jog to catch up with her six fellow oneironauts.

"Come on, Neria."

Barkface's hand closes around Neria's wrist. He pulls her gently after him, and she lets him lead her in the opposite direction of the oneironauts. The two of them stop once they reach the shade of the trees, out of sight of the Face of Pale.

"I'm not going with them," Neria mumbles. She tries to wrench herself out of her father's grasp, but he's holding her too tight.

"Neria," Barkface says.

She turns to look up at her father, at his seven-foot height, his massive elk antlers, and the mossy mane where he once sported a wispy white beard. "Dad?" she breathes.

"Listen, it seems I've made a bit of a miscalculation," he says.

"What?"

"The *Jericho Cascade* has over six thousand oneironauts on board. That's enough to make a difference. But they're not gonna help us." He pauses, then adds, ponderously: "This isn't good."

"No, it sure fucking isn't!" Neria mutters.

"We lured the Face of Pale here to see them destroyed. That was always the plan."

Neria turns to stare at her father. She glares into his stony green-brown eyes. "You lured everyone here," she spits. "The Face of Pale, the *Jericho Cascade,* me and Auntie August—all so you could erase your mistakes from history. You're sick, Dad. You're sick. And I'm tired of playing your nightmare games. Now let—*go*—of—me!" She jerks her wrist hard, and Barkface relinquishes her so suddenly that she stumbles back, loses her footing and lands on her backside in the sand.

"You have every right to feel that way, Neria Nightshade." There's a casual cruelty in the way Barkface says it. He steps forward, offers a hand, but Neria pulls herself to her feet on her own.

"Don't ever call me that again," she snarls, dusting sand from her shirt, jacket and pants.

Barkface blinks, then nods. "You're right," he says. "I'm sorry." He wavers. "I have one last request to ask of you. Father to daughter. Please."

For a moment Neria considers not turning to look at him again—considers just walking away stiff-backed into the woods.

Instead she turns to stare over the water at the lighthouse. Steadfast sentinel.

"Show me your real self, then," she says, at last, through gritted teeth. She squeezes her eyes shut, and when she opens them again, and turns to look at Barkface, it's just an old, old man she sees before her, stoop-backed and canyon-faced. Sunken eyes glimmering with old fire and rimmed with darkness. Hair like white snow suspended in midfall.

He approaches her slowly, like he's trying not to spook a wild animal. Like he's afraid his daughter will bolt at a single wrong move.

"One final request," he says. "It might save the day."

Shouts sound from down the beach. Neria cringes. So does Barkface. But neither one of them looks away from the other.

Barkface reaches into the folds of his tattered cloak. From one of its inner pockets he extracts a little glass vial filled with sand.

"Go to the lighthouse," he instructs Neria. "You'll be able to get inside—you know how to cross over, I've seen you do it. Go in and find Rusalka. The bonds I placed her under were damaged when Jack broke the hourglass, but they were not destroyed entirely. She will answer the call."

A wave of dizziness overwhelms Neria. "What?" she croaks.

"Twenty-seven steps north of this tree here, waiting on the edge of the treeline"—Barkface lowers his voice to a gentle murmur as he pats the trunk of a nearby tree—"you'll find a canoe that I recovered from the ocean floor.

Take it to the lighthouse. Go to Rusalka, and tell her we need her help. Tell her the Face of Pale must be destroyed today, or there might never be another chance."

"And what if I just turn around and run away from here as fast as I can, instead?"

"Then I'll send you to the lighthouse by force. Do not underestimate me. This is no time to be selfish."

All Neria can do is shake her head, incredulous.

Then Barkface steps back from her and opens his mouth, and a strange sound emerges, a resounding birdcall that Neria can't identify. Moments later, something rustles behind them—Neria wheels around just in time to see Dylan emerging from the foliage. He's got a machete in one hand and a long wooden staff in the other. His face is drawn and pallid, his eyes ringed with red circles. His long shaggy hair is messier than usual.

"*Dylan?*"

Neria sees it all again. The highway. The bone-white tree. Skye's body swaying in the breeze. Blood soaking into the roots of the tree.

"Get out of here!" she snaps at Dylan. Then she wheels on Barkface. "Leave him out of this!"

"No. I want to help." Dylan strides over to them and hands Barkface the wooden staff. Then he slips the machete into a leather sheath on his belt. "I want to end the Face of Pale. For Skye."

Neria opens her mouth, only to find she's got no words left.

For Skye.

"Don't worry about us, Neria," says Barkface. He turns, points down the beach. "Observe."

The three of them watch as the dark mass of the Face of Pale closes in around the seven bright-robed negotiators.

In one fell swoop the oneironauts are swallowed up by the stormcloud. The cultists' weapons, axes and knives and guns, flash like lightning in the maw of the storm, glinting in the glow of the impossible dusk.

Screams and shouts drift across the sand.

"This is it." Leaving the cover of the trees, Barkface strides out onto the sand. "The lighthouse, Neria." He speaks without turning around, without pausing in his tracks. "Dylan will accompany you."

Neria turns to Dylan, and tries to meet his gaze, but she can't, her throat's closed up and she stares down at the sand.

"Come on," says Dylan, with such unexpected tenderness that Neria's eyes fill with tears. He places a hand on her shoulder. "It's almost over."

All she can do is nod.

She and Dylan walk over to the tree Barkface indicated. "North," Neria mutters. They start walking north— following the treeline. *One. Two. Three. Four...*

"So what's it like having a shapeshifting wizard for a dad?" Dylan says.

...nine, ten...

"*My* dad's a murdering pyscho, so you can see why I'd be envious—"

"Let's just count the steps, okay?" Neria croaks.

...seventeen, eighteen, nineteen...

"Just trying to be a light in a dark place," Dylan grumbles.

*...twenty-five. Twenty-six. Twenty-***seven!**

And then it's right in front of them, sitting just beyond the treeline. Wrapped in vines, crusted with barnacles. The gold lettering still gleams faintly on the side: *WYVERN.*

"The—the cult," says Neria. "They can't see us, can they?"

"I think they're busy," says Dylan. "We're in the clear."

The two of them carry the canoe down to the water's edge, and Neria pushes it out onto the waves. She and Dylan leap into the boat, where they find a pair of oars waiting for them.

They start rowing. Neither of them says a word during the crossing to the lighthouse. It doesn't take long to reach the sloping rocky shore of the islet.

"Keep watch," Neria instructs Dylan as she climbs over the rocks toward the lighthouse.

"Neria."

She squeezes her eyes shut for a second, then turns to look at Dylan. His face is drawn and chalky, but he offers a smile. Neria wants to believe it. But she doesn't.

"Be careful," Dylan says. "Don't get lost in there."

"I won't be long."

"If anyone comes—how do I warn you?"

"Just keep watch, okay?" Neria reaches into her pocket, pulls out the star marble. "Take this," she says.

Dylan accepts the star marble, cupping it gingerly in his palms and gazing in fascination at it. Neria turns to face the lighthouse door. It's hanging slightly ajar... or does it just look that way, in the light from the strange unnatural sunrise?

Are the shadows playing tricks on her?

Does it even matter?

You know how to cross over. I've seen you do it.

She walks to the door, pulls on the handle; and it's not that the door opens, but the shadows lengthen, and she realizes that she can just slide right on through.

Dark inside the lighthouse. The spiral staircase whirls dizzily above her.

Neria takes the steps two, three, four at a time. Round and round and round, step after step after step. *How long does this go on for?* It occurs to her that the stairwell might never end—might only spin higher and higher into the desolate night above, passing beyond the stars and finally, after an eternity, losing itself in the unending blackness.

No, there's something up above her now. A light?

She reaches the landing at the top of the stairs. A door before her, swinging ajar. Neria pulls it wide, and walks through, into the lantern room.

There's Rusalka, perched on top of the lantern in the center of the room, bleach-white hair falling down in front of her face. White, pupil-less eyes boring straight into Neria.

Neria holds the vial of sand up in front of her.

'Smash it on the floor, child. It is useless.'

"I don't think so." Neria's grip on the vial tightens. "*This* is the reason you're going to listen to what I have to say."

Rusalka cocks her head to the side. Her giggle sounds like seagulls screaming. *'And what is it that you have to say?'*

Neria wavers. "You're still bound by my father's spell. He sent me here. He needs your help. He's fighting the Face of Pale out there." She points through the floor-to-ceiling glass window of the lantern room, at the mass of clotted darkness on the white sand, the *Jericho Cascade* out on the water, and the mad sky blazing behind it all. "But they can't fight them on their own. With your help, though…" She trails off. "You have to help them. You don't have a choice."

Rusalka swoops from her perch atop the lantern, arcing through the air to hover right in front of Neria. *'Don't I?'*

Her icy fingers fall on Neria's shoulders. *What are they fighting for, my love? Do you know?'*

When Neria doesn't answer, Rusalka continues: *'It's because of you. It's for* **you** *that they are killing each other out there. Look at them.'*

"You—you—" Neria growls, her voice becoming viscous with anger. "What the hell even are you, anyway?"

It's only then that she spots it. *A shadow in a reflection on a windowpane in the corner of someone's eye.*

She turns on her heel, so fast that she stumbles, trips, and has to steady herself against the lantern in the center of the room.

"No," she breathes. "No, no, no, no…"

But he's right there, leaning against the wall. Old beyond old, a corpse that's still breathing. Skin stretched tight over warped bones. Eyes milky and unseeing. And a face so wrinkled, so rotted away that she barely recognizes him—

Barely.

The vial of sand slips from Neria's fingers, shatters on the floor at her feet.

She screams.

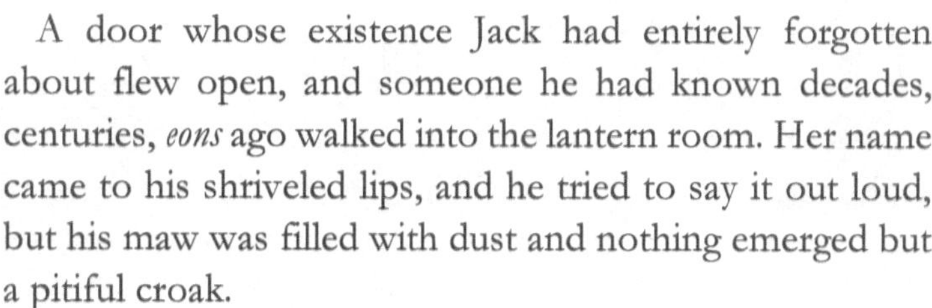

A door whose existence Jack had entirely forgotten about flew open, and someone he had known decades, centuries, *eons* ago walked into the lantern room. Her name came to his shriveled lips, and he tried to say it out loud, but his maw was filled with dust and nothing emerged but a pitiful croak.

Focus.

The girl screamed, and the sound dug talons into his chest, raked claws across his heart.

She rushed toward him, but slowed as she neared him. She hesitated a moment, before crouching beside him and taking his geriatric hand in hers.

Rusalka loomed over them, grinning a savage grin with her shark's mouth.

'You cannot help him,' she whispered. *'He is beyond saving.'*

Jack stared at the girl standing in front of him. His jaw hung agape, his teeth yellowed and crooked, drool spilling onto the collar of his soiled shirt.

He stared at Neria, and he wanted nothing more in that moment than to hug her and tell her it was all going to be okay.

Neria.

Her tattered jean jacket. Her amber eyes rimmed with dark circles. Her shifting red hair falling in front of her face.

Jack couldn't move.

He couldn't do a thing.

Neria's grip tightened on his hand, and with her other hand she pressed two fingers to his neck to try to find his pulse.

"Hang in there, Jackdaw," she whispered.

Then she turned to face Rusalka. "I'm not afraid of you," she spat.

Rusalka cackled a trickster's cackle.

"You don't have any power over me," Neria continued. "You're not real. You're just someone else's nightmare. *His* nightmare." She pointed straight at Jack. "I'm not afraid of nightmares, especially when they're not my own. But *you* should be afraid." She swallowed. "You should be afraid of me because—"

'I am not afraid of you in the slightest. You are minuscule.'

"You *should* be afraid of me, because you destroyed someone I love."

'*You know nothing of love, child.*'

"Yes I—"

'*I have watched you since you first arrived on Morgana Wynd.*' Rusalka pointed to Jack again. '*You know nothing of love, and yet here, before me, you pretend to? You puzzle me.*'

Neria drew in a sharp, painful breath. "Well, I'm not here for him. I'm here because you still have a debt to pay my father."

'*Your father?*'

"You know who my father is. He needs your help."

'*No, child.* **You** *need my help. You did not choose for any of this to happen. You did not choose bloodshed. You did not choose for those people out there*'—Rusalka gestured to the window—'*to fight for you. They chose all of that. Your father, and his cult, and those visitors who came on the* Jericho Cascade. *Even Ara Augustine. They all chose blood, and death, and hate. But not you, Neria. You chose nothing of the sort. You* **are** *nothing of the sort.*'

Jack gritted his corroded teeth. If he could only muster the energy to *speak*…

"I—but I—" Neria broke off. "No, you're right." Her face crumpled, but she kept going. "I'm so tired of running. And not only that. I'm just—so—*tired.*"

Rusalka smiled with her shark's mouth. '*I have watched the goings-on of this strange, strange place for a long time,*' she said. '*I have come to admire you. You have something that many others do not. And I can help you. I can stop all of this madness.*'

"You can?"

'*I can hide you. I can make it so they will never find you.*'

Jack realized that neither Neria nor Rusalka was watching him anymore.

It took all of his strength—*all* of it, every last fiber, every pore, every atrophied muscle straining against the massive weight pinning him to the cold stone floor.

Up.

He rose slowly. Shakily. Fell back to lean against the wall as his knees knocked together—but remained standing.

Rising is the hardest part.

He started limping across the lantern room.

Rusalka tilted her head back, pointed up at the ceiling. *'I can scatter you,'* she murmured to Neria. *'Scatter you to the winds of time, to the unending heights and the most distant depths, to the furthest reaches of the cosmos and further still, so that no matter how hard they look, even if they scour every corner of the Earth, they will never find you. They will never catch you.'*

"But—"

'You will be everywhere and nowhere. You will be within everything, but you will be hidden from sight, hidden from everyone save those who know what to look for. And perhaps… perhaps the world will be just a tiny bit brighter for it.'

Rusalka turned to face Jack, her milky eyes dug into his soul and his legs folded beneath him. He slammed onto the floor, screaming in agony. Pain flooded him like he had never felt before, white-hot and eternal.

Rusalka turned back to Neria.

'You are a child of more than one world. Do you know where you belong?'

Jack couldn't move. Couldn't feel his arms or his legs. Rising again was out of the question.

Don't do it, Neria.

"Nowhere," Neria said, with sickening certainty, "and everywhere."

Rusalka laughed, then, and it seemed to Jack that she never stopped laughing, that it went on forever, an everlasting cackle that had existed before the universe began and would be the only thing left after the stars went out and all of time and space collapsed.

But somehow Neria was there beside him again, after the end of the universe, crouching next to him as he lay curled and broken on the floor of the lantern room. The smell of her snuck into his brain as she took his head in her hands.

Her fingers traced patterns on his wasted face. She kissed him on his withered lips, her hot breath spilling down his throat and into his altered depths.

"You don't think I'd really do it, do you, Jackdaw?" she whispered.

She kissed him again, and this time he kissed her back, and pushed himself up on his elbows so he could kiss her for longer.

Neria wrapped her arms around Jack and pulled him closer, as the mask of age began to retreat from his face, the colour returning to his cheeks, the wrinkles fading. His white hair became grey, then grey-brown, then brown with a silver streak, and it grew to cover his entire scalp once more.

Neria drew back from Jack, far enough that she could pull his face into focus. She smiled for him, warm and tired, and her amber eyes crackled like hearty campfires.

She helped him to his feet and took his hand in hers. Jack's back cracked as he stood up straight for the first time in what felt like at least a lifetime.

"Don't say a word," Neria whispered.

Then, keeping a firm grip on Jack's hand, she turned away from him and fixed her gaze on Rusalka, who was hovering in the darkness nearby. Watching them. As Rusalka always was.

"He's leaving," Neria declared. "He's not yours to play with anymore."

Rusalka drifted slowly toward Jack and Neria. *Leaving?*

Neria nodded.

In my time here, on this little island, Rusalka said, *three people have come to see me, besides the two of you. Do you know who they are?*

Jack frowned.

"My father's one of them," said Neria.

Something twitched deep inside Jack. "This is a trick," he said. "It's always a trick with you, Rusalka. Isn't it?"

The accusation hung in the air, an echo that didn't want to fade.

Neil Faulken was the first. He deceived me. He took a piece of me, and bound my consciousness to the body of his dead wife. Your mother, the oneironaut.

Neria swayed, but Jack's grip on her hand tightened, and with his other hand he gripped her shoulder to steady her.

The next people to come see me were Jacob and Gabriel Brecker. They asked me if I could help them. They wanted to bring their god to life, to make it real: a physical, breathing organism. I told them I could help them. But they would have to give me something in return.

Rusalka was staring right at Jack now.

It was you, Jack Brecker. The Face of Pale would hand you over to me, and I would plant a god inside you. Those were the terms. And I intended to honour them, until I laid eyes upon you. I decided the god they had fashioned was not worthy of you. And I could not possibly let them condemn you to such a heinous fate. So I brought you here, instead.

Jack stared back at Rusalka. He stared into her impossibly ancient face, into those milky white pearl eyes that had seen millennia.

Then he pried his hand loose from Neria's, and stepped toward the witch. He planted his feet and gritted his teeth, and said, with hardened resolve:

"I want to do it."

Even Rusalka fell into stunned silence, then.

"What?" Neria gasped.

"Put the demon god inside me," said Jack. "Like my father wants." His voice was heavy with weary bitterness, and he refused to look at Neria as she burst out in protest:

"No! Jack, think about what you're saying! Are you insane?"

She reached for his hand again, but he jerked it away.

Rusalka's grin was wide and ghoulish as she swept through the dark toward Jack, coming to a halt directly in front of him. She stuck her face in his.

'That is truly wonderful to hear, my love.'

Rusalka's lair was shrinking back down to a small, recognizable circular chamber again. The lantern room. Neria tried to say something, but Rusalka silenced her with a long, bony finger pressed to her lips.

'Yes,' she said, without blinking once or turning her gaze away from Jack's face. *'Wonderful. And just in time, too: they are all waiting for us outside.'*

Chapter Seventeen: The Ends of the Earth

ylan sat on the rocks at the foot of the lighthouse and peered through a pair of binoculars at the scene unfolding across the water on the beach.

The seven oneironauts who had gone to negotiate now lay dead, dark blood painting the sand beneath them. Blood spilling over polished golden armour, soaking into their colourful robes.

They die just like we do.

Around the seven golden-armoured corpses were the scattered bodies of the cult members they had taken out on their way down. Dylan counted the dead cultists— twenty-nine. *Not bad,* he thought, though it had barely put a dent in the Face of Pale's forces, which were milling about at the edge of the water now, while even more of them continued to emerge from the woods in a steady stream.

How can there possibly be this many psychopaths in the world?

Here came a group of them now, carrying canoes out onto the sand and down to the shoreline. Three canoes.

Dylan watched them load into the boats, six cultists per canoe.

Shit. He lowered his binoculars. There was nowhere to hide.

As the canoes cut through the waves toward the Cursed Rock, the rest of the cult members gathered at the water's edge, while still more of them trickled out of the woods to join the rest.

There are too many of them.

Dylan turned to look at the *Jericho Cascade* sitting out on the water, anchored in place. Absurdly gigantic, and inexplicably silent.

Raising his binoculars again, he scanned the myriad buildings sprouting from the ship's deck. There were clay hunts and castles. Temples, shrines and churches. Shacks. Chapels. Villas. Cathedrals. A whole city crouching on the deck of the ship, beneath those seven blazing masts.

Would it be possible to swim to it? Dylan lowered the binoculars and scanned the water that lay between the Cursed Rock and the *Jericho Cascade*. And it was only then, in that moment, that he truly understood how colossal the *Cascade* was. As he stared over the water at the otherworldly ship, he could have sworn that the ocean was sloping down toward it from the Cursed Rock—as though the ocean's surface had somehow gone from flat to inclined.

He blinked. No, that wasn't it, was it? The ocean was level, as always. It was Dylan's vision that was being distorted. The *Jericho Cascade* was simply too big for him to truly comprehend, so his brain had to *curve* the rest of reality around it for him to be able to make sense of what he was seeing.

"Unreal," he breathed.

Behind him, he could hear shouts echoing over the water as the canoes drew nearer to the Cursed Rock.

Rusalka led Jack out of the lantern room to the landing at the top of the spiral stairs. Neria tried to follow them, but Rusalka stopped her by turning and raising a desiccated palm.

'You cannot leave the lighthouse. They are here to give you to their god. It is not safe.'

"But my father will—"

'Neil Faulken has been overpowered. He is their prisoner now. He is no longer in control.'

"But—but the *Jericho Cascade*—" Neria's voice was getting increasingly hoarse. "Alaya, she—"

'Alaya is dead. The rest of her people will not take up arms. They do not fight anymore.' Rusalka lifted off the floor to hover over Neria. *'You must stay here and wait. It is not safe for you out there. You must stay hidden.'*

Neria glanced from Rusalka to Jack. She rocked back and forth on the balls of her feet.

"All right," she said at last. "Go, then." Her gaze locked with Jack's. "Go."

Rusalka nodded to Jack. *'Go down to the rocks,'* she commanded. *'I will be right behind you, my love.'*

Jack looked past Rusalka to Neria. Her disheveled hair hid her eyes, but even this far away Jack could see that her bottom lip was trembling.

"Good luck, Jackdaw," she whispered, so quietly the sound didn't make its way to Jack's ears. But he read the words on her lips. He nodded. Then swallowed loudly, squeezed his eyes shut, and started down the spiral stairs. The lantern room door swung closed behind him.

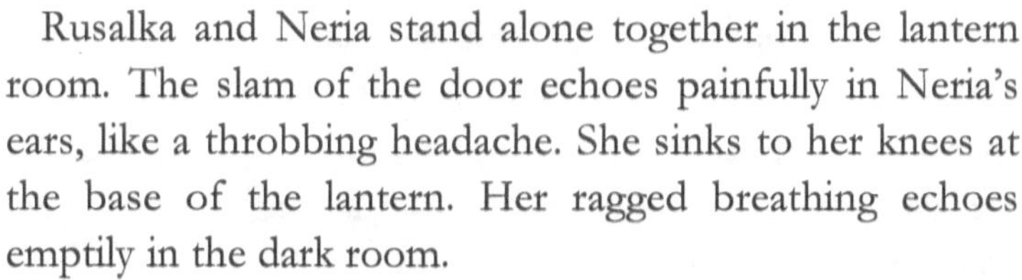

Rusalka and Neria stand alone together in the lantern room. The slam of the door echoes painfully in Neria's ears, like a throbbing headache. She sinks to her knees at the base of the lantern. Her ragged breathing echoes emptily in the dark room.

Nowhere, and everywhere.

Finally she turns to look up at Rusalka. Looks dead into Rusalka's sagging grey-blue face, her time-blind eyes, her half-rotten lips peeling back to reveal rows and rows of razor-point teeth.

Neria growls to herself, to stoke up the fire inside her.

"Rusalka," she says, but it comes out as a piteous croak, so she gives it another shot, trying her best to make it a command:

"Rusalka."

Rusalka's shark smile widens ever so slightly. Neria draws the cool air of the lantern room deep into her lungs, deep as she can. She savours it: closes her eyes, exhales slowly.

I'm sorry, Jack.

She opens her eyes.

"Scatter me," she says.

———— •.◆.• ————

Jack pushed the lighthouse door open and stepped out into the strange alien twilight. The glow in the sky seared his eyes, drew tears and sent pain throbbing to the back of his skull. There was a steady ringing in his ears, and every step he took out onto the Cursed Rock felt altogether too heavy.

Maybe the Earth's gravity had increased while he had been away.

"The man of the hour," someone said. Though part of Jack's mind started in sudden terror, it was mainly relief that washed through him, as he looked up and squinted at the dark mass crowded on the rocks, and the two men standing in front of him.

All of the cultists were wearing their pale slit-eyed masks, except for Jack's father and uncle. Jacob and Gabriel Brecker looked haggard and exhausted. Uncle Gabe's long hair was explosively unkempt, he black dye was starting to come out in streaks, exposing the grey he had hidden so successfully all his life. He was holding Dylan hostage, a knife to his throat.

Jacob Brecker, for his part, looked like he hadn't eaten or seen sunlight in weeks. Chalky skin, plump black circles under his eyes. His clothes were stained and wrinkled, and marred by patches of drying blood. He strode slowly across the rocks toward his son.

As Jack's eyes adjusted to the light, he took stock of the other cult members gathered on the Cursed Rock. Sixteen of them in total, not counting his father and uncle. Near the water's edge, where the three canoes had been secured, one of the cultists was holding Barkface in place, a knife to his throat, duct-tape covering his mouth and nose, his hands bound by rope behind his back.

A quick glance toward shore showed that the rest of the Face of Pale was waiting on the beach.

"Jack."

He turned to look at his father, who was standing just feet away from him. Jack screwed up his face as he tried to bring Jacob Brecker into focus, but his eyesight simply wouldn't cooperate. His father remained a vague Jacob Brecker-shaped blur.

"Dad."

"Do you know why we're all here, son?"

Jack nodded.

"Good." Jacob Brecker smiled, and stepped back, turning slightly so that he could address Jack and the rest of the gathered cult members at the same time. "You see, my friends—I told you he just needed time."

"Hear, hear!" someone called out.

"Don't piss your pants this time, kid," another cult member guffawed, and laughter erupted on the Cursed Rock.

Jack straightened his back, and forced a chuckle. "I'll try not to this time," he said, and was surprised to hear his voice emerge loud and clear as a bell toll. "But you all know how it is." This prompted more laughter from the onlookers—but not from Jacob Brecker, who had only then, in that moment, realized that his son was taller than he was. *When did that happen?* he wondered.

Jacob stepped back from Jack, turned his back on his son. "The history of our species is filled with warfare," he declared to the assembled cultists. "A constant, unrelenting tide of bloodshed, all in the name of a million and one gods and goddesses and ways and paths and truths. But you know why they all fail eventually? Because their truths are all lies. *Their* gods never show up. They all leave their faithful hanging, sooner or later." He paused. "But our god is real."

Jack gritted his teeth. *Can't you just get it over with?*

"That's what we have given the world: the great, eternal circle. Gods make us, and then we learn to make gods. Now imagine this, my friends. An army of devoted disciples of Pale, such as us, marching to conquer a city, with the very god we champion leading the march— leading us into battle. A god that no weapon can stop, not even an atomic blast. Imagine how they'll all bow, all the presidents and emperors, children and grandparents, beggars and CEOs—imagine how they'll all bow when they behold the divine truth of Pale. In the *flesh.*"

Jacob turned to his son again. "That's what you will be. You are the vessel. You will *be* the Face of Pale. You will lead us to world dominion, and at your command we will build the kingdom of Paradise right here on Earth. *Do you hear that?*" Jacob Brecker didn't look away from his son, but he raised his voice loud enough that it was clear he was addressing everyone gathered there on the Cursed Rock.

"Do you hear that?!" he cried again, staring unblinkingly into Jack's eyes. "We are going to steal paradise back from all the pretender gods, once and for all time!"

Cheers erupted behind him, and clapping, and a muffled protest from Barkface. Overhead the sky began to darken. The ethereal, unearthly glow that had suffused the sky for so long was receding now toward the horizon. A glacial wind whipped up, and as one the people gathered on the Cursed Rock shivered, and turned to look at the *Jericho Cascade*—which they only now realized was turning to point its prow in the direction of the vanishing light.

"They're leaving," Jack heard someone gasp.

Murmurs of consternation broke out amongst the cult members as the light shrank back from the sky like a sped-up sunset, and the darkness of night swept in. The *Jericho Cascade* grew smaller and smaller, until they could only make it out as a distant seven-masted silhouette against the dwindling glow.

And then it was all gone, and there was only darkness in the sky, a few distant nervous stars coming out overhead to offer what little solace they could.

"We win?" one of the cult members said, but it sounded like more of a question than anything.

Jack glanced in the direction of the beach, but even the Morgana Peninsula had vanished, eaten along with everything else by the sudden onslaught of night. As though the whole world had drowned in ink, and only the Cursed Rock remained, with everybody gathered there transformed to smoke and ash and shadows.

Jack's stomach swooped. *Neria.*

Then he heard the lighthouse door creaking open behind him, the swishing of Rusalka's robes as she drifted through the air. He could smell the rotten-fish stink of her breath. A cold glow illuminated the Cursed Rock, like a light that had come from the bottom of the ocean. It came from a lamp which Rusalka held in her hands: a cage made of coral, with a blueish-green flame burning within.

Rusalka placed the coral lantern on the ground between Jack and his father. The light made a circle around them, to encompass Jack, his father and uncle, Dylan, and Rusalka. The rest of the cult assembled on the Cursed Rock faded to greyness.

The circle of light felt to Jack like a protective bubble. Rusalka returned to hover just behind him. *'It is time,'* she said softly, placing a hand on Jack's shoulder.

"No!" Dylan shouted. "Don't do it, Jack! Don't—" But then Gabriel Brecker covered his son's mouth with a large leather-gloved hand, censoring Dylan's protests.

Jack was trembling from head to toe, but he kept his back straight, did his best to keep his feet planted steady and firm on the rocks beneath him. He could hardly see his cousin in the dim glow. "It's all right, Dyl," he said, speaking slowly in an effort to keep his voice steady.

It almost worked.

"Where's the girl?" Jack's father demanded. "Where's Neria Nightshade?"

'She is not here,' said Rusalka. She gestured to something near the water. *'Her father will have to do.'*

Jack's jaw dropped as Barkface was hauled into the circle of light. He had taken on his true form now, the way he had appeared when Jack had first seen him, emerging from his cottage on the beach: an ancient man, bent and eroded by time. Cracked lips and snowstorm hair and sunken, haunted eyes. The duct tape was removed from his mouth, and the cultist named Rika, who had been holding him in place the whole time, took her knife and sawed through the rope binding his hands.

Rusalka turned to address Jacob and Gabriel.

'On this very spot,' she declared, *'the two of you came to me once before, and struck a bargain: I would give you your god, in the flesh. Tonight, we seal this agreement in blood.'*

Rusalka turned her face to the darkened sky.

'Let us now draw Pale from the shadows.'

She swaggered over to Barkface, then, and took him by the hand, and led him toward the center of the circle of light. Barkface bowed his head. "You didn't listen," he rasped, more to himself than to anyone gathered there— yet still they heard him, and the sponge-like darkness pressed in on all sides, soaking up Barkface's voice like sand soaking up blood. "None of you listened. So I brought you here to see you all destroyed." He licked his lips, then looked back up at Jacob and Gabriel. "I underestimated you."

"You're a hypocrite, Neil!" Rika spat. "That's what you are. You taught us that Pale would become the most powerful entity in the cosmos. You taught us that one day he would consume the entire universe and everything in it. And if we served him, and served him well, then we would have a special place at his table, in his great star-palace at the center of the galaxy."

("Pretty sure he never said *that*," Gabriel muttered in Jacob's ear.)

"Then," Rika continued, moving toward Barkface, "you changed your mind."

"I found the truth," said Barkface. "The *real* truth. My wife and daughter showed me. Pale had grown beyond control." A beat. "I always thought we were doing them a favour. A service—it was a *gift*, even. Giving their souls to Pale. Laying their souls like bricks upon the edifice of our demon god. Our methods were barbaric, yes… but all human civilization is founded on savagery and brutality. And they would be reborn, wouldn't they? At the ends of the earth, when Pale finally became flesh? *I* believed it, as you all believe it still. And I always thought that each person we gave to Pale, each soul, would see, in the end, that they were blessed beyond measure for the chance to join the heart of a man-made god. To live *forever*. To see eternity from the eyes of the greatest enterprise the human race ever undertook." Barkface heaved a grotesque, retching sigh from the deepest sewers of his being. "And then I met my wife, and sometime after that I met my daughter, and I saw this whole thing for what it truly was. Naked fanaticism. A waste of the true cosmic gift: the gift of the here-and-now, and these flesh forms we've been given to explore it with. The greatest thing I could do for little Neria was give her the best chance at life here, now. Not in some impossible future. Not in the heart of a demon god. I was… wrong."

"I saw my wife murdered for Pale," Jacob growled. "I made my son watch. For Pale. So did my brother. And Rika, and Axel, and Sammy and Dack, and everyone else." He gestured to the inky darkness crowding around the circle of ghostly lamplight. "But *you*, Neil, *you* decided Pale was wrong because you didn't want to kill your own kid, and your own wife. But what about all of us, huh? What about the sacrifices we all made? *Hypo*crite." He spat on the rocks at Barkface's feet. "You don't know what it is you've asked of us. You never have."

"Kill me, then," said Barkface, without hesitation. "I've had enough. I want to die." He drew in a deep, rattling breath and raised both hands in the air. "Feed me to Pale."

For a moment no-one spoke.

Then Jacob walked up to Barkface from behind, and kicked him in the backs of his knees so that the old man fell down with a cry onto the rocks.

Jacob brushed past Barkface and crossed over to Jack. He handed his son a plastic milk jug with the top sawed off, filled with brown sludge.

"Drink," he commanded. "Now."

Don't hesitate.

"JACK! STOP!" Dylan roared, but it was too late: Jack had already lifted the jug to his lips and started drinking the foul brew. He gagged on the taste, but forced it down, screwing up his face to keep from puking it back up. His head began to spin, he could feel his heartrate increasing even as the foul liquid spooled into his stomach.

Once Jack had swallowed about a third of the liquid in the jug, Jacob patted him on the back. "Good job, son. Keep at it. Not much longer now." He kissed the crown of Jack's head. "I'm proud of you." The words came awkwardly to him, and he shuddered after he said it, as though he found it somehow distasteful.

Jack bent over double and began to retch. "Steady, steady," said Jacob, while his son spewed brown sludge onto his shoes. But then Jack straightened up, wiped his lips on his sleeve and continued drinking from the jug.

Jacob turned, leaving his son, and crossed the circle of lamplight to stand over Barkface. The old man was lying with his head against the rocks, muttering frantically to himself. "I'm sorry," he was saying. "I'm sorry for bringing you into existence. I'm sorry that I made something so wrong. Because you *are* wrong. And the thing is, you've already lost. You've already—"

Jacob Brecker drew his knife from its sheath. "Shut up!" he roared, kicking Barkface in the back. Barkface fell silent, and curled into the fetal position.

"Pale," Jacob growled. "Please accept Neil Faulken's final and eternal service. Blood, body, mind and soul." He crouched down next to Barkface. "You are the greatest offering we could hope to make," he said. "Short of your daughter, of course. But we'll keep looking for her, once we're done here. We'll find her. Don't worry."

Then he lifted Barkface's head and stabbed out Barkface's left eye, sticking the knife in the socket and jiggling it around like he was using a tension wrench to pick a lock. He did the same to the right eye.

"Do you see him now?" Jacob growled.

Barkface's breathing grew faster and more frantic, but other than that he made no indication of the pain he must have been experiencing. "I don't—believe—in you— anymore," he hissed, weeping hot blood, as the blade of Jacob's knife pressed against his neck, sinking deeper and deeper as it sawed back and forth, opening Barkface up, rinsing the rocks with his blood.

Then Jacob stood and looked over at Jack, who had just choked down the final dregs from the jub. "Atta boy," said Jacob.

Jack began to spew brown sludge onto the front of his shirt again, but he covered his mouth and managed to swallow some of it back down. His legs twisted beneath him and he collapsed onto his side. His father knelt next to him, rolling him onto his back so that he lay there spread-eagled.

Rusalka hovered higher and higher in the air, drifting several feet above them all now. She raised her hands—and the light in the coral lamp brightened, brighter and brighter until it suffused the whole islet with spectral light.

The cult members began to double over, to heave and cough and vomit.

Jack stared at the sky overhead. He didn't see his father and uncle on their hands and knees, sobbing as thick black coils of writhing darkness spilled from their mouths and crawled over the ground. Nor did he see the other sixteen afflicted cult members, bathed in harsh ghostly light—not one of them standing anymore, all of them toppling to the ground, hacking up clotted masses of black fluid.

He didn't see Rusalka drifting through their ranks, herding the strange black fluid. Nor did he see additional coils of darkness spilling toward the Cursed Rock from the shore of the peninsula. It gathered on the rocks, like rivers of tar come to life. Like black electricity flowing in slow-motion. Rusalka guided the churning fluid, directing it through gentle hand movements toward Jack. Whatever the black stuff was, it appeared to obey every twitch of her fingers, flowing and twisting, writhing and churning as it crawled toward the sprawled teenager.

No, Jack didn't see any of that. All he saw was a black sky. Unfathomably distant stars, indifferent to the madness playing out far below them.

Or perhaps those stars *could* see everything that was happening, but were too far away to help.

Jack couldn't fight back. He could hardly even move.

All he could do, as the coils of darkness reached him and began to prod at his body—and then to crawl up his body, over his legs and arms and torso, all toward his head—was open his mouth, and let the darkness sluice down his throat.

Dylan's protests had devolved into wordless shouting by now, and nobody was trying to shut him up anymore. Aside from Rusalka, he was the only person on the Cursed Rock who wasn't violently sick with darkness. Still, he couldn't move. All he could do was watch.

So he watched, eyes wide, tears streaming down his face, paralyzed—watched as the tendrils of darkness converged on Jack, as Rusalka guided the darkness into Jack's open mouth. It streamed into his mouth, sucked in faster and faster, as though it had latched onto something deep down inside him, something it was hungry for.

Jack's eyes were closed but his body shook and convulsed and spasmed, his back arching then straightening suddenly so that he slammed back down onto the ground. Blood spurted from his nose and ears, and when finally the last of the darkness had vanished down his throat, blood also came trickling from the corner of his mouth.

"Jack…" Dylan croaked.

But Jack couldn't hear his cousin. He lay there on the rocks, crumpled and still and lifeless. The light in the lantern faded once more, so that it encompassed his body, and Barkface's body, and Jacob and Gabriel Brecker, who lay prone on the rocks, coughing weakly and still spitting up little flecks of darkness. Black tar-like gobs.

"Mira…" Jacob muttered to himself, his eyes spinning deliriously in their sockets. "Mira…"

Neither Jacob nor Gabriel saw Dylan crouch next to Barkface's body, and place the star marble in the corpse's grey fingers. Nor did they see Dylan pick the blood-stained knife up from where it had fallen.

Only Rusalka saw.

Dylan turned to look at her, the knife clutched tight in one hand. Rusalka remained motionless. She said nothing.

So Dylan turned away from her, and gave himself to the darkness.

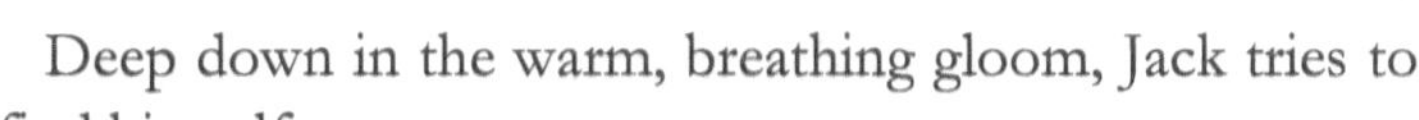

Deep down in the warm, breathing gloom, Jack tries to find himself.

It isn't easy.

Where am I? He can't feel a thing, not his hands nor his feet. There's nothing he can use to get his bearings. Just splotches of shadow, streaks of smoke.

Then something begins to come into focus. All Jack knows is that it isn't *himself*, whatever he's seeing. Before long he recognizes it: a pale rider on a white horse. A rider draped in a grey cloak.

A rider without a face, only two holes for eyes, and a knife in a sheath on his belt.

It's you, says Jack. He finds himself, then: a naked boy crouching in the shadows, climbing unsteadily to his feet. Where's his voice?

He tries again: "It's you."

The rider nods, and slides off the scaled horse's back. He straightens up and pulls the polished knife from its sheath.

Jack walks tentatively toward Pale. As he draws near, Pale presents the knife to Jack hilt-first. Jack takes it in his hand. Then he straightens up and looks the creature standing in front of him straight in its empty holes-for-eyes.

He knows that surprise will be key, and hesitation will be failure.

"Go to hell," he says—and lunges forward, jabbing the point of the knife through Pale's grey robe, into his chest on the left side, where the heart should be. There's a *crunch* as the knife drives through bone and sinew, sinking all the way to the hilt.

Jack lets go of the knife and falls back.

Pale looks down at the knife handle sticking out of his chest. Then, silently, he reaches up and pulls it out. Blood spills from the wound, darkening his grey robes.

Casting the knife aside, Pale tears the robes off, revealing the rest of his body to Jack: a well-toned male body, completely naked and hairless, looking as though it were sculpted from the whitest marble.

The gouge where Jack drove the knife in, in the upper-left of Pale's torso, splits wide into a lipless mouth. A snakelike tongue slides in and out between gleaming fangs—as though the tongue is emerging straight from Pale's heart.

'That was well-executed,' the chest-mouth says, *'but mistaken.'*

Jack lists on his feet. *Keep it together.* "Barkface?" he asks.

Pale's striding toward him now. *'Do not be afraid. This is good.'*

"Dad?" Jack tries again, notching his voice up louder, bit by bit, word by word. "Are you in there?"

'I am Pale. And you are my face.'

"Skye?"

'You are me, and I am you. They have made it so.'

Jack decides to switch tactics. "Where are we?" he asks.

'Exactly where we need to be.' Around the mouth that has opened over Pale's ribcage, other features begin to push out of the marble-like flesh: a nose, eyes, the curve of a forehead. All of it smudged and indistinct, but unmistakable. A human face. *'Do not worry. Your brain is simply trying to make sense of something it cannot comprehend. Understanding will come, in time. For soon, when we wake, we will begin the Great Conquest.'*

"The Great Conquest?"

'Of course. Surely you know this has all been building to something greater?' Pale extends a hand. His nails are long and black. *'Take my hand, and we will become one, as we were always meant to be.'*

Jack raises his hand—

But then there's a woman's voice in his ears, a woman he knows, and misses dearly. Her voice is warm but raspy with stress, dancing on his eardrums like a gust of private summer wind.

You are not the things in your head.

He can see her face, suddenly, clear as day before him: her eyes pushing out of Pale's chest, her nose, her mouth above Pale's heart, where Jack tried to land a killing blow.

"Mom," he whispers.

Remember this, Jack: whenever you feel like you've lost yourself…

He pulls his hand back from Pale. He closes his eyes.

All you have to do is find two things.

He pulls a deep breath into his lungs. Exhales, then does it again. And again. Pale's saying something, but Jack grits his teeth and focuses on finding the pounding of his heart.

They'll guide you home.

When he finds his heartbeat, he discovers that it's off-rhythm. Skipping beats. As usual.

He opens his eyes.

Pale's staring at him. The mouth on his chest has disappeared. His knife returned to its sheath. He stares silently at Jack with those implacable not-eyes.

"My mother died because of you," says Jack. "But she didn't die *for* you."

Pale pulls his knife out of the sheath again. But this time, instead of offering it to Jack, he raises it to his own face, and saws into his own flesh directly beneath his two eye-holes. Once he has sliced open a deep enough gouge, he lowers the knife about an inch and begins sawing again. And then one more gouge after that, below the second incision.

Then he slides the knife gracefully back into its sheath.

Three mouths, stacked vertically beneath Pale's eyes. They split open one at a time, and three tongues flick out between razor-sharp teeth. *'Yes,'* Pale says, in three voices speaking in perfect harmony. *'She died for you. And you are me, and I am you. So she died for me, too.'*

"If that's true," says Jack, "then show her to me."

'Take my hand, and you will see her. We are close to waking now.'

Jack sighs, exasperated. "What does that even *mean?*" He squeezes his eyes shut. *Think.* **Think.** He slips his hands into his pockets, hoping to find something useful—and that's when he discovers that his pockets have holes in them.

He growls in frustration. *What would Neria do, if she were here?*

And then it comes to him, all at once.

He tries not to show it on his face.

Keeping his eyes closed, he summons up the dreaded memory of a dim, damp room, lit by a flickering fire in a garbage can. A crowd of shadows. Pallid, unnatural, unmoving faces.

A woman with silver hair and silver eyes tied to a chair. A father and a son framed in a doorway.

A rusty steel door.

"I love you, Mom," Jack whispers.

He opens his eyes.

Pale's still standing in front of him. All three of his stacked mouths are open now, displaying razor-sharp fangs and flicking snake tongues. He's making a strange growling sound, at once guttural and soft. And his eyes aren't empty holes anymore. They've changed.

Jack almost breaks. Right then and there, he almost turns and runs.

Pale's eyes are Mira Brecker's eyes now, unmistakably. Glowing silver eyes, like rainclouds backlit by haunted moons, staring unblinkingly at Jack from above the demon god's three growling mouths.

Jack clenches his hands into fists.

'Do you see now?'

Jack nods. He forces himself to look, blinking as little as possible, into his mother's stolen eyes. "Yes," he says. He can only manage it for a few seconds before he has to look away. He turns his gaze to the cracked moldy tiles at his feet. To the ceiling, festooned with mildew.

Or—behind Pale, behind his white-scaled horse—the rusted steel door.

Jack freezes. And then, once again, he forces himself to look into his mother's eyes.

"I see," he says, "but I don't understand."

A chuckle emerges from Pale's upper mouth, a sigh from the lower mouth, and from the middle one a new voice emerges, a voice Jack hasn't heard in a long, long time.

"What don't you understand?" Mira Brecker's voice says, as clearly as if she were standing in front of him.

Jack frowns. "I don't understand *you.*"

Pale throws his head back and laughs—laughter coming from three mouths, demented cackling mixing with furious giggling and good-natured chuckling. And as he laughs, more mouths begin to open all over his statuesque body, along his arms and legs, all up and down his torso, marble-like flesh splitting as dozens of tongues taste the air, sliding between sharpened fangs. Each and every one of these mouths starts laughing, too, until the hallway echoes like it's filled with a jeering crowd.

Jack backs away. He can't help it. The laughter spikes in pitch as it wears on, louder and louder, until it's not laughter at all anymore but screaming filling the hallway, desperate, anguished screaming coming from each of the mouths lining Pale's body. And between all the screaming, Jack can make out words. *"Somebody, help! Please! I'm so scared, I'm so scared I just wanna go home I wanna go home…"*

Then, behind Pale, Jack sees Barkface.

What?

Impossible.

But it *is* Barkface. Not the stooped old man Jack saw butchered on the Cursed Rock, but tall, youthful, elk-antlered Barkface, draped in a massive black cloak.

Jack's jaw drops as Barkface pulls the steel door open with a squeal of rusty hinges, to reveal the dim room beyond. He looks over and winks at Jack.

Jack turns back to the demon god. The screaming is winding down, but now the many mouths lining Pale's body like lesions are baring their teeth, snarling like angry dogs.

Pale advances on Jack, and the three mouths on his face speak, all three of them reverting to the demon god's original voice:

'Do you oppose me, then?'

Jack backs away, slowly and deliberately, curving his retreat in a U so that he's now walking backward toward the open steel door. "Yes," he says simply. He doesn't bother looking for Barkface—he knows he won't find him. His heart's on jackhammer mode, his pulse pounding like a bass drum, his blood rushing in his ears like torrenting rapids.

"Yes," he says again, for good measure.

'No. You will not oppose me. You are merely a vessel, Jack Brecker. This has always been your destiny. A vessel to hold a god. It is why your father got your mother pregnant in the first place: in service to me.'

Jack passes backward through the doorway, into the concrete-walled room beyond. The garbage can still sits in the middle of the room, the fire still crackling away inside it, lighting them with its flicker. Aside from that, the room is deserted.

Pale has to stoop to pass through the doorway. Jack continues backing away from him, clenching his teeth and his fists as he disobeys every instinct of his entire being and moves with slow, deliberate steps. *Come on… come on…*

The demon god advances into the room, and now his many mouths are murmuring things, different voices all tangled up in knots. The voices swarm Jack like a cloud of flies, amplified and reverberating harshly in the gloom:

"…don't understand where we are, I don't…"

"…but I'm telling you it doesn't make any sense, I mean, I know what it feels like to **die,** *yet here I am, I'm still here, I'm still… breathing…"*

"…sometimes manage to forget who I was, but then something will come back…"

"*…just can't condone killing that girl the way they did—putting her in the tree like that—and she was here with us, for a moment, wasn't she? Where did she go?*"

Jack keeps his gaze locked on Pale's eyes. On his mother's eyes. Here in this room where she died, buried at the bottom of his mind.

He understands, then, what Neria was trying to tell him before. That this room will always be here. That there's nothing he can ever do about that.

And he doesn't *want* to forget it.

Jack smirks as he comes to stand beside the garbage can fire. Pale sweeps across the room toward him, and Jack moves so that the garbage can now stands between him and the demon god.

Both of them come to a halt. Pale's screaming rises in pitch, getting shriller and more feverish. Jack winces.

'I know,' the three mouths on Pale's face say in unison. They sound strangely sympathetic. *I know. So loud. So* **infernal.** *They never shut up. It would drive anyone mad. It will drive you mad, too.'*

Jack takes a deep breath. The acrid smoke from the garbage can fire stings his nostrils. His eyes smart. But he grins at Pale, wide and true, his off-kilter heart stirring inside him now. The fire in the garbage can burns hotter, the flames reaching higher.

For the first time, Pale falters. And Mira Brecker's stolen eyes blink.

For Skye. Jack's grin widens even more. *For Neria.*

"I'm already mad," he says.

For Mom.

He kicks the garbage can over—its sizzling, smoking contents spill over Pale's feet, and Pale barely reacts, but Jack's already sprinting for the doorway. The demon god launches into pursuit, his many body-mouths all shrieking wordlessly again, his three face-mouths ripping open wide to reveal dark, gaping maws.

Jack lunges out into the hallway—slams his back into the steel door and knocks it shut with a CLANG! Keeping his back pressed to the door, he glances frantically up and down the hallway. "Barkface?" he cries.

Pale starts pounding on the door behind Jack, each knock shaking the doorframe, denting the steel and rattling Jack down to the atoms of his bones. Behind the door, Pale's thousand voices wail and roar with unbridled fury.

"Barkface!" Jack cries.

And then Neria's there too, next to him, for a split second, throwing her weight against the steel door. Gazing intently at Jack with those amber eyes.

She straightens up without a word, swings a ring of three keys out of her pocket, and locks each of the deadbolts, one after the other. *Click. Click. Click.*

Jack falls away from the steel door. "Where did you—" he gasps—then frowns. Neria's nowhere to be seen. Like she was never there at all.

He's alone in the hallway.

He looks down at the prick of coldness in his hand, and sees the ring of keys.

What?

Pale continues pounding on the other side of the door. BANGBANGBANG. *"LET ME OUT!"* several of his voices shriek in unison. *"OPEN THIS DOOR NOW!"* And though the door rattles on its hinges, shaking in its frame, it holds.

Jack turns to face the steel door head-on. He summons up his last memory of Pale, the tall marble-skinned demon riddled with snarling mouths, wearing his mother's stolen eyes.

"I know you're real," Jack says, and in an instant the voices behind the door cease, the banging stops, and at long, long last there's silence in the hall.

"All it takes to make a demon god real is one true believer. But I'm in charge here. And *I* don't believe in you. To be perfectly honest, I never really did. You know, I think if you gave your believers a chance to really sit down and think about it, I'm pretty sure they would all realize you're not real, either. You're just a nightmare. That's all."

A low chuckle seeps through the steel door and finds Jack's ears. *'And you are a vessel, Jack Brecker. That is all.'*

"Yes." Jack nods. "That's my destiny, we are all powerless before fate, blah blah blah, all that horseshit. I know. I'm a vessel."

He turns away, then, and starts walking down the dim hallway toward the exit. The voices start up behind him, muted by rusty steel—rustling murmurs at first, then pitching suddenly to that familiar chorus of harmonizing shrieks. The pounding resumes on the door. *'DO NOT IGNORE ME, JACK BRECKER!'*

Jack resists the urge to look back. He keeps his gaze locked stoically on the exit door up ahead, on the seam of daylight visible around its edges.

Your breath, and your heartbeat.

He breathes deeply as he walks down the hallway, each breath pulled in slowly, released even slower. And in his ears, overtop of the screaming and metallic pounding behind him, he finds the pulse. Erratic, as always. Off-beat. And undoubtedly his own.

When Jack reaches the exit, he allows himself one glance back.

The steel door stands firm, way at the end of the corridor. Pale's muffled protests echo alongside the backbeat of his fists pounding against steel, but to no avail.

The door will hold. Jack knows this.

And eventually, Pale will starve.

Not soon. Not easily. But eventually. As long as the demon god doesn't get fed, it will starve.

Eventually is enough.

Jack turns away, pushes through the exit door and emerges into the dusty grey sunlight of a forgotten town in a blurred, tarnished memory. Continuing to breathe deeply, and walking to the rhythm of his heart, he sets off into a maze of abandoned streets, even though there's no abandoned town left, and he's already floating upward toward waking like a diver ascending to the surface of the ocean.

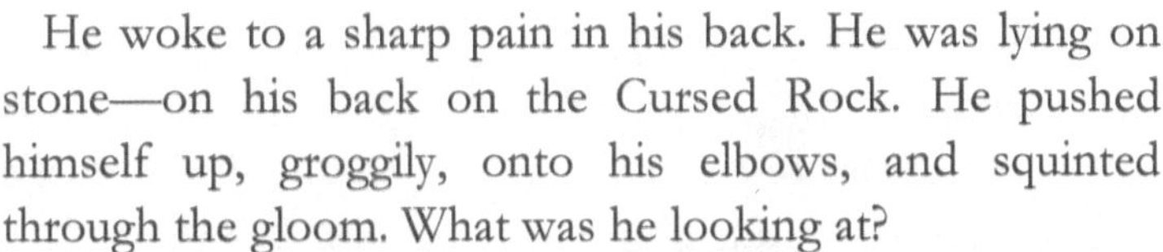

He woke to a sharp pain in his back. He was lying on stone—on his back on the Cursed Rock. He pushed himself up, groggily, onto his elbows, and squinted through the gloom. What was he looking at?

Rusalka's ghostly lantern was still sitting on the rocks nearby, flickering with that turquoise glow. Barkface's mutilated body—well, the mutilated body of an old man— lay where Jack had seen it fall. The Cursed Rock was littered with black forms, cult members sprawled on the ground. None of them were moving.

Jack wrinkled his nose. The air was heavy with the stench of blood. He saw the glimmer of lantern light reflected in dark puddles strewn about the islet. Splashes of dark liquid.

He frowned. "Dyl?" he grunted.

'He took one of the canoes.'

Jack jumped, startled, and tried to scramble to his feet as Rusalka floated up behind him—but he didn't have the strength, his limbs flagged under the strain and he fell back, *hard,* onto the cold stone.

"But… but…" Jack spluttered. "Wait…"

Rusalka slid her arms under Jack and gingerly lifted him into the air, cradling him to her chest like a baby. *'Rest, my love,'* she whispered. *'Sleep…'*

Jack's eyelids were already falling shut, and he knew he wouldn't be able to get them back open for a while. "Barkface…" he said, and that was the last thing he had the strength for.

When he next woke it was to glacial wind teasing his hair, the sound of distant waves crashing. He had to open his eyes slowly against the brightness, and the wind blasting his face.

He was flying. Soaring high above an empty ocean, through gauzy wisps of cloud lit by milky sunlight.

Rusalka was still carrying him in her arms.

'It is beautiful, don't you think?'

Her voice slithered into his ears, drove into his brain like needles. He stared up at her ancient face, but she wasn't looking at him; she was gazing straight ahead, her milky eyes focused on the curve of the Earth.

Jack tried to turn his head to see the rest of her, but he couldn't—could only catch glimpses of her fluttering sail-and-scale robes in the corners of his vision. Above the roar of the wind he could make out a rhythmic, leathery flapping noise. *Wings.*

Of course she has wings.

"Let me *go,*" he managed.

Rusalka laughed. *'But we have come so far.'*

"LET ME GO!" Jack squirmed in her grasp but it was no use. "HELP!"

'You would rather fall to your death than accompany me?'

Rusalka banked to the side to avoid a flock of geese.

"Where are you taking me?"

'To a place where you can find Neria again.'

The mushroom cloud of panic growing in Jack's chest subsided, vanished, replaced by a bout of laughter. Cold, painful laughter. Or maybe he was crying. Somewhere along the way he seemed to have forgotten how to tell the difference.

How long did they fly for? How long *had* they been flying for, before he had awoken—with Rusalka cradling him like that, miles and miles above the surface of the waves?

Soon the sunset swallowed them and there was nothing around them but gaping tracts of moonlit ocean. The waves far below were growing larger, choppier, more muscular. Above them, a bank of black clouds whirled in and strangled the moon. *Go back!* screamed the wind. *Go back!*

Rain swept in and drenched them to the bone. A thousand winds screeched at them, and Rusalka howled loud enough to be heard above the din: *'Let us through! Let us **THROUGH!'***

Something else was filling Jack's ears, lurking behind the shriek of the wind and the thrash of the surf. In fact, it was more like silence than any sound. A yawning, unending silence.

He blinked the stinging misty spray from his eyes and tried to catch a glimpse of what was ahead.

That was when he saw it.

His breath deserted him.

It was the end. The end of the ocean. It just *stopped,* and beyond it was an immense chasm, a measureless gulf of *nothing.* And there went the ocean, cascading helplessly into it, heaving itself over the edge in unceasing torrents.

The edge of the world.

The nothingness beckoned as Rusalka soared toward it.

"No!" Jack shouted. "NO! STOP! TAKE ME BACK!"

Impossible things happen all the time.

The rushing, hissing silence from beyond the edge of the world flooded his ears. It was almost deafening… and he realized then that it wasn't silence at all. No, it was a noise: a noise so ferociously, hideously loud that it was nearly indistinguishable from silence. It was louder than anything Jack had ever heard, it screamed it bawled it *thrashed* with the behemothic chaos of eternity.

'Look at it, Jack.'

"NO!"

'You sadden me. Do you not wish to know what it is to sail on the Circling River? Do you not wish to see the Unspeakable Beyond with your own eyes? Do you not—'

But then a booming voice cut her off, shaking the supercharged air, louder than the shrieking din surrounding them on all sides:

"LET HIM GO."

Barkface was ploughing through the air toward them, speeding upward from the waves, rising until he was level with them. He was more majestic now than he had ever appeared to Jack before: towering and muscular, his face glowing and youthful above his long brown beard. Antlers sprouting from his forehead.

"Give me the boy," Barkface said—and though he was shouting to be heard over the wind, his voice somehow sounded gentle.

'*He is not mine to give,*' Rusalka answered, and she dropped Jack.

It happened so fast he barely had time to process it: falling. Toppling through the air straight down toward the waves—but he was slowing down, and something was reeling him in, like he had been caught on a fishing line.

He fell slower and slower, until he was merely drifting down, as though he had an invisible parachute.

He landed on an atoll, a tiny rock thrusting up above the surf in defiance of whatever deranged cosmic creature had created this place. The rock was several meters wide, enough for one person, maybe two to stand on.

The water lashed at Jack, struck him, tugged at him, but he clung on tight to the little rock, and clambered up to its highest point, where the flogging waves couldn't reach him—only the vicious, stinging spray.

Barkface alighted down on the atoll next to Jack. He sat next to him, and put a hand on top of Jack's hand, which was gripping onto the rock for dear life.

"You've done far better than anyone could have expected," Barkface said.

Jack emitted a shaky laugh that he neither intended nor enjoyed. "I still don't get what—what *happened,*" he said. But Barkface was already launching himself back up into the sky.

Jack growled in frustration, adjusting his position on the atoll. Soaked in spray and sweat, shivering to his core, hacking and spitting up slime and saltwater, heart thrashing double-time under the off-tune piano keys of his chattering teeth—Jack turned, pushed his sodden hair out of his eyes, and stared out at the impossible scene unfolding before him.

High above him floated Barkface and Rusalka, circling each other like eagles poised for a duel.

And behind them: the end.

The end.

The ocean, flinging itself over the edge of the world in a vast waterfall that stretched on as far as the eye could see in either direction. Jack saw, then, that it wasn't *nothing* that lay over the edge, not entirely; no, it was *madness.* Swirling chaos that couldn't seem to make up its mind about what it was. One moment it was gaping blackness, then a mass of writhing, lightning-frosted clouds, then a hurricane of stars and suns and whizzing comets, a chasm of dazzling, shifting, unearthly colours. And it was filled with voices. Screaming and crying and singing and laughing and chanting and—

No. Jack squeezed his eyes shut. *No.* There was nothing there for a boy like him. The abyss was trying to trick him, to fool him into thinking that he wanted to let go, to get swept away beyond the ends of the Earth.

But he knew what it really was, lurking beyond the edge. It was death. Plain and simple. Perhaps the howling, thrashing abyss was not *the end.* But he knew without a doubt that it would be the end of Jack Brecker.

Another glance back: once again it was just an empty chasm.

This place shouldn't exist. It **can't** *exist.*

The ocean roared around him. He was still full of seawater, and now it came leaking out of him from all his pores and orifices. He craned his head back, looked in the opposite direction of the waterfall, trying to see back to the world he had come from. But all he could see was Barkface and Rusalka colliding in mid-air, wrestling, tearing into each other, both of them shrieking loud enough to raise the dead.

Raise the dead.

Lightning bleached the sky and Rusalka was on fire. Jack tilted his head back, watched as she jetted up into the vortex of sky above them, higher and higher, until she was only a pinprick of light—

Barkface was standing beside Jack on the rock again. "Listen, boy," he shouted. "I know you must have a great many questions, but there's not much time, so I will answer you this one."

He bent to bring his face close to Jack's, and in Barkface's eyes Jack saw through the youthful veneer to the spiraling depths of age and anguish.

"There is only one reason that I came all this way for you," Barkface continued. "You hear them, too, don't you? The voices, I mean. The same ones my daughter hears."

Jack's heart leapt. Barkface gripped his shoulders. "You must find her. I don't where she is, but I know she doesn't want to be found. Still, you must find her, and you must tell her something."

Behind him Jack could see Rusalka descending out of the clouds, smouldering and trailing smoke as she dropped toward them, her hands and hair still on fire—

"—you must tell her that everything is going to be all right from now on, because everything I created has now been destroyed. And I will never return to Earth. I can't. I have no body there anymore. So that's it. That's all. You must tell her that. But it's not enough to simply tell her— you must *convince* her. Because I guarantee she will not believe you at first. Still, Jack, you have to try. Got that?"

Jack nodded fervently. Barkface reached into the folds of his cloak, fumbled for a second, then pulled something out and held it out to Jack in his upturned palm: the star marble. Jack took it, closed his fist around it and held it tight.

"It will get you home," said Barkface. "I promise. Just keep a grip on it like your life depends on it." He patted Jack's shoulder once more, smiled reassuringly. "Good luck, Jack Brecker. I promise that I will see you again, at the place where myth and memory meet."

With that Barkface turned and leapt off the atoll. He took flight, his cloak billowing like wings as coils of unseen energy launched him high into the air. He soared up like a missile to meet Rusalka far above the waves—once more they collided, and the ensuing shockwave shook Jack from his perch on the atoll. He grasped at the slippery rock with his free hand, and only just managed to hold on as waves buffeted him and abyssal winds tore at him. The whole while he kept a firm grip on the star marble. It was heating up in his fist, its silvery glow stabbing out through the gaps between his clenched fingers.

Above him, Barkface and Rusalka were locked together. The wind picked up, and for a moment it looked as though they were kissing passionately. Then the gale carried them both over the edge of the world, and they vanished into the abyss.

It was the last the world ever saw of them.

Jack spat saltwater out of his mouth. He tried to stand up on the atoll, but suddenly a wave bowled into him and knocked him off; he plunged into the surf. The seething cold surf swallowed him. His breath was knocked from him, saltwater filled his eyes and he was whipped forward, impossibly fast now, faster even than before. The water was brutally cold, piercing to the marrow of his bones, freezing his limbs in place—carrying him inexorably toward the edge of the world. It *wanted* him to go over.

He was nearing the edge. Almost there, almost—

—there—

—over the edge, flung straight out into nothingness.

Then, for a time, there was just numbness. A vast, resonant tranquility.

And a voice. Soft. Faraway. A voice he recognized.

"Jack? *Jack!*"

He knew that voice, didn't he?

"Come on, Jack—oh, *god,* man, not you… not you…"

But soon it was subsumed by a distant chorus of screams, and another voice rasping in his ear, like a caustic river slowly but steadily eroding the bedrock of his mind: *'Let me out… let me out… I am the god, you are the vessel… let me out…'*

"Please, Jack, just open your eyes!"

He jolted upright. There was sand beneath him, soft, cool sand, and someone was crouching beside him.

"Dyl?"

"Oh, thank god." Dylan rose to his feet, and laughed a giddy, unhappy laugh. "I knew it couldn't be *everyone.*"

Jack licked his lips. *So thirsty.* "How…?" he attempted to ask, but the rest of the question slipped back down into the pit of his stomach where it had come from. *How did I get back here?*

"You don't look good," Dylan was saying. "I'm glad you're alive, but—damn, you don't look good."

"Thanks," Jack grunted. He ran his fingers over his face. The wrinkles were still there, though they weren't as deep as he remembered.

"How *do* I look?" he said.

"Like you're sixty freaking years old. How do you feel?"

Jack shrugged. "That's only fair, I guess. I feel... I feel like I've lived a few lifetimes. Compared to that, sixty's all right. Don't you think?"

He chuckled at his own quip, but Dylan didn't.

Jack frowned. "Dyl?"

Silently Dylan extended a hand; Jack let his cousin pull him to his feet. For a moment they both surveyed the scene around them. The beach was littered with bodies: the black-clad bodies of the faces of Pale, some of them still wearing their masks, others showing their frozen death-faces. And there were the seven blue-robed, golden-armoured oneironauts who had gone to negotiate with them, lying among them.

Jack turned to look at Dylan, and for the first time he took in the dark circles around his cousin's eyes, the brown splotches of dried blood staining his clothes. "What... happened?" he said slowly.

Dylan met Jack's gaze. "After they put the demon god inside you, they were all... they were...." He bit his lip. "They were weak," he said. "Delirious. They couldn't stop me."

Jack said nothing. He met Dylan's gaze, steadfast and stoic. "Tell me," he said.

"I cut my dad's throat first," Dylan muttered. "Then your dad's. Then I figured—I figured I would see how many I could take down before they managed to stop me." He paused, and took a deep breath. Tears welled in his eyes. "They didn't fight back, Jack. It was like they couldn't see me. Or couldn't see *anything*. And you know…" He sniffed, and wiped his eyes on his sleeve. "Your dad kept saying your mom's name. Over and over again—like it was all he could say now. It was his last word."

Jack narrowed his eyes as he gazed into Dylan's. For reasons he couldn't explain, he was suddenly angry at his cousin standing before him—angry at the last family he had left in the world.

Don't.

"There were eighteen of them on the island," Dylan added. "I counted. It doesn't sound like a lot, but… it's a lot. Some of them had guns, too, so I took those, and rowed back to shore, and by the time I got here some of them were starting to stand up, all groggy and dizzy and shit. I shot those ones first."

Jack nodded wordlessly. The anger was gone, passed like a quick-burning flame, replaced with a dark cloud of smoke and the grim perfume of ash.

"I stopped counting at sixty," Dylan continued, his voice brimming with fury now, as though whatever Jack had felt moments ago had transferred to his cousin. "Thankfully some of them started coming to their senses. By then it must've looked—it must've been—well, the point is, a good few of them ran away."

"You brought me back," said Jack, sensing that Dylan wanted him to change the subject. "From—" He jerked his thumb over his shoulder at the rocky islet out on the waves, but he didn't turn to look at it. If he had, he would have noticed that the lighthouse had vanished from it.

Dylan frowned, and shook his head. "What are you talking about?"

"What?"

"I found you here," said Dylan. "Right there, where you were lying." He pointed to the impression Jack's body had left in the white sand.

Jack opened his mouth, closed it. Then he slipped a hand into the pocket of his shorts, and his finger grazed the warmth of the star marble.

It'll get you home, Barkface had said. *I promise.*

"Your turn, then," said Dylan.

"What?"

Dylan snorted. "What do you mean, *what?* They put a demon god inside you, Jack. What—how did—how'd that work out for you?"

Jack wavered. Then he laughed, uneasy and humourless. He tapped the side of his skull. "He's in here somewhere. I think he always will be. But I've got room for him. And I'm not planning on feeding him, so I'm sure he'll starve before too long."

Dylan's eyes were narrowed, and he scrutinized Jack anxiously. "But how do you *feel?*" he said.

"Are you asking," Jack said slowly, "if I feel like going on some kind of murderous psycho rampage and sacrificing innocent people to the demon god in my head?"

"Well—"

"I say hell yeah, cousin! Let's go slaughter some kids!"

Dylan's eyes bugged out of his skull, and Jack burst into raucous, unhinged laughter. "Kidding," he wheezed through cackles. "I'm kidding. I'm *kidding,* Dyl."

Dylan chuckled, but Jack could tell it was a pleasantry, and his own laughter faltered as he once again took in the darkness around Dylan's eyes, the dried blood caking his clothes.

"Sorry," he mumbled sheepishly. "That was horrible."

"Yup," said Dylan.

Jack looked away from his cousin—and only then did he see it.

"What the hell?" he said. "Where's the lighthouse?"

Dylan shrugged.

"Dyl…" Jack sighed a deep, coarse sigh, the sigh of an old man. "I think… I think I'm less *Jack*, now. I've lost bits of myself. Rusalka has some of me. And part of me got lost beyond the ends of the Earth. And—"

He broke off. For a moment that familiar metallic banging echoed in his ears, alongside his heartbeat. A voice, far, far away, buried somewhere deep and dark, screamed for him to open the door.

Fists pounding on a rusty steel door. The sound rumbled in his ears, loud enough that Jack wondered if Dylan could hear it too.

For a moment neither of them said anything.

Leaves rustled softly. Waves lapped calmly at the shore.

"Skye's dead," Dylan murmured.

"I know. I saw her, in the—in the *other* place. She said—" Jack's voice caught. "She said she'll miss you, wherever she's going next." He breathed in sharply.

Dylan nodded, and nodded again, and said nothing.

"So what happens now?"

"Let's go back to the Wynd," said Dylan. "We'll get some food, gather some supplies. And then we'll go."

"Go where?"

Dylan fixed Jack with a penetrating stare. "Somewhere else. Morgana Wynd has nothing for us anymore."

Jack wavered. "That's not true."

"Jack. We can't stay here. We can't come back, at least not for a while." Dylan paused. "We know that there are forces at work in this universe that defy the laws of nature as we know them. I don't know about you, but I wanna learn more about these forces. I want to learn to use them. And Morgana Wynd is just one place of many."

Jack frowned. Then he nodded, too. "You're right," he said.

So with that the two cousins turned and left the beach behind. They walked through the woods, let memory guide their feet, and for a time they lost themselves in the walking. The air was ripe with birdsong, the lingering scent of woodsmoke and pine, and beneath it all the dark iron stench of blood evaporating in the summer sunshine.

After a while they emerged from the other side of the woods onto the Wynd. And it was only once they had put some distance between themselves and the woods that Jack looked back. He frowned.

"Hey, Dyl—"

He could have sworn, looking at it then, that it was just a little copse of skinny trees swaying in the breeze, on the other side of which he could just make out a small pebbly beach.

They shared a puzzled glance, but neither of them could think of anything to say, so they left it at that, and went to find something to eat.

Epilogue

Neria's almost finished her map. There's just a little bit left, the place between where Morgana Wynd ends and the water begins. But this is the trickiest part. The part she doesn't fully understand.

And she knows that she can't finish the map on her own. Not in this place.

This way…

The voices lead her down the street. As she passes by number 7 she spots someone she's never seen before. A boy with tousled mouse-coloured hair, fast asleep on the sloping lawn.

She laughs. She dresses up like a memory and strays into his dream—but she slips away just in time, so that when he stirs and sits up with a half-whispered name on his lips, she's nowhere to be seen.

THE END

We hope that you enjoyed this title and look forward to many more to come. Please, leave us a review! Reviews matter to all of our authors.

Take a look at some of our other award-winning series at https://threeravenspublishing.com/series-universes/

Visit us at https://www.threeravenspublishing.com and sign up for our newsletter for the latest and greatest news on upcoming titles and events.

Other series and titles you might enjoy.

DECLAN FINN
DECLAN FINN
DECLAN FINN
DECLAN FINN
Demons are Forever
Honor at the Stake
Live and Let Bite
Good to the Last Drop
The Dragon Award Nominated Series
FREE on Kindle Unlimited!

AVAILABLE ON
AMAZON
JOINT TASK FORCE
13
HOLDING THE LINE
BETWEEN HEAVEN AND HELL
13

MYSTERY,
MAGIC &
MAYHEM
WITH A TWIST
OF ROMANCE
J.F. POSTHUMUS
ON AMAZON
FIND ME
B.E.N.T.
BIOLOGIC
ENHANCED
NASCENT
TALENT

THE RAVEN
AND
THE CROW
MICHAEL K. FALCIANI
FIND ME
ON AMAZON

STARFLIGHT

IT CAME FROM THE
TRAILER PARK

3R
Three Ravens Publishing
Are you looking for fun, new fiction?
The FEATHER and the LAMP
CROSSWAYS
THE WAYMAN CHRONICLES
MICHAEL J ALLEN
DARK STORM RISING
LEGENDS
J.F. POSTHUMUS
STAFF OF CHAOS
The Written Word Will Never Be The Same…
https://www.threeravenspublishing.com
Veteran Owned and Operated

And don't forget to check out the latest edition of *Car Wars*

http://www.sjgames.com/car-wars/

Or the other amazing titles from
Steve Jackson Games

http://www.sjgames.com

...or the latest in the Car Warriors: Autoduel Chronicle fiction series.
https://threeravenspublishing.com/car-warriors-autoduel-chronicles/

You can also keep up to date with our latest release announcements on <u>Scifi.radio</u> and get some of the best fandom programing on the planet.

Scifi for your Wifi

And don't forget to check out our other Sponsors and Affiliates

A southern Appalachian jewel for craft beer lovers, Buck Bald Brewing offers something for everyone. With delicious, locally brewed beverages from across the spectrum, Buck Bald Brewing offers craft brews that are consistently amazing.

From the dark and smooth Shesquatch Scottish ale, to the intense hops of Hippibilly IPA, to the puckering sour of the blackberry and cinnamon in Berry My Heart at the Trailer Park, and more than 60+ rotating brews, you'll find what you're looking for and more.

With smiling faces behind the bar ready to help you find your next favorite brew, a constantly rotating selection of delicious craft beverages, toe-tapping tunes always playing, and the biggest games on TV, you can kick your feet up in either Copperhill, Tennessee or Murphy, North Carolina and immerse yourself in the Buck Bald Brewing experience. So, come out, fill a pint, fill a growler, and fill your mind at your new favorite family-owned craft brewery.

To discover more visit us at buckbaldbrewing.com or follow us on Facebook @buckbaldbrewing and @buckbaldbrewingmurphy.

Vesper Wren's
TRAILER PARK
PIXIE
PUNCH
· A PEACH STRAWBERRY SELTZER ·
BUCK BALD BREWING

9 781966 650738 3